SUSPICIOUS THREADS

SUSPICIOUS THREADS

A Virginia Davies Quilt Mystery
Book Three

By
David Ciambrone

Names, characters, businesses, places, events, and incidents are either the products of the author's imagination or used in a fictitious manner. Any resemblance to actual persons, living or dead, or actual events, is purely coincidental.

No part of this publication may be reproduced, stored in a retrieval system, or transmitted in any form or by any means, electronic, mechanical, photocopying, recording, or otherwise, without the written permission of the publisher.

Text Copyright © 2022 David Ciambrone

All rights reserved.
Published 2022 by Progressive Rising Phoenix Press, LLC
www.progressiverisingphoenix.com

ISBN: 978-1-958640-11-1

Printed in the U.S.A.

Book and Cover design by William Speir
Visit: http://www.williamspeir.com

This title was originally published by
White Bird Publications
ISBN: 978-1-63363-228-8
LCCN: 2017941381

ACKNOWLEDGMENTS

Authors will tell you writing is a solitary affair. This statement is mostly true. But, any author will also tell you their writing depends on a host of others who have provided needed information, ideas, inspiration, critiques and just plain support when we needed it. To this end, I'd like to thank the following people and groups for their support bringing this book to life.

The Williamson County Coroners critique group for their sound critiques and support.

My publisher, Amanda M. Thrasher, at Progressive Rising Phoenix Press.

My wife Kathy for her support, and wonderful ideas for the story.

CHAPTER 1

Ann North Greenwald crept down the back staircase from her second-floor bedroom, one hand gripping the banister.

The noises had come from the front room area, Ann thought. She wasn't frightened, just slightly angry. Ann looked up at the large bedroom and into her quilting studio. It was her sanctuary. She loved being in there. The fabrics spoke to her. *Something was wrong.* She had never been afraid at home in her Victorian mansion, *Borealis*, for as long as she'd lived there. She had just celebrated her sixtieth birthday and had lived in *Borealis* for fifty-five years. The past ten had been the hardest since her husband died. She had been depressed. Because of what she learned a few days ago, she was now tense and angry. It wasn't right. It shouldn't have happened. That was possibly why she was hearing things.

She glanced out the high, narrow, windows along the staircase that looked out over the moonlit lawns and gardens of *Borealis*. The garden directly in line with the window was laid out in a quilt pattern with different flowers making up the large quilt blocks. The sight relaxed her a little. A bang beneath her, halted her near the bottom of the stairs. She thought she'd locked the doors and windows after she brought in the cat, Poseidon. Maybe the cat knocked something over.

Her brown eyes fought the haze of darkness in front of her. Her bare feet felt the smooth, cool, planked flooring at the bottom as she stepped to the wall and flicked on the lights. The front entrance hall looked normal with the side table, with a vase of flowers, and coat rack still in place. In the living room, the yellow light bounced off the overstuffed couch and chairs arranged in front of a huge, stone fireplace with an eighty-inch flat screen TV mounted above it. The Persian rugs set around the floor were arranged in exacting lines as if placed by an Army drill sergeant. On the far wall hung a copy of Picasso's Woman with a Baby. Ann looked around the room and out across the wooded back yard. No branches moved. The sky was black and studded with stars and the crescent moon.

She turned and edged her way to the kitchen. She turned on the lights.

Suspicious Threads

The glow reflected off the stainless-steel appliances and the thick granite counter tops. She spotted the back door ajar. She sucked in a breath of air. *Open? I'm sure I locked that door. How'd it get open?* She looked through the window in the door. "Poseidon?" She smiled at the overweight black cat. She let the cat back in, closed the door, and locked it. She watched Poseidon stroll to his food dish and eat a couple of bites then amble into the dark dining room.

Ann stepped to the counter, took a cookie from a plastic container, and ate it. She then moved to the refrigerator and took out a small bottle of water, drank it, and tossed the bottle into the trash. Ann turned to go back upstairs. As she walked, the anger returned. She gritted her teeth. Tomorrow she'd address the issue. She pulled herself up the first stairs to the landing where the stairs turned back on themselves. At the landing, she paused. A dreamy haze settled over her. The quilt hanging on the wall above her seemed to change; it swayed and changed colors like a kaleidoscope.

Poseidon stood at the foot of the stairs, his green eyes watching as Ann's body turned slightly, then doubled over, and slowly somersaulted down to the planked floor. She was still. Poseidon meowed.

CHAPTER 2

The news of Ann North Greenwald's murder caused a stir in the Georgetown, Texas, community where her family had lived for a number generations, especially among the quilters. The bigger news causing a stir, Virginia Davies Clark thought, was when the controversial and scandalous, Hollywood actress, Natalie North arrived and announced that she had inherited the Victorian mansion, *Borealis,* built in 1903. *Borealis* was located on two hundred acres of prime land, with oaks and elm trees, a stream, and small lake, outside the city limits. Natalie North planned on selling off most of its old furnishings and renovating the mansion.

Virginia spotted Natalie speeding west down TX29 in her bright, cherry red, Jaguar XF convertible, toward the mansion. Natalie reminded Virginia of Melissa Rauch, Bernadette, of the *Big Bang Theory* TV show. Except for being seen in her movies, on TV shows, and HBO movies, Natalie's years in Hollywood had made her an unfamiliar figure to most residents. In the space of two weeks, she had buried her cousin, Ann North Greenwald, taken over *Borealis,* shocked some of the local church-going ladies, and gained the admiration of the men by the way she dressed, acted, and drove. She also disturbed the grand plans of some prominent people in the community, like the big developer Bryon Weedon. She wasn't making a lot of friends.

Virginia Davies Clark, at thirty-three, the youngest member of the Bee Hive Quilt Bee, leaned back in her kitchen chair and adjusted her blonde ponytail. "Who could have imagined a quiet, nationally famous, award winning quilter like Ann North Greenwald having a famous, wild, good looking, sexy cousin in the movies? And since she's been here, she's managed to send some of the local planners and developers into a tizzy, especially that sleazy developer, Bryon Weedon." Virginia glanced around the cluttered table for a pair of scissors.

Linda Chambers, a good-looking blonde, and at fifty-seven, the oldest member of the group, handed them to Virginia. "Bryon Weedon has had his eye on the *Borealis* estate for some time. He kept pressuring Ann to sell it to him so he could develop it into high-end homes and set a portion aside for a mix of low-income housing, for the betterment of Williamson County. More like the betterment of his own pocketbook. But the new owner, Natalie North, is scandalous; that's what she is. Natalie's been here a little over two weeks and has upset the whole community. She's all over town. She dresses indecently. Very un-Christian. Now, she's redoing *Borealis* into a bed and breakfast with some land for use as a wildlife sanctuary. Ann must be turning over in her grave. The only thing fast around there is her." Linda picked up a square of blue fabric and examined it. Today she was finishing a wall hanging. "But I have to admit, Natalie North has added some excitement to the area." She bit off a piece of thread.

Virginia looked across the table at Mary Watt. "What do you think of the situation, Mary?"

Mary, fifty-one, with prematurely gray hair and a round figure, pushed a strand of hair from her eyes.

"I remember when Natalie would come to stay at *Borealis* some summers when she was young. I think she lived between Liberty Hill and Burnett with her mother. If I remember right, she was a handful then. She was… well a nice kid, but into everything, a real handful. It was because of Ann that I got into quilting, as I think the rest of you did, too. She was an excellent and patient quilting teacher. And that Bryon Weedon is a slick developer. As soon as Ann died, he went straight to Natalie North and tried to get her to sell it to him. A rich, low-life. Ms. North has sure thrown a wrench into his plans. I do like her for that."

Claire Barnes, forty-eight, with short red hair and rail-thin, quickly tested the surface of the iron with a wet finger. Satisfied the iron was hot, she stood by the ironing board near the back door and started to iron a small stack of quilt blocks. "I lived in Liberty Hills back then. If I recall, Natalie liked acting in school. She got into plays, and then commercials. She went away and turned up in Hollywood. Now she's a big celebrity. I'm glad she's been successful at it."

Mary turned and frowned. "Yeah, she really likes being naked and doing "it," on the big screen. Shameful is what she is."

Prude. Virginia listened, put the scissors down, and pushed back from the table. "Can I get you ladies anything?"

They shook their heads.

"I'm getting some water. You sure I can't entice you with some iced tea or something?"

They again said no.

Virginia pushed her chair back and stood. She brushed some thread off her shorts and went to the refrigerator. She returned with a bottle of water and a scone. She gave a quick glance toward the hall to the master bedroom. *Good thing Leo doesn't like a lot of people here and hides out in the* closet. He'd be in heaven playing with all this thread and fabric. He's a good cat.

Claire shook her head. "Virginia, how can you eat things like that and stay so slim?"

"Genes, I think."

Claire continued, "Well, like Mary said, Natalie North's being here is scandalous. Think of the impact she can have on our youth."

Virginia picked up a spool of thread, looked at it, and then set it down. "Oh, come on. Kids today know more about sex than you did when you got married. I've seen most of her movies and a couple of shows on HBO. Her wardrobe doesn't usually involve a whole lot of fabric, most of which is ultra-thin, and she definitely doesn't have anything on under them. Natalie's out of her clothes most of the time. She has no problem with nudity. Her nude sex scenes are very graphic, and she's skilled at them. She is a good actress though, and has made a whole lot of money."

"Right." Mary shook her head. "Most of her films are R, N-17, or MA on TV. Is she really acting in those scenes, or are they real? There's talk in the movie magazines and on late-night talk shows that raise some moral issues. And look how she dresses here." She measured a piece of fabric, marked it, and started to cut. "But good actress or not, Natalie's here now, and I hope she doesn't cause too much strife. She has drawn a lot of attention from the male populous. Too much for my taste." She picked up a sheet of paper with her table runner sketched on it. "This is the last block before I have to piece them together."

Virginia moved a stack of fabric fat quarters to the side. "Just because Natalie has absolutely no problem taking all her clothes off on screen and elsewhere, doesn't make her a bad person. A whole lot of name actresses willingly and enthusiastically do nude and sex scenes: Anna Paquin, Kate Winslet, Ann Hathaway, Sharon Stone, Heather Graham, Eva Green, Nicole Kidman, Helen Mirren—who was knighted by the queen—and Julianne Moore. I could list a whole lot more. No one has any problem with them. Some, if not all of them, are married and have won major awards. Natalie's won acting awards, too. A woman does not need to be modest to be respected. Anyway, it must have been emotionally hard on her to have to come from Hollywood to bury her cousin and take over the estate. She doesn't really know anyone around here any more. I feel sorry for her."

"It's nice of you to defend her, Virginia. You have a good soul." Mary shook her head. "I don't know anyone else around here who would stick up for her like that." She adjusted the collar of her blouse. "My pastor said she's not a good, righteous, Christian woman. He said she is sinful and has no modesty. He said she should not be allowed in our Christian community."

Virginia chuckled under her breath. *Moral issues? Good, righteous,*

Christian woman? I bet Natalie could care less about being a good Christian woman. Modesty? Give me a break. Not be allowed here? Says who? Some religious fruitcake? The woman came and buried her cousin, and all they can think about is her somewhat spicy movies and how risqué she dresses. Some of these women and their pastors are so prudish that they would make the Puritans look like serious sinners. Aren't these Christian ladies, and especially their pastors, supposed to forgive? Good thing they don't know about my college engineering school's monthly magazine with the nude centerfolds I modeled for. I bet these ladies would have heart failure if they knew. "Mary, does your pastor personally know Natalie? Has he ever actually met her?"

"Ahh… I don't think so. But he's seen her and heard about her."

"So, your pastor publicly passes judgment on a person's character he's never actually met? He decides who is good or who is a good Christian and who isn't? That doesn't sound very Christian to me."

Mary stiffened. "Why are you defending her so much and attacking a man of God?"

Virginia leaned forward. "I'm attacking prejudice and people who pontificate before having all the facts, like your pastor. So-called religious people are usually the quickest to judge others. She may act in movies and dress in a manner he doesn't approve of, but it isn't any of his business. Saying she shouldn't be here is wrong. Natalie has every right to be here and do as she pleases. She hasn't broken any laws. He's supposed to be a man of God and be big on forgiving. From what you said, I don't see it. With her money, she could sue him for slander if he isn't more careful. I don't think his God would be able to, or want to, help him in court."

"You have a point, Virginia," said Claire. "And you're right, Mary, like it or not, Natalie's here now. Do any of you know if she started to gut *Borealis*, yet?"

"I don't know," Linda said.

Mary shrugged. "There have been a lot of construction types out there. I think she's getting bids to do work. She must play hardball, because Sam, down at the county records office, said she's the wicked witch of the north."

Virginia smiled. "She has to be sexy or a ball buster to get anything done with this county's construction companies. Same with some of the government agencies. They are nice guys, but it's a testosterone world, and she has two X chromosomes."

"You may be right. However, she is pretty, has a reputation from Hollywood," Mary chuckled, "and they way she dresses and carries on, all that testosterone doesn't have a chance."

Virginia nodded. "You're probably right."

"Ann had quite a quilt studio. I wonder what she'll do with all Ann's quilting tools and fabric. How about all her quilts?"

Virginia stretched. "I think someone said Ann had been around town doing a lot of writing in a couple of notebooks and on her computer this past year. Any idea what she was involved with? Did that have anything to do with her murder?"

"I don't know. I heard," said Claire, "she'd been spending a lot of time with Jenny Parker, the owner of the *Quilters' Corner* quilt store, the Southwestern University, and the University of Texas libraries."

"The quilt store I get, but the college libraries, what's with that?" Virginia dusted some more threads off her tight green t-shirt. "She usually used the quilt store here in Georgetown on Williams Drive, why frequent the *Quilters' Corner*? It's in Cedar Park just north of the Lake Line Mall."

"I have an idea." Linda looked at Virginia with a Cheshire cat grin. "Virginia, you're our Bee leader. You're the Bee Keeper of the Chisholm Trail Quilt Guild and librarian of the Main Street Quilt Guild. You're also wonderful quilter. Because of your leadership positions in our quilting community, and being a curator at the San Gabriel Museum, I nominate you to go see Natalie and ask about her plans with Ann's quilting studio, her quilts, and with *Borealis*."

Mary and Claire quickly agreed.

"Well..." *Leadership positions my ass. These busybodies are just curious. They're too chicken to ask themselves and tried flattery to get me to say yes.* Virginia rubbed her forehead. "Maybe I could convince Natalie to donate some of Ann's quilts to the museum. Okay, I'll do it. But only if you go with me, Linda."

Claire added, "Virginia, you have friends on the police force, don't you? Can you see how they're doing with Ann's murder investigation?"

Virginia took a swig of water and set the bottle down. "Police? Why me?"

Linda put a rubber band around a jelly-roll of fabric. "You know people. You're pretty, and as nice as you are, people like you. From what I've heard, the cops like you, too."

Virginia sighed. "I'll see what I can do. I think the sheriff is doing the investigation though. I can ask the guys at the Georgetown PD if they know whom to contact at the sheriff's office. You do know they usually don't give out much information about an ongoing investigation. But, Linda, you're going to *Borealis* with me."

"All right." Linda wrinkled her nose. "If I have to."

Mary looked at her watch. "Ladies, we've been at it for over three hours. I think it's time for us to help Virginia clean up and take our leave." She looked at Virginia and Linda. "When are you two going to see Natalie? Oh, don't forget to ask about Poseidon."

Virginia frowned. "Who or what is Poseidon? Ann had a Greek God living there?"

"No. Poseidon was Ann's cat." Mary looked around. "Speaking of cats, where is yours?"

"Leo is hiding. He doesn't like company. Okay, we'll ask about Poseidon. I guess we can go tomorrow, say mid-morning. After that, I'll call a friend in the police. What do you think, Linda?"

"Sounds like a plan. What's the worst Natalie can do?"

CHAPTER 3

Virginia stepped from the shower and dried off. After dressing in tan slacks and a snug, light blue blouse, and applying minimal makeup, she combed her hair, so it came to her shoulders with a slight turn under. She strolled into the kitchen. Her husband, Andy was sitting at the table munching a slice of toast and reading the newspaper. She poured a cup of coffee and sat across from him. She slipped a piece of bread into the toaster. "What's on your schedule today, dear? Anything special at the university?"

Andy, a professor of engineering at the University of Texas-Austin, lowered the paper and pushed up his glasses. "I've got two classes this morning, a faculty meeting right after lunch, and a lab later. I'll probably be a little late for dinner. I should be home by six or so. You?"

Virginia removed the toast from the toaster and spread some peanut butter on it. "I've got a meeting at the museum early this morning, then Linda and I are going out to *Borealis* to meet and talk to Natalie North."

Andy set the paper down on the table, his eyes wide. "You're going to meet Natalie North? Can I come?"

"Andy Clark, you are a dirty old man. You have a busy schedule today, so you can't come along. You just want to meet her because she dresses risqué and because of her movies."

Andy's head bobbed up and down. "Yeah. She's a famous, award-winning actress."

"Right. I bet you don't know what awards she has. Tell you what. If things go well today, I'll see about getting you an introduction."

"Great. Don't forget."

Virginia shook her head. "You're hopeless."

After a brief meeting at the museum about a new display, Virginia drove her new silver Honda Pilot to Linda Chambers' home. Together, they drove to *Borealis*. Virginia turned off the county road onto a long, gravel drive-

Suspicious Threads

way, between two large stone structures, and through an open black iron gate. Continued up the slight hill to the two-story Victorian mansion of twelve to fourteen rooms with a towering gabled roof nestled in oak, elm, and fruit trees. She gazed at the upstairs balconies and downstairs porches on the south and east sides. A lone palm stood at the far side of the building. She maneuvered around a number of pickup trucks and a couple of cars and parked under a large sprawling oak tree. In the back of the house, Virginia spotted Natalie's cherry red, Jaguar XF convertible. They walked up the walkway to the front porch. They heard pneumatic nail guns and other construction noises.

As they started up the steps, the front screen door flew open, and two burly men in western shirts, jeans, cowboy hats, and a black portfolio burst out almost running into Virginia and Linda. As they stormed past, one man said to the other, "She's pretty and sexy and all, but a first-class bitch. Now, we've got to redo that bid with her changes and fast. I thought this would be a simple deal. What would she know? She's an actress for God's sake. Can you imagine what working for her will be like?" Linda stopped and watched the men hop into a pickup truck and speed down the long driveway. She turned to Virginia. "Maybe this wasn't such a good idea."

"Too late now. Let's see what we can find out." Virginia found the doorbell and pushed the button.

A voice yelled from inside. "Come in; I'm in the kitchen."

Linda ran her hands down her skirt, opened the screen door, and motioned for Virginia to go in first. Virginia entered and walked down the planked floored hall with boxes piled along one wall with Linda behind her. A side table on the right held a clipboard and white hardhat. They walked into the large open kitchen.

Off to one side was a large drawing board with documents, blueprints, and pictures on it. A couple of plastic crates sat next to the drawing board. Short, blonde, Natalie North, barefoot, dressed in very short shorts and a blouse, unbuttoned and tied closed, with large braless breasts and barely covered by her open shirt, sat on a stool in front of the drawing board. She was flipping through a three-ring binder. Virginia still thought she strongly resembled Melissa Rauch, Bernadette of the *Big Bang Theory* TV show. Natalie looked up at the women and smiled. "Hi. I'm Natalie North. Who are you, and what can I do for you?"

Linda stood in shocked silence. Virginia stepped toward Natalie. "Hello. I'm Virginia Davies Clark, and this is Linda Chambers."

Natalie straightened causing Linda to suck in air as Natalie's open shirt billowed out exposing a lot more of one of her breasts. "You're not from another damn church or civic group here to chastise me again or want money, are you? If so, just turn around right now, and go."

Virginia shook her head. "No. We're from a quilt guild, and I'm a curator at the San Gabriel Museum in Georgetown. Ann was well liked in the community and a great quilter. She was generous with her talent and nurtured a number of us. We'll miss her."

Natalie nodded. "Thank you. What can I do for you, ladies?"

"We'd like to talk to you about your cousin, Ann's, quilts, her quilt room, and what you're doing with *Borealis*. That is, if you have the time."

"Wait a minute... Natalie tilted her head and then smiled. "Did you say you're Virginia Davies Clark?"

"Yes."

"I'm glad to see you. My cousin spoke highly of you and your quilting. She said you're also some type of investigator. I was going to give you a call or stop by your museum later today. Your coming here is timely." She looked at Linda who was standing, her eyes wide, and her mouth agape. "Is your friend okay?"

Virginia looked at Linda. She stood, staring at Natalie's chest. "I think so. She's not used to celebrities—Starstruck, maybe."

"Oh. Okay. Why don't you ladies follow me into the front parlor? It's in the best shape of any room right now. I've just started the renovations, and things are a little on the hectic side. And these contractors are something else. Most of the men seem to think I'm some dumb, blonde, actress who will be a pushover. I have managed to charm some, and bust the balls of others. I've spoken to some who talk down to me. I may be blond, and an actress, but I'm not stupid. I've graduated from college. Virginia, you're a blond and quite pretty, I bet men don't treat you like your stupid."

"You'd be surprised. But that usually doesn't last long. They learn really quick."

"I knew I'd like you."

They walked around boxes and crates to the front parlor. Virginia noticed, through an archway, two workers were in the dining room. The parlor looked like something from the nineteen forties. They sat in upholstered chairs next to a fireplace with a mantle finished in pink and green tile. The original builder put Italian tile on the face of the fireplace. A modern seventy-inch flat screen TV sat on a wooden credenza.

Virginia looked around, then at Natalie. "The TV seems out of place, but I love the old time feeling in here."

"It is cool. But I had to get a bigger TV. Got a great deal at Target. I like to watch football on it."

"You're right, it does look strange in here, and it's big." Virginia smiled at Natalie. "You said you were going to contact me. Why and how do you know about me?"

Natalie sat back and crossed her tan legs. "I've made inquiries. You're a curator and a highly-regarded quilter in these parts. You even teach some

Suspicious Threads

quilting and sewing classes. You also came from southern California, where I live. I don't know much about quilting. I'm more of a seamstress. As you know, my cousin was a nationally famous quilter and teacher. She mentioned you a few times when I'd call her from California. She really liked you. So, I would like you, Virginia, to assess my late cousin's quilts, her quilt room, and stuff and tell me what to do with it. In other words, I'd like you to appraise the estate's sizable collection of quilts. You can select some for your museum if you like."

Virginia sat, stunned. "You want me to assess the quilts and stuff?"

"Yes. Obviously, we'll be working together. I think you and I can work well together. Would that be an issue with you?"

"No, not at all. I'm honored you would want me to do it. It'll be interesting to see what you're doing with this place." Virginia frowned. "You made inquiries about me?"

"Yes. As I said before, my cousin spoke highly of you and said she'd like us to meet someday. I want to be sure to get the right person. I need someone I can relate to. I hope you don't mind."

"Well, I'm flattered you selected me. But there are women around here who are registered quilt appraisers who could do it."

"I've talked to some." Natalie pulled the fabric of her shirt back over more of her breast. "As soon as they see me they run, or they try to change me and save my soul, or want to charge me a fortune. You, on the other hand, are a well-known, award-winning quilter who my cousin thought highly of. I also found out you have a background at your university, UCI, I think it was, that in some ways parallels mine. Now that I've met you, I'm comfortable with you. Oh, how much do you think it will cost?"

"For the privilege of doing it, and with your agreeing to donate some of the quilts to my museum, I won't charge you anything." Virginia gave her a puzzled look. "You know about the university?"

"Yep. Got copies of the engineering department magazines with you in them on line. You were great." Natalie leaned forward. "You should be in Hollywood with me. You'd make a fortune."

"Thank you. That would be nice, but I can't act. When would you like us to start?"

"As soon as possible. Ann's quilt room is upstairs. I moved the quilts she had in there and in one of the bedrooms. You can come and go as you please. I'll give you a key before you leave. Would you like to look around? You know, get the feel of the place."

"Yes. That would be great." Virginia rose. "Can I start with the quilt room?"

"Yeah." Natalie looked at Linda. "Are you okay Mrs. Chambers? Can I get you anything? Water, tea, soda?"

Linda shook her head. Her voice squeaked. "No. I'm fine, thank you.

I'll just go with Virginia."

"Okay. Stop by the kitchen when you're ready to leave, and I'll give you the key." Natalie got up and with a pert wiggle, strolled out of the parlor.

Linda looked at Virginia and spoke in a low voice. "Did you see how she's dressed? And when that shirt flew open and bared almost all of her breast, it didn't faze her at all. She didn't even try to cover up right away. I almost had a heart attack. What if some of the workers saw her? There are men working in the dining room. I see why Mary was so upset. That woman has no shame. She wasn't humiliated, embarrassed, or self-conscious about it. It's sinful."

"No, she wasn't humiliated, embarrassed, or self-conscious. She doesn't have to be modest for her to be respected. That should be based on her character and actions." Virginia crossed her arms. "And so what? She has no reason to be, and she isn't hurting anyone. It's normal for her. I'm sure that has happened with men around, and I bet she gets some really good bids from the contractors. It keeps them off guard, too. And she wants me to appraise all the quilts, the notebooks, and the quilt room. I'll be able to watch her transform *Borealis* and report to the Bee about it. That's what we came here hoping for. You are going to help me, aren't you?"

"I... I... I don't know."

"What?" Virginia frowned. "Don't be such a damn prude. Get over yourself. You going to help me or not?"

"I guess so." Linda swallowed. "What will I tell my husband and my pastor?"

"Nothing. What she does and what happens here is none of your husband or pastor's business. None. Nada. What happens at *Borealis* stays at *Borealis*. And for the record, your pastor's opinion doesn't matter one iota. He's never met her, so his thoughts on the matter don't count." Virginia motioned toward the hall. "Let's have a look at the place." They wound their way through the first-floor rooms stepping around boxes, construction materials, and cloth and plastic covers over furniture. When they got to the bottom of the front stairs, Virginia turned to Linda. "Remind me to ask about Poseidon." They climbed the stairs and explored the second floor.

A half hour later, Virginia and Linda entered the kitchen. Natalie was bent over the drawing table looking at some papers. She straightened. "Had a look around?"

Virginia nodded. "Yes. You've got quite a job ahead of you."

"Don't I know it? I could use some help evaluating some of the bids and engineering drawings. I'm an actress, not an engineer or contractor. I've got a BFA, not an engineering degree." Natalie picked up a key ring with R2D2 on it with a key. "Here's the house key. You can use it if I'm not here when you arrive. The work will be done on this floor first. My rooms are upstairs."

Virginia took the key. "Thanks. I'll get started quickly. Linda here may help me if that's all right."

"Sure."

"Is Poseidon still here?"

"Yes." Natalie gestured toward the ceiling. "He's a good cat and stays upstairs when there are people around. He's in my bedroom watching TV. He likes the Cartoon channel. He's a big fan of Bugs Bunny."

"That's funny. My cat likes the weather channel. I think he wants to become a meteorologist." Virginia looked at the papers on the drawing board Natalie was looking at. "You said you could use some technical help?"

Natalie waved her hand over the papers on the drafting board. "I sure could."

Virginia set a book from the quilt room on the drawing board. "My husband is a big fan of yours. He's also an engineering professor at UT. If you would like, I'll ask him if he'd be willing to help you."

"You will? Great! Thank you. An engineering professor?"

"Yes."

"Wonderful. Since he's your husband, it makes me feel better. I've gotten offers to help oversee this from men working for engineering companies who were total losers, or they think I'm a pretty, dumb, actress and they'll charge me a bundle, or they want to go out with me." Natalie sat on the stool. "Do you think your husband would like an autographed picture?"

Virginia grinned. "Are you kidding, he'd love it." She glanced at Linda, whose hand went to her chest as if in shock.

Natalie hopped up, hurried to another room, and returned with a portfolio. She set it on the drawing board and opened it. Pick one your husband would like."

Virginia examined the pictures and selected two, one of Natalie topless, and one of her nude. "Could he have two?"

"Of course." Natalie asked what Virginia's husband's name was, and then signed the pictures. "I hope Professor Clark likes them."

"Are you serious? He'll have them in his home office next to mine. Thank you. I'll be back tomorrow afternoon, and I'll see when Andy can come." Virginia picked up the book from the drawing board. "This book is a proof copy of a new book by Jenny Parker, the owner of the *Quilters' Corner* quilt store in Cedar Park. It looks like your cousin put a big X on the cover with a Sharpie. Any idea why?"

Natalie took the book from Virginia and examined it. "I haven't got a clue. Could be she didn't like the book. Is it important?"

"I don't know. We'll look into it once we get started on the quilt room. We should be going and let you get back to work."

"I look forward to seeing you again and meeting your husband." Natalie turned slightly and smiled at Linda. "I hope to see you again too, Linda."

As they drove back toward Georgetown, Linda regained her senses. "Did you see how she was dressed? There were men there just before us, and they saw her that way, too. And how about the workers in the dining room? Her breast just popped out of her shirt, and she didn't care. Scandalous, that's what she is." Linda tugged at her seatbelt. "I guess that happens with the contractors around, too."

"Probably. I bet they think, with her around; they have a great working environment. You know they'll try and get pictures of her on their cell phones."

"Disgraceful. And what did she mean when she said you and her were alike and something about your university?"

Virginia tightened her grip on the steering wheel. "Natalie seemed nice. She welcomed us, and we get to assess the quilt room, the quilts, and notebooks Ann had. And we get to see what she's doing to the estate. Isn't that what we came to do?"

"Yes… right… that's what we came for, but… will she be like that all the time? She will dress differently now that we're going to be there, right?"

"I don't know. I doubt it. She'll probably be pretty much the same as today. But it's none of my concern."

"Well, it should be. She may be working close with your husband. Doesn't that bother you?"

"Nope. Andy will love it. And he will really love the pictures I got him."

"You're actually going to give them to him? She's topless and… and… naked."

"No kidding. She's not a self-righteous, stuck-up prude like some people around here. And yes, he's getting them. This is the twenty-first century, not the sixteen hundreds. He may even scan them into his computers, too."

"What are we going to tell the others in the Bee?"

"Exactly what we did here. And that we're going to help Natalie with the quilt stuff and my husband may help her, too. That is all we'll tell them. We do *not* mention how she was dressed. Don't worry. It'll be fine."

Linda swallowed. "I'm not comfortable in this type of situation."

"You got me into this. You said you'd come and you said you'd help me. Now you're chickening out?"

"Well… I don't know."

Virginia shrugged. "Okay. Shall we stop by the police station on the way back and see what we can find out? Maybe they can tell us who in the sheriff's office to talk to."

Linda's face brightened. "If they can tell us who the sheriff's detective is, when do you want us to talk to him?"

"Us? I thought by now you would be thinking of a thousand reasons why you couldn't go back out there. Isn't she the spawn of the devil to you?"

"I thought that, yes. She shocked me. But I just considered what you said. Ms. North did seem nice, at least to us... you. She really liked you and will let me help. Natalie's excited about meeting your husband. I'm not sure I'd like my husband to meet her. And I think you're right. She said she's getting some really good bids for the work she needs done, and has been a ball buster for those who try to take advantage of her. Those men that almost ran us down when we arrived are a good example. I'd like to work on the quilts." Linda twisted in her seat toward Virginia and grinned. "Now what happened while you were in college that's like her? Were you in movies or plays? She said she has copies of the engineering department magazine issues with you in them? You wrote engineering articles? I thought you were a historian. You have a deep, dark, juicy secret?" Linda rubbed her hands together. "Tell me all about it."

"Look, we're almost at the police station. I hope they can point us in the right direction."

CHAPTER 4

Following a quick lunch, Virginia and Linda entered the police station on D.B. Woods Drive in Georgetown. After talking to the volunteers at the reception area, and to a captain, they were escorted to the office of a detective.

He rose as they approached. "Hello, ladies. I'm Detective John Morison." He looked at their nametags. "Mrs. Clark, Mrs. Chambers, how are you ladies today?" He motioned toward a couple of chairs. "Please take a seat."

"Good, thank you." Virginia cleared her throat. "Well, Detective, your captain referred us to you. We were told you knew who the Sheriff's detective was who is investigating Ann North Greenwald's murder. We were hoping you would give us his or her name so we could follow up."

He looked sharply at Virginia. "You're direct, that's refreshing. Yeah, my captain called while you were being escorted here and said to give you the name of the sheriff's deputy in charge, and any information we have. I have to admit, I've never been given instructions like that before. You must have some serious influence on the captain."

Virginia grinned.

"Okay, I have copies of what we know that you can have. One of our officers got to the scene of the crime before the sheriff's deputies. He happened to be closer. This file doesn't contain much. It's in the sheriff's jurisdiction, not ours. The sheriff's lead detective on the case is Detective Dan Grover. He's a crusty old guy with a lot of experience. He's a good homicide investigator. He teaches classes on the subject at the academy." He handed Virginia a couple of business cards. "Here is my card, and Dan's. When you leave, I'll give him a call to vouch for you. I'll also mention to him that our captain would appreciate him working with you. That should make it easier to talk to him."

"Thank you, Detective Morison. I appreciate your help."

"The captain told me about some of the work you've done in the past with the Smithsonian Central Security Service. He said you've worked with us before, too. Is this an official Smithsonian investigation?"

"No, at least, not yet. My friend here and I are doing some things out at *Borealis* for Natalie North and figured we could look around and ask questions easier than the police. People are more prone to talk to us than a police officer."

"Sounds good to me, but Dan Grover may not take kindly to you snooping around. Good luck with him."

"Thanks, detective, we can use all the luck we can get. And thanks for the information." Virginia rose. "I know you are busy, so we'll run along. Thanks again."

Morison stood. "I'll escort you out. Please keep me informed of anything you find."

"Will do."

Virginia slid into her Honda Pilot and looked at Linda as she fastened her seatbelt. "That went quite well. We even got a copy of their reports. That's something that is not usually done."

"I knew you had some pull with them. So, what now? Are we going to the Sheriff's office?"

Virginia looked at the clock on the dashboard. "No. We can contact the Sheriff tomorrow or the next day. We should call first and set up an appointment. I need to go the museum and then home. I want to prepare for our visit with the Sheriff, and our first official quilt appraisal visit to *Borealis*." She drove out of the parking lot and headed south on Williams Drive. "Natalie is selling some of the furnishings, giving some things away, and trashing other things. Besides the quilt things, I'd like to see what else she's getting rid of. Who knows, maybe my museum would be interested in some of the stuff. *Borealis* is an old place, and there are some unusual pieces there. I'm not sure Natalie knows the good stuff from trash. Maybe we can help her with that, too."

Linda sat in silence and then took a breath. "You like her don't you?"

"Yeah, I do. I think she's out of her element here and getting in way over her head in what she needs done. Maybe we can assist her."

"By throwing your husband into the lion's den?"

"Oh come on, Linda. Natalie is a really nice lady. She just buried her cousin, and now she wants to do something good with *Borealis*. Natalie is not going to try anything with Andy. And just because she doesn't dress and act like you think she should, doesn't make her a bad person. You've met her. Hell, the mafia guys went to church every Sunday, and they weren't saints. She's here and free to what she wants, and that's that." Virginia took a breath. "She's pissed off some developers and county officials who were counting on developing her land and the increases in associated property taxes. I'm glad she's keeping it. I like her spunk. She has a lot of self-confidence. They will try to stop her, so I'm hoping you, Andy, and I can help her."

Linda took a breath. "She is unusual; I'll give her that. I've never known anyone quite like her. You are right, though. She did seem nice while we were there, and she sure liked you. I agree. I like her taking on the developers and the government. Spunk and confidence, she has in spades. I said I'd be more open-minded, and I will. I really want to help."

"Good. What time do you want me to pick you up tomorrow?"

"How about nine? Will your husband be with you?"

"Nine is fine. I don't know about Andy. When I give him Natalie's pictures, he'll probably rearrange his schedule to go with us. We'll have to wait and see. But with or without Andy, nine it is."

About six pm, Andy stepped through the garage door, entered the kitchen, and set his keys on the counter. "Hi beautiful, I finally made it."

Virginia came into the kitchen from her quilt room. "Hi. You're just in time to take me out to dinner."

"We're eating out? What happened today? Something bad?"

"No." She hopped up on the island counter. "Linda Chambers and I went to see Natalie North today and the police."

"Oh, yeah." He removed his UT baseball cap and rubbed his bald head. "How'd it go with Ms. North?"

"Great." Virginia leaned back on her arms. "Natalie looked me up and was going to call me. She asked me to look over and appraise Ann's quilts, notebooks, and quilt room stuff. She's even going to donate some things to the museum."

Andy smiled. "Wow. That's wonderful. She looked you up?"

"Yes. She wanted to make sure she could work with me."

"When do you start?"

"Tomorrow. She even gave me a house key. I'd like to go out, eat something quick, and get back. I need to plan on what I'm going to do tomorrow."

"Fine. Let me put my briefcase and my computer in the den."

"I'll grab my sweater and meet you here." She sat and waited.

"Virginia!" Andy called from his home office. "Where did you get these pictures of Natalie North? They are great!" He hurried into the kitchen waving the pictures. "Wow. She even autographed them and dedicated each one to me."

"I know. I figured you'd like them."

"Oh yeah. I'll scan them into my computer, too. Some of the other professors at the university would love to see theses. Then I'll put them with the ones of you."

Virginia slid off the counter. "Great. I'm now displayed with a famous and award-winning actress in the same attire. I guess that's good."

"You bet. Where do you want to go eat?"

"What sounds good to you?"

"Panda Express?"

"Good idea." Virginia gave him a sly look. "Andy, there is one other little thing for you to consider about Natalie North."

Andy leaned on the counter. "Oh? What's that?"

"She's getting quotes for work at the estate and has construction drawing and specifications, and she's having a hard time with them. She's an actress, not a contractor, nor an engineer. So, I kind of... well... I sort of volunteered you to be her technical consultant. Her engineer. She's hoping you'll agree." Virginia smiled. "I'll grab a sweater and be right back."

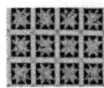

Andy slid into his dark-gray Honda Odyssey and fastened his seatbelt as Virginia climbed in and hooked her belt. He slowly turned and looked at Virginia. "She really wants me to be her project engineer on the redo of the estate?"

Virginia nodded. "Yes."

Andy started the car and backed out of the garage. He pressed the button on the dash that closed the roll-up garage door. "I'd love to help the lady."

"She does have some problems. So you're going to do it?"

"Hell, yes. We can both help her. When would she want me to start looking at things?"

"What's your schedule like? Linda and I are going back tomorrow at nine."

"I have classes until noon. A grad student is covering my two-day labs as part of his graduate program, so I'm free tomorrow afternoon."

"Good. You drive us to dinner, and I'll give Natalie a call." She dialed Natalie's cell.

After three rings, the phone was answered. Natalie's voice sounded strange. "Natalie North."

"Hello, Natalie. This is Virginia Davies Clark."

"Virginia. Hello. Glad you called. Is there any chance you can stop by here tonight?"

"Sure. Why?"

"After everyone left today, someone tried to break in."

"Did you call the Sheriff?"

"Yes. Five deputies came, took a report, and looked around. But I'm concerned about being here. I don't really know anybody around here. I could use someone to talk to and maybe give me some advice as to what to do next."

"Andy and I were just headed for Panda Express at the Wolf Ranch shopping center to eat. Care to join us?"

"I'd love to, but I'm nervous about leaving the house unguarded right now."

Andy spoke up. "Tell her we'll get dinner and bring something for her, and we can eat together there."

"Andy said —"

"I heard him. Sounds good. I can't wait to meet him. I'll get drinks ready. Can you get me some orange chicken with chow mien and some spring rolls? I'll pay you when you get here."

"Sure. We'll be there shortly."

"Oh, Virginia, did you ask him about helping me? You know what I'm like, so if you, or he, isn't comfortable—"

"Natalie, I asked him, and he said yes. He will be there tomorrow afternoon to start going over the stuff you have problems with."

"Wonderful. I'll see you shortly." She hung up.

Virginia put her phone way and smiled at Andy. "It looks like you made new a sexy friend."

Forty-five minutes later, Virginia, Andy, and Natalie sat around her kitchen table eating dinner. Natalie, dressed in tight jeans and a red blouse, smiled at Andy. "I can't thank you enough for agreeing to help me, Professor. The remodeling of this place involves a lot of stuff I'm not familiar with, and I'm afraid of being taken advantage of or making a colossal mistake. Your agreeing to help me is wonderful, Dr. Clark."

"It will be my pleasure, and call me Andy."

Virginia finished her food and sat back. "You said someone tried to break in. What happened?"

Natalie swallowed some chicken. "One of the sheds was broken into. Nothing was taken. One of the deputies fixed the door. Someone also tried to force the side door of the house. The construction of the house is... well... over done. The framework around the door is extra thick and solid oak. The two by fours are really two by four inches and not like today's wood. In the outer wall framing, they used four by six in boards. The screws holding the lock jam are four inches long. The oak is old and almost like iron, so the door and the framework around it didn't budge. If you look at it, you can see where they tried to use a crowbar or something like it to open it. The sheriff's people took imprints. I heard the noise and when I came downstairs and yelled, whoever it was, fled. I called the Sheriff."

Andy looked around. "After we finish, I'd like to look around and then look at your plans and ideas. That way I have a better idea of what you need me to do."

"Okay. I'll give you a tour and show you the drawings and specifications I've got."

"Great. But can I use the restroom first?"

Natalie pointed. "It's down that hall on the left."

After Andy had exited the kitchen, Natalie turned to Virginia. "You husband is really nice. I like him. I can see why you married him. Does he know about the magazine? I won't tell."

"That was a few years ago." Virginia laughed. "Oh yeah. He knows. He was the faculty advisor and was there for each and every photo shoot."

"Well, good for him. I'm glad you are letting him help."

"You said you're having problems with the bids and some engineering. Are the contractors trying to rip you off?"

"A few I'm sure are trying. Others, I think, are low-balling the bid, and when there is a problem, they'll stick it to me. I'm also afraid they'll do something to cost me more money. I've had it happen in LA. But I think I've got some honest bids from some really good companies and contractors, too. I think most are honest."

"Why didn't you hire a general contractor to oversee the whole project for you?"

Natalie finished eating. "Again, I've had issues with them in LA. I know this is Texas and not California, but once burned, twice wary. When I was going to come here to handle my cousin's estate, the construction guys at the studio gave me some guidance and a notebook with suggestions on what to look for, and watch out for, when I left Hollywood. But with burying my cousin, the legal stuff with the property, that damn pesky contractor who insists I sell it to him, county officials, and the remodel... well, this is a huge job. I did interview a few general contractors. They either wanted me to sell the estate to them or had conditions I couldn't abide by. There were some I just couldn't work with. There were a couple of them who seemed competent and such, but... well... I wasn't the kind of woman those Christian men thought they should be working with. Maybe their wives wouldn't like it. There were a few really nice ones, but by the time I met them, I had already started to do this myself." She took a sip of her iced tea. "This turned out to be a bigger job than I thought."

Virginia pushed the chair back and stood. "Let me help you clean up." She scooped up some of the plates and plastic bags and take out containers. "Don't worry. Andy and I, and to some extent, Linda, will help you. We have other contacts around here who may be able to assist when necessary, too." She headed for the sink.

Natalie picked up the remaining glasses and utensils and took them to the sink. "I know what was wrong with your friend today. I shocked her. She didn't approve of the way I was dressed."

"Yeah, you're right. But she'll get over it. Don't change anything or do anything different just because of her, or anyone else that's around. Be yourself and do what you think you need to do. I'm on your side. Linda wants to assist me with the quilt stuff, so she'll get over it. She's pretty nice."

"She seemed nice." Natalie sighed. "I've alienated a lot of people around here by my conduct and don't know anybody besides the people related to the construction. You and your husband are the only ones I feel real comfortable with and really like. I know I was presumptuous asking you to come tonight when you called, but I was nervous."

"Don't give it a second thought. I'm always willing to help a friend. And I do consider you a friend. And Andy couldn't wait to meet you in person. He thinks you're beautiful and great. By the way, he's seen all your movies." Virginia looked around. "Speaking of Andy, what can be keeping him?"

CHAPTER 5

Virginia pulled her cell phone out of her pocket and dialed Andy's number. She heard it ring in the side of her backpack. She hung up and looked at the pack on the floor. Sticking out of a side pocket was Andy's phone with a Mickey Mouse cover. "Why the hell did he leave it here?" Virginia rose from her chair and reached for her backpack. She opened it and withdrew a black, 9mm semiautomatic pistol. "Because of what's happened around here, I think I'd better go look for Andy."

Natalie stared. "You can carry a gun?"

"Yes." Virginia looked at Natalie. "I have a Texas concealed carry license, and I'm also a reserve special agent with the Smithsonian Central Security Service."

"You're a fed? I'm glad you're here." Natalie glanced down the hall where Andy went. "Let's go find your husband."

"Okay, but stay behind me."

"No problem. I'm only heroic in movies with lots of people on the set." She followed Virginia down the hallway.

Virginia looked at the dark bathroom, *not here*. She went to the front of the house, glanced at the parlor, and then went to the front door. She switched on the outside lights and looked through the ironwork and glass. "He doesn't appear to be out front. Where the hell is he?" She spun around at the sound of a creaking door and raised her weapon. In the middle of the hallway, a door slowly opened. A black cat ran through the doorway and to the stairs and shot up to the second floor. Andy came into the hall and shut the door. Virginia lowered her pistol and stuck it in her pocket. "Andy! Where have you been?"

Andy turned, pushed his burnt orange UT baseball cap back, grinned, and closed the door. "This place is not built on post and beam."

"Okay. Whatever that means. I'm happy for it. What have you been up to?"

"It actually has a cellar. I didn't think they used them in Texas."

Natalie stepped next to Virginia. "Yes, it does. The heating and AC units are down there along with the hot water heaters, washer and dryer, and a lot of shelves and stuff."

"I saw them. There's no sign of water having leaked into it. It's dry. That's great."

Virginia walked toward him. "Is that important to Natalie's project?"

"Yes. Now that I've looked around, I'll be better at looking at her plans." He smiled at Natalie, "Oh, yeah, I was thinking about the attempted break in. At home, I have the materials to set up a burglar alarm system for you."

Natalie smiled. "That would make me feel safer, Andy."

"Let's go in the living room." Virginia motioned for Natalie to proceed ahead of her and Andy. Once seated in the overstuffed chairs near the fireplace, Virginia asked, "Andy, when can you build the alarm system for her? Tomorrow?"

"If you will stay here with Natalie, I'll run home and get the materials. It's all in the garage."

Virginia tilted her head. "Where did you get the stuff?"

"I brought it from California when we moved here. It was the system I had on my... our house there. It's in those boxes in the garage you've been wanting me to do something with."

"So that's what's in those boxes." Virginia thought for a second and then chuckled. "Oh God, that will be funny."

Natalie looked at Virginia. "Why would it be funny?"

"Well, we had it in California. When it detects someone near the building, it tells them to leave. If they don't go away, it tells them to repeat after it, and the system says, 'Our father who art in heaven...' and finishes the prayer. Then the trespasser hears the sound of a shotgun being ratcheted. If they still don't leave, it gives off an extremely loud wail and a screech that *will* cause severe bodily harm, especially to their ears. It's exceptionally disorienting and quite painful. If the crook actually makes it into the house, everyone inside will be awake, and that isn't something most crooks like. Oh, it will also turn on some lights, and if Andy hooks it up right, it'll call the sheriff. I think he'll just set off the loud wailing sound system on yours."

"Sounds great." Natalie beamed. She thought for a second. "But Andy, you don't have to do it tonight. It's dark outside, and you have to go to work tomorrow."

Andy glanced at his watch. "I'll run home and get the necessary stuff to at least set up a temporary system this evening. Tomorrow I can finish it. That way you'll have something to protect you tonight."

Virginia looked at Natalie. "Discouraging him will be impossible. It looks like you'll have an alarm system tonight." She glanced at Andy. "What are you waiting for? Go get what you need. I'll stay here."

"Good." Andy jumped to his feet. "I'll be back shortly."

He hurried down the hall. A minute later, they heard the back door close. Andy's car started and drove down the driveway.

Virginia looked at Natalie. "He really likes you. He wouldn't do this for just anyone."

"I like him, too. He's smart and funny, and he obviously loves you. Does he by any chance have a single brother?"

"No. No brother."

"Too bad."

Virginia leaned back in her chair. "I just thought of something. How'd your cat get in the basement? I thought you said he was upstairs watching TV."

"He was. I don't know he got down there. The cellar door was closed."

Virginia rubbed her forehead. "When was this place built?"

"Originally it was constructed in 1903. But it has gone through several remodels and updates. Ann had all the wiring and plumbing updated in the late nineties. The AC was added when she changed out the old furnace around the time she did the wiring and plumbing."

"So, the remodel you are doing will not include a whole house rewiring, right?"

"Correct. But what's that got to do with Poseidon?"

"Well, this is an old house. Back in the old days, in big houses, they sometimes build secret passages. Maybe Poseidon found one and used it, but he got stuck in the cellar. There could be more."

Natalie stared at the far wall for a few seconds. "If there are any, they're not on the plans I have."

"I didn't think they would be. So, we may have complicated your work a little. We may have to find them before some of your workers come across them. This way we can figure out what to do if a remodel involves one. It won't be a surprise to the contractor, or you."

Natalie sat back. "I'm glad you and your husband are around and helping me."

"You know, this could be a fun project. But my main job is the quilts. Andy's your engineer." Virginia got up and moved next to the fireplace. "I was meaning to ask. I know your cousin was murdered. May I ask how?"

Natalie looked down, then back at Virginia. "She was poisoned. The medical examiner in Austin said she was poisoned with something from the Panther mushroom. The sheriff's people are investigating. I don't think they've gotten very far."

"Well, I must confess something." Virginia gave Natalie a sorrowful look. "I got a copy of the Georgetown PD's file on the case and the name of the sheriff's detective. I had thought about doing some snooping around to see what I could find. I feel awful. I went behind your back. It was because

Ann meant so much to us quilters. She was more than our teacher and great quilter. She was a friend."

Natalie got up, went to Virginia, and gave her a hug. "Wow. That means a lot. I knew she was big in the quilting community, but I never guessed how much. Can you investigate without causing the sheriff to arrest you?"

"I'll look at her quilts and stuff. If I can find a historical connection, I'll ask the Smithsonian for authorization. They may be willing to let me officially investigate. If not, with your permission, we'll do it ourselves."

"Okay with me. Anything I have that you need, it's yours. Just ask."

Virginia chuckled. "Just don't say that to Andy." She looked out the front window. "Do you have a gun?"

"A gun? Ahh… yeah. Ann had one. It's upstairs. It isn't loaded."

"Get it and let me look at it. You might need it if Andy's alarm goes off."

"Right. I'll run up and get it." Natalie bound up the stairs and retuned a minute later. "Here. It's a revolver."

Virginia examined the weapon. "It's a six-shot Ruger .357 Magnum revolver with a six-inch barrel. It's clean, and it's heavy. Your cousin was well prepared. Any bullets?"

"None that I've seen."

"We'll fix that." Virginia hurried to the kitchen to get her cell phone from her backpack. She called Andy. "Andy. Bring a box of .38 special bullets for Natalie. She has a .357 that Ann had, but no bullets. This way it won't kick so much if she shoots it."

"Okay. I just got home, so I'll be back there in about forty-five minutes or less."

"That's fine. We'll be here."

Virginia turned to Natalie. "Ever fire a handgun before?"

"Yes. I had a boyfriend once who was into guns. He took me to the range and taught me how to shoot and safely handle a firearm. The studio also made sure I could handle a gun for movies, too. I'm actually a pretty good shot."

"Good to know."

Andy brought his boxes into the mansion's kitchen from his van and set them on the floor near the door. "I've got the whole system in these boxes. But tonight, I'll set up a screen system. I'll have it cover the sheds, too. It'll alert you if anyone tries to get in, but it isn't the whole thing. I'll finish connecting the rest of it up tomorrow afternoon. Then you'll have the total Andy Clark alarm system."

Natalie looked at the boxes and crates. "How are you going to get power and do the connections?"

Andy grinned. "That's the beauty of it. Tonight's system is wireless and runs on batteries. The batteries can keep it going for at least six months before they need to recharge. So, you'll be good."

Natalie sat on the stool near her drawing board. "How much do I owe you for all this?"

"Nothing. Our house has an alarm system that came with it from the builder, so we didn't need this one anymore. It was just collecting dust. Virginia will be happy to get the boxes out of the garage."

Virginia nodded. "You've got that right."

"If you ladies will excuse me I'll get this set up." He reached into a small box. "Oh, here are the bullets you wanted. You'd better show her how to use that gun, so Natalie doesn't shoot herself." Andy opened the boxes and started to pull things out. "This'll take me about an hour or so."

Virginia motioned for Natalie to follow her into the parlor. She took the gun from her and showed Natalie how to load it. "Be sure to hold this with both hands like so." Virginia demonstrated how to hold the weapon. "You aim using these sights and squeeze the trigger. Hold the gun tightly as it will kick a little. The weight of this model will minimize the recoil, but you'll still get some. Remember to look behind your target and don't shoot if there is something that can get hurt. You may miss, or the bullet may pass through the target and hit it. So be careful. Also, it doesn't have a safety so it will fire if the trigger is pulled. Until you are ready to shoot, keep your finger *off* the trigger." She handed the gun to Natalie. "Here. Hold it and try aiming."

Natalie took the weapon and held it as Virginia instructed. She practiced aiming it. "I see what you mean. It's heavy. The ones I've fired are smaller. I think they were .22 and .25 caliber. I'll keep it close tonight."

"Maybe sometime soon, we can go to a shooting range so you can get the feel of it."

"I'd like that."

Virginia heard Andy going in and out of the house. "I have an idea. Let's go see if we can find Poseidon's entrance to the secret passage, if there is one."

"Okay. Follow me." Natalie led Virginia upstairs to one of the larger bedrooms. She placed the revolver on the bed. The room held a king size bed with ornately carved cherry wood head and footboards. Two, heavy looking, matching, nightstands stood on each side. A matching dresser sat on another wall, and a huge wooden armoire was across the room from the bed with the TV in it. A floor to ceiling bookcase was on the other wall next to a closet door. "See, the TV is still on. He was in here watching it." She looked around. "How do we find a secret door?"

"We can feel along the walls for any air movement." Virginia pointed. "Also, that bookcase is a built in. The passageway could be behind it, same thing for that armoire. Are there any other features built in?"

"Just that seat under the gabled window. I use it as a reading spot. The cushion is soft, and there is a light right above the window."

"Okay, let's have a look." Virginia headed for the bookcase. She started to push and tug on shelves and the framework. She was poking knotholes when there was a ping on an iPad resting on the bed.

Natalie walked to the bed and picked it up. She touched an icon for the E-mail app and looked at the list. She opened the new E-mail and read it. "This is interesting."

"Is it important?" Asked Virginia.

"It's from a Jenny Parker."

"She's the Owner of the *Quilters' Corner* quilt store."

"Yeah. That's what the note says. She says she's a certified quilt appraiser and wants to come here tomorrow morning at ten, to talk to me about assessing my cousin's notebooks, her quilts, the tools, and materials in Ann's quilt room. She adds that she has reasonable rates." Natalie looked at Virginia.

"What are you going to tell her?"

"Just a second." Natalie quickly typed a response and sent it. Then she tossed the iPad back onto the bed. "I told her I have a friend assessing my cousin's quilting things and her quilts, so her services are not required."

"She'll love that."

Natalie looked at the bookcase. "Find anything?"

"Not yet." Virginia moved around the bookcase. "I'll try pressing and pulling more. See if the armoire is fixed to the wall or free standing."

"Okay." Natalie examined the armoire. "It's about four or five inches from the wall. I don't think we are going to find a door here."

Virginia walked to the closet door and opened it. There were poles down two sides and built in wood shelves in the back. They were framed, with the shelves attached directly to the wall as a back and to the side framing. "This door was closed when the cat was in here, wasn't it?"

"Yes, and he can't open doors with round doorknobs, just handles."

Virginia closed the closet door. "It has to be the bookcase."

"Try looking really low. Poseidon can't reach very high unless he jumps on a shelf."

"Good point." Virginia got on her knees and examined the bookcase. "Uh oh." She heard a soft click, got up, and stepped back. A section of the bookcase started to open. She dropped back and looked at Natalie. Natalie had her revolver in her shaking hands, aiming at the widening opening.

CHAPTER 6

Virginia watched the bookcase continue to open another few inches and then stopped. Andy's voice called out. "You ladies in here?"

"Andy! You scared us to death. What are you doing in there? How'd you get in there?"

Andy slid into the room. "I was setting up the alarm in the basement in case someone tried to get in through a small window, or the outside cellar door. Oh, I added some reinforcement to the exterior door down there and secured it, so no one will be able to open it from outside. If anyone were to try, they will seriously regret it. They won't get in anyway. It must now be opened only from the inside. I found the other end of this tunnel in the cellar. It's behind the furnace in what was once a root cellar. One of the shelves was ajar. I figured I'd see where the hidden hallway went. There seems to be a number of them that intersect."

Natalie inspected the opening. "How'd you happen to pick this one?"

"There's dust on the floor. Using my Maglite, I followed the cat's footprints. He's used it before. When I got closer, I heard you talking." Andy closed the bookcase then looked at it. "How does it open on this end?"

Natalie stepped closer to him. "We haven't a clue."

Virginia looked at the bookcase. "We'll have to figure this out later and explore where they all go."

Natalie nodded. "I agree. It might be fun."

Andy glanced at his watch. "It's getting late. The temporary alarm system is set up and operational. If you will follow me, I'll show you how to operate it."

Virginia and Natalie followed Andy down to the kitchen. He picked up a small laptop computer and showed it to Natalie. She moved close to him and looked at the screen. He took the next ten minutes to explain how the system worked and how to turn it on and off. "It's all wireless so you can take this control system upstairs to bed with you, and anywhere else you go in the house. The sheds are on a separate system, and you control them like the house. Trust me, if anyone sets it off, you will know about it, and they will be in extremely serious pain."

Natalie took the computer and tried turning the systems off and on. "Looks like I've got the hang of it. "Thank you so much, Andy." She stood on her toes and gave him a quick kiss on his cheek.

Andy blushed. "Don't mention it. I'll be back tomorrow to finish installing the rest of it, and start going over your construction stuff." He looked at Virginia who was sitting on the stool at the drawing board. "You almost ready to call it a night?"

Virginia nodded. "Yeah. I'm tired." She yawned, stood, picked up her backpack, and turned to Natalie. "With Andy's alarm system and your gun, you should be okay tonight. I'll be back tomorrow morning to start the quilt analysis. If anything happens tonight, call us right after you call 911."

"Will do." Natalie smiled. "Great. I'm glad I met you two. Thanks for coming tonight and for everything. I'll see you tomorrow." She stood on the porch and watched Virginia and Andy get into the van and drive down the driveway.

As Andy drove, he said to Virginia. "She is short, maybe five feet tall. She sure is pretty and sexy. She's prettier than her photographs show her."

"You would notice."

"Hey, I'm a guy. We notice these things." He quickly peered at his cell phone. "She returned inside, locked up, and set her new alarm systems."

Virginia frowned. "How do you know?"

"I have a backup control on my phone and computer at home should anything go wrong. It just told me."

"I don't know if I should be happy or concerned."

"Happy, dear."

Andy reached into his jacket pocket, removed a rock, and handed it to Virginia. "Take a look at this."

Virginia switched on the dome light and examined the rock as she turned it in her hands. "Looks like quartz. Where'd you get it?"

"In a box on a shelf near the furnace. It is quartz but look at the inclusions."

She held the quartz closer and squinted. "The light isn't very good, but it looks like gold."

"Yeah, and the note on the side of the box said the specimens came from *Borealis*."

At nine the next morning Virginia, dressed in brown shorts and a blouse loosely tied closed over a bright-red, thin, tank top, picked up Linda and headed for *Borealis*.

Linda, dressed in tan slacks and a dark blue blouse, was silent for part of the trip and then turned to Virginia. "Did you give the pictures of Natalie to your husband?"

"Yep."

"Oh. How did he like them?"

"He loved them like any normal, red-blooded man would."

"I bet he'd like to meet her."

Virginia chuckled. "He did."

"What?" Linda's eyes widened. "When?"

"Last night. Someone tried to break into her house. I called her right after the sheriff left to tell her Andy agreed to be her engineer and to see if she'd have dinner with us. But Andy and I took dinner with us, and we all ate at her place. Andy installed an emergency alarm system for her and will be back this afternoon to finish it and start being her engineer for the renovation. He likes her, and she likes him."

Linda sat with her mouth hanging open. "So, he's seen her in the flesh."

"She was dressed very nicely, and Andy has seen her pictures, so how she dresses today won't surprise him any."

"So, after the sheriff left, you went there?"

"Yeah. Like I said, someone tried to break in, and she was upset, felt alone, and needed a friend. She doesn't really have family or friends here. Oh. While I was there, Jenny Parker from the *Quilters' Corner* quilt store E-mailed her. She wanted to do the appraisals of the quilts and stuff."

"What did Natalie do?"

"She told Jenny she has friends already doing it, so no thanks."

"Wow. You've gotten in good with her."

"And I told her about looking into her cousin's murder. Natalie's happy we're doing it and said she'd help if she can. Her cousin Ann was poisoned with something from the Panther mushroom. We'll have to learn more about it."

"You've been busy."

"We're here." Virginia turned off the main road and headed up the driveway. She parked next to a gray Buick and a new, white, double cab, Ford F-150. "Looks like someone's visiting. I wonder who."

Virginia and Linda climbed out of her Pilot, went up the short steps to the porch, and to the door. Virginia knocked.

"Come in," called Natalie, her voice strained.

Virginia and Linda opened the door and went inside. Natalie sat on her stool by the large drawing board looking sexy, but browbeaten, eyes red. She bit her lip. Jenny Parker, Owner of the *Quilters' Corner* quilt store, stood to one side, glowering. Bryon Weedon leaned against the table, fire in his eyes, yelled at Natalie. He stopped when Virginia and Linda entered.

Virginia marched to Natalie and turned facing Jenny and Bryan. "Good morning." She dropped her backpack on the floor.

Jenny stared at Virginia. "So, you're the friend who's doing the quilts."

"Yep. I'm starting right now. And," she pointed toward Linda, "Linda Chambers is assisting me."

"I don't see how *you* think *you're* qualified to do it." Jenny sneered. "Whereas, I'm a certified appraiser and quilt judge. I'm far more suited, and far more qualified for the job, and—"

Natalie brightened. "Wait a just a minute! I'm the person who decides who's qualified and who will do the work. I chose Virginia and her friend, Linda. I asked them. They didn't seek the job. Now, if there is anything that you want to know regarding the quilts, Ann's stuff in her quilt room, or her notebooks, you'll have to go through Virginia."

"I'll talk to you later, Virginia." Jenny fumed as she pivoted on her heel and stormed out of the house.

Natalie took a breath. The fabric of her tight, thin, white, wife beater t-shirt, stretched over her more than ample, braless, breasts, which easily revealed through the fabric. It was tucked into a pair of black shorts. "Virginia, this is Mr. Bryon Weedon. He's the developer I told you about. He doesn't think I'm qualified to undertake this rehab job on my property. He insists I sell *Borealis* to him for what *he* thinks is a reasonable price. Mr. Weedon says he has great plans for the land. And he said, he, and the community, think I don't belong here and want me to go back to California."

Virginia eyed him and chuckled. "Sell you her property? Like that's going to happen. Natalie, you've got the right stuff. You also have a staff, including technical support. And you sure as hell do belong here. You have friends here, too. Don't let this jackass tell you different. If he's that hot to get this place then maybe there is something about it you don't know."

Natalie gave Virginia a questioning look. "Like what?"

"We can discuss that later. Right now, you have a construction project to complete."

Weedon glared at Virginia. "Who are you exactly, and what makes you an expert at contracting and real estate development?"

"Like it's any of your business, but I'm Virginia Davies Clark. I'm a quilter and museum curator," Virginia said acidly.

Weedon laughed. "This only gets better. Look at you two. Two indecent broads. A scandalous actress, and now a... a quilter who runs a damn museum. That's quite a construction and development team. You will royally screw this up. Then I'll buy it."

"Not going to happen." Virginia stepped close to him and straightened, her blouse opening further, offering him a view of her tight, thin, red tank top. Weedon's eyes widened as he looked at her. He swallowed and took a step back. Virginia continued sharply, "This place is hers to do as she pleases. Now, you've bothered her enough." Virginia poked Weedon's chest with her index finger. She noticed perspiration beading on his forehead. "And I don't like being called a broad."

He gulped and then turned toward Natalie. Before he could say anything, she pointed at the door. "Get off my property, Mr. Weedon."

Weedon, his face deep red, turned, and marched out. At the door, he said, "You'll hear from me again. I want this land, and I intend to get it, one way or another." The door slammed shut behind him.

Virginia watched him go. "Looks like we didn't make any friends so far this morning."

"Batting a thousand." Natalie sagged and caught her breath, then grinned. "Thank you, Virginia. Your timing was perfect. I wasn't expecting them. They came in at the same time and caught me off guard. I got flustered. They were so belligerent." She closed her eyes for a moment then glanced at her calendar on the work surface. "Well, I have a couple of county people scheduled for later this today. Your husband sent me an e-mail. He'll be here around one-thirty. He said he and I could start going over everything after he finishes the alarm system. You know, Virginia, after you guys left, I locked up, set the alarm, and had the best night's sleep I've had in a long time. Thank you for last night." She glanced at the door. "And thanks for this morning. You saved me, again."

"It was our pleasure. Now, Linda and I will head upstairs to start inventorying all Ann's quilt-related stuff. If you need me, just yell." She grabbed her backpack.

"Okay." Natalie smiled at Linda standing near the kitchen sink. "Nice to see you again, Linda."

Virginia led Linda upstairs to the quilt room.

After they entered the quilt room, Virginia set her backpack on a chair. She turned toward Linda who still stood in the doorway.

Linda cleared her throat. "Virginia. Did you see how she was dressed again with that man here? And I heard the workers in the other room, too."

"Yeah. So what?"

"I... well it was more conservative, if that's the right word, than yesterday. Her attire didn't seem to faze that Mr. Weedon. Even your... a... your outfit didn't bother him."

"Oh, we fazed him all right. He was sweating and kept looking at our chests and tried to act like he didn't notice. Just like a man. He was trying to hide the fact that he was getting uncomfortable."

"He buckled when you verbally attacked him. You poking him really unnerved him."

Virginia chuckled. "He did get a little taken back, didn't he? I made him more nervous when my blouse opened. I also pissed him off."

"What if that didn't get him to leave, what would you have done then?"

Virginia untied her blouse and removed it. "He was already sweating and nervous with her attire and my blouse opening a little. I think, between Natalie and me, if I took off my blouse and just had my thin, tank top without a bra, we would have given him a stroke. Oh yeah, you do know that Weedon guy is an active member of a Baptist church in town. That shyster is a... never mind."

"Would you really have taken your blouse off and let him see that... shirt... and you?"

"Absolutely. He saw it anyway. I'm helping Natalie with the difficult workers and officials who come by. Most men become little boys when they see women dressed like us, or like she was dressed yesterday. They'd be *Silly Putty* if we were nude. Now, where would you like to start?"

"Aren't you going to put your blouse back on?"

"No. No telling who might show up. And Linda, give it up."

"What will your husband say?"

"He already knows, so don't sweat it. He picked out this top."

"Oh." Linda took a breath. "What exactly did you do in college that Natalie was talking about? I don't think it involved engineering."

"It did in a way. I'll tell you later."

"From the way you and she are dressed around men, I can hazard a guess." She looked at Virginia. "Well, I guess I should start inventorying all the quilts and put them in categories, like art quilts, serious quilts, wall hangings, etc."

"Good idea. They are in those two room over there."

"I'll get right on it." Linda hurriedly left the room.

She's such a prude. She probably can't wait to tell the others in our bee and the guild. Maybe I should just tell her about college and show her the pictures. Maybe later. Virginia turned and surveyed the quilt room. *Where to start?* She saw the book with the big X Ann had drawn with a Sharpie and set it on the far edge of the six-foot-long, two-and-a-half-foot-deep, wood cutting board cabinet with two blue cutting boards on top. "I'll get to this later. I guess I could start inventorying her tools." She looked at the pegboard panel attached to the rear of the cutting table. It was about three feet high and as long as the table. On it hung special quilting rulers, triangles, plastic forms, scissors, rotary cutters of assorted sizes, and pictures. *There may be more.* Virginia started opening drawers in the cabinet and the two big doors in the center when she heard the loud shrill of Andy's alarm. *Oh boy.*

Linda came running in, "What is that awful sound?"

Virginia rushed to her backpack, pulled out her semiautomatic pistol, and started for the stairs. "It's Andy's alarm. Stay here."

"Okay. I'm not going anywhere."

Virginia tore down the stairs and into the kitchen. She spotted Natalie looking at the little computer Andy left her. "Where's the problem?"

Natalie looked up with wild eyes. "It says the shed. I forgot to turn off the alarm for the sheds. It's the first one closest to the house."

"Grab your gun, sister, but you stay here in case it's a decoy. I'll check out the shed."

"Who could be breaking into the shed?"

"That's what I'm going to find out."

CHAPTER 7

Virginia hurried out the door and down the steps. She moved cautiously around the side of the house and spotted the shed with the small flashing red light above the door. It looked like a small version of the house. Something darted away from the door into the trees. Virginia hung close to the side of the mansion, maneuvering around shrubs, mountain laurels, and a large crepe myrtle, as she edged toward the shed. No one seemed to be around. She darted across the grass to an elm tree near the front of the building. She warily looked around. The door had scratch marks near the base and around the locked door handle. She glanced at the dirt. Fresh pawprints were visible. Virginia turned her head sharply at a sound from a large, near by, peach tree. A raccoon's head appeared from behind it and looked at her.

"So, you're the culprit. It's daytime; what are you doing here? You're nocturnal?" she said to him. She lowered her weapon and stepped out into the open. The raccoon turned and scampered away. "I'll have to tell Andy. He needs to change the settings, so that little guy doesn't keep Natalie up at night." She checked the door to see if it was secure, then returned to the house.

Virginia entered the kitchen. Natalie and Linda were leaning against the counter talking. *Now that's a first. Linda seems fine with Natalie. Maybe she's loosening up… that, or accepted her fate.*

Natalie held her revolver and glanced at Virginia. "Did you find who set off the alarm?"

"Yeah. It was a large raccoon. He was cute. Andy can fix the system so he won't turn on the alarm in the middle of the night." She pointed to Natalie's gun, "You can put that away now."

Virginia watched Natalie walk to the drafting table, open the bottom drawer, slide the pistol in, and then close it. "I'm glad it was just an animal and not some snooping photographer or a burglar." She sat on the stool and looked at the clock on the microwave. "The county people will be here in an hour and a half. When they leave, would you two let me buy you lunch?"

Virginia nodded. "That's nice of you. Sure." She glanced at Linda. "You in?"

"Yes. Where you two go, I'm going. But now I need to get back upstairs and work on organizing and indexing all Ann's quilts. Call me when you're ready." Linda turned and went down the hall to the stairs.

Virginia looked at Natalie, "She seems quite comfortable now, what did you do?"

"Just had a little woman to woman chat. Linda's nice."

I wonder what they chatted about. "That's good. Well, if you need me for anything while the county people are here, just yell."

"Okay."

Virginia went back to the quilt room, slid her gun back into her backpack, and looked around the room. She noticed Ann's laptop computer and stepped to it. She booted it up and waited. *I hope this thing doesn't have a password.* The computer home screen appeared. She looked at the files shown. *Let's see... recipes, files for the quilt guilds, home repairs, gardening, expenses, pictures, teaching schedules and notes, classes, and book.* Virginia sat back. *Book? What book?* She clicked on the file. It opened. The file was empty. She typed on the keyboard. *The file was erased. Funny, it was erased the day after she died. How'd that happen? Natalie wasn't here yet.* She started opening the other file folders, and they seemed to be intact. *Just the book folder stuff is missing? Her cat may be able to open doors, but I don't think he can operate a computer, even with a mouse. What's this?"* She tried to open a file labeled 'concept.' It was locked and needed a password. *What's in here?*

She turned off the computer, leaned back, and looked around. "Okay, now to see what else we've got here. She opened large cabinets against one wall. In shelves were clear plastic containers holding various color and types of fabric. There were color chips facing the front of the containers depicting the range of colors of the fabrics inside. *Nice idea. I'll have to do that.* She opened a number of boxes to see exactly what was in them. Some boxes held fat quarters, others, jellyrolls. Some had pieces of fabric of certain colors, and a couple had what appeared to be quilt squares ready to be pieced together to form quilts. A couple marked for classes Ann taught. They had precut fabric, and in some cases, patterns Ann had made, complete with her copyright. *Okay. I've got an idea as to the scope of this project. I'll ask Natalie if I can use Ann's computer to do the inventory. It'll be easier to do searches that way.*

Close to two hours later, Virginia stood and stretched. She heard a car approaching the house and went to the window. She opened the blinds and looked down at the driveway. A county vehicle stopped. Two men in suits got out of the car. One carried a portfolio. They started toward the house.

Virginia returned to her work. In a drawer in the cutting workbench, Virginia found some sticky notes and numbered the cabinets and all the boxes inside. She opened one of the boxes and pulled out a slender piece of cotton. The pattern was gentle, a couple of wavy lines that added more texture than a pattern to the piece. Virginia looked at the fabric in the box and found quilt blocks that would form an outdoor scene with foxes. Ann had picked fabrics that created texture and feelings and added interest. She put the fabric back in the box and closed it, then started toward the closet when she heard Natalie call her. Virginia hurried down the stairs to the kitchen. She walked in and saw Natalie sitting at her drawing board and the two men standing across the board, in front of her.

Natalie motioned for Virginia to come closer. "Virginia, these men are from the county development department. They seem to think *Borealis*, which includes all my land, needs to be developed into much-needed housing. They are telling me that my resistance to development will be met with opposition from developers, the community, and the county government."

Virginia frowned. "So what? It's your land to do as you please with."

Natalie cracked a smile. "They also have some sketches showing me how to divide my land, so I keep a small section and the rest is open for development. What do you think I should do?"

One of the men stared at Virginia's chest then looked up at her. "Who may I ask are you? I take it you're *another* woman from California or Hollywood? What is your connection to this?"

Like it's any of your business who I am. Virginia took a deep breath and grinned. "I'm Virginia Davies Clark, a close friend of Ms. North. I am also a curator at the San Gabriel Museum. Ms. North has engaged me to appraise Ann's quilts and things, and she's hired an engineer to assist her with the technical and contracting aspects of the project and obtaining necessary permits, most of which she already has. As to the development, you're more interested in the property tax increases you'll get." She glared at them. "And maybe you're helping a certain shyster developer who's been pressuring, and as of this morning, threatened, Ms. North to sell out to him or else. How much has he paid you to put pressure on her? Or, is it campaign donations to some officials?"

The man looked at the fellow next to him who was staring starry-eyed at Natalie and Virginia. "The county feels she must use her land for the highest and best commercial use. Bill, what do you think?"

"Huh? Oh," He blinked then looked at his partner. "Yeah, best use is the policy."

"I've heard this crap before when the counties or cites want more tax revenue." Natalie pointed to her map. "It's my land, and I'll do as I please. To me the best use is for what I'm using it for. I refuse to allow it to be turned into a California style, cookie-cutter development, on very small lots, like your drawing shows."

Virginia jumped into the conversation. "Oh, yeah, Ms. North and I have been talking to the U.S. Department of Wildlife and the Army Corps of Engineers, about some endangered flora and fauna around here and her artesian spring and stream. What she's doing won't harm any endangered plants or animals in this area or the water, but any development definitely will."

The fist man's lip twitched. "Did you say you've communicated with the federal wildlife folks?"

"Yes, and the Army Corps of Engineers. Next, we'll be talking to the IRS, that's another federal agency you do not want to get sideways with."

The second man, still staring at their chests, stammered. "Wildlife? Army engineers? I think we've taken up enough of these ladies time. We should go." He cracked a smile, "Thank you both for your information. We'll be going."

They folded up their portfolio and started to leave when the first man turned. "Is the engineer you hired a registered professional engineer? That would be a requirement."

Virginia frowned. "He's a registered engineer in Texas, California, Florida, Arizona, and New York. Anything else?"

He shook his head. "No. Thank you for your time." They hurried to their car.

Natalie smiled at Virginia. "I'm not on my game today. My nerves need a rest. They started in on me as soon as they walked in, and I got rattled. I wasn't too sure if I could tell them to get off my property without any more trouble with the county. I guess I'm still shaken from Weedon and that quilt woman this morning. Thanks again for your help."

"No problem. You've been under a lot of stress without any support, until now. And yes, you can tell anyone to leave your property, including government officials."

"We're talking to the U.S. Department of Wildlife and the Army Corps of Engineers? I don't remember that. When did we do it?"

Virginia winked. "Not we, I mean you, haven't. At least not yet, but they don't know that."

"Oh." Natalie grinned. "They were having trouble concentrating with both of us dressed as we are, and when you told them about the federal agencies, that sure took the starch out of them." Natalie looked at the clock. "How about lunch? Call Linda and see if she'd still like to go, too."

"I'll run up and ask her, and slip on my blouse. Can't have the local natives too upset."

"Okay. I'll go put something else on, too. Meet you and Linda here in a couple minutes. We need to go somewhere close. I want to be here when your husband comes to upgrade my security system and start on the engineering stuff." Natalie got up. "I'll check on the construction guys in the other room and see what they're doing."

"I'll call Andy and see if he's still coming at one-thirty." Virginia darted for the stairs.

Fifteen minutes later, with Natalie and Linda in Virginia's car, they pulled into *Jardin Corona's*, a Mexican restaurant in Liberty Hill, and parked under an oak tree. They entered and took a table toward the back. As they waited for their order, they munched on chips and salsa.

Natalie sipped a grande margarita. "Those county guys were pompous asses. I don't know how to stop this harassment."

Virginia nodded. "I have some ideas. We go on the offensive. First thing, we get some no trespassing signs and put them up out front. Post an armed guard. Maybe get the construction guys to act as bouncers. If that Weedon guy comes back, while one of us talks to him, the other calls the sheriff."

Linda finished off a chip. "Ladies, that might be a little overkill. I think you two doing what you're doing will eventually work. You two are quite a team, and you're getting good at unnerving them and throwing them off base. You have seized the upper hand with them with what you're doing. Stick to your guns."

Virginia smiled. "Well, you're part of this team, too. I'm glad you're helping." *What happened at the house? Linda isn't the same. This is great.* Virginia's cell buzzed. She looked at the message. "Andy will be at the house at one thirty. We have a lot of time before he gets there."

Natalie smiled. "Good. I think I'll have another grande margarita." She waved over their waiter and placed her order. She sipped the last of her existing drink and sat back. "I feel better already with you two and Andy helping."

"I have a question for you." Virginia picked up her backpack and fished out the quartz sample. She handed it to Natalie. "Have you seen this before?"

Natalie took the quartz and rotated it. "Looks like some rocks in a box in my basement. Why?"

"I think we may have found a reason why Weedon and others want your property."

Natalie sat expressionless. "Because of some rock?"

"Yes, that rock is quartz with gold in it."

"Gold?" Linda leaned close to Natalie and gazed at the rock.

Natalie reexamined the quartz and noticed the gold striations through it. "I never noticed this before. I really never paid much attention to that bunch of rocks Ann had in the basement."

Linda took the sample and looked at it. Where'd it come from? I didn't think they had gold around here." She handed the quartz back to Natalie.

"I didn't either. It's a mystery." Virginia pointed. "Looks like lunch is coming, let's eat.

They finished lunch and returned to *Borealis*.

A large delivery truck was pulling up when they arrived. Natalie raised an eyebrow. "I wasn't expecting the hot tub until tomorrow."

Linda's eyes widened. "A hot tub? You bought a hot tub?"

"Yes. It's a big one, too. I have one in California. I've had a concrete slab poured, and there is a water line and power box already set. It's got its own drainpipe, too. Just didn't expect the delivery today."

Virginia noticed a couple more pickup trucks pulling in. "Looks like the workers are back from lunch. We made it back just in time to let them in."

Virginia and Linda resumed their work on the quilts. Virginia started inventorying the quilt room after setting up a spreadsheet on Ann's computer. When she entered the last information for the day and sat back, she realized it was 4 pm. *Andy's been here all afternoon and hasn't come to see me. He must be busy. I wonder how the hot tub is coming?* She backed up all the new information in the spreadsheets on a Two Terabyte jump drive, and climbed out of the chair, stretched and went down to the first floor. She heard conversation in the living room. She strolled in. Natalie and Andy were sitting across from each other looking at some papers and a drawing.

Andy looked up when she entered. "Hi. We're going over some materials for Natalie to use in a request for quote packages. How are you doing?"

"Fine." Virginia plopped into a soft chair. "Did you finish with the alarm system?"

"Yes. It's up and running. I made adjustments for raccoons, too. I watched over the men putting in the hot tub. We've been going over what she needs done on the house and put together a first cut at a schedule, so things get done in order, so she won't have to redo anything."

"Did she tell you about the county people that were here this morning?"

"Yeah. Sounds like you took care of that. She mentioned the quartz sample, too. We'll look into that later. This construction project and the quilts are more important right now. Oh, when are you going to see the sheriff?"

Virginia closed her eyes. *I forgot about that.* "Maybe tomorrow. I'll be a little late coming here. I've got an early meeting at the museum, and then I'll run by the Sheriff's office. I bet that call won't take long."

Natalie smiled. "That's fine. How's it going with the quilt stuff?"

"Okay. Linda and I have found about everything, and we're doing an inventory. We'll then start valuing things then. I'm using Ann's computer. I hope you don't mind."

"No. Go ahead and use it."

"I just remembered, there's a locked file on it. It's labeled 'concept.' Any idea what's in it?"

Natalie shook her head. "None."

"It's locked. By any chance, do you know the password?"

"No. But Ann had a short memory for some things. You may find the password written down somewhere up there."

"I'll keep an eye out for it. One other thing, there is a file called *book*. It was erased the day after her death."

Natalie sat up straight and brushed some stray blond hair from her eyes. "How could that have happened? No one was here. The police locked the house up when they were through with their investigation here the day they found Ann. I had to get the keys from the sheriff's detective."

"Either someone else has a key, or they broke in. The question is who?"

"I'm glad Andy finished with the alarm system, now. Oh, here's the code to disarm it if you come and I'm not here." Natalie handed Virginia a slip of paper with numbers on it.

"Thanks." *I bet Andy already has it.* Virginia took the paper and stuffed it in her pants pocket. "How's the hot tub coming along?"

"They'll be finished installing it tomorrow. Andy said he'd pick up the chemicals I'll need. We can start getting it ready for use then. There is a concrete patio around it, so I'll put an umbrella table, chairs, and some lounges around it as soon as I can. At least the house construction won't hurt it. Maybe it'll do my nerves some good. Once I get it ready, you and Andy will have to be the first guests to use it, with me."

"That would be fun. Oh yeah, I've transferred everything on Ann's computer to a portable backup drive, so nothing happens to her files and our work."

Natalie wet her lips. "Good idea."

Linda walked into the room. "I'm bushed. Ready to call it a day?"

Virginia nodded. "Yes. I'll take you home. Tomorrow you'll have to drive here yourself. I have to go to the museum and stop by the sheriff's office first."

"Okay. Let me know how it goes with the detective."

Virginia rose. "I'll get my backpack, and we can go. How much longer will you be, Andy?"

He looked at Natalie, then back at Virginia. "I've got a couple things to finish up for her for tomorrow. I'll be home in about an hour, or so."

The phone rang. Natalie rose and darted to the kitchen. She returned a minute later. "That was my agent in Hollywood. He has a part in a new movie he thinks I should look at. He's talked to the producer, and they're

Suspicious Threads

looking for locations, and he wants me to send pictures of *Borealis.*"

Virginia frowned. "Will you have to go to Hollywood for this? If you do, we can keep things rolling around here while you're gone."

"No. He's sending me the script by FedEx. I'll e-mail him pictures. Oh, I asked if there was a chance you could be in the picture, Virginia. You too, Linda."

Virginia gave her a quizzical look. "You didn't."

"Yep. He said to send him some pictures of you two and information on any acting or modeling you've done. You want to try for a part? It would be a minor part."

She looked at Andy. He nodded.

"Sure, that would be a blast. I've never acted before, so I'd settle for an extra or a walk on."

Natalie looked at Linda, You in?"

Linda looked stunned. "I... I couldn't. I haven't acted since high school. Where will they be doing the filming?"

"In Hollywood, I guess, and also on location. Probably some of it here."

"Well... sure, I'd like to do it if you two are. I'll tell my husband. I'm not sure what his response will be though."

"Okay. Tell him Virginia is going to do it, maybe that'll help."

Virginia looked at Linda. "Let's get our things and head out." She glanced at Andy. "See you at the house, dear."

Linda started for the stairs then stopped and turned. "Ms. North, I'm using my *Surface* computer to do the inventory and backing it up on a flash drive. I'll leave the flash drive with the quilts. Is that okay with you?"

Natalie smiled. "Hell, yes. Thank you, Linda."

A few minutes later Virginia and Linda drove down the driveway and stopped at the road. Virginia pointed at a gray Chevy parked, idling, on the side of the road, by the fence, in front of *Borealis.* The person inside set their camera with a big lens down. The vehicle spun around and roared down the highway away from them.

Virginia turned onto the road. "Who the hell was that?"

Linda held up her iPhone. "I don't know. But I got a picture."

CHAPTER 8

Virginia dropped Linda off at home. She kept an eye out for anyone following her as she proceeded to her house. She parked the car in the garage and went in. She took Ann's computer to her quilt room and plugged it in. She then attached a one Terabyte backup drive and downloaded all the files from Ann's computer. *Doesn't hurt to have a second backup at a different location.* She then opened her E-mail and downloaded the picture Linda took of the mysterious car and person with the camera. *I'll look into this later.* She transferred the pictures to her cell phone.

About an hour later, Andy came in from the garage. He found Virginia and Leo, her cat, in the family room watching TV. He sat on the couch near her and stroked Leo. "Boy, Natalie has a lot of work to get done. She's not in as bad a shape as she thought, and even though she's new at this, she's actually accomplished a lot."

Virginia turned the TV down. "Will you be able to help her?"

"Yeah. I worked out the order she needs to do things and made a tentative timeline. Her drawings for the work look pretty good. I think, from some of the dates on them, Ann started the project before she died. A lot of background work is pretty well done. There are some aspects that will need my attention. She's concerned about the contracting. I can help her with that, too. This will be a nice distraction for me."

"The work or her?"

Andy put his hand on his chest and feigned hurt. "Why the work, of course."

"Of course." Virginia cracked a smile and sat back. "You said Ann might have started the work? She was going to turn *Borealis* into a B&B?"

"From what I saw on the papers and drawings Natalie showed me, yes."

"Was there any correspondence from the developer Bryon Weedon?"

"A bunch of letters. In one letter, he mentions some E-mails he had sent to Ann. He's obviously none too happy. There is correspondence from other developers, too, and someone at the university. I wonder if they knew of the gold. But who knows where those rocks came from. Oh, yeah, there was some scathing letters from some church, too. And I'm going to help Natalie get her new hot tub ready for use, too. She wants you and me to help her christen it."

"That's what she said. That could be interesting." Virginia rose, clicked off the TV, and looked at Andy. "To protect my interests, I think I'll show you some very personal attention tonight."

Andy looked at the clock on the wall behind the couch. "But we haven't had dinner yet."

"You'll have a much bigger appetite after I'm done with you." She started to take off her clothes as she walked toward the bedroom. "Coming?"

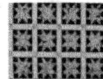

The next morning Virginia drove to the museum. In her office, she had just opened her computer when her boss, the museum director, entered and sat in a chair. "Good morning, Virginia."

"Good morning, Dr. Doverspike. What can I do for you?"

"I was curious how things are going at *Borealis?*"

"We have started the inventory of the quilt stuff. Natalie said I could take some for the museum and she's getting rid of some of the furnishings. There are pieces that are very old. She said the museum could have first right of refusal so we can pick out anything we want that she's disposing of."

"Wonderful. But, Virginia, you're on vacation. What are you doing here this morning?"

"I have a meeting with a couple of anthropologists and the display builders. Then I'm going to see a sheriff's detective about Ann's murder. That probably won't take long. He'll probably get mad and throw me out or just refuse to see me."

Doverspike sat thinking for a minute. Then spoke. "Before I forget, I did a little literature research on the mushroom you asked about. I don't think she ate a bad mushroom as much as someone either purchased the poisonous agents in the Panther cap mushroom as reagents or concentrated it from a number of them. That would take an organic chemist or biochemist. If the ME said that's what killed Ann North Greenwald, then she was poisoned. The Panther cap contains the psychoactive chemical compounds ibotenic acid, muscimol, muscazone, and muscarine. Ibotenic acid is a powerful neurotoxin. Muscimol is the product of the decarboxylation or drying of ibotenic acid, and it is thought that muscimol is as much as ten times as potent as ibotenic acid alone. The others are pretty nasty in high concentrations, too."

An organic chemist or biochemist? Virginia raised an eyebrow. "So, someone went to a lot of trouble to make her death look like an accident. Someone who is a chemist, or got the procedure from a chemist."

"Right."

"So, it actually is murder."

"Yes. That ME is sharp." Doverspike rose. "Virginia, go investigate and help Ms. North. I'll handle your meeting this morning."

"That's nice of you, sir."

Doverspike chuckled. "There's a price. I want to meet Ms. North."

"I can arrange that. Thanks. I'll go see the sheriff's detective, then go to… maybe I'll also go to a certain quilt shop first." She rose, grabbed her backpack, and headed for the door.

She turned as Dr. Doverspike called to her. "Virginia, Dr. English, from the archeology department, said he wants a picture of Ms. North."

"Of course he does. I'll see what I can do. Eight by ten glossy okay?"

"I guess so. Get one for me, too."

"Okay." Virginia hurried out of the museum.

Sitting in her Pilot, she dialed sheriff detective Dan Grover, on her cell phone. *This probably won't be a long call. He'll say hello then go to hell. I tried anyway.* He answered on the fourth ring. "Grover."

"Detective, My name is Virginia Davies Clark, and I'm—"

"You're the broad who thinks she's investigating the murder of Ann North Greenwald."

Virginia swallowed. *Broad?* "You've heard about me?"

"Oh yeah. Let me guess; you want to talk to me, see how well we're doing, and investigate yourself."

"Well…"

"Can you come to the Monument Café in about fifteen minutes?"

She looked at the phone. "Huh?"

"The Monument café; you know, the one on Austin Avenue. Everyone knows the place."

"Sure. I'll be there." *This sounds strange.*

"Good. You're buying me breakfast, and we can talk." He hung up.

Virginia looked at the phone. *I'm buying him breakfast? Now? He didn't sound mad. Gruff, but not mad. Maybe this'll work out. Then again, maybe not. He may still tell me to mind my own business and to go to hell.* She started the car, drove to the Monument Café's parking lot, and went in. She told the woman up the front to send Detective Grover, an older, man with a Sheriff's badge who may ask for her, to her booth. After a short wait, a man about sixty with a white cowboy hat in a blue, striped, western shirt and jeans, entered. On his belt were a sheriff's star, sidearm, and a leather case for handcuffs. He carried a stuffed, red, file folder with a wide rubber band securing it. The woman at the front desk pointed toward

Virginia.

He marched to her table. "You Virginia Davies Clark?"

She looked up at him and smiled. Her heart thumped. "Yes, sir."

"Detective Dan Grover, Williamson County Sheriff's Office. I'm a homicide investigator. Glad to meet you." He sat opposite her and set the folder on the table. "You ordered yet?"

"Just coffee."

"Fine." He waved a waitress over. "I'm having an order of pancakes, a side of extra crispy bacon, large orange juice, and coffee." He looked at Virginia. "You having anything besides that coffee? I was joshing you on the phone. I'm buying."

He doesn't seem all that mad. Virginia looked up at the woman. "I'll have an order of scrambled eggs and a side of hash browns, wheat toast, and bacon like his."

Grover stared at her for a few seconds. "I like a woman who's not easily intimidated and knows what she wants. Good."

Virginia nodded. "Thanks, I think."

He removed his hat, exposing gray wavy hair, and set it on the side chair. "So, I understand you're helping Ms. Natalie North with her construction project."

"That's correct."

"You're also doing something with the quilt stuff Ann North Greenwald had, right?"

"Yes." *How'd he know?*

"From what I've heard you've become quite close with Ms. North. You've helped her run off some big mouth assholes, including a couple of county jerks."

"Yes." Virginia leaned forward. "May I ask why you're concerned about my relationship with Ms. North?"

Grover ran his hand through his hair. "There are a lot of people who coveted the land Ann North Greenwald had out there at her place. There are contractors, county, school, and various other officials who drooled over the possibilities of development and a large increased property tax inflow. Then, there are possible personal vendettas or maybe something else on that land I don't know about. She was a nationally known quilter, and I'm sure that garnered a few unhappy competitors. Your assessing the quilts out there, I heard, pissed off someone, too."

"Yes, sir." *Has he got the place bugged?*

He took a sip of his coffee. "There's some folks at the university that had designs on something out there, too. Exactly who and what I don't know. Then, there is a very vocal, really far out, church group who wants her property and doesn't approve of her at all. Any, or all of them, could be the one that killed Ann North Greenwald and maybe get Ms. North killed, too. Ms. North has gotten some folks in and around these parts worked up because she doesn't fit their idea of what she should be, and with what she's doing with the property. She hasn't had any friends here, and she's under a lot of pressure. Some of these people, thinking God's on their side, of course, could, and probably will, cause her some serious problems. The pompous, uptight, self-righteous religious jerks are sometimes the most dangerous. So, I'm glad Ms. North has a friend now."

Wow. He's done his homework and seems to genuinely care about Natalie's safety. "You're worried about Ms. North?"

"Yes. I've heard she's intelligent and rather spunky and spicy. I think she's a breath of fresh air around here even if she has tongues waging. I like that. She's different. She's doing what she wants and is sticking to her guns. I like her. I've never met the lady, but that'll change."

"She's intelligent and really very nice." Virginia nodded. "I agree with what you said about the people you mentioned." Her facial expression soured. "Does Bryon Weedon sound familiar?"

"Oh yeah." Grover nodded his head. "He's at the top of my list. I take it from the expression on your face, you've met him."

"Yes. He has sent Ann, and Natalie, some nasty e-mails and letters. He's pestered them both over the phone, too. He was browbeating Ms. North at her house when I met him. He was being rude, obnoxious a bully and a bastard, so I jumped in to help her get rid of him. He threatened her, too. Ann had some serious run-ins with him before she died."

"You've got him pegged right. He's a rich, well-connected, asshole. He operates just inside the law."

Virginia noticed their food coming. "Shall we eat, then get more into business?"

"Sounds like a plan."

As they ate, Grover asked Virginia what her interest was in investigating Ann North Greenwald's murder.

Virginia finished her food first. "Ann was a friend. She was a famous quilting teacher, and my mentor, and was well liked by those that knew her. I was curious as to any progress you've made in the investigation. I know you guys don't tell us civilians about ongoing investigations, but I figured I'd give it a try."

"I like your honesty. You're right. We usually don't give out information about ongoing investigations." He ate a slice of bacon. "But there are a few reasons I'm going to make an exception for you."

He is? Virginia's eyebrows rose. "You are? I mean… there are?"

"Yeah. One, the Georgetown PD asked me to. Two, they vouched for you. Three, I checked you out and found out you do work for the U.S. government as some sort of reserve special agent or something, and your agency thinks you're really, really good at it." He gave her a bewildered look. "I never heard of a reserve federal special agent before, but I guess you're one. They said you can be a little... how'd they put it... oh yeah, somewhat unorthodox sometimes. But if we want the killer, it would be a good idea to give you space and look the other way while you do your thing. They mentioned something about you bending rules now and then, but you get results. You'll have to tell me more about that some time." He finished his pancakes and pushed the dish away. "Forth, I'm stumped. I could use the help. People don't like to talk to the police. And the quilters are pretty protective of her. So I figure people, like the contractors, friends, and the quilters, would talk to you. Finally, you are a friend of Ms. North and helping her. If anything unusual turns up there, you'll be privy to it. Together we might actually stand a chance to apprehend the killer."

"I wasn't expecting this, detective." Virginia sipped her coffee. "Thank you for agreeing to let me help. If I do help you, I want you to take any, and all, the credit for finding Ann's killer."

"From a fed, that's unusual, but we'll jointly take the credit."

"Okay."

"It's unofficial you understand. That is, unless, or until, my request for your assistance to your Smithsonian Central Security Service gets approved."

He asked them to let me investigate with him? Wow. "Of course, sir."

"Okay." He slid the red folder to her. "Here are copies of everything I've got on the case. You understand they are confidential, you do not have them, and you never saw them. If you are sanctioned by your agency to investigate, then you will officially have them."

Virginia pulled the folder to her and slid it into her backpack. "What file?"

"I have a question. Does Ms. North really dress as racy as they say? To hear what some of my wife's church friends say, she's an immodest, uninhibited, unembarrassed, seductive, scandal on two beautiful legs. Of course, they've never actually met her, and probably never seen her either."

"Yes, she's all that. She's from Hollywood, and there a woman doesn't need to be modest to be respected. Think of the actresses on Showtime and HBO movies at night and the nudity and sex. I bet you watch. You don't dislike them. But she is smart, spunky, and as sweet as you can get. And you're right. I've noticed the people who are the most vocal about her haven't actually met her. I'm really glad I'm her friend."

"Me too. I'm glad she has you."

Virginia pulled out her cell phone and showed a picture to him. "Detective, this is a picture of a car and someone with a camera with a huge lens, who was parked outside Natalie's place yesterday. Can you trace it? You may have to enlarge the license plate."

"I'll see what I can do. E-mail it to me." He gave Virginia his e-mail address. "I'll let you know what I get as soon as I can."

"Thank you." Virginia sent the e-mail. "You've got it."

Grover waved for the waitress. He took the check and presented her with his credit card. "Virginia, it was very nice meeting you. Stay in touch and let me know what you find. I'll do the same. Also, if you need anything else traced or anything you need local law enforcement to do, call me. I'll let you know what your agency says."

"Okay." She got up, picked up her backpack, smiled, and shook his hand. "I'll keep you posted on any new developments. Thanks for the grub."

"Don't mention it. We never had this meeting."

"Understood." She walked out of the restaurant past one of the county men she had spoken to at Natalie's place. She glanced over her shoulder and saw him pull out his cell phone. *Is his being here a coincidence? I bet he can't wait to report back to whomever he works for. Change of plans. I think I'd better go straight to Borealis.*

CHAPTER 9

Virginia drove to *Borealis*. She swung into the driveway and parked behind Linda's car. Three pickup trucks and a panel truck were parked further ahead. She slid out of the Pilot. She walked around back, opened the tailgate, and pulled out Ann's computer while hiding the folder from Detective Grover under some red insulated grocery bags and a blanket. She started for the house when she heard some men talking around the side.

Virginia strolled toward where the voices came from, stopped just before the corner. She listened to the men finishing the hot tub installation. She chuckled to herself and hurried inside.

Natalie, in a very thin blouse and shorts, was standing near the sink rinsing out a glass. She turned. "Hi, Virginia. How'd it go at the museum?"

"Great. My boss is covering for me, but he has a price. He wants to meet you. And there is an anthropologist; he's a great guy, who wants a picture of you."

Natalie nodded. "Okay. You know where the binder is with the photos. Get whatever you need. I'll sign them."

"Okay. I met with the sheriff's detective who's working Ann's murder."

"How'd it go? You thought he'd stonewall you."

Virginia sat on a chair at the kitchen table. "He actually agreed to meet with me and bought me breakfast." Natalie set the glass down, dried her hands, and tightened the knot holding her shirt immodestly closed.

"He did? Why?"

"Yes. He gave me a file on what they have on the case and agreed to let me help."

Natalie moved to the table and sat across from Virginia. "Oh. That's unusual, isn't it?"

"Yes, it is, but he needs help. He's also asked the Smithsonian Central Security Service, it's the one I'm a reserve special agent for, to authorize me to investigate with him."

"Reserve agent? How does that work?"

"I'm a special agent, but I'm on duty when they need me, or authorize me, to investigate something, like in this case, helping the sheriff."

"Oh." Natalie leaned forward. "Do you think they will?"

Virginian nodded. "If the Sheriff asks, my guess is yes."

Natalie jumped up. "Great! You are wonderful."

"Maybe, but I've got some quilt stuff to work on right now."

"Okay." Natalie smiled. "I'll be around if you need me."

"Oh, by the way." Virginia got up. "The men finishing installing the hot tub have obviously seen you today, and are speculating on your attire when you use the hot tub."

"Oh? That's funny. Maybe to tease them, I'll wander out there again and see how they're doing and casually mention I don't wear anything in hot tubs."

"That will make their day and probably cause you to have some peeping Toms with telescopic lenses on their cameras. Talk about sexual fantasies."

"That's okay. I'm sure they would enjoy the pictures. They said they should have it filled with water by this afternoon."

"You can't go in until the chemicals have been added and had time to filter."

Natalie nodded. "I know. Andy told me. The paperwork that came with it says so, too."

Virginia pulled out her cell phone and looked at a message. "This note from Andy said he'd be back this afternoon to add them. He said he'll add the initial chlorine and when it dissipates, he'll add the enzymes. I'm sure the guys out there would be more than happy to help you adjust the chemicals and hand you a small towel."

Natalie laughed. "I'm sure they would."

"Well." Virginia picked up Ann's computer and her backpack from the table. "I best be getting upstairs to work. I see Linda is here."

"Yeah, she arrived early, around seven-thirty. Well, have fun."

Virginia climbed the stairs and went to the quilt workroom. She set up the computer and started her inventory when her cell phone rang. She pulled it out of her backpack. "Hello?"

"Virginia. This is Detective Grover. I just got a call from the Smithsonian Central Security Service. They have authorized you to work with me. The written authorization will be here shortly. You'll get an e-mail. You're now on active duty."

"That was fast. That's good news."

"There's more. I just got the information you requested about that car you took a picture of."

"That was also fast. Who was it? Should Natalie be concerned?"

"I think you, your friend who's helping you, and Ms. North should be

Suspicious Threads

concerned. The car belongs to an ex-P.I. He had his license jerked by the state a year ago. He's an alcoholic thug. It's been rumored that he does... side jobs for certain people."

"Like Bryon Weedon?"

"Among others. He is suspected of some break-ins and some heavy-handed work, too. He's been implicated in some Assault and Battery type stuff. Likes to rough people up, especially women. But we can't get enough on him to arrest him."

"What's his name?"

"Jack Blake. He's also known as Mad Jack, JB, and Meat. Be careful around him."

"Thanks. We will. I'll look at the files you gave me and start investigating from there."

"Okay, bye." Grover hung up.

Virginia put her phone away. *This is getting interesting. I had better tell Linda and Natalie.*

Virginia went down the hall and found Linda, in jeans and a Polo shirt, sorting through a stack of quilts. "Hi, find any interesting ones?"

"Yes. I found some Welch style quilts and some from the early nineteen hundreds. She has some vintage aprons in here, too. It's a nice collection. What's up?"

"I just got a call from the sheriff's detective. I need to tell you and Natalie what he said. Come downstairs with me."

"Sure." Linda placed the quilt she was examining back on the bed and followed Virginia.

Virginia and Linda entered the kitchen and stopped. Papers from the drawing board were scattered on the floor. A muscular man, about six feet tall, with dark hair in a short ponytail, and a goatee, wearing a black t-shirt, tan cargo pants, and work boots, was standing extremely close to Natalie. He pinned her to the kitchen cabinet with his body. He had her arm in a vice-like grip. She was shaking. Fear and pain raked her face.

Virginia yelled. "Who the hell are you? Get away from her, now!"

He turned slightly and glared at Virginia. "More broads? Get lost bitch. This is a private conversation."

He's the guy from the car. "I don't think so, asshole. Now get away from her, or I'll—"

He stepped away from Natalie, balled his fists, and stomped toward Virginia and Linda. "You'll do what? You stupid, nosy, bitch. I hope your health insurance is paid up because I'm going to teach you a painful lesson, too."

Virginia bristled. *No one calls me a bitch and lives long.* She quickly grabbed a magazine off the kitchen table and rolled it as he approached.

He stopped a few feet from Virginia, looked at the rolled magazine, and frowned. "You stupid broad, what are you going to do with that, read me to death?" He tossed his head back and started to laugh when Virginia suddenly rammed the end of the rolled magazine as hard as she could straight into his throat, and twisted it.

He stumbled backward grabbing his bloody throat. His eyes widened in panic as he tried unsuccessfully to breathe.

Virginia stepped close, grabbed his shirt, yanked him forward, and then kneed him twice, between his legs. She let go of his shirt. He doubled over and tumbled to the floor. After a minute, with his face distorted, eyes bulging, and his lips turning blue, he finally started to gasp for breath while still holding his groin. She bent over him. "Like beating up defenseless women, huh? Well, this one fights back. Get up and get out, Mr. Blake. Snooping with a camera wasn't enough? If I ever see you around here again, I *will* cause you more pain than you have ever imagined. This will feel like a love tap when I'm through with you. Understand?" He slowly nodded, and then moaned, as he gradually sat up. She moved in front of him. "Can you talk yet?"

He shook his head. His breathing was labored.

She leaned over. His throat was red and raw; blood oozed where she slammed the magazine into it. "Stay put."

He gave her a painful look and slowly nodded. Virginia hurried to Natalie, who was bent over, hanging onto the counter top. "You okay? Why didn't you call me?"

Natalie straightened, wrapped her arms around herself to try and stop shaking. "He... he barged in, dumped my papers on the floor, and next thing I knew he had grabbed me and dragged me over here. He pressed me against the cabinet. He... he was telling me to reconsider what I'm doing, or else." Natalie swallowed. "He looked angry. Then suddenly he asked where the quilt stuff and a computer file were. He's big, and strong, and was so close he pinned me with his body. I was bent back. It hurt. When I didn't answer, he grabbed my wrist and twisted it until I thought it would break. I was terrified. I tried to scream, but nothing came out." She held her hands in front of her. "Look, I'm still shaking. My wrist is bruised, and it hurts."

"I'll take care of this." She stepped to Blake and looked down. "Get up."

After a couple of unsuccessful tries, he gasped, and grunted, and very slowly climbed to his feet using the kitchen table for support. Bent over in obvious pain, Blake leaned on the table. He looked at Virginia with teary eyes.

Virginia leaned closer. "I'm Special Agent with the Smithsonian Central Security Service. You're under arrest."

Blake tried to speak, but his words came out as muffled squawks and gowns.

"You have any ID?"

He nodded then whispered slowly, "I... in my car."

"Is it out there by the garage?"

He nodded again.

She pointed at the door. "Let's go get it." Stooped over, he slowly shuffled out.

Virginia watched him hobble through the door, then followed him. When she got to the doorway, she swung around. "Linda, stay with Natalie. I'll be right back. Call the sheriff. Tell the dispatcher to get a deputy here before I take that bastard apart."'"

Linda, wide-eyed, with her mouth hanging open, nodded. "O... Okay," she whispered as she wiped her hands on her slacks, and went to the phone.

Virginia turned back towards the door. Blake was moving a little faster in the direction of the garage. She bolted out the door, jumped past the steps, and raced to Blake's car. As she reached the car, Blake leaned on the vehicle, opened the door, and reached inside. He picked something up. As she got closer, Virginia spotted the black, semiautomatic pistol in his hand. She slammed into the car door smashing his arm between it and the frame. He howled in pain and dropped the weapon inside. She released his arm and kicked his feet out from under him. He fell, banging his head on the side of the vehicle. She kicked him in his groin, again. Blake opened his mouth, but only a muffled scratchy sound emerged. He crumpled over, landing on his broken arm that Virginia had smashed. He rolled off it, gritting his teeth, and moaned.

The three men installing the hot tub rushed over. They looked at Blake, then Virginia. The leader shook his head. "I was going to see if you needed assistance, ma'am. But it looks like you can take care of yourself."

"Yeah. I'm fine, but he's hurting in more than one place. He attacked Ms. North. Keep him here until the Sheriff arrives. If he tries anything or tries to leave, go ahead and beat the crap out of him with something really hard, like a crowbar, or better yet, a heavy sludge hammer." She opened the door and carefully picked up the weapon so as to avoid putting her fingerprints on it. "I need to see about Ms. North."

"Yes, ma'am. He ain't goin' nowhere." Virginia returned to the house.

Natalie was sitting next to Linda at the table drinking a glass of water. She looked up at Virginia. "Is what I'm trying to do worth it? Maybe I should just sell out and go back to California. People here don't like me anyway."

Virginia sat across from her. "No way! Natalie, your dream is important. You're doing this for you, and for Ann. You must stick with it. You're a strong, intelligent, beautiful woman. You can stand up to these thugs, the stuck up, uptight, self-righteous prudes, the religious nut cases, and the developers like Weedon, Jenny Parker, and all the others. You have every right to be here and do what you're doing. You must be yourself, too. Go for your dreams. You're not alone here anymore. You've got friends now. Linda, me, and my husband, like and care about you. We are your friends. We're going to stick with you all the way. Don't give up. You have to stay and finish this. Furthermore, my boss would fire me, and Andy would kill me, if I let you give up and leave. You don't want that to happen, do you?"

A tear ran down Natalie's cheek. She cracked a smile. "No."

Linda patted Natalie's hand. "Virginia's right. Don't give up. You have friends here now who care about you. We're here for you. We *will* make this happen with you. Don't let anyone intimidate you."

Virginia leaned closer. "She's right. Even Detective Grover said, from what he's heard about you, he really likes you, and he hasn't even met you yet." She looked around. "You by any chance got any plastic ties."

Natalie frowned. "Plastic ties? Like cable ties?"

"Yes."

She nodded, her color returning. "Yeah, in the top drawer next to the sink, on the right."

"Good." Virginia rose and got the plastic ties. "I'll be right back." She hustled back out and found Blake sitting, leaning against his car, his eyes watering. He cradled his arm, with the two men watching him. She walked up. "Stand up and turn around, Mr. Blake."

He looked up at her and responded in almost a whisper "I don't know if I can."

"You're supposed to be a tough guy, try. Try real hard. You don't want me to encourage you more, do you?"

"No." He hesitated, then, using the vehicle for support, slowly rose and turned around.

"Put your hands behind your back."

One of the men shouted. "Do as the lady says."

He looked down at her, then whispered, "I think my arm's broke. Hurts like hell."

"Too bad. Turn around and put your hands behind your back, or I'll make sure your arm is slowly, and painfully, broken into multiple little tiny pieces."

He groaned as he slowly followed her instructions. She placed two ties around his wrists and pulled them tight. She leaned close and said. "I hope that hurts, a lot. Not used to a woman hitting back, are you? Don't even think of ever returning." She smiled at the sound of a siren. "If you're stupid enough to come back, you might be leaving in a body bag instead of a police car."

He turned around and started to speak.

"Shut up, Mr. Blake. Remember, you're under arrest." She recited the Miranda rights. "Now sit."

He slid down the side of the car. He spoke slowly with a low, raspy voice. "You can't arrest me, bitch."

"You're a slow learner. Mr. Blake. I'm a federal officer. It isn't nice to threaten or attack a federal officer, or illegally enter a private establishment and attack its owner and threaten her. Breaking and Entering, Assault and Battery are felonies. Attacking me is a federal felony. I'm sure the sheriff and I can think of a few more things to charge you with. And if you call me a bitch once more you'll need long-term intensive care at the hospital and speak with a very high pitched voice." She looked at the men guarding him. "Sounds like the sheriff coming. Keep him here and direct the deputy over here when he arrives. I'll be right back with my badge."

The men looked at each other and nodded. "Okay."

Virginia rushed back inside and returned with her badge and official ID as the deputies pulled up. After a few minutes of conversation, and the deputies verifying her credentials, they took Blake's gun from Virginia and took him in. They said they would return later to get a statement from Natalie.

Virginia walked back to the house. Linda and Natalie were picking up the papers on the floor.

Natalie stopped. "Virginia, what just happened? You took that big, scary man down like he was a toy."

Linda picked up the magazine from the floor. "You took him out with *Better Homes and Garden*? He must be embarrassed."

"Yeah. It was all I had. The sheriff detective, Grover, said he's the one you and I saw watching this house yesterday. Now he barges in and attacks Natalie. Not good form. I just arrested him. Detective Grover will handle him now. Maybe we'll find out whom he works for. Oh, the deputies will want to talk to you later."

Linda looked at Virginia with a quizzical expression. "You arrested him?"

Natalie grinned. "Yes. She's a federal special agent. I guess the Smithsonian agreed to let you help."

"Yes. I was coming down to tell you that when I saw what he was doing to you. Now we have a possible lead to who's behind the murder and your harassment. But in the meantime, we'll need to make sure no one just barges in again. Linda, will you please lock the door?"

"Linda walked to the door and locked it. She turned. "How about the workers in the other rooms?"

"I'll handle them." Virginia walked into the rooms where the construction workers were located and told them what had happened.

She returned. "I agreed we'd leave one door, this one, unlocked, but closed, for them to come in and out. I also told them if they see anything unusual, to tell us right away. After I showed them my badge, they agreed to more than cooperate. They said if anyone tries something like that again, you can just yell and they'll come right away and help you. I told them if someone is attacking you, or scaring you again; they are free to do anything they want to *terminate* any threat. They eagerly agreed. But from now on, at least one of us will be in here during the day. Natalie, keep your gun closer. But for now, keep that alarm control near you, and show Linda how to trigger it from the little computer Andy gave you. The noise will summon help and probably drive away a would-be attacker."

Natalie and Linda both nodded.

Virginia stepped to the table and plopped onto a chair. "Now, will one of you please get me some water? My adrenaline is wearing off. I think my nerves are going to unravel."

Linda got Virginia a glass of water. She drank it and sat staring at the table. After a few minutes, Virginia looked up at the other two women. "I just thought of something. Linda, you're backing up your *Surface* computer at home on a flash drive, right?"

"Yes."

"I have a spare drive up stairs. I think it prudent to do two backups. One here and one at home. We can hide the ones here. Just in case."

Natalie nodded. "Probably a good idea. Are you expecting more trouble?"

"Yes. We all think it's the property or maybe the gold in that rock sample that is the cause of Ann's murder and your problems. What if it's the quilts?"

Linda plopped into a chair. "Why the quilts? Why kill someone over a bunch of quilts?"

Virginia looked at Natalie. "Mr. Blake asked about the quilts when he pinned you to the cabinet, right?"

Natalie nodded. "Yes."

"We don't know yet, what exactly Ann had in the way of quilts. Some may be quite valuable. Whether it's the quilts, or the land, or something else, we must be on our guard. Natalie, carry your gun with you, especially at night. Don't go outside without it, and always with one or more of us with you. Set the alarm after everyone leaves."

"Don't worry; I will."

Virginia eyed Natalie's handgun. "I think we need to get you a smaller gun. That looks funny. It's huge, and you're tiny."

Natalie looked at her gun. "Probably a good idea."

"Until you get a concealed handgun license, don't carry the gun off your property though." Virginia's cell phone rang. She reached into her pocket and pulled out her phone. "Virginia."

Suspicious Threads

"Hi, beautiful. I'm on my way. Want me to pick up some lunch for you three?"

"Andy. I'm glad you called. Yeah, pick us up some hamburgers, lots of fries and onion rings. Oh, please stop by the house and get that old leather holster you have around somewhere for the .44 Magnum you had. We need it so Natalie can carry her .357 revolver."

"Okay. Something happen?"

"Yeah. I'll tell you about it when you get here."

"Tell Natalie I've got the chemicals she needs for her hot tub, too."

"I'll tell her. Hurry." Virginia stuck the phone back in her pocket. "Andy's on the way with lunch and your chemicals."

Linda jumped up. I'll help with the drinks."

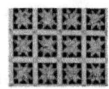

Andy arrived, unloaded the chemicals, and gave Virginia the holster and food. During lunch, they told Andy about their adventures and Virginia being authorized by the Smithsonian Central Security Service to assist the sheriff.

Natalie found a belt, attached Andy's holster, and strapped on her gun. At barely five feet tall, the Ruger on her hip seemed like a canon. She glanced at the gun, then at her breasts, and laughed, "It does look a little oversized on me, doesn't it?"

Virginia turned to Andy; I think we need to take her gun shopping for a smaller weapon."

Andy looked at Natalie. "You're right. Natalie, it looks like you'll fall over with that on your hip."

When they finished and were clearing away the paper plates, napkins, and bags, a car pulled up. Linda looked out the window. "Oh boy. Things just went from bad to worse."

CHAPTER 10

Virginia looked at Linda. "Now what? Someone pull up in the driveway?"

Linda continued to watch the car. "It's a van from a church. There are two men and a woman in it."

"Which church?"

"The sign on the side says, Calvary Evangelical Chapel." Linda shook her head. "They're the most fundamental, and rigid, so-called Christian church in the area. They make the Puritans and the Pope look like swingers, and their political views make the Tea Party look like left wing radicals. This can't be good."

Virginia got up from her chair. "I think I'll meet them and see what they want."

Natalie sighed. "I know this church. I know what they want. They have insisted I donate *Borealis* to them as a retreat and spiritual center for…" She gazed at the ceiling, then nodded, "that's it… the glory of the Lord and the redemption of my immortal soul. I told them no, but they keep pestering me. The pastor has made incessant phone calls, written to me half a dozen times, sent me almost daily e-mails. One of their brazen assistant pastors even approached me at the cemetery the day I buried my cousin. They want my land; they are upset with my behavior, and the way they've heard I dress. The head pastor also wants me to go back to California. He said, if I must sin, do it in California with the other heathens, sluts, and harlots. Can you believe that? I keep telling them no. They don't give up. They've hounded Ann for years for the property, too."

Andy stood. "I'll get rid of them."

"Thank you, Andy, but I guess I need to put this to bed once and for all."

Andy gave her a concerned look. "After what Virginia said you've been through lately, are you up for this?"

"I think so. At least this time I have you guys for support." Natalie sat for a second collecting herself. "I'm not dressed to meet a church group, especially them. This outfit will cause even more trouble."

Andy grinned and jumped to his feet. "Don't worry about it. You're dressed just right. You want to put an end to this?"

She gave him a sad look. "Yes."

"Okay, then. Remember, this is *your* territory. It's *your* home. You can dress and do as you please here. They are the outsiders, and they weren't invited here. Under the circumstances, the way you are dressed is perfect for meeting these self-righteous pests. You can enjoy unhinging these self-centered religious prudes. You *will* get your point across."

"Thank you, Andy, for the support." Natalie cracked a smile. "I'll just slip into something just slightly less provocative, but will still blow their rigid minds. With you guys around, I feel better facing them again. Thanks."

"We're here to support you." Andy glanced at Virginia, "You ready?"

Virginia nodded. "He's right. We're right here with you, Natalie. We're your friends. You are not alone anymore. And I'll really help. Stay as you are. I'm going to quickly change. This could be fun. Linda?"

"Right." Linda started for the door. "I'll see what they want."

Natalie nodded. "I know what they want, but okay."

Linda looked at Virginia. "Should I stall them for a minute or two while you change?"

Virginia nodded as she walked toward the hall. "Yes. Hold them for a few minutes, and then show them in."

Linda opened the door and went out onto the porch. She looked at the two men in dark suits and the woman in a long dark skirt and a high-buttoned, cream-colored, blouse, approaching. Linda smiled. "Can I help you?"

One of the men, in an expensive-looking suit, white shirt, bright red tie, and slicked-back, black hair with touches of gray at the temples, stepped out from the others. He looked at Linda like she was a lower life form. "Yes. I'm *the* Reverend Edward Nesbitt." He turned toward the woman. "This is Mrs. Blair, and this gentleman is Mr. Heller. We are from Calvary Evangelical Chapel."

Linda calmly stated, "I saw the sign on your vehicle. Nice to meet you. Now, what do you want?"

"We are here to see Ms. North. Is she available?"

This could be fun. "Do you have an appointment?"

"No. We shouldn't need one. We are here doing God's work."

"Doing God's work?" Linda gave them a quizzical look. "Does God have an appointment? Did God give you a work order?"

Nesbitt's eyebrow went up. "Huh? Work order? God doesn't need an appointment."

"Maybe God doesn't, but you do." Linda raised an eyebrow. "What exactly do you want to see her about?"

Nesbitt gave her a condescending look. "This is a private matter."

Natalie's right, these people are as arrogant as hell. Linda put her hands on her hips. "In that case, get back in the van, turn around, and get lost."

"But…" Reverend Nesbitt stared at Linda for a second, and then folded his hands in front of him. "I see. Well, we want to offer her a chance to save her immortal soul. We want to give her the glorious opportunity to make a God filled, tax-deductible donation of her land to our church, and for the Army of the Christ. That way she can go back to Hollywood where she belongs and spread the good news to other pagans."

Linda frowned. "Go back to Hollywood?" *I'll stall this jackass a little longer. This is getting good.*

"Yes. She'll be among others of her ilk there."

Linda slightly tilted her head and lowered her arms. "Her ilk? You know any *real* Hollywood actresses personally? Have you ever been to California, or Los Angeles, or Hollywood?"

"What? Ahh… no, I've never been to California. I've never met any Hollywood actresses either. But I've talked to other pastors; I've seen pictures and movies, read about it in the newspaper and religious journals."

Linda chuckled. "Really? They actually have religious journals? That can't be real. I thought only *real* science, medicine, and engineering subjects had journals that are based on facts, not mythology." She looked down off the porch, as he turned red. "You've never been to southern California or LA. You don't even know anyone there, and you're an expert? You're no expert; you're a complete self-righteous idiot."

Nesbitt stiffened. "You can't—

"Oh, you said something about good news. What good news? You leaving?"

"Leaving? No. The good news is the glory and the light of Jesus and the salvation of her soul." His voice grew impatient. "Now can we see Ms. North?"

These people must be crazy. Hell, they're certifiable. Back to Hollywood where she belongs? Good news? Make a donation of her land? Like that's going to happen. Hell will freeze over first. If they are as pompous inside as they are out here, I hate to think what Natalie and Virginia are going to do to them. I vote for shooting them. I know Natalie and Virginia are going to be risqué, but how much? What will Dr. Clark do? Linda took a breath to calm her nerves. *I guess I should go ahead with what I planned. If Natalie and Virginia can do it, and these people are complete jerks, I will too, if I can still muster the nerve.* "She is engaged with her engineer and with a quilt consultant doing some appraisals for her projects at the moment. But I'm sure she can spare just a few minutes to visit with you. Come in."

Linda entered the house and held the door for the church group. As they walked in Linda heard a collective gasp. She closed the door and turned. Andy was seated at the drawing board pouring over some engineering drawings. He looked up and smiled. On either side stood Natalie and Virginia looking at the drawings. Natalie's tight, sheer, yellow blouse amply displayed her braless chest. Virginia had changed into a pair of tight, short, jean shorts, and a white, sheer, tight, t-shirt, with nothing under it. Linda grinned. *Bingo. We're off to a good start.*

Andy looked up. "Linda, who are these people?"

Linda casually introduced the church people to him, Natalie, and Virginia. *This is going to get interesting.* She wiped her sweaty hands on her slacks. *I might as well do what I planned when possible.*

Natalie stepped away from the drawing table and walked to the group. Her big gun pressed tight against her hip. They stood, wide-eyed, staring at her. Mr. Heller's eyes watched Natalie's breasts move under her blouse. She noticed Reverend Nesbitt's cool manner collapse as he stared at Virginia's thinly covered breasts. He began to sweat. Natalie shook their hands. "Maybe we should go into the parlor. It would be more comfortable."

Reverend Nesbitt puffed up, "Ms. North. I *demand* that you and this... this other... hussy, go and put on some more modest clothing for meeting with good, righteous, Christian people."

Natalie waved Andy down when he started to rise, then glared at Nesbitt. "You demand it? Who the hell do you think you are?"

He stared at her for a second. "We represent the moral God-fearing community here in the Georgetown area."

Natalie's jaw tightened. "In that case," she pointed at the door, "get lost."

Nesbitt bit his lip. "We have some important business to discuss with you. But we *insist* you two to be more modest."

"Not happening." Natalie pointed. "There's the door, buster. We're busy."

"Buster? I'm the..." Nesbitt looked at his companions, then back at Natalie. "I see. Well, because of the importance of our mission here today, we can overlook our feelings of indignation at your behavior."

"You can overlook your feelings of indignation at my behavior?" Natalie put her hands on her hips. "Meaning?"

"In spite of how we feel, we would like to sit and talk to you... as you are."

"Okay, but don't press your luck. You're on very thin ice right now. This way." She led the silent group, followed by Virginia, Linda, and Andy, into the front room. Once they were seated, Natalie leaned back in her overstuffed chair facing them, making no effort to cover her thin top.

"Now, what can I do for you?"

Reverend Edward Nesbitt straightened his tie and cleared his throat. "A couple of things, actually. We... we... ah..." He unbuttoned his jacket and shifted in his seat. "We are here to investigate rumors we've heard about your salacious behavior. Sadly, it seems the stories we've heard are true. We also want to save your immortal soul from damnation." He glanced at Mrs. Blair and Mr. Heller and then continued. "Then, there is the subject of you making a Lord-pleasing, gracious, tax-deductible, donation of this beautiful property to the Calvary Evangelical Chapel for a retreat center, to expand our outreach, and to facilitate the training of our Army of Christ."

"I see." Natalie pursed her lips. "You think because you're some sort of ultra-rightwing church, and you're a highly visible pastor around here, and you and your cronies have been first class pests, I'll just buckle under and hand everything over to you? Guess again, buster. Oh... how do you know what's Lord-pleasing?"

"I'm a..."

Mrs. Blair interrupted and gave Natalie and Virginia an icy look. "You two women do not go out in public dressed this way, do you?"

Virginia smiled. "Define out in public."

"I mean around people."

"Sure we do. You're here, aren't you? I'm not sure, but I think you might somehow qualify as people." *This is fun.*

Linda giggled.

"Yes. I see." Blair continued in a condescending tone. "I would have assumed you would have been willing to put on more modest attire when accepting visitors, especially those of us Christians with obvious higher moral standing than you. And I noticed there are male workers around. What must they think?"

Natalie's eyes narrowed. "Christians with obvious higher moral standing? That's rich. I question your so-called high moral standing. I briefly looked into your church. You are egotistical, self-righteous prudes and give more credence to mythology than science." She grinned at their shocked response. "And you're arrogant and came here unannounced, uninvited, and without an appointment. So, you get what you get. What we wear around here is our business. As to what the workers think, they're men; I'm positive they like what we wear. They haven't complained." She had a mischievous expression. "And I bet they've had every lustful, double X-rated sexual fantasy they can muster about us. I also bet they would love to watch us naked around here, too. But they seem to enjoy working here, I pay them well, and they do excellent work. They routinely beat my expectations."

Reverend Nesbitt looked at Andy. "Their wanton behavior makes you feel uncomfortable around them, doesn't it, sir?"

Andy shook his head. "Not in the least. They're beautiful. And for the record, Virginia is my wife, and Linda and Natalie are my friends. I have nothing but the highest respect for both of them."

"Oh! Your... your wife? Friends?" Reverend Nesbitt swallowed. "I see." Regaining his composure, he sat straight. "I'm sure you, Dr. Clark, and you women, can understand our concern for our community of good Christians."

Natalie took a breath and then said in a flat tone, "We've been over the attire thing long enough. I'm tired of it. If you can't get beyond it, you can leave. You came to see if we were really as bad as the rumors said. Now you know. I think we've also settled the donation question. There won't be one, so what else is there to discuss?"

Nesbitt looked at Virginia. "May I ask if you have ever been baptized in Christ?"

Virginia responded coolly. "No, you may not. It's none of your damn business."

He shifted in his seat. "I hope there are no obscene activities going on here. Our Army of Christ would definitely not approve and would have to take action."

Virginia stiffened. "What kind of action would your so called army take, exactly? Violence? That sounded like a threat to Ms. North's safety, and that, Reverend, would be a felony."

"I... I didn't mean it like that."

Virginia leaned forward. "How did you mean it?"

"Public protests. We would have denouncements from churches, articles in the news, and on Facebook, pickets, and those kinds of thing. You must resist temptation. You know, the devil works in strange ways."

"Maybe he does, Rev," said Virginia. She stifled a chuckle. "Ms. North just installed a hot tub. Who knows, maybe she'll make it swimsuit optional. There's no telling what kind of debauchery will take place in it."

Nesbitt paled.

Mrs. Blair smiled. "Ed, she's teasing you." She looked back at Natalie. "I understand you are trying to change this place into a bed and breakfast and not let the land become another housing development."

Finally, they're changing the subject. My answer is still no. Natalie nodded. "That's correct. I don't want the land to become another Southern California with cookie cutter houses and apartments close together."

"Good for you. You're doing good things. But by donating this wonderful building and the land to the *Calvary Evangelical Chapel,* you'll be doing God's will, furthering our outreach, and assisting the Army of Christ."

"Did God personally talk to you and tell you his will? You know, they have meds for that condition." Natalie sat back and crossed her arms. "The answer is still, no." She looked at her watch, then at Nesbitt. "For the record, Reverend, and for the fifteenth and *final* time, you're *not* getting my property. I'm *not* donating or selling it to anyone, especially *you*. Period. We're *not* repenting, and we're *not* joining your church, either. So, was there anything else you wanted to know before you leave, Reverend?"

Nesbitt's eyes darkened. "If you were to donate your property to the church, you would be free to return to California to be with others who share your moral code."

Natalie glared. "Donate my land to you and move back to California? Don't you understand English? I'll keep the words to one syllable. No way in hell."

Mrs. Blair pointed at Natalie's gun. "Is that firearm normally part of your immodest attire?"

"It is since someone tried to break in, and after that, someone barged in here and physically attacked me. Was he one of your Army for Christ members, Mrs. Blair?"

Blair's neck muscles tightened. She flexed her fingers. "Ahh... no. I... uh... surely not."

"For your sake, I hope not." Natalie patted her gun. "I'll send the next intruders to God sooner than God's expecting them. Or, maybe it'll be the devil that *is* expecting them. Then there is the lawsuit."

Virginia noticed Mr. Heller staring at her breasts. "You've been quiet, Mr. Heller. What's your part in this little inquisition?" *Never seen tits before?*

Heller fidgeted. He glanced at Reverend Nesbitt, then back at Virginia. "I'm the leader of the Bible study ministry and our salvation outreach program at *Calvary Evangelical Chapel*." He wet his lips. "I was hoping to possibly sign Ms. North up to join us and start her on the road to Christ to gain her redemption."

They just don't give up. Virginia glanced at Natalie, who was shaking her head. "Nope. Not going to happen. Thanks for asking though."

Heller started to sweat. "I hear there are a number of quilts and fiber art pieces here that are valuable. Would you consider a donation of them to the church?"

Virginia sat back and looked at the church people. "Let's see what we've got here. You have come uninvited, and unannounced, to try to get Ms. North to give you her property. You have harassed her by mail, e-mail, coming here, and over the phone. You've told her she's going to hell. One of the low-life, unfeeling, self-righteous, assistant pastors even approached her at the cemetery the day she buried her cousin. You keep giving veiled threats about your so-called Army of Christ. You also want what could be some of her valuable quilts. You disparaged her, and my attire, called us hussies, sinners, heathens, harlots, and sluts. By the way, you left out jezebels."

Natalie chuckled.

Virginia continued, "You say you want to save our souls and mold us into non-thinking, science hating *fools,* like you. After all that, do you really think Ms. North is going to join, or donate her home or any other property, to your church or any other church? She told you *no* before, and she just said it repeatedly again today, absolutely not. So give it up. Oh, for the record, we're not joining your church, and we don't want to be saved, especially by you."

Reverend Nesbitt raised an eyebrow. "Well, I never—"

"You heard the ladies." Andy stood. "Their answer is *no* to any donations and *no* to all that church and religious stuff. It is time for you to leave; we have a lot of work to do. If you want to come back, which I definitely don't recommend, I suggest you try to make an appointment, if you can, first. That way Ms. North may not shoot you. By the way, her land is posted, so *no* trespassing or she might use you for target practice."

Everyone rose. Mrs. Blair looked around. Where is Mrs. Chambers?"

Natalie pointed at the stairs. "She went up there a while ago. I'm sure she'll be right…"

Linda came gracefully down the stairs. She stopped a few steps from the bottom and smiled. "Ya'll leaving already?"

The visitors stared, jaws agape.

CHAPTER 11

Virginia turned toward the staircase and looked. *Oh boy. This will be the cherry on the cake.*

Mrs. Blair stepped backward and leaned on the armchair for support for a second, then stepped forward. "M... M... Mrs. Chambers." Blair's voice carried an edge of indignation. "You're a married, Christian woman. You have married children. You're dressing like these... these other... harlots is... is indecent, and degrades you in God's eyes. Cover yourself up at once."

Linda stood straight. "No. And I seriously doubt I'm degraded in God's eyes. God's supposed to be a man, isn't he? The Bible is full of murder, incest, adultery, lust, and sex, too." Linda swallowed, her heart raced, and with sweating hands, she folded the edge of her thin blouse back a little further and smoothed her tight shorts, as she finished walking down the stairs. As she descended, her blouse opened more, exposing her breasts. "Yes, I'm married. Virginia is married, too. And I'm their friend. I stick with and support, my friends. So, if you consider them... what did you call them? Oh yeah, hussies, harlots, sinners, and sluts. Then so am I. Saying that stuff to them was no way to make friends or influence people, Mrs. Blair. So far you and your associates have done nothing but alienate all of us. If high pressure, insults, and threats are how you try to get people to turn to God and make donations to your so called church, you're either stupid or crazy."

Blair's voice was tinged with menace. "Mrs. Chambers, I know your pastor. What will he think when I tell him about this? And, I most surely *will* inform him about your scandalous behavior in front of this assembly. For that matter, what will your husband think?"

Linda noticed Nesbitt and Heller fidgeting and staring at her chest with sheepish grins. She took a breath and gripped the railing. "You know something, Mrs. Blair? Go ahead and tell my pastor. Be sure to describe my clothing and what I'm doing in excruciating, graphic, detail. I don't give a damn what you think, and I sure as hell don't give a shit what my pastor or anyone else thinks."

"Mrs. Chambers! Your language." Blair's eyes widened. "How could you not care? He's a man of God."

"Easy. Man of God, or not. I just don't care what he thinks. So, go ahead and tell him. As to my husband, he will either approve, like Andy does, or he'll have to get used to it. I'm with Virginia and Natalie. Before I came here, I, like you, didn't approve of the way Natalie behaved. I thought the way you do. I was a stuck-up, self-righteous, prude, but *not* any more. When you arrived, Andy said he thought they were pretty, smart, and sexy and was proud of them. I hope he feels that way about me, too. And if I had a vote, I'd vote *no* to any donations. Now, let me show you out."

Natalie raised her hand and stopped them. "Before you go, I'd like to inquire, since I couldn't figure it out from your website, or your approach, what denomination, cult, or sect, are you?"

"Cult? Sect?" Reverend Nesbitt turned a light shade of red. "I'll have you know; we are not a cult or a sect, we are an evangelical, non-denominational, Bible and faith-based, Christian church."

"Figures. I guess even the Baptist didn't want you."

"I... I never—"

"This way, folks." Linda led the church group to the door and said good-bye. She returned to a stunned Virginia and Natalie. Andy beamed. Linda looked at them. "What? You don't like my outfit?"

Andy nodded. "Are you kidding? Linda, I love it. You look beautiful, radiant, and confident. You're fantastic. And you're very sexy. You lost your inhibitions. That's fabulous. And when you told them off, I thought you were wonderful."

Virginia poked him. "Down, boy."

Virginia and Natalie went to her and hugged her. Virginia smiled. "This is something I never expected. Like Andy said, and he's a man, he's the expert on these matters, you look fantastic and very sexy. I approve."

Linda twirled around. "Me too. A few days ago, I never would have dreamed I'd do something like this. But watching you two and seeing how comfortable you are this way, and seeing the effect you have on people, men, and especially these crazy folks, I thought about trying it. These religious nut jobs gave me the strength to join in with you. At fifty-seven, I didn't think I could pull it off. I didn't think I was pretty enough or had the body for it."

Andy nodded. "You look beautiful to me."

Virginia poked him again. "You would notice."

"You bet."

Linda smiled at Andy. "Thank you, Andy. I'd been thinking about it but didn't have the nerve. I decided, when they came, to give it a whirl. Halfway down the stairs, I almost chickened out. My nerves were all firing. I was scared. I'm surprised I made it to the bottom. But it was fun and exciting. Their reaction was more than I hoped for. Did you notice Blair almost choked and the Reverend and Mr. Heller were embarrassed and dumbfounded, but they couldn't stop looking at me? Who would have thought I could do this and get that reaction?" She turned to Andy. "Thank you again for the compliments, Andy."

Andy smiled at Linda. "I'm sure they can't wait to tell others in their congregation, their friends, and your pastor, Linda. They'll probably put something on their website and Facebook, too. I'm sure Nesbitt and Heller wish they had a camera. Now I'm glad I installed the alarm system, and you have that pistol, Natalie."

"I agree." Natalie leaned against the doorframe and grinned. "Thank you, guys. I think we got across to them that I'm here to stay, and *Borealis* is not for sale, nor is there going to be a donation. This is what I've been putting up with all this time without any support. I can't thank you enough for your help. Now to get that idea sunk into that developer Bryon Weedon's thick skull."

Andy nodded. "I think you got across the fact that there will be no donations. Now we need to get back to work. Natalie, you have the material to send to the contractors to bid on to go over. Virginia, you and Linda have your quilt stuff, and I'll see to the chemicals in the hot tub."

Natalie straightened. "I think we got the message across and upset their apple cart. I think though I should start behaving in a little less risqué manner to not alienate all the people around here. At least not more than I have already."

Linda looked down at her chest then at Natalie. "Now you decide this. I'm just getting the hang of it, and it's fun."

"Okay, maybe more selectively."

"Good. I better get back to work."

They all separated and went to their respective areas to work.

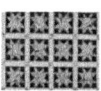

After an hour, Virginia came downstairs from the quilt room and went to the hot tub. Andy was measuring the chlorine levels. She sat on the edge and watched him. "What did you think when you saw Linda coming down the stairs in that outfit?"

"What did I think? Wow! She surprised the hell out of me. But I thought she looked fantastic. She's pretty and very sexy. And when she came down, I thought she was going to cause those religious idiots to have heart attacks. Too bad she didn't. She now fits right in with you and Natalie. But I didn't think she had it in her."

"Me, too. I think we're a bad influence on her. Natalie was doing it to

Suspicious Threads

unnerve the contractors and developers and keep the locals on edge because they pissed her off. I've been helping her. Maybe Natalie's right; we should tone it down. Maybe we're overdoing it."

"Not from where I sit. This community can get quite… ahh… dull at times. You guys have livened things up and caused some controversy, and this time it isn't about an endangered animal in the way of development."

Virginia poked his shoulder. "What am I thinking talking to you, you're a man." She looked at the hot tub and made circles in the water with her finger. "How's it looking?"

"Everything is working fine. The heater, pumps, and filters are working like they should. I added the chemicals per one of the chemists at the university. He was right about the hot tub company."

"How's that?"

"If you follow what they said to do, the chlorine will never get past the breakpoint. The chlorine will never reach the sustained level it needs to be. If that happens, the enzymes won't work. So, they'll tell you that you need experts to handle the chemicals and try to sell you their service. I've got it running, and the chlorine did its thing and is now evaporating. I'll start the enzymes shortly. Tomorrow I'll check it again, and if all goes right, tomorrow evening, it will be ready for use. I set the timer on the pump so it will go on and off on a schedule."

Virginia hopped off the side. "I'll go tell Natalie and Linda."

Andy put the test kit away. "I think I'll go scout around the property and see if there is anything else we may need to address during Natalie's construction projects."

As Virginia started for the house, Natalie stepped out onto the porch. She spotted Virginia. "Hi. That session with the church group was fun. And I hope final. I'm sure there will be repercussions."

"I bet there will be repercussions. Let's hope it isn't from the Army of Christ. No telling what fundamentalist fruitcakes like them will do in the name of their God. It's too bad, because they give the majority of really good pastors and priests an undeserved image. Most are honest, nice folks, sincerely trying to help people. The good ones are a benefit to the community."

"You're right. I know a couple of priests and a rabbi in L.A. who are really good guys. They even have coffee, lunch, or even dinner with me. Sometimes I cooked for them."

"That's what I mean. They see the good in you. Oh, Andy said the hot tub should be ready for use tomorrow night."

"Good. Let's invite Linda and her husband, too."

"That should be interesting. Oh, Andy's out exploring the property and the outbuildings to see if there is anything else to do besides what you two think needs to be done."

"That's good. The reason I came looking for you is I found this." She handed a small, black, spiral notebook to Virginia. "It has what looks like a bunch of passwords in it. Maybe one will unlock that file on Ann's computer you mentioned."

"Thanks, I'll give it a try."

Natalie walked to the hot tub and looked at the swirling water. "There are a number of passwords. She must have a lot of things on the Internet that requires them. Either that or there are more things to find around here."

Virginia thumbed through the book. "Maybe the secret tunnels lead to things that need passwords." She looked at her watch. "I've been meaning to go to *Quilters' Corner* quilt store and see Jenny Parker. There is still time today; I think I'll drive down and talk to her."

"May I ask what about?"

"Of course. I'm curious why it was so important that she do the assessing."

Natalie sat on the side of the hot tub. "Probably just ego."

"Maybe. Tonight, I'll go through the Smithsonian Central Security Service computers and check into this Army of Christ group, too."

"Maybe it's just the people," Natalie made air quotes, "they 'saved.'"

"You may be right. But Jenny, that guy Blake, and the Reverend's people all inquired about quilts. That could mean something. And they all could be dangerous. We also have the developer Bryon Weedon to consider, too."

"You're right." Natalie turned and looked at the acreage behind her. "I got a message from Southwestern University. Some professors would like to make an appointment to see me."

Virginia frowned. "More trouble?"

"I don't think so. I found some inquiries they had made to Ann before she died. It's about some studies or something. Ann had let them do some science stuff here about a year ago. At least there was no mention of any donations. I should respond and set up a time so we can see exactly what they want."

"Another group to worry about. What will you tell them?"

"Come at ten tomorrow. Will you be here?"

Virginia nodded. "You bet."

"Good. Do you think they could have anything to do with Ann's murder?"

"I don't know. I doubt it. Give them a call."

Ten minutes later Natalie walked into the living room and sat near the fireplace across from Virginia. "I talked to a nice woman at the university. She wanted to set up a meeting with two biology professors, a geologist, and an anthropologist to see me. They wanted to come here."

Virginia chuckled. "I bet. Besides their real scholarly intentions, I bet they're hoping, in an academic way, of course, to witness you in your risqué attire. What's the meeting about?"

"You're probably right. The woman said it has to do with some science studies they are interested in conducting. They have grants, so I won't need to give them anything except permission to come on my land. I guess there's something special about this place that they'd like to use in their study. She was very polite, so I told her to send all four of them tomorrow morning at ten. That way we can get that over with and explore more tunnels."

"Good, once we meet with them we can see if we'll add them to the list of suspects. But what worries me is, who else is out there we don't know about?"

CHAPTER 12

Virginia changed clothes, drove to Cedar Park, and pulled into the strip mall of US183. She nosed into a parking place and went inside. The shop had racks of bolts of various fabrics, quilting and sewing tools, needles, notions, and patterns. Sample quilts hung high on the walls. A large cutting table was off to one side. Two women were shopping. A woman stood near the cutting table waiting as a clerk cut fabric off a bolt. Virginia walked around looking at the various items when she heard her name called. She turned. "Hello, Jenny."

Jenny Parker marched toward Virginia and stopped. "Well, well, what brings you here, Virginia? Finally realizing you are in way over your head with Ann North Greenwald's quilts and come seeking my help?"

"No. I came to ask why you were so insistent on being the one to assess her quilts."

"Ann taught some classes here, and I liked her. Just offering my expertise."

"I see. She was a friend, right?"

"Yes."

"In that case, is there something particular you were looking for? Maybe a memento?"

Jenny stiffened. "What? That's… that's none of your business."

"True. I was just curious. But if there is something you specifically are interested in, let me know, and I'll keep an eye out for it." Virginia looked around the shop then back at Jenny. "If I find whatever it is, I can ask Natalie if she wants to part with it. She's a very nice lady and can be quite generous."

"It's… nothing." Jenny swallowed. "I'll think about it."

"Okay. If you change your mind, let me know."

Virginia started to walk out, then stopped, and turned. "One more quick question. Do you know a man named Jack Blake? He was arrested after he broke into Ms. North's house and attacked her. He's a two-bit thug who'll sell his mother out for the right price. He was taken to jail after a visit to the hospital."

Jenny's face grew tight. "The hospital?"

"Yeah. He was attacking Natalie when I caught him. He started to attack me, too. I smashed his windpipe. While he tried to regain his ability to breath, I kicked him hard in his balls, twice, took a gun away from him, and broke his arm. The deputies had to assist him into the patrol car."

"Holy cow." Jenny leaned on the edge of the cutting table. "You were able to do that to him? He's big."

"Yes. He pissed me off."

"Is he still in jail, or did he make bail?"

"I don't know. Do you know him?"

Jenny stuffed her hands into her apron pockets. "You said his name was Blake?"

Virginia nodded. "Yeah."

She shook her head. "No, I don't think I've met anyone by that name."

"Good. He's not the type to take the rap for anyone else. So, if someone put him up to it... I'd hate to be him or her. I'll talk to you later." Virginia turned and exited the shop. She sat in her car for a couple of minutes. *I got a rise out of her. There is something in Ann's quilting stuff she wants but won't tell what it is. So, what is it? From her reaction, statements, and questions, and that she knew he was big, she knows Blake, too.* She looked at her watch. *It's getting late. I'll call Natalie and Andy, then head home. Tomorrow could be interesting.*

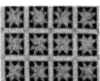

Virginia noticed Andy's car in the garage. *He beat me home?* She parked, shut the garage door, and went into the house. Andy was in the kitchen cooking dinner. She sniffed. "What are you cooking that smells so good?"

He looked up from the electric frying pan on the kitchen island. "My famous Swiss steak, mashed potatoes, and green beans almandine." He set the spoon he was stirring with down and leaned on the counter. "How'd it go at the quilt store?"

Virginia started for her quilt room. "Let me drop this stuff, and I'll tell you." She returned and opened a bottle of white Zinfandel wine. She looked at Andy, "Want some?"

"Sure." He took his glass and sipped. "Okay, how'd it go at the quilt store?"

"Jenny definitely wants something in Ann's quilting stuff, or a particular quilt. She wouldn't say what, but she is a lousy liar. She said Ann was a friend and taught classes at her store. That part I know is true, the teaching I mean. She also lied about not knowing Blake."

"Why would she know him?" Andy stirred the Swiss steak in the pan.

"I don't know. Maybe she hired him to get something that Ann had. He is just a thug. Low-cost muscle."

"What are you planning for tonight?"

"I'll try going through the Smithsonian Central Security Service computers and see what they have on the Army of Christ and *Calvary Evangelical Chapel*. I might turn up nothing, but it's worth a try. I'll also run a background check on Bryon Weedon." She looked at the Swiss steak and the potatoes in the pan on the stove. "When's dinner?"

"Give me another fifteen minutes. Oh, call Linda. She wants to talk to you. I guess she told her husband about her transformation and the church folks today. She's dying to tell you about it."

"Okay." Virginia went to her desk and called Linda. She returned to the dinner table fifteen minutes later. "You'll never guess what?"

Andy finished placing the serving dishes on the table. "What? She's getting a divorce?"

"No. Her husband is tickled pink. He's really happy. Linda said she was nervous and almost died trying to tell him and then was in shock when he was so supportive. He thinks her new attitude and doing what she did is fantastic. He told her she should to do it more. She's relieved. She wanted to know about tomorrow. I told her we have the quilt stuff to do, and professors from the local university coming, so be ready. I told her about my meeting at *Quilters' Corner*. Linda's driving alone to Natalie's tomorrow because of a doctor's appointment in the morning." Virginia sat and helped herself to the food and started to eat. "How'd it go at Natalie's after I left?"

"Fine. I found a few more items that need attention, and we put them on her schedule. I rechecked the hot tub, and it's doing fine. When I left, she said she was going to lock up, set the alarms, and try to get some rest. She wants a quiet evening eating chocolate and watching TV."

"Good for her." Virginia ate her steak and potatoes. "This is good. It's been a while since you've made this. What's the occasion?"

"No occasion." He dabbed his mouth with a napkin. "You cook most of the time, and I enjoy doing it once in a while. Anyway, I figured you'd be busy investigating on your computer this evening, so I'm the chief cook and bottle washer tonight. I'm giving you a break."

"Thank you. That's sweet." Virginia finished dinner, went to her computer, and booted it up. She logged into the Smithsonian Central Security Service and started her searches. After an hour and a half, she shut it down and took a handful of printouts to the family room.

Andy was on the couch eating popcorn and with Leo, her cat, watching NCIS when she walked in. He looked at the papers in her hand. "Looks like you hit pay dirt." Andy turned the TV volume down.

"You could say that." She went to the couch and after moving Leo, sat next to him. "For openers, I did a check on the *Calvary Evangelical Chap-*

el. It seems the IRS is more than a little interested in them. Their 501C (3) is at stake. They are being investigated and are about to be audited by the IRS. The file said the IRS is looking at filing criminal charges after the audit. The Texas Attorney General and the FBI are looking into the church for using high pressure, threats, and fraud for embezzlement as a means obtaining large contributions and something about a money trail to offshore banks. They are suspected of recruiting and training a few, selected, young folks, their Army of Christ, to carry out the high-pressure, and very physical—strong-arm stuff to gain membership and high-value donations. They are also a sort of security for the church and enforcers. Basically, they are a den of snakes. Pastor Nesbitt is being investigated for these things and some other felonies. But because he runs a religious organization, Nesbitt has a certain amount of… leeway. That may change sometime in the near future."

"We've seen some of their tactics. What else you got?"

"Jack Blake's got issues. He's an alcoholic, likes pot, and likes to beat up women. Been arrested for drunk and disorderly conduct. One charge in Travis County for misdemeanor assault, and he beat a felony assault with a deadly weapon. Three arrests, two convictions in Houston, the last one nine years ago. He has an A.A. degree from Austin Community College in anthropology. Texas stripped him of his P.I. license when they discovered he was… shall we say… unethical and suspected of theft, assault, battery, and fraud. They couldn't prove it all so they couldn't arrest him, but they could limit his activities. Since then, he's been arrested for a couple more misdemeanors, and now Williamson County is charging him with a couple of felonies. He's basically a low-life thug and likes to beat people up, especially women."

"He's the guy you sent to the hospital and jail, today, right?"

"Yep. That's the guy. And I also checked into Bryon Weedon."

"What did you find on him?"

"Not much. He has, or had, oodles of money from a family inheritance. He thinks he's hot shit. He's a ladies' man. Thinks he's God's gift to women. He's got lots of political connections, mainly due to large contributions to election campaigns. He's got a B.A. from the University of Houston in chemistry. Worked for a chemical company when he got out of college. He's a real estate developer, and he's been arrested for trespassing and drunk and disorderly. The police and DA think he's a scumbag. He operates just inside the law. Some of the homes he built used substandard materials and poor construction techniques. He's been sued a number of times for his home quality, business tactics, and deceitful practices. He's lost every case. There are still some suits pending. It is rumored that he keeps some muscle around to enforce his wishes. Oh, yeah, he also fancies himself as a modern-day Indiana Jones. He likes to explore and dig up ancient artifacts and minerals for sale on the black market. The authorities haven't been able to get enough evidence to arrest him, yet."

"Minerals, huh?"

"Yeah. That's what the report said."

Andy finished his popcorn. "You've learned a lot about these people in a short time."

Virginia shuffled the papers. "Yes, but this will interest you. Remember Jenny Parker?"

"She's the woman who owns the quilt store you were just at."

"Right. She doesn't have an arrest record except for some minor traffic stuff. But she just published a quilt book. It's the one Ann had a large X on it from a black Magic Marker. She's a certified quilt judge and appraiser. She's had the quilt store for eight years. Jenny's got a B.S. and several M.S. degrees from the University of Texas at Tyler. Her degrees are in biology. She has a temper, likes booze, and has been sued a couple of times when she caused some property damage."

"Okay, so she's a hot head. Anything else on the woman?"

"No." Virginia set her papers on the table. "I e-mailed Detective Grover what I found. He probably already has it. I'll tell Natalie about this tomorrow. I was surprised the county moved so fast on Blake."

"Grover?" Andy sat back and gave Virginia a sheepish look. "Oh boy. I forgot to tell you."

"Tell me what?" She straightened. "What did you do? What about Grover?"

"I didn't exactly do anything. That sheriff detective you mentioned, Grover, he came to Natalie's place, as I was finishing up. Nice guy. He talked to her for a while. I sort of stuck around and managed to run into him again as he was leaving."

She settled back against the cushions. "Of course, you did."

"Well, from what he said, he really likes Natalie. As far as he was concerned, Blake should be hung, drawn, and quartered, for attacking her. He's glad you took Blake down. He also said Blake is a big guy and was very impressed you decked him with just a magazine. Grover said you should have smashed Blake's throat a number of times with that magazine, and saved the county some money. He thinks you're something, too. Detective Grover let some of the prisoners at the county jail know tough guy Blake was taken down by a pretty, blond woman with a ladies' magazine. He figures Blake's stay in the county jail will not be pleasant. Oh, yeah, Detective Grover said he explained things to the JP. The judge also set Blake's bond at fifty grand cash bond for the breaking and entering, the assault charge, and the battery charges against Natalie."

"He did?"

"Yep. All fifty grand must be posted in cash or a cashier's check for him to get out. It seems Natalie has a growing fan club around here."

"Did you tell her?"

"No. I'll leave that for you." He looked at the clock on the far wall. "I've got a class starting at eight tomorrow morning. I'm going to bed. Oh, Grover had two of Natalie's pictures with him when he left. Tell Natalie I'll be there tomorrow around two or so to help her."

Virginia sat and stared. "Uh. She gave him some pictures?"

"Yeah."

"Well, how about that. I'll tell her you'll be there later."

The next morning Virginia drove to *Borealis* alone. As she pulled into the driveway her cell phone rang. She parked under a huge oak tree next to a shed and near a couple of pickup trucks. She quickly rummaged in her backpack for the phone. "Hello?"

"Virginia. This is Mary Watt."

I wondered how long before the other two members of the Bee Hive Quilt Bee would start asking questions. "Hello, Mary. What can I do for you?"

"I was wondering how are things going at *Borealis?*"

Her voice sounds strange. "I take it you haven't spoken to Linda?"

"Just briefly. We have texted. After her doctor's appointment this morning, we're getting together with Claire Barnes for coffee. I just wanted to see about anything going on out there."

"Linda and I are working on Natalie's quilt stuff and... helping her with other things. My husband is now her engineer on her projects. You're having coffee?"

"Yes. That's one of the reasons I called you. Want to join us?"

Mary's up to something. "Can't. I've got things to do here at *Borealis.*"

Mary's voice changed to a whisper. "Just so you know, a Mrs. Blair, of the Calvary Evangelical Chapel, posted an article on their website and some rather... immodest pictures of Ms. North."

Oh shit. "That bitch. That church has tried to pressure her into giving *Borealis* to them. They are very unscrupulous and unchristian in their methods."

"Virginia," Mary hesitated, her voice becoming a whisper, "there are some interesting, and rather immodest, pictures of you and Linda posted along with Ms. North, too. What will your husbands think?"

"Oh?" Virginia turned off the engine.

"Yes. They show the three of you in... indecent attire with men around."

"Indecent?" Virginia said testily. "We were just *almost* topless. That's nothing these days. And our husbands don't care. One of the men in the pictures *is* my husband. The real question is how'd she get pictures? I didn't see a camera. Blair must have either used her cell phone or had a miniature camera hidden on her. I think that's illegal. Natalie's been pressured by a lot of men around here, and Linda and I have been helping her."

"I figured that, Virginia. I understand. I know that church. They are weird, and I don't consider them true Christians. By the way, you and Linda look great, and Ms. North is short, beautiful, and it looked like she had a canon on her hip. She wears a big gun?"

"She's got a .357 Magnum for protection. Andy gave her .38 Special bullets for it, so it doesn't knock her down when she shoots it. The gun is big, and she's short. Makes for quite a sight."

"Yeah, it sure does. Are you there now?"

"Yes. Just pulled in."

"Well, tell her for us, we support her."

"Huh?" Virginia sat, stunned. "Ahh… thanks, Mary." *The other day Mary thought Natalie was the spawn of the devil for her behavior and manner of dress. What caused the change? V*irginia undid her seatbelt. "From your rather vocal negative views the other day at our Bee, I thought you didn't approve of her."

"I didn't. But after hearing of her issues, seeing the pictures from that so called church, and what and who she's up against, well, she's young and can pull it off. I like her spunk, even if I'm not too keen on her approach. If she's impressed you, Linda, and your husband, then she must be pretty nice. She's okay with me."

"She is. Thanks for that. I'm sure Linda will fill you in on everything."

"Virginia, Does Ms. North quilt?"

Now what? "I don't think so."

"Does she sew?"

"Yeah, she does. She's a really good seamstress. Why?"

"Invite her to our quilt guild and our Bee. Oh, here comes my ride. Call a meeting of our Bee so we all can all meet her. Gotta go." Mary disconnected.

Virginia sat staring at her phone. *What the hell just happened? Am I dreaming? Mary was convinced Natalie was the devil incarnate and would corrupt our whole community. Now Mary thinks Natalie's great. Well, better get with it.* She grabbed her backpack. As she started to slide out of the car, gunfire erupted from behind the house.

CHAPTER 13

Virginia pulled her nine-millimeter semiautomatic pistol out of her backpack as she exited her car. She ran to the house, slipped around the side, and carefully, she maneuvered around some shrubs, a large oak, and a couple of elm trees, to see where the shots came from. Virginia cautiously looked around the side of a tree and spotted Natalie holding her revolver at her side as she walked to a wooden sawhorse. Natalie set the gun on the rail of the sawhorse, picked up some tin cans, and placed them back on the sawhorse. The cans were full of holes.

Virginia stepped from behind the tree. "Practicing?"

Natalie, dressed in tight jeans and a blouse, picked up her gun and turned. She smiled at Virginia. "Oh, hi. Yeah. I had some time and figured a little practice couldn't hurt. It's fun. If anyone hears the shots maybe they'll get the message that I'm armed."

"I don't think that's a problem."

"Huh? Why?" Natalie quickly reloaded.

"Mrs. Blair posted pictures of us with her group here last night on the Internet. It shows us in good, *intimate*, detail, and there are photos of you with that gun strapped on."

Natalie fumed. "That bitch. Now the rest of the community will hate me. Maybe, if she comes out here again, I'll just shoot her. She'd make a great target. She has a body like a fifty-five-gallon drum. Couldn't miss. Look." Natalie pointed at a can with a picture of Mrs. Blair taped to it. It had a couple of holes in it. "Told you I couldn't miss."

"I don't think everyone will dislike you. Matter of fact, I know they won't. The detective who was here yesterday really likes you."

"Detective Grover. I liked him, too. He wasn't judgmental or anything. He asked questions, and then we just talked. I liked him."

"You gave him some pictures, too, I hear."

"Yeah."

"Well, a justice of the peace seems to like you, too."

"He does? That's nice. Having a judge like you isn't all bad."

"You're right about that. He set Blake's bail at fifty-thousand cash bond."

"Wow. I don't think Mr. Blake will be walking the streets anytime soon." Natalie shoved her gun into the holster on her hip. "Let's go inside. I have something for you and Linda. Oh, how do I clean this thing?"

"I'll have Andy get you a cleaning kit and show you." Virginia retrieved her backpack from the car, entered the mansion, and followed Natalie into her parlor. Virginia stuck her gun back inside the backpack as they walked.

On the floor were stacks of notebooks and papers in groups of three.

Virginia looked at the three stacks. "What's all this?"

Natalie looked at Virginia smiled. "My FedEx from Hollywood arrived early this morning. I sorted things out, so you, Linda, and I have what we need, so we can look at the scripts and requirements my agent sent for the movie I mentioned. My agent made some notes as to possible parts for you and Linda. He wants pictures of both of you both, and information about any acting or modeling you've done. Remember, this is Hollywood."

"Okay. Let me take my pile. I'll be upstairs working in the quilt room."

"Grab one."

Virginia took a stack of folders, notebooks, papers, and her backpack, and then proceeded up the stairs to the quilt room. She set her backpack on the floor, near the custom-made sewing table, with a *Bernina Virtuosa 163* sewing machine on it. Virginia eyed the machine. *Ann and I have this in common. I love my Bernina.* She looked at a quilt hanging on the far wall, went to it, and fingered the fabric. Her eyes soaked in the fine detail, the perfect curves of arches, the blend of applique and piecing, similar to a quilt she was making. Virginia stared at the vines wrapped around the sides, twirling and curling like fairies. She pulled Ann's laptop computer from her backpack, opened the project file, and reviewed what she had done and the inventory to date. She had just started to work when Natalie came in. Virginia glanced up. "Hi, what's up?"

"We've got a little time before the university folks arrive, how about some coffee and some cinnamon rolls? I just took them out of the oven."

Virginia looked around. "This stuff isn't going anywhere, so why not?" Virginia gave Natalie a mischievous grin "It's low calorie, right?"

Natalie smiled. "Of course. There are no trespassing signs posted, so calories can't come on my land."

"I like how you think. Let's go. Oh, I'm not sure if calories can read." As they walked down the stairs, Virginia asked, "You bake?"

"Yes. I like to bake from scratch. I'm a pretty good cook, too. I've even created some of my own dishes."

"With you liking to cook, your brain, fun personality, great looks, and sex appeal, how come some young man hasn't managed to get you to marry him?"

Natalie had a lost expression. "Some have tried. I haven't found anyone yet who measures up. Most of the guys I meet, especially in L.A. and in the Hollywood acting community, are shallow, full of themselves. They drink or use drugs, they're chronically unemployed, and live paycheck to paycheck. That is, if they even have a job. Most are back stabbers, have maxed out credit cards, are gold diggers, and don't make good husband material. They live over their mother's garage and park cars to earn any money they may have. I'm holding out for the right guy. You're lucky you've got your husband. Andy's really great."

Virginia smiled. "I know."

Natalie gave her a hopeful look. "I think I asked already, but does he by any chance have an unmarried twin brother?"

"No. Afraid not. Sorry."

Natalie shook her head. "Too bad."

Virginia continued as they walked downstairs. "Maybe you're looking in the wrong places."

"You are more right than you know. Maybe some Texas cowboy will ride up to *Borealis* on a white horse."

"You never know. Maybe one of Andy's colleagues at the university would be a good match."

Natalie brightened. "If they have a clone of Andy or even a reasonable facsimile, I'd love to meet him."

"I'll ask him. Can't hurt."

As they drank coffee and ate a few of the cinnamon rolls, Virginia told her about visiting Jenny's quilt store, her computer investigations into Blake, the church, and Weedon.

Natalie took a drink of coffee. "You've been busy. Sounds like the self-righteous church folks are in for serious trouble from Uncle Sam and the State of Texas. Good. Weedon is a constant pest, too. I expect to hear more from his camp before long."

Virginia sat back, finished her coffee, and set the cup down. "Linda will be here later. She had a doctor's appointment and was meeting with the other members of our quilting Bee. It seems they have seen the Internet pictures of the three of us."

Natalie looked shocked. "Oh. I'm sorry. What must they think? You and Linda don't need that. What people think of me doesn't matter. But I don't want you and Linda to get into trouble with your friends." She looked down. "What have I done? I'm so sorry."

Virginia patted Natalie's hand. "Not to worry. First, Linda told her husband about yesterday, and he's thrilled. That was a surprise, but a good one. She and I did what we did on our own. So don't worry about it. Second, this morning one of the members of our Bee called and asked me to invite you to our guild and especially to our Bee. They now seem to think you're pretty and spunky, and they're dying to meet you. She particularly liked you wearing your gun."

"They do? Linda's husband is okay with her behavior yesterday?"

"Yes to both questions. You do sew, don't you?"

Natalie stared at Virginia. "Your friends like me?"

"Yes. They want to meet you."

Natalie grinned. "I'd love to go to with you to your guild and meet the ladies in your… your Bee. And to answer your question, yes, I do sew. I'm a pretty darn good seamstress. I've been sewing for years. I started in in junior high school. I've made clothes, dolls, costumes, and repaired countless dresses and blouses. I also knit and felt wool to make purses and bags. Just never got around to quilting. My cousin was the quilter in the family. But it's something I'd love to learn. Once I get all this stuff here at *Borealis* finished, I want to take lessons."

"Good. I'll call a meeting of our Bee shortly. I noticed you've got a blouse and jeans on for today's visitors."

"Yeah. Like I said yesterday, I think I should tone my behavior down a little and save the risqué stuff for when I need it."

"Probably a good idea." Virginia patted her backpack. "I won't have to change into my sexy war attire. I'll join you at ten." She looked at the clock on the microwave. "It's almost ten now; I'll stick around." She looked at the second tray of cinnamon rolls. "They still smell heavenly. Going to offer coffee and warm rolls to the university professors, too?"

"Why not. They're men, and most men like food, especially hot, fresh, cinnamon rolls. They won't be expecting that. And they're probably going to expect us being naughty. The food, my gun, and dressing normally will throw them off base a little. The professors don't sound like they are obnoxious like the church people. The rolls should help keep things civil in case there are any difficulties or misunderstandings. When they leave, we can go over the stuff my agent sent, if you want to."

"Sounds like a plan." Virginia was helping clean up their dishes when she heard a vehicle pull into the driveway. "Sounds like show time."

Natalie went to the door and watched four men exit a large white van with Southwestern University printed on the side and walk toward the front of the house. She opened the kitchen door and yelled. "Over here, gentlemen."

The four men looked at her standing on the porch in her cream-colored blouse, tight jeans, and a six-gun on her hip. They seemed nervous as they hurried to the door and followed Natalie inside. She noticed the change in their expressions when they smelled the cinnamon rolls. Natalie nodded toward Virginia. "This is Virginia Davies Clark with the Smithsonian Central Security Service."

The leader's eyes widened as he stepped toward her and shook Virginia's outstretched hand. "You're... with... the Smithsonian?"

Virginia smiled. "Yes."

"I'm Doctor Charles Morrison." His gaze froze on her tight green shirt and shorts. "You really are with the Smithsonian?"

Virginia smiled. "Yes, Doctor, I'm really with the Smithsonian." She pulled her badge and credentials out of the side pocket on her backpack and showed it to them.

Morrison examined her credentials, and then looked at her up and down. He got a confused look on his face. He cleared his throat. "I... I see. May I ask why the Smithsonian has a... representative here today?"

"I'm helping Ms. Natalie North with some of her things and with the sheriff, investigating a murder."

"A murder?"

"The murder of Ann North Greenwald."

"Oh." He swallowed. "So, you're like... undercover or something, and not here with a scientific interest?"

"No, Doctor. The Smithsonian, at this juncture, has no interest scientifically in *Borealis*." Virginia gave him a hundred-watt smile. "What's your discipline, if I may ask?"

"I'm a biologist. My colleagues and I are here to discuss some funded research we'd like to conduct here based on previous studies of the ranch."

"I see."

They sat and opened their briefcases.

Natalie pointed at the table. "Can I offer you fellas some homemade, freshly-baked, cinnamon rolls and fresh coffee?"

They all quickly agreed.

Natalie and Virginia hustled around the kitchen getting plates, silverware, cups, cream, and sugar, as the men watched. Virginia poured the coffee as Natalie brought the fresh cinnamon rolls to the table.

Natalie sat, looked at the men, and smiled. "Help yourselves, gentlemen."

Virginia pulled up a chair between Morrison and another professor and poured herself a cup of coffee. She glanced at Morrison. "You have a request of Ms. North?"

He finished chewing and swallowed. "Yes. Oh, this is excellent. Thank you, Ms. North. I haven't had homemade cinnamon rolls in years."

Natalie pointed at the doorway from the front of the house. "Here's another of my friends who will be sitting in on our discussion, today. This is Mrs. Linda Chambers."

Linda entered the kitchen in tight jeans and a tight, tank top. "Hello." Linda stepped to the wide-eyed Doctor Morrison and shook his hand, then sat on the right of the gentleman who identified himself as Doctor Emerson

Dunlap, the archeologist.

Natalie sat and looked at the other two men. "Who are you?"

A bald-headed man of about sixty grinned. "I'm Professor Ian Manahan of the biology department."

The other man cracked a smile. "I'm Doctor Aaron Shaprio. I'm with the geology department."

Natalie pointed to a tray on the table. "There are sweet rolls and coffee for you gentlemen. Now, the nice lady at the university said you wanted to discuss doing some science stuff on my land, and you had some sort of grant?"

Dr. Morrison cleared his throat. "Ahh… yes. A year ago, with some grants from the National Science Foundation, we did a preliminary study of some interesting features on Ms. Ann North Greenwald's estate. We had her permission, you understand. She had stated that if we were able to obtain further funding, she would grant us access to her land again. We were very careful not to disturb much and not cause any destruction or harm to her ranch."

Natalie nodded. "Okay." As she moved, her gun shifted and rose slightly in her holster. She noticed Morrison's eyes widen.

He swallowed. "We have received another grant to further our studies, but Ms. Greenwald died. We were not sure what to do. So, we figured we'd approach you and see if there was any way to continue our research."

Natalie looked at Virginia and Linda. They shrugged.

Virginia spoke up. "How many people are we talking about traipsing across Ms. North's land?"

Dr. Dunlap finished a roll, and then spoke. "The four of us and a few graduate students."

"Define a few."

"Six or seven."

Virginia rolled her neck from one side to the other to work out the kinks. "So, as many as ten or eleven people?"

"Yes. Usually not all at once though."

Linda sipped some coffee. "What is this study that involves biologists, geologists, and anthropologists? That seems like a strange mix of disciplines."

Dr. Shaprio smiled at Linda. "You are right. But there are some caves, caverns really, that some very early pre-Columbian people inhabited. That's Dr. Dunlap's area of expertise. The caverns and the surrounding area have some unique geology, flora, and fauna. There are also some fault lines that cross the property we'd like to study. They may have been active more recently than anyone suspected."

Natalie looked at the four men. "Do you know a Mr. Weedon?"

They paled. Professor Manahan set his coffee cup down. "Yes. We've run across him before. When it comes to the land, trees, animals, and natural features, he's like the proverbial bull in a china shop. He will destroy anything that gets in his way to develop land for housing. He'll destroy the landscape, disrupt the delicate balance of nature, destroy animal habitats, then plants a couple little trees with his cookie cutter houses, and call the development an estate. He's natures number one nemesis in these parts."

Virginia chuckled. "I see you've met him."

"Like I said, unfortunately, yes." Manahan rubbed his hands together. "You haven't sold this beautiful ranch to him, have you? We know he wants it."

Natalie shook her head and chuckled. "No. I haven't sold him anything. We also warned off a church bunch that has been a pain in the ass. They wanted my land, too."

Morrison wiped a napkin across his mouth and said, "I take it that church group outside your fence is the one you're referring to. I know they don't approve of you."

Natalie chuckled. "You've got that right. They want some donations from me, like my estate and some quilts. That isn't going to happen. Of course, we do our best to tease them."

"Good for you." Morrison sat straighter. "They're a strange group. About a year ago, I had a student who was in their church. He subsequently left it. He said they were really strange and that he didn't take to their brand of uptight, weird theology, and beliefs. They believe the earth is about four thousand years old; the Bible is all literally true, they think there really was a worldwide, 'Noah' type, flood. They believe in creationism and man has always looked like we do today. They don't believe dinosaurs existed and think evolution is the work of the devil and some other weird stuff. They demand their parishioners provide the church with fifteen percent of their income. Fifteen percent. Can you believe that? He said they had some branches in other states and countries, and have a corporate headquarters somewhere in the Caribbean. A lot of their money goes to a bank down there."

Natalie, Virginia, and Linda exchanged glances.

Virginia rose and pulled her cell phone from her backpack. "That was interesting. If you will excuse me for a minute, I have a call to make." She hurried toward the dining room.

Natalie looked at the men who were watching Virginia leave. "Okay, gentlemen, you said you have a new grant to continue your studies here."

They nodded.

She raised an eyebrow. "There are really caverns on my property?"

Shaprio took a bite of a sweet roll, chewed, and then spoke. "Yes. Four that we've found. We have evidence for more."

She leaned forward. "Old people lived here, too?"

Dunlap chuckled. "Yes. Really old people. They were here about eight or nine thousand years ago."

"That's old." Natalie sat back. "How much money did you professors get to do this research?"

Manahan gave her a sheepish look and swallowed. "Two hundred and sixty thousand dollars. About ten thousand of that goes to the university for their support."

"So you get to work with two hundred and fifty thousand dollars." Linda shifted in her seat. "How long will you be working out here?"

"Five and a half months. But fifty thousand dollars of the money in the grant is to go to you, Ms. North, for permission to trespass."

Linda nodded. "I see. And you and your students will be the only ones out here?"

"Yes. Well, there could be some administrators who like to poke around, and possibly some reporters who could come by once in a while. But usually, no one is interested in what we do."

Natalie jumped to her feet, startling the professors. "Sounds good to me. I'm interested, even if no one else is. I guess the foundation providing the funding is, too. Do you have some documents for me to look at and some agreements?"

Morrison's jaw dropped with her sudden outburst. He took a tentative sip of coffee. "Yes, ma'am. Dr. Dunlap will you please give the papers to Ms. North?"

Dunlap pulled a file from his briefcase and handed it to Natalie. "Everything should be there and in proper order. Our statements of work, copies of the proposals, and I've also included a copy of the agreement we had with Ms. Greenwald for you to see. There are also maps showing the location of the caverns we are aware of on it. There is the master of a tentative agreement for you as well."

Natalie moved to Dunlap and took the folder. "Thank you. I'll have my lawyer look at it, but I think it will be safe to say you will be allowed to conduct your research here at *Borealis*. I do have a few conditions though."

The professors exchanged glances. Morrison wet his lips, and then spoke. "What would they be?"

Natalie sat back down. "One, if you're going to be here, please call me Natalie. Two, I want the names and a photo of everyone who will be working for you on this site. Please have them wear ID badges so I can keep track. Anyone else will need my prior authorization to come on my land." She twisted slightly in her seat and patted her sidearm. "I'm a good shot. Third, my friends and I want to see the caverns. And lastly, do no damage to *Borealis*, or I'll throw your asses out." She looked at the four shocked men. "Do we have an accord?"

Shaprio sucked in a short breath He cleared his throat. "Ahh… yes, ma'am."

Natalie got back up and stood in front of them. "Oh yeah, there is one more thing. I seem to have a bad reputation for dressing and acting unconventionally. My friends here do to. Get used to us dressing how we damn well please."

"But our students…"

Natalie glared at him. "Your students haven't seen tits before? I know you're from a Christian university, but young college people are still young college people, and they screw."

"I'm… well, I'm sure… I mean… ahh…" Morrison mumbled, then stood. He extended his hand. "Ms. North, we agree." The other professors nodded.

Natalie shook his hand. "Call me Natalie, this is Linda, and the woman in the dining room on the phone is Virginia. We aren't formal. Like I said, I'll have my lawyer look at the materials you gave me, and we should be back to you in about two weeks. Is that agreeable?"

"Yes. Yes." Morrison nodded. "That would be great."

Natalie smiled. "Oh, you can keep the fifty thousand dollars you were going to give me. You can use it towards your project. I'm pretty sure your research needs it more than I do."

The men stood dumbfounded. Manahan almost choked. "You don't want the money? It's fifty thousand dollars."

"Let's just say I'm also giving you a grant by returning the fifty thousand dollars to you for your research. You understand we'll probably come to your project sites from time to time, to see how things are going. We're intrigued. Anyway, Virginia is a historian and works for a museum."

"That's wonderful. Thank you. Come by our work sites anytime."

"When would you like to start?"

"In three to four weeks. That is, if that's okay with you."

"Sounds good to me." Natalie set the papers on a side table. "If there is nothing else, Linda will show you out."

After escorting then men to the door, Linda returned to the kitchen where she found Natalie and Virginia sitting at the table. Linda chuckled. "That was fun. Now we'll have scholars running amuck. I bet the students and the professors will be hoping they'll see us dressed topless or naked like Playboy models this summer. I'd love to see the caverns and the anthropology stuff." She took a seat next to Virginia. "Who did you call?"

Virginia sat back. "Detective Grover and the Smithsonian. I told them about the church's offshore offices and bank the professors mentioned. They're on it."

Linda took a bite of a sweet roll. "How did they get anything on them when you or the sheriff couldn't?"

"Someone at the SCSS had either connections with the IRS or had something on someone there. They are emailing me what they found out."

Natalie smiled at Linda. "You came in just after the professors arrived. I didn't get to ask you how it went at the doctor's?"

"I'll live. I've got a slight infection in one lung. He gave me some antibiotics and decongestant."

"I'm glad it isn't too serious. I have something for you in the living room."

Linda ate the roll quickly as she followed Natalie and Virginia to the parlor. She looked at the stack of folders, notebooks, and papers on the floor. "What are these?"

Natalie pointed. "Take a pile and look through it. That's the stuff from my agent. Virginia can tell you what else my agent will need from you." She watched Linda pick up a stack. "I heard you met with some of your quilting friends. I'm sure they wanted the latest dirt about me."

"Oh yeah. I told them how nice you are, what you're up against, and what we've been doing. They asked about our attire in the pictures. I told them about that crazy church group and us. They were hesitant at first but agreed that what you, Virginia, and I do here is really no one's business. They also agreed that if Virginia and I think you're great, then you must be great, and they have to meet you." Linda put the papers, folders, and notebooks on a side table and set her purse next to it. "They think you'd be a good addition to our Bee, and possibly, if you want, to our quilt guild. I agree."

"That's really nice. Thank you, Linda, for telling them. I'll have to invite them out here." Natalie turned to Virginia. "Can you do it? Let me know when they can come."

"Yes. I'd be happy to."

Natalie got a playful look on her face. "I have an idea. I don't have anyone scheduled to see me the rest of the day. The contractors are already here and busy. So, instead of doing our normal stuff, how about exploring the secret tunnels, see, what we've got, and where they go? We can go over the stuff my agent sent later."

Virginia and Linda exchanged glances, and then both nodded.

Linda looked around. "Where do we start?"

Natalie shrugged. "I guess the basement where Andy found the entrance he used."

"I agree." Virginia rubbed her hands together. "We'll need flashlights. Natalie, you have your gun, give me a minute to get my pistol and penlight from my backpack. No telling what we'll find in old tunnels."

CHAPTER 14

Virginia returned to the parlor with her semiautomatic tucked into the belt on her jeans. She spotted Natalie and Linda both holding flashlights. Virginia motioned for them to follow her. "Let's get started." She unlocked the cellar door, flicked on the stairway light. Holding the banister, they descended the steep squeaky, wooden, steps. At the bottom, Virginia turned on the overhead florescent lights. The ballasts hummed. Virginia looked around. The concrete walls were coated with a thick layer of an organic substance. She pointed. "What's on the walls?"

Natalie shrugged. "I was told it's a coating that provides moisture-proofing and some insulation. I'm not sure what it's made of. Ann had the floor coated, too, to help keep things dry and clean. Why she picked gray for the color is beyond me."

Virginia noted the new washer and dryer, two clean-looking furnaces, and AC units. Two large water heaters stood on short, coated, metal stands. "You've got two water heaters and two heating and air conditioning systems?"

"Yeah. Ann had them installed. They are only a year old. I think only one of each is on. That's what your husband said. The others are backups for some reason."

Virginia headed for the furnace. Near it, she noted shelves with various items on them including light bulbs, packages of paper towels, canned goods, and plastic containers. Near the washing machine and dryer were two long tables with cabinets above them.

A wooden box sat on the table full of rocks. "That must be the crate Andy found the quartz with the gold in it."

Natalie nodded. "Yeah, it was on the bottom shelf of the shelves over there. I hadn't looked at it with everything else going on."

As they approached the first furnace, Linda directed the beam of her flashlight at the wooden shelves behind it. "Look. That must be what Andy saw. The shelf is angled slightly away from the wall. If you weren't looking for it, you'd never see it." She stepped to the shelf and tugged. It swung out enough for a person to slip behind it. Linda aimed the light down the dark passage. "I wonder where this goes." She slid inside. "It's chilly in here."

Natalie entered the opening. "Oh, yeah. It's a bit brisk."

Virginia ran her hand over the stone and wood walls then cast her light on the floor. "Watch your step; these stones are old and worn."

The passageway went straight for about twenty feet before coming to a junction where another tunnel crossed. Their tunnel continued straight another twenty feet through spider webs and dust to an archway and stairs down to another level. Virginia slid past the other two and descended the stairs.

At the bottom, Virginia said, "It smells somewhat musty in here, but not as bad as I imagined it would." She wiped a cobweb off the low, stone arched, ceiling. "The walls aren't as cold as I expected either." Virginia turned. "Let's see where this goes."

Natalie waved her light around. "Spiders. I don't like bugs."

Linda swung her light across over the floor. "I'd be more worried about snakes."

Natalie stopped, her voice cracked. "Snakes? Maybe this wasn't a good idea after all." She shone her light toward the ceiling. "Look. There are lights. If we can find the switch, it'll be easier to get around, especially if there are snakes and bugs waiting for us."

Virginia swung her light around the walls. "If there's a light switch, it'll be near an entrance, like where we came in. Since we weren't looking for one, we might have passed it. Let's see what's ahead. Maybe we'll find another door and a light switch."

They followed the dusty tunnel until they came to a three-way split. Ahead a few feet was a rusty ladder. Virginia shined her light up. "There's a wooden door up there. Must be a trap door someplace. Let's see where we are."

Natalie moved next to her. "I don't know if that ladder is safe."

"One way to find out." Virginia turned off her flashlight. Linda and Natalie shined their lights on the ladder. Virginia grabbed the sides of the ladder and shook it. Some specks of rust settled. "It didn't fall apart. Give me some more light." With Natalie's and Linda's flashlight beams showing the way, Virginia, using her hands to grip each rung, cautiously scaled the ladder. At the top, she pushed on the door. The door creaked, as it swung open. She climbed a couple more steps and peered into the darkness. Hanging on to the side of the ladder, she pulled out her flashlight and swung the beam around.

Linda called up to her, "What do you see?"

"A John Deere lawn tractor, a trailer for it, a weed whacker, and shelves with some garden tools. There are a few sacks of potting soil. There are a couple of bags of fertilizer and spools of plastic cord for the weed whacker. There are two cans for gasoline, too."

"That's my garden shed," said Natalie. "That's the one the raccoon you scared off wanted to get into."

"Okay. We know where this end of the tunnel goes. Virginia stepped down the ladder pulling the trap door closed above her. She climbed down and looked at Natalie. "Did you know that door was in the shed?"

"No. I've been in there multiple times and I never noticed it. I wasn't looking for it though. Later we'll have to go in and see if we can find it." She shined her light down the side tunnel. "Where does this go?"

They aimed their lights down the musty tunnel. Natalie knelt and examined the floor. The dust had not been disturbed. She took a breath. "Looks like no one, and no animal, has come this way, including my cat Poseidon." She stepped ahead, flashlight aimed at the stone floor, and moved slowly into the dark. She abruptly stopped waving her hands and wiping her face and hair. "God, Damn it! Oh, shit!"

Virginia waved her light around. "What is it?"

Natalie stopped her frantic movements and stood, her hand on her chest. "I... I'll tell you as soon as my heart stops pounding." Natalie stood for a couple of seconds. "Okay. I ran into a huge spider web. I'd hate to see the spider that made it. It must be a man-eater. I hate bugs. I hate them more than mayonnaise and salmon." She turned slightly. "I really hate mayonnaise and salmon."

Virginia nodded. "I understand. Leo, my cat doesn't like salmon. I don't like mayonnaise and salmon either. Let me go first."

Natalie stepped aside. "Be my guest." She wiped a section of webbing from her sleeve. "Your cat doesn't like salmon?"

"No. He hates it."

"I like your cat."

Virginia, followed by Linda and then Natalie, continued down the tunnel for another hundred feet. At the end of the tunnel was a set of stairs made from heavy timber. Virginia tested it with her foot, and then slowly climbed the ten steps to the top. She faced a sturdy looking wooden door with an iron handle. She grabbed it and pushed. It didn't move. She tried pulling on it. Nothing happened. "Okay, there has to be a trip mechanism around her somewhere."

Linda mounted the stairs and stood next to Virginia. She and Virginia waved their lights around the door and sides. Linda shrugged. "I don't see anything."

Natalie stood looking up at them then swung her light around the stone tunnel walls near the steps. She climbed the steps, stopped two steps below the top, and carefully moved the light around the wall next to the door. She pointed at a smooth square rock sticking out slightly from the rest. "That stone looks different from the others."

Virginia bent forward for a closer look at a stone. She pushed. The stone moved slightly inward with a cracking sound. The door creaked; it swung inward as it opened. "Bingo." A musty, barn smell hit their nostrils. She panned her light inside over a number of dusty tables. She moved the beam around at the walls and found a light switch near the secret door. She stepped to it and flipped the switch. Lights came on in the building. Virginia stepped further inside followed closely by Linda and Natalie. Virginia looked at the door from the building side. "It looks like a large cupboard from here."

Natalie chuckled. "This is what Ann called her barn." She pointed at items scattered around. "That's the tractor for use out in the acres. I like the scoop on the front for digging and picking stuff up. That thing over there on the floor is a large grass cutter that attaches to the tractor for the high brush. The backhoe attachment is in the corner. There's the cart. It has a name, but I think it looks like a golf cart on steroids. It's great for roaming around the land. Two thousand acres is a lot of real estate." She turned and pointed to the far end of the building. "There is a workbench and tools; over there is shelving for piping, house and farm repairs and stuff." She indicated an area to their right. "That's for repairs of the tractor and other equipment."

Virginia looked at the tractor. It looked clean. The areas around the large pieces of equipment looked dirt-free. The floor was clean. "The tractor and stuff looks well maintained."

"Ann took good care of them, and I've run around on them to see what they're like."

Virginia nodded. "I hope this is secure. There's a lot of valuable equipment and things in here."

Natalie nodded. "Andy put alarms on this building and the other sheds. He said he added more special locks to this one and the shed we were in. We can look."

They walked to the big doors and examined the locking systems. Natalie pointed. "There are the locking mechanisms. The dull handle with the keyhole is the original. Your husband said it was pretty good. These shinny... thingamabobs are what Andy added. I can open it from inside or outside, but trying to break in would mean dismantling the building and setting off the alarm."

Virginia nodded. "Good to know. He's been busy." She turned and looked around. "Where is Linda?"

Linda called out. "I'm over here." She waved from the seat on the tractor. "This is really cool. My grandfather had a tractor similar to this, much older of course, but I use to ride it with him when I was a kid. This brings back memories."

Virginia took a glance around the barn. "Looks like we found out where this tunnel went. We should get moving; there are more tunnels to go."

Linda smiled. "I could use a break and get some water. Let's head back."

Virginia looked at Natalie and pointed at the big doors. "I can shut this cupboard and seal the secret door. Can you unlock those doors so we can stay in the light going back?"

"Yeah. Andy showed me how." Natalie walked to the doors and fiddled with the apparatus. It clicked, and the doors swung open. "Let's go. I'll re-lock it from outside."

They hurried out of the barn and waited while Natalie closed and re-locked the doors. They walked back to the house. Inside, Linda and Virginia pulled plastic bottles of water out of the refrigerator and headed for the parlor. Natalie turned her head and looked out the front window. "What's that noise?"

CHAPTER 15

Linda stepped to the window and peered out. "Looks like there're a few demonstrators out there. Shall we go see what they are up to?"

Virginia nodded. "Let's see who's behind this. Who knows, it could be Reverend Nesbitt's so-called army."

They walked out the front door and strolled down the driveway to the stone pillars marking the entrance. They stood and watched the people marching back and forth carrying signs near the driveway.

Linda raised an eyebrow. "Looks like there are two groups." She pointed. "That bunch is obviously from that crazy church."

Virginia nodded toward the second batch of protesters. The gathering was mainly men in jeans and hard hats protesting the lack of development opportunities. "Looks like you just heard from that developer, Bryon Weedon. He's over there talking to that huge man. I hope they don't start anything."

Natalie pulled out her cell phone, tapped the screen a couple of times. "Hi, Detective Grover, this is Natalie North. I'm fine, thank you. I just wanted to tell you I've got two groups picketing my property. You said to call if I had any concerns." She listened. "Yes, Virginia, Linda, and I will wait here. You said, if they come onto my land Virginia is to arrest them?" She listened. "I'll tell her." She disconnected.

Virginia stared at Natalie. "You've got Detective Grover on speed dial?"

"Yes. He said to do it in case I had any trouble and call him anytime. He was really nice."

Linda shook her head. "You've got another admirer. Is he sending anyone?"

"Yes. He said deputies would be here shortly. The deputies can't do anything unless the protestors trespass, or get violent. But he said the deputies stopping by more frequently might discourage any trouble."

Virginia pointed at the construction group. "That's a new one on me. This isn't a union issue. What can Weedon hope to gain?"

One of the men from the church assembly, dressed in dark blue slacks and a white shirt and red tie, strutted up to the women. "Ms. North. We are members of—"

Natalie cut him off. "The Calvary Evangelical Chapel. Dressed the way you are, and with those signs, you stand out like a sore thumb." She put her hands on her hips. "Your arrogant pastor sent you, didn't he?"

The man stiffened. "Arrogant? Pastor Nesbitt is a great man. He leads his flock in a righteous manner to the glory—"

"Cool it. I've heard this stupid drivel before. Just stay outside the fence and don't block the driveway. You could get hurt doing that. Oh, step back a few feet, you are trespassing."

"If... if you will just consider—"

"Stay off my land, buster. Better yet, go away." Natalie turned and looked for Virginia and Linda. She spotted them talking to Weedon and a couple of tough-looking men, then hurried to them.

When she got there, Weedon looked at her. "Ms. North. I see you've cleaned up your act.

Natalie looked up and glared at him. "Shove it up your ass."

"No need to get hostile. If you will just see the inevitable and stop your stubbornness, we can sit down and discuss terms of the sale of *Borealis*. I assure you, I can be most generous."

Natalie bristled. "And if I don't?"

"Then, we will join that assembly of good Christians and picket. We'll go to the media and bring down the social and government leadership in our community to entice you to sell me the land. Then you can return to California."

"I suppose the use of your union construction men on the picket line is to stop my nonunion workers from returning to work."

Weedon smiled. "You bet."

Virginia stepped in front of him and moved within inches. In a low, steady voice, she said, "Get this straight. I'm going to say this just once. If you, or any of your bozos, causes *any* disruption of work here or intimidates any workers, I'll come looking for you. When I find you... well, I hope your medical insurance is paid... in full."

"You... you just threatened me. That's illegal. You'll hear from my lawyer. I can have you arrested."

Virginia smiled. "Go ahead and try. It's your word against mine."

Weedon leered. "You could have an accident out here."

"Now that was stupid. Did you ladies hear him threaten us?"

They nodded. Natalie smiled. "Yes. Maybe I should call the sheriff."

Linda pointed down the road. "No need, they're here already."

Two sheriff's cars arrived. Weedon turned and strutted to the deputy exiting his vehicle, then hustled away.

A sergeant walked to Natalie, Linda, and Virginia. "Hello, ladies. I'm Sergeant McCutcheon." He looked at Natalie and smiled. "Ms. North?"

She nodded.

"Detective Grover informed me of the situation here. I'm posting a deputy here for today and this evening. For the next few weeks, we've increased the patrols around here. If you have any problems, just call, and we'll get someone here pronto." He gave her his card.

Natalie took the card. "Thank you, Sergeant. I appreciate your help."

"No problem, Ms. North." He looked at Linda and Virginia, then moved closer to Virginia. "Are you Special Agent Virginia Davies Clark?"

She nodded. "Yes."

"I heard from Detective Grover what you did to Jack Blake. Good for you. He's big, strong, and mean. Likes to pick fights and especially beat up women. That took a lot of courage. From what I've heard, his reputation as a tough guy is not holding up too well at the county jail. He's been harassed since he's been there. Someone seems to have mentioned to a couple of trustees that Jack Blake was beaten up by a pretty blond woman. He still has the throat contusions and sore testicles to prove it. Since he's been in jail, there have been a few new bruises added."

"We may be women, but we aren't pushovers. Please be sure that sentiment gets out to the criminal world."

Sergeant McCutcheon pointed at Natalie's gun. "I don't think we need to add much. Pictures of her with that gun on are all over the county. She's been labeled the short, sexy, six shooter." He looked around. "I don't think you have much to worry about from the church folks, other than them being annoying. The construction guys are another matter. Keep an eye out for them. Call if there are any confrontations."

Virginia nodded. "We will." She watched the sergeant go talk to the other deputies and then to Weedon. He climbed back into his cruiser and left. The other deputies pulled their car up next to the driveway.

Natalie walked up to the patrol car and spoke to the deputies inside. "You can park in my driveway if you like. And if you want anything, water, food, snacks, just call me, and we'll bring it out." She gave them her cell number. "You can also use the restroom in the house if you need to."

They gave her a surprised stare, then grinned. "Thank you, ma'am. We'll also check on you tonight to make sure everything is secure."

"Please give my number to the deputies that relieve you and tell them that my offer applies to them too."

The deputy nodded. "We will, thank you."

Natalie, Virginia, and Linda returned to the house and sat in the parlor. Linda leaned back. "Looks like you are popular with the local gendarmes."

Natalie nodded. "Yeah. Who would have guessed? Short, sexy, six-shooter, I like that."

"I was surprised the sergeant didn't say anything about my threat to Weedon. I'm sure Weedon told him."

Natalie nodded. "I'm sure he did. But I wouldn't be surprised if the sergeant didn't tell him, in great detail, about what you did to Jack Blake. I think Weedon was a little shocked when he walked away from the sergeant."

The phone rang in the kitchen. Natalie jumped up and hurried to answer it. In a couple of minutes, with a despairing look, she returned.

Linda rose. "Natalie, what's wrong?"

"Someone just posted bond for Jack Blake. That's scary."

"Who posted the bond?"

"I don't know. The sheriff's deputy said a lawyer came in with a cashier's check and posted the bond. All fifty grand."

Virginia got on her cell phone and called Andy at the university. She left a message for him to call her right away. "Tell you what; there are a couple of sheriff's deputies outside. I'll tell Andy to pick some stuff up at home and come here tonight. With the deputies outside, your alarm system, our guns, and Andy here, you will be protected."

Natalie sat. "No need for all that, Virginia. It's kind of you to do that. But with Andy's alarm system, the cops, and my gun, I think I'll be fine."

Linda looked at Virginia. "Who could, or would, put fifty thousand dollars at risk for Blake?"

Virginia sighed. "My first guess is Weedon. Next, would be Jenny Parker. I suppose that church group could, too. Religious nut-jobs are dangerous, especially if they believe they are doing for their god."

Linda sat back down. "Come to think of it, Weedon is the only one who hasn't mentioned, or asked, about quilts. Didn't Blake ask about them?"

Virginia and Natalie nodded.

Linda shrugged. "Maybe it was Jenny Parker or the church group."

"But Blake is big and violent." Virginia looked thoughtful. "Blake's someone Weedon could use in his picket line, and someone who would not hesitate to try and get revenge."

"True." Natalie unsuccessfully tried to speak with courage. "But he'd have to be stupid to try that again."

Linda fiddled with her wedding ring. "Yeah, but he's a violent sort of criminal. He didn't impress me as the intellectual kind of crook. More of a vicious, caveman crook."

"You may be right." Natalie shook her head. "We've got a lot of theories, but nothing solid to pin any of this on someone. So far, it's only been harassment and one physical attack. Even Blake getting out of jail on bond can't be traced."

Virginia looked at the floor, then back at Natalie and Linda. "But something is bothering me, and I can't put my finger on it. It's lurking at the edge of my brain." She looked around the room. "You guys up for more secret tunnel exploring?"

Natalie and Linda didn't respond.

"Come on, the afternoon is almost shot, and we can't do anything about the groups outside. Why not explore. No telling what we'll find. It looked like there were more tunnels that ran underground. Where do they go?"

Natalie slowly rose. "I guess we could explore some more. At least, for a little while."

"Before we go, I have a question. We explored the tunnels that went to the shed and the barn. There wasn't one for the garage. Why not?"

Natalie shrugged. "The garage was built to have the same architecture as the house, but it was built in the nineteen sixties. It was probably made after the original tunnels were constructed. I have my car in there."

"That could explain it. Let's go tunnel exploring." Virginia got up. "Coming Linda?"

Linda pushed herself out of her chair. "I guess so. Let's go see where more of those passages end up."

Virginia led them down to the basement and back into the tunnels. At the entrance, Virginia found a light switch and flipped it on. Most of the incandescent bulbs came on, illuminating the tunnel. The light bulbs that were out allowed the others to cast shadows in sections of the stonework and crevices in the sidewalls. At the cross paths, they turned left. Farther down the tunnel, it came to an abrupt halt. Ahead of them was dirt. Boards were stacked nearby. Virginia walked to the wall of soil and hit it with her hand. "Looks like someone wasn't finished with this tunnel. Doesn't go anywhere." She pointed at the electric wires above. "Even the power terminates here. Let's go the other way."

They turned and headed back. They followed the path back past the crossroad where they came from and continued. Then they climbed a wooden ladder to the next level up.

Natalie looked around, her mood brightening. "We must be on the first floor. Over there is a ladder that looks like it goes to the upper floors. I wonder what rooms are connected to this one and how you access the tunnel from the other side."

Linda started down the tunnel and stopped about thirty feet away. "Two bulbs out down here. Kinda dark." She waved her flashlight around. "Looks like we're at the end of the line. There's another ladder over here, and... let's see... what looks like a release lever here." She pushed on it. A section of the wall quietly rotated open.

CHAPTER 16

Light streamed into the dark tunnel. Linda stepped through the portal and screamed.

Virginia pushed past and spotted someone in dark pants, and a dark hoodie, turn and dart out of the parlor room. She ran toward the fleeing man, grabbed a heavy bronze bookend as she ran past a shelf, and threw it at the person ahead of her. It hit him in the back between his shoulder blades. He arched his back, yelled, and stumbled. He caught himself and lurched ahead. He missed-stepped and tumbled into a side table in the hall. He faltered, and then slowly regained his footing, and with Virginia almost on him, he staggered toward the kitchen. The cellar door suddenly flew open in front of him. He ran squarely into it.

Virginia ran into him from the rear, knocking him down. She quickly pulled her gun and aimed it at him. "Stay perfectly still, and maybe I won't shoot you."

Natalie stepped into the hallway from behind the cellar door. "Looks like we got him."

Virginia looked at the door, then Natalie. "Good job. How'd you get back so quick?"

Natalie grinned. "When you're both scared and mad, you can do wonders. I ran like hell."

"I believe you." Virginia looked down at the man on the floor. "Okay Mr. Weedon, sit up and put your hands on top of your head."

He slowly moved to a sitting position, lowered his hood, and put his hands on his head. "How'd you know it was me?"

"Your shoes. Those are L.L. Bean walking shoes. They're great by the way, but distinctive to someone who knows their products, like me. You were wearing them outside when you spoke to us, and the sheriff."

"I didn't think of that. Can I put my hands down now?"

"Not if you don't want to get shot. What are you doing inside Ms. North's house?"

Weedon glared at her with disdain. "None of your business."

Natalie kicked his leg. "It's my business. It would be a shame if the sheriff found you with a knife in your hand and a bullet in your head. Self-defense from a man who's been harassing me." She patted the gun slung on her side.

He looked up at Natalie, then Virginia, and her gun. "Okay. I was looking for something."

"We guessed that." Natalie leaned over. "What was it?"

"Are you going to have me arrested?"

"Maybe," Natalie shrugged. "Then again, maybe not.It depends on your answers."

He gave them an arrogant look. "Either have me arrested, or let me go. I'm not talking."

"We just want to ask you some questions. But if you want to continue to be an asshole, I can just have you arrested."

Weedon gave her a smug look. "You can't intimidate me. I have a lot of high-powered connections. I've got lawyers. You won't get far."

"He has a point." Virginia sighed and winked at Natalie. "I don't think anyone out in the street will hear him scream from the barn, do you?"

Weedon looked up at Virginia and Natalie. "What? What do you mean? Scream? Barn?"

Natalie knitted her brow in a confused look, and then she cracked a smile and shook her head. "I don't think so, but we could gag him to make sure he can't be heard."

Linda ventured down the hall. "This was on the floor where he was standing when I caught sight of him. Must have dropped it." She handed Natalie a copy of Jenny Parker's new quilting book.

Virginia glanced at the book then bent down slightly. "Now, Mr. Weedon, why would you have a quilting book? You a quilter, too?"

Weedon's jaw tightened. "None of your business."

"That's the second time you've said that. It's getting old."

Linda handed Virginia a small paperbacked book on prospecting. A page was earmarked. Virginia flipped it open. A picture of a piece of quartz with a gold vein through it and a brief description of how this was formed in and near volcanoes was underlined. "This is interesting. Looking for more than just a quilt book?"

Weedon snarled. "None of you damn business."

Virginia waved her gun. "Get up and start walking. I'm sure you'll find the inside of Ms. North's barn to be both very fascinating, and extremely painful."

He frowned. "What are you going to do? I don't want to go. I demand you release me."

"Demand we release you? Guess again, mister. You're not in any position to demand anything. I'm thinking of using enhanced interrogation techniques. I think that's what the CIA called it when they did it. The news folks called it torture, but they have no sense of humor. We're going to ensure you experience some extremely excruciating pain."

His eyes widened. "You wouldn't dare. That's illegal. I have high-placed friends."

"Big deal. They won't be able to help you in the barn." Virginia grinned. "Get up and start walking." She looked at Linda. "Bring a couple of knitting needles and sewing needles for the quilt room. Natalie, do you have any foam oven cleaner? It's mainly caustic soda."

Natalie grinned. "Yeah, it's under the sink, I'll get it. The stuff's in a spray can."

Linda leaned close to Natalie. "What are you two doing? You can't kill or torture him."

"You're right. We know that, but Virginia is convincing him otherwise. Watch and play along. From what I've seen of Virginia, she'll get him to cooperate if we all act like we're together in this and going to actually do it."

Weedon's hands shook, sweat beaded on his brow as he stood. "Knitting needles? Oven cleaner?"

Virginia poked him with her gun. "Start walking that way." She struggled to contain her laughter. "The knitting needles are long and sharp on the ends. They can make their own holes in things, like you, or they can be used very effectively, and very painfully, in *all* your existing orifices. The caustic soda is sodium hydroxide or lye. Burns tissue like hell and can make body fat into soap. It's especially bad for the eyes. Very painful. You'll go blind. There are various tools in the barn we can improvise with like pliers, screwdrivers, bolt cutters, and electric drills. And then we can use the jumper cables. Attach them to the battery on the tractor and the other end to various parts of you, like your balls, and… well you get the idea. It gets real interesting if we wire you to the headlights, start the tractor, and turn on the lights that will be painful, and then gun the engine. That will be extremely painful. We can cut things off you with the bolt cutters, like fingers, toes, ears, penis, and your balls. Just think of what we can pull off you with pliers. And just think, no pesky lawyers, no Constitutional rights, and no cops to worry about. Oh, and your big, strong, construction buddies won't be around to help you either."

Weedon swallowed. His lip quivered. "Bolt cutters? Jumper cables?"

Virginia smiled at him. "Yeah, they'll carry twelve volts from the battery on the tractor, and quite a lot of juice. Amps I think they call it. Lots of those. Hurts like hell when you can't pull away. Burns tissue, too. Parts of you will be smoking." She glanced at Natalie. "Natalie, get the oven cleaner and some plastic ties."

"Okay." Natalie hurried to the kitchen and returned with the ties and a spray can she held in her hand by her side, slightly out of Weedon's sight.

She smiled at Weedon. "Mr. Weedon, in case you hadn't heard, Virginia took Jack Blake down with a just a magazine. Better Homes and Garden to boot."

"Jack Blake? He's huge, violent, and mean." His head swiveled around as he looked at the women. He stared at Virginia. "You're the one who decked him and got him arrested? I heard a woman did it. He was almost killed."

Natalie nodded. "Yeah. And like I said, she did it with just a magazine. She ruined his throat, busted his arm, and smashed his balls, three times, too. A sheriff's deputy said he's still a high soprano. You don't stand a chance with her if she uses the things in my barn on you. The barn will be perfect. She can find new uses for the tools I have in there."

Virginia tied his arms behind his back. "Almost ready to cause you a lot of serious pain and lingering discomfort. A dentist pulling your teeth out without knocking you out will seem pleasurable by comparison."

Weedon stammered, spittle coming out as he spoke. "I... I'll... sue you for everything you've got."

Virginia grinned. "Sue us? Might be hard to do. Finding a body buried on two thousand acres is a daunting task. Since you broke in here, I assume you didn't tell anyone of your pending felony. Natalie, Linda, and I are each other's alibi, and we never saw you." Virginia winked at Natalie. "That tractor of yours has a backhoe attachment, doesn't it? Wasn't it in the corner of the barn ready to go?"

Natalie stifled a laugh. "Yes. I've been *dying* to try it. Should dig a nice, deep, hole fairly fast."

Linda returned with the metal knitting needles and handed them to Virginia.

Virginia held the needles in one hand and made a show of carefully examining them while keeping her pistol aimed at Weedon. "These will be way more fun than a magazine."

Linda swallowed, leaned close to Natalie with a nervous look, and whispered, "Virginia's not really going to torture him, is she? She's eyeing those needles like she intends to use them."

Natalie shook her head, and said, under her breath, "No. But she's making him extremely uncomfortable. He knows what happened to Blake. After what he's done to me, this is fun. Maybe I should encourage her to... ahh... use our enhanced interrogation tools on him for the fun of it."

Linda turned pale. "Please don't."

"Don't worry; she's going to get him to talk, or scare the piss out of him. Look." She pointed at Weedon pant leg. "Looks like she accomplished that already."

Virginia noticed the growing wet crotch and pant leg. "Natalie, get a napkin and a dish towel to gag Mr. Weedon before we take him to the barn.

Can't have him calling out for help or screaming." She pointed the handful of needles at his pants. "Guess you've got a weak bladder. You should see a doctor about that. Well, that is, if you live through the day."

Natalie returned with two cloth napkins and two dishtowels. "I've got lots of duct tape in the barn to secure him with." She used the towels to gag him.

"Excellent." Virginia stopped Weedon in the kitchen and told him to kneel on the floor. "Mr. Weedon. You have tormented Ms. North. You have threatened her. You've had various officials who you either bribed, or contributed a lot to their re-elections to harass her. You've been making her a nervous wreck. Now it's her turn to return the favor. As to suing us, you will have a lot of trouble. Dead people usually can't go to court. You inherited a lot of money. A boatload of money. But typical with someone of your mentality and ego, you spent it all. Now we are going to take you out to the barn where, one way or another, you will answer a few simple questions. If you talk right away, we'll consider some sort of leniency, like not killing you, or breaking too many bones, maybe not painfully probing too many places with the knitting needles, or hurting vital organs beyond repair, or frying your testicles. Get up."

Natalie and Linda helped him get to his feet, as Virginia went to the side door and peered out. "The church group is milling around and mostly facing the street. His gang is looking at them, and at the house. We need a distraction."

Natalie nodded. "I'll distract them while you two take this scumbag to the barn." She hurried away. A couple of minutes later she retuned wearing his loosely tied, thin blouse gaping open exposing a lot of her breasts, and short shorts. She smiled. "Risqué time again. I think I'll go talk to the boys and keep them busy while you get him to the barn."

Virginia looked Natalie over. "Yeah, that outfit will do the trick. They'll never even see us. As soon as you get their attention, we'll move. Don't stay out there too long."

"Okay. Flash the light over the barn door once you're inside, and I'll come back."

"Okay."

Natalie strutted out the door and down the driveway. Weedon's construction men turned and watched as she approached. The church group started to yell and berate her, but the construction men quickly shut them up. Natalie leaned against a fence rail and talked to them.

Virginia and Linda took Weedon, gagged and bound, by the arms and pulled him toward the barn. Upon entering, they pushed him down on the floor near the tractor. Linda returned to the door and flashed the outside barn light. She pushed the door open a crack and looked out. Natalie was walking toward the barn with a smile on her face.

Virginia looked down at Weedon. "First, who's behind your efforts to get *Borealis*?"

He fidgeted, but remained on his knees, quiet.

"Mr. Blake was a really big, mean, man. A lot tougher than you. As you have heard, it took less than a minute to bring him down. He had trouble breathing for quite a while. He still can't talk above a high-pitched whisper. He almost squeaks when he talks. His balls were swollen and hurt like hell because I kicked him there really, really hard three times. The sheriff said he's still walking slow and bent over. I even broke his arm. Compound fracture. We'll go slow with you and have more fun. We'll induce an extraordinary amount of pain in you, too." Virginia tucked her gun in her waistband, then selected one of the long, thin, knitting needles, and laid the others on the floor in front of him. "You understand I can ram this up your nose, into your eyes or your ears without much effort on my part, but inducing a hell of a lot of pain on your part. If I push it too far into your skull, I'll probably turn you into a vegetable, or you will be dead. I can use them on your other end too. That will be most unpleasant for you. You can talk or else. We really don't care which." She leaned closer. "Personally, I hope you're stubborn for a while and let us have some fun watching you in agony."

She turned and watched Natalie enter the barn and close the door. "Good job with the distraction."

Natalie smiled. "Thanks. Are we ready to have some fun?"

"Yes." Virginia set the needle down and went for the jumper cables. "Get the other tools girls."

Natalie and Linda exchanged glances and giggled as they went to get pliers, bolt cutters, a power saw and a portable propane torch.

Natalie looked at Linda then spoke loud enough for Weedon to hear her. "Do you have any idea how many air fresheners it'll take to get the smell of his dead body and his shit out of here?"

"No." Linda held up both hands. "I'd guess quite a few. Maybe we should buy a few cases."

"Good idea. I can get them at Costco. Won't cost too much."

Virginia returned with the cables. "Natalie, hook the terminals on these ends to the battery on the tractor and start it. I think we should start with something that will shock him." She stepped closer and dropped onto one knee. "Linda, hold him while I press this end against his head. When we're ready I'll attach the other one to his balls. Good thing he's gagged. Oh, use that rubber mat over there to do it, won't conduct electricity and shock you, and don't touch him with any part of your body."

Weedon's breathing rate increased. His jaw quivered. He squirmed. His head jerked around, peering wide-eyed at the three women, and the tools that lay out in front of him.

"This is going to be extremely painful for him. He'll probably squirm, and then pass out, so we'll need to revive him. Who know, maybe this will also fry his brain some. After this, a cabbage will be able to do more than him. It can carry on photosynthesis. He'll most likely be a stupid vegetable. Sex will definitely be out of the question."

Linda took a lead from Virginia, and using a section of the rubber mat, held it against Weedon's head while Natalie was opening the tractor's hood and doing something in the engine compartment with the other ends of the jumper cable.

Virginia held the other cable and smiled. "This is going to hurt you a hell of a lot more than me. Matter of fact, I'll actually enjoy it." She moved closer and raised the cable so he could see the end. I'll try and limit how long we juice you, but I'd love to see what part of you smokes first. What the hell, you're an asshole anyway."

Weedon struggled and tried to talk. His pants got wetter. His face turned white. He started to waver under Linda's grip.

CHAPTER 17

Virginia lowered the end of the jumper cable and frowned. "Take the gag off for a minute, girls. He seems to want to say something. Maybe a last request."

Linda set her end of the cable down next to Weedon, quickly undid the gag, and stepped back as Weedon fell onto the floor. His breathing still labored, he tried to speak, but just garbled noise came out.

Virginia put the jumper cable down, picked up a knitting needle, and stroked it. "Help him sit up."

Natalie and Linda struggled to get him into a sitting position.

Virginia kept the knitting needle in plain view. "Now, Mr. Weedon, do you have anything of real interest to say to us to forestall us from going to work on you?"

He sat, his pants wet, his breathing slowing. His head swiveled around taking in the barn and the tools arranged on the floor near him. A tear ran down his cheek. "Plea... please don't do this."

"Okay, talk to us, but make it real good, or we will get creative."

"All right. All right. You win." He swallowed. "You're correct. I spent all my inheritance on cars, clothes, gambling, expensive trips, and women. I got into the development business before I ran out of cash. I started with spec houses then got into small housing developments. Now, I get large tracts of land and either sell lots to custom builders, or contract the building some of the houses myself. To accomplish this, I obtain investors who make money when we sell either the lots or the houses."

Virginia smiled. "You have investors for Ms. North's property?"

He nodded. His voice wavered. "Yes. I couldn't afford to buy all two thousand acres myself once I got her to sell. I got investors. Rather, they approached me about it. But they're getting antsy. They have invested in what was to be called *Mission San Gabriel*. They want to get started. They have capital tied up and aren't happy. They see themselves making millions on this project."

"They are pissed off at you because you spent a lot of their money and have nothing to show for it?"

He shivered. "Yes."

Virginia changed position so she was kneeling in front of him. "Who are your investors?"

He leaned back. "I can't tell you."

Virginia gave him a sneer. "You're more afraid of them than me?"

He nodded. "Frankly, yes."

"I see. Okay." She held a knitting needle close to his face then stuck the end into his nostril. "I'll ram this nice, sharp, stainless steel needle, up your nose, puncture your skull, and stab your brain, making you a docile idiot forever, or kill you. Then, if you still can, you'll remember, that I'm less of a threat than they are. Would that be better than what your investors will do to you?"

He sat teary-eyed looking at the three women. He swallowed. "I see your point."

Virginia pulled the needle out of his nose sat back on her heels, and waited. "And?"

He took a breath. "They've told me that my trying to get Ms. North's property, and to get her to leave Williamson County has taken much too long. They want finalized results in the next two weeks, or they'll skin me alive. I believe them."

"Blake works for them?"

"I think so, yes." Weedon nodded. "One of them anyway. I've used him on occasion, but he scares me."

"Which one of the investors hired him?"

He shook his head. "I don't know."

"So, you do have some dangerous partners. Where'd you find them, a nut house?"

"Not exactly, but close. There's one who scares me as much as you do."

"Oh? Who's that?"

"I... I don't know their names. They're called The Solomon Group. They invest through corporations. I tried tracing them once. They are a rat's nest of privately held companies with offshore activities. I couldn't do it. I receive my instructions over the Internet and by phone. The money is electronically routed to my business accounts from offshore banks. I'm to get Ms. North's property, or they'll take back their money and get the money I've already spent on the project out of me. They said I'd pay in cash or with body parts. I believe them, especially after Ms. Ann Greenwald's murder. There is one of them I've listened to on the phone who scares the hell out of me."

"Male or female?"

"The phone messages and conversations are... well... sound like a computer voice, mechanical, or sometimes like... I don't know how to describe it... not real. I can't tell if the speaker is a man of woman."

Virginia stood. "You don't exactly know who your partners are? You don't know if they're men or women? That's kind of stupid. For being a college graduate and a big-time developer, you're pretty dumb."

Weedon nodded. "Unfortunately, you're right."

Virginia chuckled. "You're screwed, aren't you? They'll hurt you and kill you, or we'll do their dirty work for them. Either way, you lose. Ever feel like you're between a rock and a hard spot?"

"Ye... yes."

Natalie leaned over. "Why did you break into my house?"

He glanced up at her. "I... I was told there is a file here one of the Solomon Group investors wants. Badly. I was to get it, or some rather damaging information about me would be leaked to the media and the Internet."

Natalie frowned. "What files?"

"I was told it was probably on Ann North Greenwald's laptop computer or on a flash drive that looked like R2D2 from Star Wars. I saw you, Mrs. Clark, with the computer the other day, so I figured the flash drive must still be here. My investor said it would be either in Ms. Greenwald's quilt room, or the parlor in a secret hiding place."

Virginia rubbed the needle. "Does the file have a name?"

"Yes. Concept or book. That's all I know." He looked at the three women. "Honest, that's it."

Linda held out the prospecting pocketbook she had found. "How about this little archeology book you had?"

"The person who told me to get the file said there was someone else who had left that book here and wanted it back. That book was all I found before you came charging in and caught me."

Linda looked at Natalie and Virginia then asked, "Who left it, and when?"

Weedon's body shook. A tear ran down his cheek. "Hon... honest, I don't know."

Virginia grinned and set the needle down. "Now, doesn't telling us all this without experiencing a great deal of pain make you feel better?"

He squirmed. "Not really. You won't let any of what I've told you get out, will you? It could get me killed."

Virginia patted his head. "We'll see. We'll release you, and you *will* stop harassing Ms. North and forget about her property. You will deal with your investment partners any way you choose, but remember; we can be most unpleasant, too. If you cause us any more trouble, you can be sure we *will* cause you a whole lot of pain, and we *will* do it fast. Understand?"

Weedon looked pale. He slowly nodded. "Yes."

Virginia ran her hand across the back of her neck. "Mr. Weedon, you have a degree in chemistry, right?"

He cocked his head. "Yes. Why?"

"Do you know how to make ibotenic acid, muscimol, muscazone, or muscarine?" Virginia looked at his uncomfortable position. "You can stand up."

Weedon clumsily climbed to his feet. "They sound like biochemical compounds. I wouldn't know how to do that. Where do they come from?"

"Mushrooms. Why not? You're a chemist, aren't you?"

"Yes, but you would need to be a biochemist with at least a masters, or an organic chemist with one to do that. I was an analytical chemist. I actually didn't like organic chemistry when I took the classes at the university. I never studied biochemistry. When I started out after college, I worked for a chemical company in the northeast. We made industrial chemicals. It wasn't a drug company. On top of that, I haven't worked as a chemist for well over a decade."

Virginia pointed at Weedon's wrists. "Cut him free."

Linda cut the plastic ties with a box cutter. He rubbed his wrists.

Virginia pointed at the door. "You can go. We'll be watching you leave and drive away. I just hope none of your he-man thugs out there see your wet trousers. It might also be a good idea to take your men with you and make sure they don't come back."

Weedon gave her a sad look. "I'm being paid, in a way, to have them here."

"Let me guess. That church group that's also out there."

He nodded.

"Give them back their money and get your men out of here."

"It's not about money." He stared at the floor. "They have pictures of me in… in some… some rather compromising situations and positions. Almost like you ladies do, but worse."

"More pictures? You really are an idiot." Natalie put her hand on her gun. "Let me guess. Someone took photos of you having some recreational sex with a certain young woman who is definitely not your wife. In them, you're doing something that church group considers an abomination. Your wife probably won't approve of the eight by ten glossies of you doing it with your new lady friend either. They're going to send copies to her and let them out for public viewing on the Internet if you don't do what they want."

He hung his head. "Yes."

"Okay, you didn't find the disk or computer. That you can tell them, and it's true. But how you handle them is your problem. Stay away from me."

He nodded. "I will."

"Good. You're in a lot of trouble." Natalie sniffed and wrinkled her nose. "I think Virginia scared more than piss out of you. You need a change of diapers. Next time, it'll be worse."

Virginia held up her hand. "Wait. Mr. Weedon, you forget about getting Natalie's land. If you agree, I want you to write down everything you know about your investors including e-mail addresses, banking information, any phone numbers, or anything else you can remember, and give me your cell phone. I will try to find your investors and try to fix your, and our, problem. You're on your own with the church though."

He cracked a weak smile. "Okay. Deal. I'll give you everything I know. Anyway that you can help me, I will appreciate. Ms. North, I'm sorry for the hell I've caused you."

"Thank you for that." Natalie gave him a piece of butcher paper from a workbench and a pen.

He stood next to the workbench and wrote out the information. He handed the document to Virginia. "This is it." He gave her his cell phone. "Please return it soon. I need it."

"Thank you. See how easy that was? Now, go before we forget we're ladies."

They watched him hurry out the barn's side door.

Linda sighed. "I'm glad we didn't actually torture him."

"We weren't going to, but his imagination worked as I hoped." Virginia closed the door and grinned. "I have some ideas. I think I know who his unknown investor is that wants the file. The geology book may be linked to that quartz rock Andy found."

Linda helped Virginia gather up the plastic ties, gags, and papers. Linda deposited them in the trash as Virginia stuffed the papers Weedon had provided the information on in a canvas tote bag she found near the backhoe attachment in the corner of the barn.

Virginia looked around. "Where's Natalie?"

Linda pointed at the door. "Last I saw her she had a big grin on her face and was headed for the house."

CHAPTER 18

Linda and Virginia walked into the house. Hearing a noise, they moved into the parlor. They looked across the room at the shelves that were standing open like a door. Natalie was bent over, examining it.

Linda watched for a second, and then asked, "Did you find the release mechanism?"

Natalie straightened and smiled. "Yeah. Finally. It's a plank behind a book on the fourth shelf." She swung the bookshelf closed with a soft click. "I don't know about you two, but I'm done with tunnel exploring and scaring the shit out of people for the day. But I have to admit, I think things went rather well with Mr. Weedon."

Virginia and Linda agreed.

Natalie leaned against the bookshelves. "How about we order dinner brought in here tonight and you two invite your husbands to join us to eat and christen my new hot tub?"

Linda and Virginia exchanged glances, and then nodded. Virginia pulled out her cell phone and called Andy as Linda called her husband. After getting agreement from their husbands and telling them to bring their bathing suits, they discussed what to have for dinner. At six, Linda and Virginia headed out to pick up take out Chinese for dinner as Natalie went to change clothes.

They entered the restaurant, went to the counter to order dinner, and then sat at a nearby table. They got iced teas to drink while they waited. A middle-aged couple came in and sat at a table. The woman stood, strutted to their table, and stopped.

Virginia swallowed. *Here we go again. Another moral do-gooder who doesn't like the pictures that damn pastor posted.*

The woman cracked a smile. "I heard what you ladies did to that overbearing pastor, Nesbitt. Good for you. People like him get away with being self-righteous and telling people what to think because no one will stand up to them. The SOB lives in my neighborhood. Thanks." She turned and walked back to her table.

Virginia pinched her arm, and then looked at Linda. "Did that woman say what I think she said?"

"Yes." Linda nodded. "How about them apples?"

They sipped their tea as they watched customers' come and go. Virginia sat back and asked, "How are you coming with the quilt inventory?"

"I'm almost done. I've got them all on the computer numbered and sorted by quilt type and size. I've also categorized the table runners, art quilts, and wall hangings similarly. I should be done in a day or two. I've got them physically sorted as well."

"Good."

"How are you doing?"

Virginia ran her hand across the back of her neck. "I've got all the tools, notions, and sewing machines categorized and accounted for. The furniture is also identified and described. I'm working on all the fabrics Ann had. It seems like Ann had enough fabric to open her own store. When you're done with your project, maybe you can help me finish."

Linda nodded. "I'd love to." She looked at the take-out counter. "I think that man is motioning for us to get our order."

"Looks like it. Let's go."

They arrived at *Borealis* fifteen minutes later and set the kitchen table. As they finished, Andy and Linda's husband arrived.

Linda introduced her husband to Natalie. "Natalie, this is Brian, my husband. He's been anxious to meet you. Brian, this is Natalie North."

Natalie gave him a thousand watt smile and hugged him. "Nice to finally meet you, Brian. Linda has been a great help and a good friend. I'm glad you didn't have any problems with her being here."

Brian beamed. "I'm thrilled to meet you, Ms. North. In spite of all the things that have happened, Linda's been really happy being here, and I think it's wonderful she has you as a friend."

"Thank you." Natalie then hugged Andy. "Good to see you again, Professor. Thank you for everything you've done for me. We have dinner ready, and then, we can christen my new hot tub."

Andy nodded. "Sounds like a plan. Let's eat. Anything exciting happen while I've been gone?"

"Yes. We'll tell you over dinner."

After dinner, Brain and Andy changed into their bathing suits and got in the hot tub while the women dumped the empty take-out containers and paper plates. Andy and Brian were peering around the edge of the house at the street and the church protesters when Natalie, Linda, and Virginia came out, all three in bikinis.

Andy smiled at them. "Looks like the developer's workers are gone. You three must have *really* scared Weedon. He's such a pompous ass I didn't think anything, or anyone, could intimidate him."

Virginia chuckled. "I think he has a new-found respect for the three of us."

"You're probably right." Andy pointed. "But there is a guy over by that tree at the fence line. He has a camera on a tripod, with a big lens. I think he's shooting pictures of us."

Linda climbed into the hot water. "I bet he's hoping for some scandalous behavior he can photograph for their church website."

Virginia looked toward the fence. "I see him."

Natalie looked, too. "Yep. There he is. Isn't that Mr. Heller from Calvary Evangelical Chapel?"

Virginia squinted. "You've got better eyesight than me. It may well be. He was a real piece of work. Like the last boy in high school to see boobs."

"He was odd bird, and very determined." Natalie snickered. "He wants something scandalous, let's give him something scandalous."

Andy touched her hand. "Natalie, you may want to rethink that."

She turned and gave him a quizzical look. "Oh? Why?"

"You're playing right into their hand. Think about it. They want you to do something they consider disreputable or distasteful, and then they'll use it against you."

Natalie stood, water dripping off her short, curvaceous figure staring at Heller and his camera. "You're right, Andy. Thank you. I have a better idea. I'll be right back." She climbed out of the hot tub and disappeared into the house. A couple of minutes later she returned and climbed back into the water. "Okay, I've fixed them."

Linda tilted her head. "What did you do?"

"I called Detective Grover. He's sending deputies to handle the situation."

"They're outside your fence; what can a deputy do?"

Natalie sank down into the water next to Andy and smiled. "Watch."

A couple of minutes later, a sheriff's car pulled up and a deputy shined his spotlight on Heller.

Heller hopped off the fence and started hurriedly walking for the church group.

The deputy exited his car and stopped him. "Stop right there."

Heller froze. His hand holding the video camera and tripod shook. "What do you want, deputy? I haven't done anything."

"Step over here, and hand me that camera."

Heller moved to the deputy. "The camera belongs to my church, the Calvary Evangelical Chapel. I haven't broken any laws."

The deputy held out his hand. "The camera."

Heller puffed up. "It's church property. It's above the law. It belongs to God."

"Then you can explain to your God why *you* are in jail and I have His camera."

Haller sighed and slowly handed it to him. "The Lord will not approve of this."

"Tell Him to file a complaint." The deputy opened the memory compartment and withdrew the memory chip. He handed the camera back to Heller. "Here is your, and your God's, camera. The memory chip now belongs to Ms. North."

Heller straightened. "You can't do that."

"Yes, I can. You were on her fence, and that constitutes trespassing. Just so you and your friends know, she actually owns the land to that little silver surveyor's peg in the ground at the edge of the street. So, if you want to get huffy, I can arrest you and the rest of your bunch over there for trespassing. It's either the chip, or jail, your pick. Trust me, a guy like you won't last a day in the county jail, and I seriously doubt God's going to protect your sorry ass in there or pay your bail."

"Fine. You can have the chip. Can I go now?"

"Yes."

Heller spun around on his heel and stormed toward the others church members. They quickly climbed into cars and drove off.

The deputy chuckled, got back in his vehicle, and slowly drove up the driveway. He stopped next to the back porch.

Natalie, Virginia, and Linda climbed out of the hot tub, slipped into their flip-flops and hurried to the police car. Natalie stopped in front of the deputy. "Hi. Glad to see you. Thanks for coming."

He looked at the three women in wet bikinis and grinned. "No problem, ma'am, no problem at all."

They smiled.

He reached into his shirt pocket, pulled out the memory chip, and handed it to Natalie. "I took this from that guy on your fence. I scared them off, at least for now."

She took the chip. "Thank you."

"I'll increase my patrols around here tonight just to be safe. If anyone else shows up, we'll just arrest them." He eyed Linda and Virginia. "Have a nice evening, ladies."

Andy and Brian were all grins as they watched the three women saunter up the driveway toward them. Andy helped Virginia climb in. "Looks like the sheriff got them to go away, at least for now."

Natalie tossed the chip on a side table as they returned to the hot tub and hopped back in. "Yeah. They're gone. Unfortunately, they'll be back tomorrow."

Linda sat back next to Brian and looked at Natalie. "Think they had another camera?"

Natalie shook her head. "No. Probably not."

"I think we disappointed them." Linda turned to Brain. "You haven't said a word. You okay?"

He grinned. "Hell yeah. That was something. I hope the sheriff scared them from returning, period."

Andy chuckled. "You upset their plans. They were hoping for pictures of you girls topless or nude, and didn't get any."

Natalie laughed. "This time I finally out smarted them. Thanks for your assessment, Andy."

"Changing what they expected upset the apple cart. The churchwomen will still hate you, and the men there will secretly adore you and were probably very disappointed. With your new tact, the community will slowly get used to your new persona and not the Hollywood hottie they've come to expect." Andy shifted in the water toward Virginia. "How's it going with the inventory and appraisal?"

Virginia splashed him. "We've got the inventory pretty well cataloged. Shortly, we'll start putting a value on everything."

"From what you've told Brain and me, it looks like Mr. Weedon won't be bothering you anymore, Natalie."

Natalie wiped some water from her face. "I hope you're right."

Virginia sat on the edge of the hot tub. "But his investors are still out there, and we don't know who hired or bailed out Jack Blake either. I think one of them is Ann's murderer. I sent the information we got from Weedon to Detective Grover. Maybe he can run something down for us. I'll check with the Smithsonian Central Security Service, too."

Brain wiped the top of his blond crew cut with his wet hand. "Think this Blake guy will come back?"

Virginia shrugged. "No telling. But the last time he was here, it didn't go to well for him."

"Is what you did to Weedon today really legal, you being a fed and all?"

Virginia shook her head. "Probably not. We didn't actually hurt him. I didn't arrest him. But he did break into the house. And it's his word against ours. We did scare the shit out of him. I'd hate to be in his shoes right now. When he walked to his car, in front of his men, he was shaken up, his pants were soaked—"

"Soaked and smelled." Linda laughed. "He shit his pants, too. His diaper *really* needed changing."

Natalie climbed out of the hot tub and took a drink of water from a bottle she had set on the table. "Virginia, earlier today you said you had an idea who one of his investors was, and maybe that person either murdered my cousin or could somehow lead us to the killer. Who is it?"

Virginia rubbed her nose then held up her fingers. "Let's look at what we've got. One, both Jack Blake and Jenny Parker have inquired about the quilts and something there that she wants. Two, Mr. Weedon, until today, hadn't. But he was blackmailed by someone in the Solomon Group into breaking in and trying to find a computer file relating to quilts and/or a book and had a book relating to quartz and gold he said the blackmailer had accidently left here. The blackmailer knew about the file and computer in the house and about the gold. Three, Jenny Parker just published a quilt book and wanted to assess your quilts. Four, Weedon said an investor was interested in that file he was looking for. Five, the church people who were here asked about the quilts too, and wanted some quilts as a donation. Everything seems to revolve around Ann's quilts or something related to them on her computer. Then there is the gold and the university folks wanting to go into caves around here. From all that, my money is on the Solomon Group, one or more of the university people or Jenny Parker. The questions are, what is it that is so important someone would kill over it, and if I'm right?"

Andy frowned. "Was the file he was looking for on that flash drive you gave me?"

"Yes."

"The locked one labeled Concept?"

"Yes." Virginia's expression brightened. "Did you show it to some computer science faculty at the university? Could they open it?"

"Yes, I had them look at it. They tried but couldn't unlock it. The encryption is really tough. They said the encryption was about NSA quality. Whoever put it on the computer file really knew their business."

Virginia sighed. "Bummer."

"However, one of the faculty recommended a certain grad student who is a notorious, and quite good, hacker. Maybe he can unlock it."

"When can you give it to him?"

"He'll be back tomorrow from an... ahh... extended trip. I'll ask him then." Andy turned to Natalie. "I don't know how much it would cost. I'm guessing not much. Maybe meeting you would help entice him."

"No problem, Andy. Just let me know how much it'll cost, and you can bring him here, if that will help."

Linda chuckled. "Bribery usually works."

Andy nodded. "I'll give the grad student the file. I'm sure him getting to meet you will greatly encourage him to get that file open. He's a college student, so meeting you will probably be better than money, but I'll inquire about the cost."

Virginia slipped back into the water. "He's coming back tomorrow? Where has he been?"

"Well... Jail. He got picked up for minor hacking. Did thirty days."

"Only thirty days? That's all? Who'd he hack?"

"The computer at a strip joint near the Austin airport. The judge thought hacking was something he shouldn't be doing but thought hacking that particular place was funny. The judge said they don't usually show a great need for privacy there. The student wasn't interested in, and didn't get, any personal files or Social Security numbers, banking information, or anything serious. Just pictures and some other stuff. Could have been worse."

"I guess it could. The judge was pretty lenient." Virginia tipped her head back and stared at the sky. "I have the book of passwords that Ann had. I'll try them as well."

Natalie hopped back into the water. "You said everything hinges on that file and the quilts. The obvious suspect then is Jenny Parker."

Virginia nodded. "Jenny Parker, the Solomon Group, one of the professors, or someone at that church. I think we can rule Weedon out for now. Like I said earlier, my money is on the Solomon Group or Jenny Parker." She glanced at Andy. "If that grad student can crack the encryption on that file, we may be able to figure this out faster. That file may answer why Ann was murdered and by who. I'll see what I can find out about the Solomon Group, more about that church, and Reverend Nesbitt and his elders, or peanut gallery, or whatever they're called. Could be interesting."

CHAPTER 19

Later that night, Andy padded down a hallway that was illuminated by a nightlight. Farther down the hall, light shone from Virginia's quilt room. He walked to the doorway and leaned against the doorframe. He watched her hunched over her cutting table working on her laptop computer. A cord connected it to the printer she had situated by the back pegboard holding her quilting tools. "What are you doing in here at three in the morning?"

Virginia looked up at him, straightened, smiled, and ran her hand through her hair. "I couldn't sleep. I've been trying the passwords in Ann's book that Natalie gave me to see if I could crack the file." She leaned back against the cutting board. "So far no luck." She picked up the copy of Jenny Parker's book with the big X through the cover. "I'm getting the feeling this has something to do with all this."

Andy tilted his head. "A quilt book?"

Leo, Virginia's black cat, walked into the room, looked at them, turned, and strolled out toward the family room.

Andy watched Leo leave. "I guess we disturbed his highness."

Virginia nodded. "Looks like it."

"What about the quilt book? Is it what this whole thing is about?"

"Maybe. The book, or the gold. What I don't know is if it's the actual book or something to do with a real quilt." Andy stepped into the room and leaned against a cupboard. "Could Ann's murder have to do with all the land Natalie now has? Maybe your thoughts about the gold being the issue are good."

"Some people are interested in it, of course. The big builders and developers would love it. Weedon was one. He was the most aggressive, but I don't think any of them, even Weedon, would resort to murder. Maybe a lot of pressure, pushing public officials to intervene, and being an asshole, but not murder."

"How about his… ahh… investors?"

"Good question. I don't know if the gold really is an issue, or just in our imagination. But it would play a part if it were why the developers wanted the place." Virginia rubbed her eyes. "I tried getting some background on the Solomon Group on the computer. What I found was sketchy at best. It has the usual PR crap, but nothing I can hang my hat on. I forwarded the information, and what I had so far, to Detective Grover and the Smithsonian Central Security Service."

"Good." Andy looked at the papers scattered on top of some quilt squares. "Those quilt blocks reminded me, weren't you supposed to schedule a time for Natalie to go to your quilt Bee?"

"Yes." Virginia yawned. "I did actually. It's tomorrow afternoon. Natalie is hosting them at her house."

"This should be interesting."

"The other two members *now* seem to think Natalie is okay. We'll see tomorrow."

Andy took a deep breath. "What else can you do, especially tonight?" He looked at the big clock on her wall. "This morning?"

"Nothing, I guess." She tossed her pen on the cutting table. "I'll turn everything off and come back to bed." She switched off the computer and then reached for the printer.

"Okay." Andy turned and headed back to the bedroom.

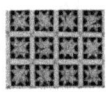

The next morning Virginia drove back to *Borealis*. She turned onto the county road and spotted the church group picketing outside the fence. Virginia drove past them, turned up the driveway, and parked next to Linda's car. She grabbed her backpack and strolled to the rear door and, after knocking, entered. She found Natalie and Linda in the parlor discussing Weedon's recent run in with them and his complaint to the sheriff.

Linda looked up from her chair as Virginia entered. "Natalie got an e-mail from Detective Grover that said Weedon had visited him and complained about our…" she made air quotes, "torture of him. Weedon wanted to file a complaint. Are we in trouble? Have you talked to the detective?"

"Yes, I talked to him, and no, we're not in trouble." Virginia sat and leaned back in an overstuffed chair near the fireplace, and grinned. "Grover asked Weedon why he was here in the first place, and what he was doing. Weedon said he was just looking for some lost materials. Grover didn't buy the story. Grover told Weedon he obviously picked on the wrong women. He informed Weedon that breaking and entering is a felony. And you, Natalie, because he has harassed you, and he broke in; you could have feared for your life and could have shot him, or at least, had him arrested. He told Weedon, *if* we ladies really wanted to hurt, or kill, him for breaking in and bothering you, he'd either be still suffering in a hospital intensive care ward as a eunuch, or he'd be dead. As to us using tractor jumper cables to fry his balls, Grover told him *if* we were that upset with him, we'd have probably done it and enjoyed doing it. He also told him, in reality, we'd most likely just tie him down and slowly cut his balls and dick off with a dull, rusty knife and use a red-hot poker to cauterize the wounds. Grover said Weedon cringed at that. As to the knitting needles, well, Grover thought that was quite creative. But since Weedon exhibited absolutely no evidence of physical harm or injury, and it was Weedon's word against ours, there was nothing he could do. Grover advised Weedon to give us a wide berth, not piss us off anymore, and stay away from *Borealis*. Grover told Weedon, if he came back, we'd probably actually do those things to him and bury his body in a really deep hole somewhere on the ranch." Virginia looked at Natalie. "I told you the detective liked you."

"I guess so." Natalie looked at her watch. "Ladies, I suggest we get ready for your Bee Hive Quilt Bee meeting. Virginia, didn't you say they are coming about one this afternoon?"

"Yes." Virginia stood. "I said we'd have lunch here. Natalie has some things ordered from the tearoom place in Georgetown. They will be here in a half-hour to set up. Didn't you see that on my e-mail?"

"Probably. Just forgot. I've got my sewing stuff in the car. I'm not sure exactly how much sewing we'll actually do. Probably gossip more. Let's get ready."

At one in the afternoon, Mary Watt and Claire Barnes arrived at *Borealis*. They brought their bags of materials, tools, and portable sewing machines inside.

Mary hugged Linda and Virginia, then went to Natalie and gave her a hug, too. "Ms. North. I've heard a lot about you."

Natalie looked at the floor, then at Mary. "I bet."

Mary gestured toward Virginia and Linda. "Virginia and Linda think very highly of you, and that's enough for me. I want to join them in welcoming you to our community. I hope you like our Bee and will consider joining us. Virginia is our leader… our Queen Bee."

Claire stepped to Natalie and shook her hand. "It's nice to meet you, Ms. North. You've been through a lot since you came, and you've added some… well, spice to things around here. I'm glad you, Virginia, and Linda put that church group in their place. Never did cotton to their ways. You know something? You remind me of the actress on The Big Bang Theory TV show, Melissa Rauch. She plays Bernadette. She's a good actress. You're as pretty as she is."

Natalie smiled. "Thank you. I've been told I resemble her."

Claire turned toward the kitchen table. "What's for lunch?"

Natalie motioned for them to go to the table. "I had the tearoom in Georgetown send over a sampling of foods. I hope you like it."

Mary scurried to the table. "Smells wonderful. Let's eat before we get down to business."

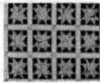

Three hours later, the group sat around the dining room table working on the lesson Virginia was teaching.

Virginia explained the steps and showed them the samples she had prepared. She helped them with their projects and samples. "Okay, now you can see how easy it is to add a hidden zipper to the bag. You can do this on a lot items." She sat and watched them using their sewing machines.

Mary was done first and held her sample up for the group. "This is great. I've been afraid of adding zippers, but this way is super and easy."

Linda was next, followed by Claire. Natalie finally finished and held up her wool-felted handbag for show. "I've been nervous about zippers too, but this is great. It even works for this type of bag."

Virginia looked at their samples and smiled. "I told you it wasn't hard. Now, do you believe me?"

They all nodded.

Virginia pointed to Natalie's wool-felted bag. "Natalie has agreed to show us how she makes her wool-felted handbags next month."

Claire smiled. "That will be interesting. I've wanted to try it but... I hope it's easier than it looks."

Natalie set her sample down. "Yes, it is. It's actually a lot of fun."

Mary turned her chair around and looked at Natalie. "What's it really like in Hollywood?"

Claire scooted in her chair and leaned on the table, looking at Natalie. "Yes, what's it really like there?"

Natalie sighed. "That's what I get asked all the time. People also ask about the movies and... and other things." She sat back, wet her lips, and told them her canned Hollywood speech about movie making and an actress's life. They were mesmerized. When she finished, she turned toward the commotion at the front of the house. "Is that those pesky church picketers making noise again?"

Virginia jumped to her feet, sprinted to the living room, pulled back a curtain, and looked out the front window. "Yeah. It's that Calvary Evangelical Chapel group again. Looks like they have more people this time. They've got a big cross out there. Maybe something's happened. It's kind of stupid; there isn't a lot of traffic on that county road. If we keep ignoring them, maybe they'll eventually go away."

Natalie's expression brightened. "Maybe we should do to Pastor Nesbitt what we did to Weedon. Then maybe he'd call it quits."

Claire jerked her head around. "Weedon? You mean that developer fella?"

Natalie nodded.

"That man is a disgrace to the community. He's a bully, a cheat, a shady developer, and a poor builder."

Natalie grinned. "You know the gentleman?"

"Gentleman?" Claire took a breath. "Not by a long shot, honey. He calls himself a businessman and developer. Snake in the grass is more like it. A rattlesnake has more principals than him. He's gotten a lot bigger in the past couple years. I've seen him a few times at a small restaurant and bar out in Liberty Hill. He sits in a booth at the back, where it's darker, with a man and a woman. They each leave a few minutes apart. Last night, he was there when two men came in. One was that Reverend Nesbitt guy. The meeting didn't last long, and Weedon stormed out."

Virginia scurried back. "Claire, did you say he met with a woman?"

Claire looked confused. "Yes. Why?"

"Did you recognize her?"

"No." Claire frowned and rubbed her chin, thinking. "She had a big floppy hat, dark glasses, wore a loose-fitting dress with a belt, and kept to the shadows. The hat and glasses seemed out of place there. She hurried out without looking around. Must not have wanted anyone to notice her. Maybe she'd seen too many spy movies, or is married and doesn't want to be seen with the men."

Virginia pulled out a chair and sat next to Claire. "How about the man? Anything remarkable about him?"

Claire looked up at the ceiling, then back at Virginia. "Not really. But I've seen him some place before. Can't rightly think of where. Maybe it'll come to me. Is it important?"

"Yes. Very. You said Nesbitt went to see Weedon there, too? I take it the meeting didn't go too well."

"No, it surely didn't. Mr. Weedon was obviously tense. Nesbitt seemed… I don't know… smug. He showed Weedon some documents, or pictures, or something. He had them in a big manila envelope. Weedon seemed to get madder and pounded the table."

"What were they saying?"

"I don't know. The place was a bit noisy. A youth or school soccer team had won something, and the kids were excited. Nesbitt and Weedon were on the other side of the room."

Virginia nodded. "That's interesting."

Mary looked back and forth between them then said, "You saw all that from across the room?"

"Yes." Claire stiffened. "I don't care for either man. Watching them feud was kind of fun."

Mary looked at Virginia, then Natalie. "What did you do to Mr. Weedon to get him to stop pestering Ms. North?"

Virginia smiled. "He took part in a painfully convincing, and humiliating, conversation with us that persuaded him to leave Natalie alone."

"Painfully convincing? Humiliating?" Claire frowned. "Do we want to know how, or what you three did to him to accomplish that seemingly impossible feat?"

"Not really." Virginia shook her head. "Let's just say we described, in very graphic detail, what we'd do to parts of his anatomy if he returned, or bugged Natalie again." Virginia's head swung around at the sound of a hard knock on the front door. "Oh boy, now what?"

CHAPTER 20

Natalie slipped out of her chair, strolled to the door, and swung it open. Detective Grover stood in the doorway. "Hello Detective, please come in." She stepped out of the way and motioned for him to enter.

Grover walked in and noticed the women sitting around the table. He smiled as Virginia approached. "Hello, Special Agent Clark."

Virginia nodded. "Detective Grover. What brings you out here?"

"Two things. One is to tell you and Ms. North that Pastor Nesbitt has been murdered."

Virginia raised an eyebrow and then shrugged. "Oh? The devil finally caught up with him?"

"Yeah. Looks that way. Only this time the devil had some help. It seems there are a lot of people who didn't care for the man. We're looking into it. I was thinking, his murder might be related to Miss Ann North Greenwald's murder. The preliminary autopsy results said the same mushroom poison as the one used on Ms. Greenwald killed him. Can you meet me at our usual spot to discuss this? I need your help."

"Sure, we can do that. What's the second thing?"

"We can't find Mr. Bryon Weedon. He is, for now, a person of interest in Reverend Nesbitt's untimely demise. You, Mrs. Chambers, and Ms. North didn't have much love for the man. You… well… you've caused him more than a little anxiety lately. He isn't buried someplace out back here is he?"

Natalie looked shocked. "No. Do you really think we'd kill him and bury him someplace on my land?"

Grover rubbed his forehead. "No. I don't think you ladies would kill him, or bury him here. You could have shot him when he broke in, but you didn't. Had to ask."

"We haven't seen him since the visit he told you about. We figured the sheriff would probably frown on us doing him in."

"I'm not sure how the sheriff would actually feel if he was buried out back. Probably forget to look. Weedon, like Nesbitt, isn't on a lot of

Christmas card lists." Grover stuck his hands in his pockets. "Well, he's been involved with Nesbitt somehow. Funny, I never thought they would be doing any business together."

"It's not real business." Virginia chuckled. "It's blackmail. Reverend Nesbitt was blackmailing Weedon."

"Blackmail? The pompous ass... er... pious reverend was a blackmailer? Oh, that's funny." His eyes widened. "Blackmailers sometimes don't live too long. It's a hazard of the profession. That's a good motive for murder. We need to talk, Virginia. Buy you a cup of coffee?"

Virginia pointed at the women in the dining room. "These ladies are in my Bee Hive Quilt Bee. We're having a meeting. Natalie has some food in the kitchen. Why don't you help yourself, and I'll be in shortly? We can talk there."

Natalie pointed toward the kitchen. "I have a fresh apple pie I made from scratch in there, Detective."

Grover looked longingly toward the kitchen. "Well, it is a little unusual... but Ms. North is a real good cook and baker... so okay, I'll see you shortly." He started for the kitchen when Natalie moved to his side and walked with him.

He knows she's a good cook? Virginia returned to the dining room and leaned on the table. "That man is a sheriff's detective. I'm helping him with the investigation into Ann's death and now it seems, Mr. Nesbitt's murder."

Claire looked at Virginia through sharp green eyes. "We knew you were investigating Ann's death and helping Ms. North. So, Nesbitt was murdered? How about that? The bastard finally pissed off the wrong person, was killed, and the Lord didn't intervene. I guess God didn't care for him either. Keep us posted on your progress."

"I think you're right," said Virginia

Claire looked at Linda and Mary, then back at Virginia. "Look, I didn't approve of her at first. I feel bad about judging her before I even met her. Now, with actually meeting her, and everything I've seen and heard, I think the lady is nice, and she needs us. I like her, and so does Mary. You and Linda know her pretty well and like her, so, we will be her friends. Have her call on us anytime. Oh, and while you were talking to the detective, we voted. We want you to ask Ms. North to be a member of our Bee."

Virginia straightened. "Oh? Great. I'm glad. I'll tell her. I know she will accept and appreciate this."

Mary stood. "Get her to come to our quilt guild, too."

"Okay. I'd better go see what the detective wants. Linda, will you help wind this up?"

"Sure, go see the detective, and send Natalie back."

"Right." Virginia scurried to the kitchen. She rushed in and skidded to a stop. Grover was seated at the table, next to Natalie, who was sipping an iced tea. He had a big plate of food from the tearoom in front of him and next to it was a large slice of the apple pie Natalie had baked. Virginia stared. "Detective?"

He looked up, finished chewing, and swallowed. "What?"

"I'll come back in a few minutes."

"Fine." He returned to eating and talking to Natalie.

Virginia walked back to the dining room and plopped into a chair.

Linda titled her head. "What happened? What did he say?" Claire and Mary leaned forward.

"Nothing. He's happily eating and talking to Natalie. He seems smitten by her and her cooking and appears to have forgotten why he came, and about me. She's got him spellbound."

Mary chuckled. "The short, sexy, six-shooter is in there with a red-blooded man. No wonder."

Virginia jerked back. "Where did you hear she's called the short, sexy, six-shooter?"

"On the Calvary Evangelical Chapel website. I've watched them post their warped opinions about her, and that phrase was on it. I thought it fit her. She is short, she's sexy, and with that canon parked on her hip, the slogan fits. The church was trying to destroy her, but it backfired. Every man under eighty within four counties loves her… and you and Linda."

Virginia nodded slowly. "Oh."

Claire looked at her watch. "Ladies, it's time we packed up and thanked our most gracious host."

They packed their materials, tools, and sewing machines, then got up, and walked to the kitchen.

Natalie looked away from Grover, saw them coming, and stood. "Leaving?"

Mary nodded. "Yes. We had a wonderful time. Claire and I are thrilled we got to meet you. The food was great; we learned about the hidden zipper techniques, and more about you. We voted to make you a member of our Bee. Please have Virginia bring you to the quilt guild, too. We're looking forward to your teaching us about the felting and making the purses."

Natalie stood. A tear ran down her cheek. "Thank you. That means a lot."

Claire smiled. "You're a hell of a seamstress, and from what Virginia and Linda said, and the detective obviously knows, you're a great cook. I'm looking forward to learning a lot from you. I'm glad we're friends."

Grover finished his food, slid the dish aside, and started on the pie. He looked up at the women. He nodded, "Nice to see you, ladies. I'll need to talk to Virginia, Mrs. Chambers, and Ms. North, shortly."

Mary had a shocked look on her face. "You can't think they had anything to do with that preacher's death."

He shook his head. "No. But they may be able to help."

Virginia motioned toward Claire. "Detective, you need to hear what Claire just told me about Nesbitt and Weedon."

He frowned as he looked at the women. "Claire?"

Claire slowly raised her hand. "I'm Claire Barnes, sir."

Grover pointed to a chair. "Pull up a seat and join us. Let's have a little chat, Mrs. Barnes."

Virginia, Mary, Claire, Linda, and Natalie sat around the table as Detective Grover finished his large slice of pie. He moved the dish to the side, sat back, and sighed. "Now that apple pie was the best I've ever had." He gazed at Natalie. "If I were thirty years younger and single, I'd be after you to marry me like there was no tomorrow."

Natalie's face brightened. "Thank you, detective. I think you are a very nice man and like you a lot." She leaned closer and kissed his cheek.

Grover blushed.

"You need to come by more. I love cooking. I'd love to have you and your wife come for dinner some evening." Natalie grinned. "Another piece of pie, maybe?"

Grover patted his stomach. "No, thank you. I've eaten more than I should already. I will take you up on that wonderful offer for dinner though. I know my wife would love to meet you. I'll call you."

"Good. I'll pack you a large slice of pie when you leave for later."

"That would be very nice." Grover nodded. "Thank you, Ms. North."

"Natalie, please. We're friends."

"Okay. Call me Dan."

Natalie smiled and nodded.

Virginia cleared her throat. "If you two are done discussing food and dinner plans, can we get back to the murder of that asshole Reverend Nesbitt?"

Grover turned and frowned. "I've had a bad week. This case has me on edge. This little interlude with this lovely lady and her great cooking is the highlight of my week. Cut this old cop some slack."

Virginia leaned forward. "Okay, you finished your food, wrangled a dinner invitation, and fantasized about Natalie; can we get back on track now?"

"Jeez, you *are* a ball buster."

"Yeah, ask Blake about that." Virginia drummed her fingers on the table. "Well?"

Grover pulled a small digital recorder out of his pocket and set it on the table. "Okay. I need to talk to you ladies about the blackmail stuff you mentioned, and what Mrs. Barnes saw and heard between Nesbitt and Weedon, and where. We can discuss the church's offshore banking, and that Solomon Group, too. Mind if I record our conversations?"

They all agreed to be recorded. Claire told Grover about seeing Nesbitt and Weedon at the restaurant and seeing their reactions to each other. Virginia told him about the Nesbitt blackmailing Weedon. Grover switched off the recorder and glanced at Claire. "Mrs. Barnes, unless you and Mrs. Watt want to spend the rest of the day bored out of your minds, at this point, you two may leave."

"Oh." Claire looked at Virginia. Virginia nodded.

"Oh, okay. I'll talk to you ladies later. Thank you for your hospitality and your sewing tips, Natalie. This was a great meeting and welcome to our Bee." Claire left the room followed by Mary.

Grover looked at the remaining pie on the counter then gave a quick shake of his head. "Okay, where were we?"

Natalie chuckled. "More pie, Dan?"

"Well," Grover shrugged, "maybe just a smidge."

"Okay. I'll be right back." Natalie jumped to her feet, cut another slice of the pie, and slid the dish in front of Grover. She refilled his iced tea glass and then sat next to him. "Can I get you anything else?"

Grover picked up his fork and started to eat. "No, nothing else, Natalie, you're spoiling me as is."

Virginia sat back and glared. "You two are killing me. Can we focus here?"

Grover finished chewing and swallowed. "Sure. Where were we?"

"Calvary Evangelical Chapel with a bank and offices in the Caribbean, the Solomon Group with offices and a bank in the same place, and Ann and Nesbitt's murder with the same mushroom extract, remember?"

"Yeah, yeah. I touched base with your people at the Smithsonian Central Security Service about the Solomon Group. They said they sent some information to you this morning, but hadn't gotten the ping from the e-mail that you received it yet."

"I haven't checked it yet. What did they say?"

"Their... ah... sources, whoever or whatever they are, said the Solomon Group has its main office and a bank account in the Caribbean, too. It's in the Cayman Islands. It's a shell corporation. It's the same island and the same bank where Nesbitt's church has offices and an account. Same office address, too. It's the bank. Cozy."

"Too cozy. But we kind of knew that already. What else? Anything on who the Solomon Group is or who their officers are?"

Grover grinned like a Cheshire cat. "Yeah, your museum folks are superb. You ain't going to believe it."

Natalie leaned forward. "Let me guess: Reverend Nesbitt, Mrs. Blair, Jenny Parker, maybe one or two people from the university and... I don't know, my agent?"

Grover sat with his jaw hanging. "You reading my e-mails?"

Natalie shook her head. "No."

"Well, you got it right. All accept your agent. You missed that one. He's not part of it. You must be clairvoyant or something. You thought your agent was part of this gang of crooks?"

"You don't know my agent." Natalie shook her head. "No, I was surprised that Weedon and Nesbitt weren't working together. They are pains in the ass, and both wanted *Borealis*. Maybe they wanted it for the same reason. Nesbitt blackmailing Weedon was the big surprise."

Linda spoke up. "Why would they be in cahoots? And why would the Calvary Evangelical Chapel and the Solomon Group have the same offshore bank and use the same office on the same island?"

Virginia rubbed her temples. "Maybe because there *is* something very valuable on this land. And the church and the Solomon Group are one and the same. Maybe the church named the company after King Solomon."

Natalie leaned back in her chair. "You're probably right, but why all the interest in the quilt stuff?"

Virginia shrugged. "Good question."

Natalie noticed Linda eyeing the pie. "Want a piece? Help yourself."

"Yes, it looks delicious." Linda got up, went and cut a slice of pie, returned to the table, and took a bite of the pie. She glanced at Natalie. "This is exquisite. I see why your new admirer here likes it so much."

Natalie smiled. "Thank you."

"You don't add calories, do you?"

"There are no trespassing signs posted around here. Calories aren't allowed."

"Good." Linda swallowed another bite then spoke. "Even though it's a possibility, maybe the murder of your cousin wasn't related to whatever is on the ranch. Maybe it has to do with the quilt book Ann put a big X on."

Virginia bit her lip. "You may have something there. Maybe Andy's student hacker can open Ann's computer file, and we can see. It seems Blake, Jenny Parker, Weedon, and Nesbitt all wanted it, and they are all somehow related to both the church and to the Solomon Group. Maybe the book Jenny wrote has to do with whatever it is the Solomon Group wants here. If the group and the church are one and the same, it answers the question of why two seemingly independent organizations wanted the same thing."

Linda finished her slice of pie. "Maybe it's just the book that is so important in Ann's murder, and the stuff here on the ranch is another thing altogether."

Virginia nodded. "You could be right."

Detective Grover sat listening. "Is this how you guys go about solving mysteries and murders? You set up scenarios, discuss and modify them, and then follow up on them?"

Virginia smiled. "Pretty much."

Grover sat back and looked at the three women. "Well, you're a little unorthodox, that's for sure. But according to the Smithsonian Central Security Service, Virginia *always* gets her man, so I'm in. What do we do next?"

Virginia leaned forward, "I suggest three things. One, I find out what Andy's hacker has done. Two, Natalie turns on her well known R-rated charm on Calvary Evangelical Chapel's weakest link, Mr. Heller, and she tells him we know about the blackmail, and what's on *Borealis*. Then, if she can entice him enough, maybe he'll spill more beans. Three, Linda visits Jenny Parker and tells her I've got a friend who opened the secret file on Ann's computer, and I'm going to bring it here to show Natalie tomorrow."

Grover sat with his mouth open. "You ladies are kidding?"

Virginia shook her head. "Nope."

He looked at Natalie and Linda. "You two are going along with Virginia's... plan? You realize what she means by R-rated don't you?"

They nodded.

Natalie, seeing Grover's nervousness, gave him a coy smile, and added, "If R-rated doesn't work, I could resort to X-rated discussions."

Grover stuttered, "X... X-rated? You wouldn't! What's... what are you going to do? No, don't tell me. Yes, tell me."

They waited.

He sat wide-eyed for a moment. "How can you... I mean... what will...?"

Natalie leaned close and patted his arm. "I'm just kidding, detective."

Grover shot an eyebrow up. "Oh. Oh! Well...in that case... yeah, I knew that." He took a deep breath and slowly let it out. "You almost gave me a heart attack. Okay, what do you want me to do?"

Virginia grinned. "Eat more of Natalie's pie, and then see if you can get the names of the professors at the university who are involved in this conspiracy and are principals in the Solomon Group."

"Your SCSS didn't know." He rubbed one temple. "How am I going to do it? I don't have their resources."

Virginia sipped some water. "Natalie will give you the names of the professors who were here to ask her for permission to do their study. Contact them with some sort of excuse and casually mention that Natalie, Linda, and I are going to see the caves on her land tomorrow evening and dig into what's so important about *Borealis*."

Grover nodded. "Okay. But you do realize this can, and probably will, get extremely dangerous. Wait a minute; you're going cave hunting after dark?"

"Yes. If we kick the hornet's nest, we expect them to swarm. That's the idea. And it'll be light until about eight-thirty or nine. We'll start about six tomorrow night. I hope we're not in the caves after dark."

"You hope? This is bat shit crazy. I'd better have deputies in the area to back us up."

Virginia frowned. "Us?"

"If you think I'm going to let the three of you go running around today and tomorrow stirring up a shit storm, and then abandon you tomorrow night, maybe under the earth in a cave, you're crazy. I'll be here."

"Why don't you and the deputies, who should be in plain clothes and in unmarked vehicles, stay close, but out of sight? If, and when, we need you, we'll use our radio and scream for help. Having you and the deputies too close around here will scare off the bad guys."

Grover pulled himself up in the chair and shook his head. "I don't know. This sounds crazy dangerous. Your radio may not work where you're going."

Natalie patted Grover's arm. "We'll be fine, Dan. Virginia and I will both be armed, and we will shoot if attacked."

Linda grinned. "I'm bringing my gun, too. And yes, I can shoot."

Grover shook his head. "Good grief. Just what I need, a short, sexy, six shooter, Annie Oakley, and Ma Barker. God, I hope you three don't shoot each other."

Natalie brightened. "Right. See, Dan, with the three of us together, and armed, what could go wrong?" She looked at the empty dish. "More pie, maybe with a little ice cream this time?"

CHAPTER 21

Late the following afternoon, Virginia, Natalie, and Linda, all dressed in jeans and tee shirts, met in Natalie's parlor. They sat in wing chairs arranged in front of the fireplace. The slow movement of cool air circulated in the room.

Linda leaned back in her chair. "That air feels good. Your new air conditioning system is working great."

"Yeah." Natalie nodded. "Most of the work here is now complete. I had them install two bigger units, each with the capacity to cool or heat the whole place. That way they aren't taxed in the summer Texas heat. Cost more, but the guys who installed them said it was smart."

"It does feel good." Virginia looked at the other two women. "Okay, time for status reports. I'll go first. Andy gave the locked file to the grad student who's the hacker. The kid wants to meet Natalie in person. The grad student said he'd do it because he liked the challenge, especially since the faculty couldn't do it. Andy also gave him $100. After that, the student took an hour and opened the file. You won't be able to guess what was on it." She looked at Natalie and Linda's faces. They were lost in thought.

Linda finally raised an eyebrow. "Okay, we can't guess, what was in the file that was so secret?"

"The file was the unedited manuscript for the quilt book Jenny Parker published." Virginia fidgeted in her chair. "Only Jenny didn't write it. Ann did. The word documents prove it. There were also pages showing which publishers Ann had been sending it to, and the dates. It looks like Jenny pirated the manuscript and published the book, with a few very minor changes. Ann found out and was preparing to go to her lawyer, but died first. There was one funny thing though."

Natalie stiffened and fumed. "You mean Jenny stole it."

Virginia nodded. "Yes. It sure looks like it."

"So that's why she wanted to work in the quilt room. What are we going to do? She can't get away with it." Natalie slammed her fist on the armrest. "I'll call my lawyer and sue that bitch."

"Sue her?" Virginia raised an eyebrow. "Think about it. Jenny may have killed Ann to stop any lawsuit or Ann going public. News of Jenny stealing Ann's book would ruin Jenny in the quilting community, and probably cause her shop to go under. She'd be bankrupt."

Natalie fumed. "I'll sue the shit out of her."

Virginia held up her hand. "There's more. On a separate Word document, there was a notation about that quartz rock with the gold. It seems Ann went exploring after the professors left the last time they were here. She found a vein of some sort of mineral with quartz and gold in it. She wanted to get a geologist to survey the situation but hadn't gotten around to it. She thought it might be fool's gold, iron pyrite."

Natalie's face became flushed. "Hell, I'll sue her, then kill her. Maybe I'll kill the professors, too."

Virginia cooed. "Natalie, calm down. Before you have a coronary, let's hear from Linda, and then you can tell us about Heller and that stupid church. We'll handle Jenny in due course."

Natalie tensed, her hands gripped the armrests. She looked at Virginia, then Linda, sighed, and relaxed a bit. "In due course. Okay. But maybe I'll just take Ms. Parker for a tour of my barn like we did with Weedon, only this time I'll actually use the stuff there and bury her somewhere out on the ranch." She sat back and grinned. "Her stealing the manuscript, publishing my cousin's book, and then being caught doing it, would be a motive for murder. I'd probably get caught. Maybe the law could handle her, and I don't have to mess up my barn. I'm glad she never got the file and doesn't know about the gold; at least I hope not."

"Yes, I agree," Virginia said. "But we aren't in a position to accuse her of murder just yet. We can't kill her either. Let's hear from Linda, and what you found out first, then see what's next."

Linda leaned forward and patted Natalie's leg. "I can think of ways to ruin Jenny for pirating the book without the courts or your barn. I'm sure Virginia can, too. We'll need more to accuse her of murder."

Natalie cracked a smile. "I can see why you two are friends, and I'm glad you're my friends. Okay, what did you learn from that... that... dame?"

"Well, when I casually told Jenny that Virginia had located the file on a flash drive and was opening it. Jenny almost fainted." Linda sat back. "She had to pull up a stool at the cutting table in her shop and sit. She asked how Virginia could open it because it was locked with a tight encryption. Jenny said it was almost like the CIA locked it. Obviously, she had knowledge of the file and that it was well locked. She must have tried to open it before sometime, or someone told her about it. I said Virginia had computer friends who did it. Jenny asked if Virginia had shown what was in the file with anyone. I told her no, and that Virginia hadn't read what was in it yet either, but would show it to us here at your house tonight about nine. That seemed to intrigue her."

"Good work, Linda. I hope it wasn't too obvious a trap, but I think it'll work." Virginia turned her gaze to Natalie. "Now, Natalie, what did you get out of Heller? You were able to meet with him weren't you?"

"Oh, yeah. I went to his apartment. It's pretty Spartan. Lots of religious books, icons, diplomas, and fancy documents on the walls. No pictures of him or family or friends. No vacation pictures either. Furniture was nice, but not expensive." Natalie shifted forward in her chair. "When Heller opened the front door, I thought he was going to pass out. I wore a tight blouse and shorts, it was a little risqué, but nothing too risqué. He said he didn't expect me to come to his apartment. He was very gracious. He was also nervous as hell. A real dweeb. I figure he doesn't have a lot of experience with women. I turned on the charm, along with a few bottles of wine I brought, and asked about the church's activities, especially now that Reverend Nesbitt had been murdered. I hinted about the blackmail and how that can be a motive for murder. At first, he denied any knowledge of it, but after a couple of minutes me flirting, and all the wine, he blabbed."

Virginia smiled. "I told you he'd be a pushover for you."

"I guess you were right. It seems the Calvary Evangelical Chapel is involved with *auxiliary* activities, too. Heller said Nesbitt was blackmailing Weedon and some other people in the community. The church has financial interests in a number of businesses around here, other parts of Texas, a few other states, and Mexico, too. They own land around Texas, especially West Texas, Arizona, and California. Nesbitt, and the church, are like a corporate loan shark. The church uses shell companies, and they make loans and then end up taking a controlling interest in things when the client can't pay. Their interest rates are awful. They demand large contributions from their parishioners, too. Being a church, it's hard for the authorities to probe into things. Weedon wanted out of some sort of agreement he had with Nesbitt or the church. Weedon was going to go to the newspaper, and maybe the cops. Heller said he's heard that sometimes people who have given Reverend Nesbitt difficulty in his *missions and plans* or with paying their *obligations* to him and the church, would turn up in a hospital, or dead, after Nesbitt asks God for help and divine intervention." Natalie shook her head. "Heller really believes God was doing the dirty work for the good Reverend. I can't believe he's that stupid."

Virginia's eyes widened. "That's interesting."

"It gets better. After a while, and a lot more drinks, and me faking interest in him, and the church, I also found out that Nesbitt, and the Calvary Evangelical Chapel, have tentacles into the Solomon Group or the other way around. They're seriously connected. So is Mrs. Blair. Also, Jenny is involved somehow with the church. Nesbitt and Jenny seem to be more than just business acquaintances. Heller said they are extremely close friends, in the biblical way. His words, not mine."

Linda raised an eyebrow. "Huh?"

Natalie gave her an exasperated look. "It's Heller's pious Christian way to say Jenny's screwing Nesbitt's brains out on a regular basis."

"Oh." Linda looked shocked. "Who would have thought that? The Reverend doing that with a parishioner isn't Kosher."

Natalie chuckled. "Honey, he isn't Jewish either. He's a low life slime ball hiding behind being a minister and *his* twisted version of religion. According to Heller, Nesbitt has filmed him and Jenny having sex to blackmail her if she got out of line. I call it extortion, but I guess Nesbitt called it business as usual."

"I bet he did." Virginia sat back. "The number of people with motive to kill him gets even bigger."

Natalie nodded and continued. "I thought so, too. Heller also said there was something here at *Borealis* that Nesbitt and the Solomon Group are extremely interested in. Nesbit wanted the land at any cost, even if it meant my life. Heller didn't know what it is, but he overheard about it from a couple of professors who were talking to Mrs. Blair. I asked about the Solomon Group. He said it's tied to the Calvary Evangelical Chapel somehow, but he doesn't know any more than that. I believed him. Heller said Mrs. Blair is heavily involved in this, too. She's also the church treasurer. Heller was upset about Nesbitt's murder, but he thinks he's in the running to replace Nesbitt as the head pastor. With his personality, I don't think that's going to happen.

"To continue, Heller said the church wanted some of Ann's quilts because Jenny said they were valuable and would be a nice addition to their treasury. And Jenny wanted some computer file, or computer, or something. Heller said Jenny was obsessed with getting that file, and he didn't think it had anything to do with the church. He didn't know why she was so adamant about getting her hands on it. He went on and on about the good works the church does and how he, as an outreach minister, can personally lead me to salvation through faith. Heller expounded on that church's teaching. I finally told him I thought Calvary Evangelical Chapel was a fraud, a den of snakes, part of a stupid cult, Nesbitt was a common crook and blackmailer, and I wasn't interested. He wasn't too pleased, but after four bottles of wine, he was so drunk I don't think he'll remember much of our conversation. That's when I left.' She sat back and sighed. "You know, it's too bad these types of people exist. They give a bad name to the real, honest churches, who are trying to help people."

Virginia rubbed one temple, then tilted her head back, and stared at the ceiling for a minute. "Okay, we've got a couple of professors, Mrs. Blair, Jenny Parker, and Nesbitt all tied together. All of them are principles of the

Solomon Group, and some are high muckety-mucks in the church. I bet the Calvary Evangelical Chapel and the Solomon Group are one and the same. Jenny and one or more of the professors are biologists, too. I wonder if they could extract the poison that killed your cousin and Nesbitt? The professors have doctorates so they might know how to do it. Why kill Nesbitt? And if I remember, one of the professors was a geologist." A bubble of laughter escaped her lips. "Hell, why not? Nesbitt's blackmailing more than one person, and he's scum. Blackmail isn't a safe pastime and sports a short life expectancy. People don't like blackmailers much." She held up both hands. "Now, who is the missing member of that group? On the other hand, is there really a missing member?"

Natalie leaned forward and rubbed her hands together. "I have an idea. Why don't we invite them all out here, really give them our version of the barn tour, and just bury them all in various locations on my two thousand acres? That would take care of things once and for all. Then, we could look for what they want on my ranch."

"As nice as that sounds, it would not be a real good idea," came a disembodied voice from the hall. "Effective, vengeful, enjoyable maybe, but very illegal."

Virginia looked around the side of the wingchair. "Detective Grover? What are you doing here?"

"Natalie said to come here for our debriefing. No one answered the door when I knocked, but I could hear you all talking, so I came in. I hope you don't mind."

Natalie smiled. "I don't mind at all. I'm glad you did."

"I wanted a first-hand update from you ladies and also wanted to tell you what I found out at Southwestern University. I heard what you all said. Good work, ladies. Oh, I'd forget Natalie's last idea though." He put his hands on his hips. "Also, if you three think I'm going to let you go, after your stirring the pot, sniffing around some cavern or tunnels, without me, you've got another guess coming. I want to be here tonight at the time when Ms. Parker thinks you're telling what's in the locked flash drive."

Natalie stood and walked to Grover and gave him a bear hug. "Thank you for coming, Dan." She patted her big gun strapped to her hip. "I'm a good shot, but I've never actually shot anyone. Just paper and tin can targets." Linda stood and went to Grover. She pulled a small, pink .380 semiautomatic from her fanny pack. "I'm a good shot, too. Been practicing. But I've never shot anyone either."

Grover looked at her gun. He struggled to keep a straight face "Pink? Pink? The bad guy would probably die laughing before you could shoot him."

Linda stuck out her lower lip. "In that case, I'd make a point of making him the first person I shoot. Teach him a lesson. Maybe his last. And, in case you were going to ask, the bullets aren't pink."

"I believe you." He held up his hands. "Just don't make me your first real target."

Linda nodded. "Okay."

Virginia strolled to Grover, and the women. "I have."

Grover looked at her. "You have what?"

"Shot someone."

"Yeah, I know."

"So, Detective, what did you find out at the ivy-covered halls of higher education?" Virginia pointed at the couch. "Have a seat."

"Thanks." He sat on the edge of a cushion. "Well, not as much as you three."

Virginia chuckled as she sat in her chair. "Then you didn't try very hard."

"What did you want me to do, torture the professors?" He held up his hands. "Wait. Don't answer that. Anyway, I don't have your assets when it comes to getting men to talk."

"True. If it would have helped, you could have called us; we'd have done it. Especially if we got them here to do it."

"That's what I'm afraid of." He got up, moved to the fireplace, and leaned on the mantle. "However, I did find out that two biology professors and a geologist are somehow involved with an international corporation. They have gotten numerous grants from it. From what others at the university said, the international corporation is the Solomon Group. From what I learned, that's the source of a lot of their grant funding."

Virginia went to the front window, glanced outside, and then turned and looked at Grover. "Who are the professors?"

"Doctor Charles Morrison from the biology department. Professor Ian Manahan, also of the biology department. And last is Doctor Aaron Shaprio with the geology department."

Natalie returned to her seat and frowned. "They are the professors who have the grant to study science stuff on my ranch."

Virginia nodded. "Yep. Remember how nervous they were when they saw my Smithsonian badge?"

"I thought they were concerned that the Smithsonian was jumping their claim. I'm glad Doctor Dunlap, the archeologist, isn't involved. I liked him."

Linda put her gun back in her fanny pack. "Did you find Mr. Weedon?"

"No. But we searched his house and garage. We got a surprise. For a man who is deep in debt, he has a nice collection of vintage automobiles in a large storage building near Liberty Hill. It's very impressive. I liked the two-tone 1956 Ford and the '57 Chevy Bel-air. He has a clean, classic, Hudson, too. Haven't seen one of those in years." He looked wistfully out the window, then back at the women. "But in a tool cabinet, we found a small, dark-brown, bottle. Guess what it contained."

Linda shrugged.

Virginia arched a speculative eyebrow. "A small amount of the mushroom extract poison?"

Grover smiled. "Give the lovely lady a Kewpie doll."

Natalie gave Grover a quizzical look. "A Kewpie doll? What's that?"

"A small, cheap, plastic doll they would give as prizes at carnival sideshows or county fairs. I meant Virginia got it right."

Natalie stared at him.

"I'll explain it later."

Natalie's brightened. "Okay." She bit her lower lip. "Do you think Weedon was a member of the Solomon Group?"

Grover shook his head. "No. I think what he confessed to you when you three... ahh... interviewed him, was the truth. I believe Nesbitt and company was using him. From what that friend of yours, Claire, said, he was blackmailing Weedon. I'd love to know what the blackmail was about."

Virginia leaned forward. "It was about some pictures of him in compromising positions with a woman who isn't his wife. At least that's what he told us."

"I see. Well, I agree with you ladies that the church and the Solomon Group are one and the same. I heard from the Smithsonian Central Security Service. They said they sent this information to your computer, Virginia. Calvary Evangelical Chapel and the Solomon Group have the same bank, and they have a common office in the Cayman Islands. Their company officers in the Cayman Islands are one and the same, too. I don't know how Smithsonian Central Security Service found that out and didn't want to ask." He rubbed one temple. "Oh, just so you know, the bottle was wiped clean of fingerprints, which makes me think Mr. Weedon, for all his faults, was not the actual owner of it, and probably not the murderer. The bottle was most likely planted. But we still want to talk to the guy."

Virginia nodded. "I agree."

Natalie looked at Virginia, Linda, and then Grover. "Okay. Now what? I have an idea."

Grover raised an eyebrow. "What?"

"For starters," Natalie chuckled, "can I have Jenny Parker come here and slowly kill her? I can use the tools in my barn. I can hide the body, too. I think she murdered my cousin, and I bet I could get her to admit it."

Virginia, Linda, and Grover all responded at once, "No."

Natalie sat back and sighed. "Too bad. I was looking forward to it." She looked at the group and smiled. "I probably couldn't pull it off anyway. It made a great fantasy."

Grover laughed. "You're not a killer, Natalie. Now if Virginia said it, I'd worry."

Virginia put her hand on her heart and feigned hurt. "Thanks a lot, Detective. You think little old me could do something as brazen as that? Murder? I'll have to take you off my Christmas card list."

Grover's hand flew to his chest. "Oh, about those pictures, Natalie mentioned. We searched Nesbitt's place. There are no hidden rooms or one-way mirrors to film him and anyone else in bed. If there are videos of him with Miss. Parker, they weren't made there. So, either someone else makes the films for him, or Mr. Heller heard about it and assumed they were made at Nesbitt's home, or they were never made, and it's just the threat that they exist that Nesbitt was using to keep Miss. Parker in line."

"I like your last idea." Virginia bit her lower lip. "Maybe Jenny Parker made them and was blackmailing Nesbitt."

Natalie chuckled. "Maybe Heller let the Reverend and Jenny use his place, filmed them without their knowledge, and was blackmailing them both."

"Nice theories, ladies," said Grover, "but we need facts, supportable facts. Now, what were you going to do?"

Poseidon, Natalie's black cat walked into the room and rubbed Linda's leg. She bent down and picked him up. Linda tunneled her fingers through Poseidon's soft black fur, scratched behind his ears and under his chin, his purring intensified, and his eyes closed in ecstasy. She looked at the group. "Now that we've upset the apple cart, I think we should go find some caverns and see what was so important that someone would kill for it. Then we come back and wait for Ms. Parker."

CHAPTER 22

The three women and Grover walked into the kitchen. On the long table was piled their exploring gear as they called it. Each woman took a flashlight, a web-belt with a canteen, a waterproof camera, rain ponchos, coiled rope, goggles, work gloves, and hard hats.

Grover went to his car and came back with much the same equipment. He handed Natalie, Virginia, and Linda walkie-talkies. "Set them all on channel six. We will be able to talk to each other, and hopefully my men stationed above ground the area will be able to monitor us." He spun around at the sound of the kitchen door opening. Andy walked in.

Virginia hurried to him and kissed him. "Andy, what are you doing here? I thought you had a lab tonight."

"I did. A grad student's covering for me." Andy put his hands on his hips. "I'm going along on this expedition. Your cat wanted me to come. Leo said he's very concerned that he'll lose his meal ticket. Leo and I can't have you traipsing around underground without me with you."

Virginia chuckled. "Leo is always worried about his food. My cat talks to you? You need stronger meds."

"He's our cat now, remember? We have stimulating conversations."

"I bet. With you two, it's mostly about food. He doesn't talk about my old boyfriends, does he?"

Andy put his hand on his heart. "I promised Leo I wouldn't tell."

Grover patted Andy's shoulder. "Glad to have you along, Professor. You'll need some supplies. And I'd like to know more about her cat sometime."

"I've got them. I'll get my stuff from the car. I'll be right back." Andy hurried out and returned in a few minutes carrying his exploring gear, plus a first aid kit and two small, gray, plastic cases.

"The first aid kit is a good idea." Virginia looked at the cases as Andy stuffed them in his backpack. "What are they?"

"I got them from the university. They're portable test kits for identifying materials and metals. Could come in handy. I've got some notebooks, pens, a camera, and a tape recorder."

"Great." Virginia noted the folded maps sticking out of a side pouch on the backpack. "Maps?"

"Yeah. I picked up some topographical maps of this area and some geo-sat images. Figured they might come in handy trying to find Natalie's caverns."

Natalie turned from the kitchen island, walked up to Andy, and smiled. "Glad to see you, Andy." She held up a map sketched on a legal-size piece of paper. "This is a copy of what was in the materials the professors gave me. It's a hand-drawn map of my ranch, and it shows the locations of the caves. I had them in a folder on the kitchen island. It's not to scale."

Virginia turned. "You said you didn't know where the caves were."

Natalie shook her head. "I didn't, not until a few minutes ago. I remembered the profs said they were giving me all the stuff from the earlier expedition, as well as their proposal, and I figured I'd take a look. I gave the originals to my lawyer but kept a copy. I rifled through them, and sure enough, among the papers was this sketched map. It's better than nothing, and it includes some notes about each cave they found. I haven't examined it, just found it. I also found one Ann had drawn. It is crude and doesn't have much detail on it. I think the professors started with her map and went further."

Grover stepped to them. "Let's make a copy, so if something happens out there, we won't lose it."

"Good idea." Natalie turned and started for the stairs. "I'll be right back."

Virginia watched Natalie hurry out of the kitchen then turned back to Andy. "Did you bring a gun?"

"Yep. I've got my .357 Magnum with extra bullets."

"Okay." She turned to Grover and Linda. "As soon as Natalie gets back, we can head out. From the quick look at her map, it will be a real hike to the first cave."

"No it won't," said Natalie as she hurried through the door. "We can use my golf cart on steroids to get there. You know, that huge, gray ATV that's in the barn. I noticed, while copying this map, that one of the caverns is a short distance from here and has the most notes. I don't understand all the geology stuff, but it looks like there is something there of interest to the professors." She handed each of them a copy. "I made copies for everyone and locked up the original. Of the other caves identified, two seem to have been studied. I think we should start with the cavern. I'm dying to see it."

Virginia took her copy and studied it, then looked at Natalie. "I wish you hadn't used that phrase."

They locked up the house and went to the barn. Grover found a full five-gallon gas can and topped off the tank on the large ATV Natalie referred to as her golf cart on steroids. They loaded their supplies on board and climbed in. Andy sat in the driver's seat and studied the controls. Natalie sat next to him with a map.

Andy glanced over his shoulder. "Okay gang, everyone strapped in? Here we go." He started the motor and eased the clumsy vehicle out of the barn doors and stopped.

Natalie hopped out. She closed and locked the doors, then, using her cell phone, set the alarms for the barn, outbuildings, and the house. She climbed back in and fastened her seatbelt. "Okay, let's roll." She glanced at her map and pointed. "That way, Andy. Head through those oak trees." She looked up at the sky. "Looks like we could get some rain. I hope it holds out until we get back."

Andy turned the vehicle and drove into the brush. As they maneuvered around trees and scrub bushes, Natalie looked around, then consulted the hand drawn map. They slowed to descend a stream bank, forged across the stream, and then drove up the other side and back onto an animal trail. Periodically she'd direct Andy to turn. After about twenty minutes, they pulled into a clearing in a small forest of scrub oak, mesquite, juniper, and cedar trees. She told Andy to stop.

Andy stopped the ATV and looked around. "Are we there?"

Natalie nodded. "According to this map, yes. The entrance should be over there in that pile of boulders."

Thunder rolled across the area.

Grover looked at the darkening clouds. "Oh boy. Just what we need. The weather folks said partially cloudy with a thirty percent chance of rain. What gives?" He glanced at the top on the ATV. "At least this thing has a roof."

"And you believed them? It's the only job I know of that pays you when you keep getting things wrong." Virginia hopped out. "Let's get moving before the rain hits us."

Lightning ripped the sky. Linda looked up at the flash. "Now *that* can really complicate things." She looked at the rocks. "We've got a thunderstorm coming, and we're going underground into who knows what. Is this a good idea? Maybe we should come back another time."

Virginia stretched. "Might as well take a look while we're here. It isn't raining yet. We can take a quick look around and then head back. This shouldn't take too long." She started for the boulders.

CHAPTER 23

As Virginia started up the dusty incline, over an outcropping, toward the rocks, Natalie called out to her. "Watch for snakes. I've got a lot of rattlers around here."

Virginia froze. "Rattlesnakes? I forgot about them. I'm a city girl. I hate snakes." She opened a bottle of water and quickly took a drink. "Too bad this isn't something stronger." She turned when she heard someone coming up behind her. "Andy. I'm glad you came." She looked around. "See any snakes?"

"No." Andy scanned the area. "But we need to be careful, especially when we go into the cave."

She looked around, wide-eyed. "Great."

"We had rattlesnakes in California when we lived there. They didn't bother you then."

"Most of the snakes I met there wore suits."

"How about when you were traipsing about in the jungles of Central America?"

"Again, the only actual snakes I saw were the two-legged kind and one very poisonous individual who wasn't interested in making my acquaintance. I went one way, and it went the other. Oh yeah, there were a couple of really big ones who looked like they could eat a whole cow, but thankfully they were headed away from us."

Natalie, Linda, and Grover caught up with Virginia and Andy.

Natalie consulted her map sketch and pointed. "The entrance should be right up there." She moved ahead of the others and climbed the rise into the jumble of rocks and boulders. "There it is." She hurried to a narrow opening in a rock formation and examined the ground. "Looks like people have been here before, so this must be it."

Grover caught up with her and peered at the dirt. "Yeah, you're right. We need to be careful, there may be someone in there, and there could be bats and snakes."

Virginia put her hand on her pistol. "If I'm not shaking too badly, maybe I can hit a snake."

Grover led the way. Before he pushed through the slit in the rocks, he switched on his flashlight. "It widens out a little in here. Someone has been here recently." He touched the rock wall. "It's cooler in here as well."

The others slipped into the cave entrance, turned on their lights, and swung them around over the cave walls.

Virginia pointed her light at a section a few feet further into the cave. "Looks like ancient wall paintings. You can tell they are old by the style, the materials used, and that they are fading and sloughing off." She sniffed the air. "Smells musty. Must be water or dampness around."

Linda moved ahead and slowly maneuvered down the tunnel. "I feel a slight breeze. There could be another entrance or vent somewhere ahead." The others fell in behind her. They slowly walked on the dirt floor of the cave and around small boulders and outcroppings. After a nine-minute hike, they entered a cavern about sixty feet long, thirty feet wide, and twenty feet high. Linda tipped her head back, so her headlamp shown on the roof of the cave. She stared at the ceiling. Stalactites of varying sizes and colors hung above. Water slowly dripped from the tips. A path wound between Stalagmites and flowstone formations. "They are really pretty, and big."

"They are pretty." Virginia's turned and illuminated a section of the sidewall of the cave. "Look at this. Petroglyphs. They look super old, and they are etched into the rock." She stepped over rubble and small stalagmites. She took out her cellphone and took pictures of the primitive drawings. "This will have to do for now." She moved around a short rock formation. Just beyond ran a slow-moving stream. "Found a stream."

Andy shone his light at the petroglyphs. "Interesting."

Natalie stared at the cave paintings and etchings. "I've never seen real ones before. Only ones I've seen are in books and magazines. This is cool. And they're on my land." She stepped to the wall and touched a few of the pictographs. "There are some that are chiseled into the rock and then colored. That's neat."

Andy swung his flashlight toward the stream. "Here's the source of your dampness. It looks like it originates in that rock formation over there. See how it just pours out of openings in the sidewall of the cave and doesn't just seep. It looks like it's coming from a fault." He turned toward the entrance. "Did you hear that?"

Natalie cocked her head. "Thunder?"

"Possibly."

She looked wide-eyed at Andy. "What should we do?"

"For now, maybe a quick surveillance, and then beat it out of here and head for home."

Virginia was stepping toward the far end of the cavern. "Well lookie here. Mushrooms." She walked to a set of long wooden benches. On them were small plastic containers with dirt and some organic mix in them. Growing from the shallow boxes were mushrooms. She looked around with her light. On the end of one of the benches was a switch. She flipped it. Above, soft, low-level lights above the benches flickered on. Under a bench, she found a set of large batteries and a timer. "Someone was growing these."

Linda went to the tables and examined the mushrooms. "They are Panther cap mushrooms. They're toxic and contain the psychoactive chemical compounds ibotenic acid and muscimol as well as muscazone and muscarine. Not nice chemicals. Poisons actually." She looked at the stunned faces of the others. "What?"

Grover cleared his throat. "Mrs. Chambers, exactly how do you know this?"

She moved her right foot back and forth on the floor and looked down for a second, then looked at Grover. "Before my husband and I retired, I was a biology teacher in Maine. I've got a Master's degrees in biology and education. When we finally hung it up, we decided we were done with work, snow, and moose crossings."

Natalie eyed the mushrooms. "Do you suppose this is where the mushroom extract that killed my cousin and Reverend Nesbitt came from?"

Grover nodded. "Probably. I'll call for a forensic team to gather some of these for analysis."

Linda picked up a book on the ground under the closet-growing table. "This is a copy of Jenny's quilt book she stole from Natalie's cousin."

Natalie stepped to Linda's side and took the book. "Yep, that's it all right. That bitch." She frowned as she stared at it. 'Why is it here?" She set the book on the edge of the table.

Grover looked around. "Where are Virginia and Dr. Clark?" He jerked his head around at a series of flashes of light. "What the hell was that?"

Virginia stuck her head around a huge flowstone formation. "I'm over here with Andy. Looks like we found something interesting. There is a section back here that is igneous rock."

Grover frowned. "Is that important?"

"Yeah, it shouldn't be here. Andy's found some rocks and is using his test kit from the chemistry department to see what they are. So far, he's found nickel sulfide, a salt of silver, and some copper. Just beyond that flow is an area of igneous rock with quartz with the same gold striations as the rock in Natalie's basement. Now that's interesting. There's a lot of it."

Natalie stepped to the flowstone and stood next to Grover. "You found the quartz and gold?"

"Yep. Andy is doing some preliminary tests. I took some pictures."

Natalie smiled. "Good. What do you want me to do?"

"Can you snap some shots of the mushrooms?"

Using her cell phone, Natalie snapped a dozen pictures of the mushroom growing stations then touched a growing bench. "Why is this vibrating, and what's that sort of rumbling noise?"

Grover looked at the surface of the stream. Small ripples formed, then stopped. "I don't know. It was a low-level shaking. Maybe the noise you heard was just some rocks moving." Dust flew into the cavern from the tunnel they had just come from. "Shit. That was either a landslide or someone has just blown up our way out."

Virginia, followed closely by Andy, returned to the group. "If I didn't know better, I'd think that was an earthquake. Felt like a small three on the Richter scale. We had lots in California."

"You're right, Virginia. It did feel like one." Natalie looked at the fading undulations in the water. "But with the dust coming from that tunnel, like Detective Grover said, we've had a landslide or an explosion."

Linda swallowed. "What do you think, Andy? Earthquake or landslide?"

Andy looked at the pictures on his camera. "There are old faults all over this area. Real old ones, but faults nonetheless. This cave, even though it's limestone, has some crossing it like the ones I found over there with the igneous rock formations. At one time, there must have been a volcano either here or close by to explain the rock formations we just found. A small earthquake is possible, I guess. It could trigger a landslide. Yes, earthquakes can make noise." Andy shined his light on the surface of the water. The ripples were subsiding. "That shaking could be from an explosion. Probably not a big one; it wouldn't need to be big to cause damage."

Virginia swung around and looked at him. "Explosions?"

"There are quarries in the area." He glanced toward the tunnel they came through. "Or, maybe someone is trying to blow up the entrance."

"The quarries are miles away. Not too likely we'd feel anything here. She turned toward the entrance to the cave. *I hope it's still intact.* "We found what we came for... and more. Let's get out of here."

Grover hurried to her and Andy. "I second that idea. Never really did like being underground. Lived in Oakland for a while. Hated going under the bay to San Francisco and back on BART. Got a little claustrophobic."

"Blow up the entrance?" Natalie swallowed. "Who would do that? No one knows—oh shit, we told everyone of our suspects what we were going to do." She touched her abdomen. "I feel weird. My stomach's knotted up."

Linda stood next to the widening stream. The water sloshed around her ankles. Her sneakers squished as she jumped back out of the water, "That's warm. Shouldn't it be cold?"

Natalie moved next to her, bent down, and stuck her hand in the stream. "You're right; it is warm. I'd expect it to be cold, too." She looked at the rocks near the edge of the water. The sides of the stream were slowly widening, as the water got deeper. "I don't like this. The stream is getting bigger. We should be leaving, and soon."

Linda looked at the cave wall where the water was streaming out. "This isn't good."

Natalie moved next to Linda. "What's not good?"

She pointed at the cave wall. "More water is flowing from the rocks."

Andy glanced at the rock opening and the water pouring out. That's igneous rock. No wonder that water's warm."

Linda twisted around and looked at him. "Why?"

"I'll tell you when we get out of here."

"Okay." She turned. "Let's go."

Grover stood near the narrow tunnel from the entrance "Time to go folks. Let's not wait to see what Mother Nature does." Grover took a few minutes less time hurry up the small, winding, inclined tunnel toward the entrance with the others following, then stopped. He showed his light up and down a pile of boulders. "Shit! Looks like Andy was right, someone blew up our way out." He jumped as Linda slid past him.

Wide-eyed, she frantically pulled small rocks from the pile. "Can't we dig our way out? Andy?"

Andy pushed past them and examined the rubble. "Not too easily. We have no tools, and some of these are really heavy. He jerked his head around. "Sounds like thunder. That stream down in the cavern is going to get pretty big soon." He looked at Grover. "Can you use your radio to call your deputies?"

"Tried." Grover shook his head. "Spotty signal. Too much rock. Cell phone isn't effective either under all this rock and dirt, and we aren't close to a cell tower or a Wi-Fi hotspot."

Virginia, standing at the back of the group waved her light. "Quiet... I think I heard someone calling."

Natalie moved closer to Virginia and listened. "I'm losing my mind with all this. If I didn't know better, I'd say that was Mr. Weedon's voice."

"Me too."

"What the hell would he be doing here?"

Virginia turned in the direction of the voice. "It is Weedon. Let's go back to the cavern and find out what's going on. Maybe he's trapped as well."

They quickly retreated to the cavern. Weedon, dressed in tan cargo pants, hiking boots, and a Green Bay Packers T-shirt, holding a large flashlight, sat on an outcropping.

Natalie rushed forward and stopped in front of him. She placed her hands on her hips. "What the hell are you doing here? This is my land. Is this your poison mushroom farm?"

Grover approached. "You have some explaining to do, Mr. Weedon."

"Hello to you, too. No. It's not my mushroom farm. But I know whose it is. And I know it's your land."

Natalie's eyes narrowed. "You responsible for the blowing up of the entrance?"

"No. If I was, do you think I'd still be inside?"

Natalie tilted her head and frowned. "If this isn't your doing, why are you here? How'd you get in here?"

"You did notice your entrance is gone and the creek's rising, right?" He stood. "In spite of what you ladies did to me, I came to save you all."

CHAPTER 24

Virginia stood next to Natalie. "Okay, just how did you get in here without us seeing you, and is there another way out?"

Weedon stood. "This cavern is only part of a rather extensive cave system that runs under Ms. North's land. There are different types of rocks and stuff in them and old native wall pictographs and even some ancient campsites. There are artifacts in here too. I think they're ancient. And there actually are a couple of other exits. That's how I got in here. I witnessed someone blow up your entrance and decided to try and rescue you before things got even worse."

Grover took a breath. "Okay, you're acting as the big hero now. Why didn't you stop the person from blowing up our way out? How do we know you didn't do it and are trying to look like the knight on the white horse?"

Natalie glared. "What's the price of our rescue? My land?"

Weedon smiled. "To answer your question, Detective, I'm not armed and didn't feel like attacking people who were obviously armed murderers with explosives. You guys want to stand around and ask questions in a cave that is flooding, or get the hell out of here and ask questions above ground?" He turned to Natalie. "No conditions, Ms. North. I may be a slime ball, but I'm not a killer."

"Okay." Natalie sighed and wrapped her arms around herself. "I'd like to vamoose. This place is giving me the heebie-jeebies, and I don't want to die in here. Show us the way out, Mr. Weedon, please."

Andy touched Weedon's shoulder. "Wait. Does anyone else know of this hidden way out of yours?"

"Not that I know of. There is actually more than one. I don't think the professors know about them either. But I don't have their map to ensure that." Weedon turned and started for a dark back area of the cavern. "This way."

They followed Weedon around more stalagmites, flowstone formations, and low-hanging stalactites. They had to detour around more igneous rock formations. The paths were sometimes wet, slippery, and narrow, and in some places, required the group to move single file, twist, and wiggle through the small openings. After about forty-five minutes, they squeezed through a short stretch of a tunnel and entered a large cave. Tired, they all sat on boulders dispersed on the floor of the cave.

Virginia swung her light around. "Hey, note the lack of stalagmites and stalactites. We're in a plain old cave."

Linda shined her headlamp on the roof of the cave. "Yeah, nothing but smooth, black rock." She held her hand up. "I feel a small breeze."

Grover stepped to Weedon. "How much further?"

Weedon shrugged. "About a hundred yards... give or take."

"Let's get a move on."

"Okay. We're almost there, and boy, do I have a surprise for you."

Linda moved next to Andy and leaned close. "I'm not sure I like the sound of that."

Andy nodded. "Me either." He stood and moved closer to Grover. "Detective, I think we should be ready for trouble."

"Way ahead of you. Keep your gun handy and tell Virginia to do the same."

They stood and followed Weedon across the cave and up a slight incline. After another few minutes, they spotted a widened area with a light on and a heavy wooden door with a locking mechanism.

Virginia hurried forward and looked at the door. "Where does this go?"

Natalie examined the door, pointed at it, and said to Weedon, "Is this how you got into these caves, through my house?"

He shook his head. "No. I came in through one of the side tunnels. This one, with the door, I think goes to some other tunnels in and around your house."

Natalie slowly lowered her arm. "This must be one of the tunnels we hadn't explored yet. How'd you find it?"

"By accident. I wanted your land, remember? I did some exploring over the years when Ann had it, and when you came. I couldn't build much on top of the caves, so I wanted to know where they were."

"How about the university professors?"

"Not sure exactly. I know they had mapped some of the network of tunnels and caves, but I don't think they got as far as I did. I had more time, and I wasn't studying the ancient drawings, flora, and fauna. I made a map of sorts I'll give you when we get out of here." Weedon looked at the door. "Can you open it?"

Natalie gave him a quizzical look. "You can't?"

"No. I'm hoping you can."

She frowned. "I don't know. I'll try."

Virginia and Linda walked to the door and stood with Natalie. Virginia spoke. "We will try." They examined the door, the locking mechanism and the surrounding rocks and doorframe. Virginia stepped back. "I don't see a keyhole or anything that seems to warrant using a key. We haven't found any external trip mechanism either. Maybe it opens only from the inside." She turned to Andy. "What do you think?"

Andy pointed at the stone blocks near the right side of the doorframe. "What are those?"

Linda turned and looked at them, then back at Andy. "Rocks."

"Yes, but they have symbols on them."

Linda moved closer to the stones and pushed them. "I tried pushing them, but nothing happened. They didn't move."

Andy stepped to the rocks and ran his hand over them. "They're glyphs. What do they mean?"

Virginia stepped to the stones and knelt. "I've seen this before. They are almost smooth and are hard to read, but they're not glyphs, they're Roman numerals. We must need to push on them in a specific order, like a date or numeric code to trigger the opening of the door. But what code? What date? I'm not all that familiar with Texas history or the history of the former owners, and I seriously doubt it's a date important to the Romans."

Andy nodded. "I agree. Whoever did this must have gotten the stones from someplace else and used them like a combination lock. I would guess that he or she was a Texan. So, my first guess would be the date Texas became an independent country. If that doesn't work, maybe when it joined the Union."

Grover nodded. "Makes sense, doc. Ladies, try pushing the following stone blocks in this order... ready?"

Virginia flexed her fingers, placed her hands in front of the stones, and nodded. "Go ahead."

"Okay. Push... one... eight... three... five..."

Virginia pressed on the stones. The figure for the number one moved almost imperceptibly. She waited, and then pressed the other numbers. "Nothing else moved, and nothing happened." She looked up at the group. "What now?"

Grover frowned as he thought. "I think Texas joined the Union about five years later so—"

Natalie rubbed her chin. "I have an idea. Try pressing one... eight... nine... two."

Virginia shrugged. "Okay. Why eighteen ninety-two?"

"That's when the oldest part of the house was built."

"I'll give it a try." Virginia pushed the one. It again moved slightly. She then pressed the eight and the rest of the numbers. They all slid back a half inch. Then there was a click, and the door moved slightly inward. Virginia climbed to her feet. "It worked. Good going, Natalie." She stood. "Let's see where this leads. The sooner I get out of these tunnels the better."

Andy started for the door and then stopped. "Wait. I just realized something. Why is this light bulb on? I don't see a switch out here. Who turned it on, and when?"

"I don't care." Linda looked longingly at the doorway. "I just like to get the hell out of here."

"You may want to rethink that, Linda." Andy drew his sidearm. "We better get ready for anything and proceed carefully. You lead the way, Mr. Weedon."

"Why me?" Weedon glanced at the door. He rubbed his palms on his pant legs. "I had nothing to do with the light bulb being on or this door."

"Simple. You suddenly show up right after someone blew up the entrance to the caves that we used and offered to rescue us. Good timing. Too good. You said there were other entrances, but brought us here. You said you knew who used explosives on the cave opening but haven't divulged that bit of information yet. Right now, we don't know who may be behind door number one, and like I said, someone has already tried to kill us." Andy pointed his gun at Weedon. "Move."

CHAPTER 25

Weedon glared at Andy. "Look who's trying to be the big man. You can't and won't shoot me, jackass. You especially wouldn't shoot me with a cop present. This is assault with a deadly weapon." He glanced at Detective Grover and then pointed at Andy. "He's assaulting me with a deadly weapon in front of you and these witnesses. I demand you arrest him."

Grover shrugged "I didn't see any assault, and I'm sure these nice ladies didn't either."

Weedon's eyes shot daggers at Andy. He stood erect in a defiant stance, and then tried to move around Andy. "You can't shoot me, and I'm *not* going in first." A sharp buzz and his back arched, he twisted and screamed, then tumbled to the dirt floor, writhing in pain. Two taser wires protruded from his back.

Virginia stepped closer. "Andy may not shoot you, but my handy taser is just as effective."

When he stopped twitching, he spoke through clenched teeth. "I'll get you for this, bitch."

"No one calls me a bitch. I guess it's time to teach you a lesson." Virginia gave the trigger on her pink taser a quick tug. His body convulsed around on the ground; his head bounced off a rock. He moaned.

"Now, Mr. Weedon, I'll tell you once and only once, go through that damn door and be as quick about it as you can. My trigger finger is getting tired, and I may just increase the voltage. The next jolt will probably give you a heart attack."

Weedon raised one hand slightly. "Okay, okay. I'm sorry." He slowly sat up; his clothes soiled with dirt. Perspiration dripped from his forehead. He looked at Grover. "I suppose you didn't see or hear that either, Detective."

Grover shook his head. "Nope. I was talking to Ms. North, and I guess missed all the action." He bent over. "If I were you, I'd do as Mrs. Clark says. We don't have paramedics or a medical doctor around in case she gets even more upset and actually succeeds in giving you a heart attack. Did you happen to notice her taser is pink?"

Weedon nodded. "Yes."

Linda leaned close to Andy and asked in a low voice, "Can she actually increase the voltage and give him a heart attack?"

Andy lowered his weapon and grinned. "No. But I don't think Weedon knows that."

Linda nodded. "I didn't think so."

Weedon sat for a couple of minutes regaining his composure and let his nerves and muscles relax. He slowly climbed to his feet and turned toward the slightly opened doorway. He glanced at Virginia and Natalie "Okay, I'll go first. Really, I have no idea what's beyond it. I came in here a different way, but it's farther. The light wasn't on when I explored the caves, so I never noticed this door. But the light was on when I came in to get you. That's when I noticed the door. I honestly didn't know it was here before."

Virginia pointed. "March."

Weedon nodded. He stepped to the door and pushed it fully open, stepped inside, stopped, and peered around. "It's clear. It's another tunnel. It's empty. There are more lights though."

Virginia moved through the doorway and looked around. She pulled the Taser cartridge off the front of the taser, reloaded it with a second that was stored in the bottom of the Taser's handle grip and tucked it back into its holster on her belt. "Okay, come on. We need to figure out where we are and fast. Someone thinks we're trapped and won't be expecting us."

Natalie looked at Linda. "Expecting us?"

"I don't know," Linda shrugged, "ask Virginia."

Natalie moved next to Virginia and leaned close. "Who won't be expecting us?"

"Whoever blew up the entrance." Virginia stepped out of the way for the others to enter.

Andy and Grover followed the women and Weedon. Andy turned and inspected the inside of the door. "Looks like old shelving, but if you look close, you can see it is fairly new and made to look old. There're a couple of dilapidated cardboard boxes on them. The door assembly looks old too, but it has been artificially aged like the selves. Someone went to a lot of trouble to refurbish this but make it still look like it's been around a long while." He pushed it closed and heard the click of the locking mechanism. He turned and examined the tunnel. "Okay, this tunnel was here for a long time. It has been rehabbed as well. You can see where the older parts and support sections are. Some of these beams are solid, old oak. As oak ages, it gets harder. These posts and beams are probably as hard as iron. The updates can't be more than five to ten years old though; the electricity is coming from somewhere. The wiring is fairly new. You can see fragments of the old cloth insulated wire on the floor. Why was this section built and then redone?"

"Originally, this may be an old way to get moonshine out." Natalie snickered. "My great uncle was a moonshiner back in the thirties." She slowly shook her head. "Maybe Ann had it redone for some reason. I don't know why she'd do it, but she could be eccentric at times." Natalie looked at the tunnel in both directions. "Which way do we go?"

Virginia looked up and down the tunnel. "I don't think it really matters. It starts one place and ends at another." She pointed to the left. "Let's go that way and see where it ends. We can always turn around and go back."

They trudged down the tunnel for about a hundred yards where it stopped at a metal ladder going up about fifteen feet. Grover looked up at the roof of the tunnel. "Another door. I'll go first and make sure the coast is clear."

Weedon sighed. "Thank God. I don't want to be first, and I really don't want to be tazed, again."

Grover climbed the ladder, yanked on a handle, and slowly pushed the trapdoor open. He climbed higher and was half out of the opening twisting and poking at something when he called down to the assembly. "This hatch is topped by a realistic looking fake rock. We're somewhere out in the woods. I think Ms. North is correct about this being a way to get moonshine or something else in or out." He tugged at the handle on the hatch, closed, and relocked it as he climbed down. Reaching the bottom, he pointed back down the tunnel. "Let's go that way and see where it ends up."

They turned, and with Weedon in the front of the column, they trudged down the tunnel for two hundred yards. They made a slight turn and walked up a gentle slope about another three hundred yards farther to the end. The overhead wires continued through the massive oaken bulkhead at the tunnel terminus. The wide doorway, with steel hinges, was secured with a swinging bar, with a wheel at the fulcrum in the middle of the door. The bar was held closed by a rusty iron angle bracket mounted to the doorframe.

Natalie stepped to the door, twisted the wheel, and tugged the door. It swung toward her opening into the basement of her house. The inside of the door was camouflaged as a section of concrete wall. She stepped into the cellar and stopped. She turned and put her fingers to her lips and motioned up with her other hand. She whispered. "There are people upstairs." She glanced at Andy. "Why didn't the alarm sound?"

Andy shrugged. "I don't know. We'll find out soon enough." He pointed at the floor. "Look, someone was here a little while ago."

Grover put his hand on Weedon's shoulder and spoke softly, "I would be very quiet if I were you. You make any sound, and I'll let Virginia and the other ladies do what they want with you in the barn. It won't be pleasant. Got it?"

Weedon frowned and sighed. He whispered. "Got it. I'm not part of what's going on up there. I'll explain everything I did when we are through with all this."

"Good. I can't wait to hear it. Now, stay in front of me. Move."

Virginia, with her gun drawn, led the group. Andy followed her with Natalie and Linda behind him. Weedon and Grover were last. They walked to the bottom of the stairs, and then quietly mounted the stairs.

Grover stopped Weedon at the bottom and handcuffed him to pipe. "Be a good boy and don't do anything stupid. Virginia or I will be back shortly to get you."

Weedon's head bowed. "Okay. Just don't forget me."

"We won't. Now be quiet."

Virginia stopped at the top of the staircase and listened. She carefully turned the doorknob and eased the door slightly open. Voices came from the living room. The sound of something being mixed in a glass container came from the direction of the kitchen. Virginia quietly moved back down a couple of steps and whispered. "There are people in both the living room and the kitchen. Andy, you and Detective Grover take the kitchen. Natalie, Linda, and I will go for the living room. Let's put an end to this now."

They all nodded.

Virginia, Linda, and Natalie slipped through the door into the hall. Linda and Natalie glided along the far wall behind Virginia to the entrance to the living room. Andy and Grover crept through the door opening and moved silently toward the kitchen. Virginia stopped at the edge of the hallway and listened. She heard rain pelting the windows and two men speaking. *The professors are in the living room. Who's in the kitchen?* She motioned for Linda and Natalie to follow her, and she stepped into the room, her gun held in both hands in front of her. "Good evening, gentlemen, Dr. Charles Morrison, Dr. Aaron Shaprio, you're under arrest."

Dr. Morrison and Professor Shaprio froze. Papers fell from their hands. Shaprio wet his lips. "It isn't what you think, Mrs. Clark. We… we can explain everything."

"I bet you can, but it'll have to wait."

Morrison tried to regain some control. He straightened his back. "And how do you figure you can arrest us?"

"I'm a federal agent. I'm with the Smithsonian Central Security Service. You do remember me showing you my badge the last time we met, don't you?"

The two men looked at each other then nodded.

Virginia smiled. "Hands on your heads. Are either or both of you armed?"

Dr. Shaprio shook his head. "No. We are academics, not criminals."

"Oh. You're in Ms. North's house without an invitation. That's a criminal act. Sit."

Suspicious Threads

They took seats on the couch next to each other. "You can put your hands down, but don't do anything stupid. Be good boys and be quiet. If you try anything, I'll let Natalie here shoot you both. You're trespassing and have burgled her house. It's after dark, there's a storm, someone tried to kill us, and Ms. North is very nervous. Under these circumstances, her shooting you would be justified. Got the idea?"

They nodded again.

"Oh, just so you know, Natalie's a dead shot with that canon." She glanced at Natalie and Linda. "Keep them covered. If they reach for their pockets, shoot. If they try to escape, shoot. If they try to get up, shoot. If they look at you cross-eyed—"

Natalie smiled. "I know... shoot."

The two professors looked at Natalie with wide eyes. "Right, I'll be right back." Virginia turned and headed for the kitchen. *Sounds like the mixer is off. I wonder how Andy and Grover are doing with whoever is in the kitchen?* As she reached the kitchen entrance, she heard a gunshot. A chill ran up her spine. *Andy!*

CHAPTER 26

Virginia stopped with her back against the wall. She held her pistol with both hands up in front of her chest. She inched forward and peered around the corner into the kitchen. She spotted Andy kneeling next to Mr. Heller who sat on the tiled floor holding his bloody arm. Mrs. Blair was slumped on a chair close to the kitchen counter and sink, with a sullen look on her face. Detective Grover stood over her. Virginia moved into the kitchen and spoke. "What happened? Why are they here?" She glanced at the counters. What's going on?"

Grover looked back at her. "Mr. Heller, or as he now seems to like to be called, the Reverend Heller, swung a knife at Dr. Clark when we came in. I shot him."

Virginia stepped to the group and looked at Heller. "So you're a reverend now, huh?"

"I… I've been one for some time," Heller stuttered. "Nesbitt didn't like anyone else using the title but him. He liked to call the rest of us *brother* or *sister*. He was a real control freak." Heller shifted position and grimaced. "Nesbitt had a big ego. He was good at raising money and at organization. But now he's gone, and no one is going to miss him." He clenched his teeth and released his hand over the bullet wound, sighed, then re-gripped the bleeding injury. "This hurts like hell. Will you please get the paramedics, I've been shot."

"No kidding. Why'd you attack my husband with a knife?"

"He startled me." Heller tensed as he adjusted his arm position.

"So you, as a good Christian, try to kill people who startle you? Good thing for you it was Detective Grover who shot you and not me. I wouldn't have hit your arm."

Grover chuckled, "I was aiming for his chest; he moved."

Heller turned even paler.

Virginia looked at Andy who was grinning. "Why do you look so happy?"

"He missed me with that butcher knife, and the good detective shot him. And look at the counter and the mixer."

She stepped around Heller and examined the things on the counter. *A mixer and an electric food chopper—normal stuff for Natalie's kitchen. Mushrooms, two bottles of some liquids? Not Natalie's stuff. There's a scale, measuring cups, spoons, a bowl with some brown powder in it, and a notebook.* She looked at Andy and Grover. "Are they making the mushroom poison? What am I looking at?"

"Yes," Andy said. "Those are Panther mushrooms from the caves we were just in. They're manufacturing the mushroom poison here instead of a lab some place else. Obviously, they knew the cave entrance was destroyed, and that made this place expedient. They probably figured no one was coming home. Oh, the poison recipe is in that notebook."

Virginia turned and regarded Blair and Heller. "Well, so much for your self-righteous, Holy Calvary Evangelical Chapel. Is murder one of your faith's beliefs and teachings?"

Blair glared at Virginia. "No. But what would a nonbeliever like you know about the one true faith? We are here under difficult and strange circumstances."

Virginia looked back at the counter. "I can see that. You burglarized Ms. North's home. You were caught mixing a poison that's been used in two murders. Who were you going to use it on, Natalie or me? Is that your poison cookbook?"

Heller groaned. "No, it's not ours, and we don't go around killing people. It's not what you think."

"You're the third person to say that. Not your poison mixing instruction book, huh? But you broke in here after someone tried to kill us, you're in possession of the book, and using it to mix the poison concoction. This story should be interesting. I bet the DA won't buy it." Lightning lit up the window over the sink followed shortly by a loud thunderclap. "Looks like your god doesn't like you either."

"That is blasphemy," Heller said through clenched teeth.

"Yeah, right. You're the one cooking poison to kill someone, not me."

"But the book isn't ours." Heller's voice cracked. "Please call for the paramedics. I'm in a lot of pain, and I'm getting woozy."

Virginia leaned close to Heller. "If the notebook isn't yours, whose is it, and how did you get it?"

Heller stared at the floor. Mrs. Blair sat with her eyes closed and arms crossed.

"Why are you here and not in a lab someplace else? Why aren't you using the church kitchen for your poison making? I figured you blew up the cave, but coming here… that's stupid."

Grover motioned for Virginia to step to the other side of the room with him. "I've read them their rights and called for backup and the paramedics.

I'm going to hold them on an assault with intent to kill charge for lashing out at Andy with the knife, burglary, conspiracy to commit murder, and for the manufacture of a poisoned controlled substance and suspicion of multiple murders. And the Blair woman had a concealed .22 caliber pistol without a license."

"Good. How about the two professors in the living room?"

Grover's head jerked back. "I was so busy with these characters, I almost forgot about professors. Who's guarding them, Natalie and Linda?"

"Yep."

"Those two ladies, especially Natalie, are likely to shoot them if they try anything, even cough."

"Yep."

"Have they said anything about why they're here?"

"Just 'it's not what you think,' but I'll go see what I can find out. In the meantime, can you get Blair or Heller to say why they were stupid enough to be here in Natalie's house mixing a poison they know nothing about, and where they got that poison cookbook? Can they tell us who else is involved? Their story should be interesting."

"I'll see how cooperative they'll be. They haven't asked for legal representation yet." Thunder shook the room. "Oh, before you go intimidate and interrogate the professors, will you do me a favor?"

Virginia nodded. "Sure."

"Here is my handcuff key, get Weedon from the basement, will you? Let's hear what he has to say."

"Okay. I'll take him into the dining room and interview him there." Virginia headed for the hallway, stopped and turned. "Andy, how'd they get in here without the alarm going off?"

Andy turned and pointed down. "They came in through the tunnel we just came through. It seems they have either explored Natalie's land around here, or had a map and knew about it. I'm glad Detective Grover locked the other end of the tunnel. I didn't find that particular tunnel when I was searching the cellar and found the other house tunnels. It's an isolated passageway and isn't connected to the other ones you explored, so I didn't alarm it like on the entrance to the others behind the furnace. I never thought to put motion detectors in the basement. That oversight will be remedied very shortly."

Virginia nodded. "Yeah, that needs to be fixed pronto. Maybe you can add a lock on the tunnel entrance." She glanced at Grover. "By the way, whom does that book belong to, if not them?"

Grover shook his head. "Don't know yet. I'll see what the Reverend and the Blair woman say and let you know."

Virginia went to the living room, told Natalie and Linda what was going on in the kitchen, and asked them to still keep the professors there.

Then, she went down the basement stairs and found Weedon sitting on a crate with his arm extended to the pipe he was handcuffed to. She smiled and held up the handcuff key. "I came to get you. Now you're going to be a good boy and not cause me any trouble, aren't you?"

Weedon nodded. "Yes... I mean no... wait... I mean I won't be any trouble. I've learned from my experiences with you that being nice and cooperative is a whole lot healthier, and a lot less painful."

"Good." She undid the handcuffs and removed them from Weedon's wrists.

He rotated his arm and rubbed his wrist. "I'm glad you came when you did. It was uncomfortable."

"I bet." Virginia smiled. "Here's the plan. We're going upstairs to the dining room. You will sit and very clearly explain to me what the hell is going on from your perspective. If you cooperate, I may be able to convince Natalie not to press charges against you. And... thank you for guiding us out of the cave and tunnels."

"Deal. I've got a lot to tell. I couldn't let you die."

"Let's go." She motioned toward the stairs with her arm, "After you."

Virginia followed Weedon to the dining room where he took a seat at the long wooden table. She sat across from him and pulled out a notebook. "Okay, start."

Weedon cleared his throat. "As you already know, I wanted Ms. North's property to develop. And as I told you before I didn't have the ready funds to buy the land and do the development myself. I have some gambling debts and other issues. That's where the Solomon Group came in. They were the money behind the project."

"How'd you know about them or contact them?"

"I was looking for financing, and they found me. They said the Reverend Nesbit knew about me and recommended that they contact me."

"Okay, go on."

"But Ms. North wouldn't sell, and I already spent some of the money on... on efforts to persuade her to sell, maps, engineering, paying off my debts, and well, stuff. The Solomon Group gave me a very short time to either get the land or return their money. I couldn't do either. They told me what they would do to me in very graphic detail, and it isn't nice. Then Reverend Nesbitt must have gotten wind of my problems and somehow managed to get some compromising pictures of me with another woman and started to blackmail me. The contact with the Solomon Group said to get the land at any cost, even Ms. North's life if necessary. I was in a tough spot. You've got to believe me, I would have done almost anything to get the property, but killing Ms. North was not an option."

"Yes." Virginia finished her last note and looked at him. "So, what else interesting do you have for me?"

"During the time I was discussing the purchase of *Borealis* from Ann North Greenwald, I did some exploring of the property." He held up his hands. "Yes, I know, it was trespassing. I had heard rumors that there were caves and an underground river here some place, and the caves had old Native American rock paintings and carvings and stuff. I found them. The issue at the time was I couldn't build on a lot of *Borealis* because of the caves and the river, just part of it. The Solomon Group didn't care if they existed or not. They had invested and wanted the place. I don't know why they were so insistent that they get the whole place, they couldn't build on all of it. They wanted to start whatever their plans were soon, and were buying off officials. They threatened me with my life. Ann North Greenwald had heard about the caves too and had an interest in exploring them. That's when the professors from the university came into the picture. They heard about the things I found and wanted to explore them, for so-called purely academic reasons, of course."

Virginia nodded. "Purely academic reasons, of course, continue."

Weedon fidgeted with the quilted table runner, then looked back at Virginia. "Ms. Greenwald gave them permission."

"Tell me about the book and computer file you tried to steal." Rain pelted the windows as lightning ripped across the sky outside the windows. Virginia looked up at the ceiling fixture as the lights flickered.

Weedon glanced at the lights while wrung his hands. "This storm is getting worse."

"I agree."

"Where was I?"

"You were about to tell me about the book and file you tried to steal?"

"Oh, yes. I was told by Nesbitt that as part of my…" Weedon made air quotes, "…penance for my adultery, I had to obtain the original manuscript of the quilt book by Jenny Parker and a certain computer file. It was supposed to be on Ann North Greenwald's computer, or a memory stick or some disk. I was to do that, and continue with my…" Weedon made air quotes again, "…monthly contributions to his church, or the pictures of me and that woman and some other less than legal business information, would see the light of day. He said something about how my getting the file could help me with my problems with the Solomon Group. I remember him mentioning something about the Solomon Group and something called 'The Arum' or something. Maybe it's some other investor." Weedon sat expressionless for a moment then frowned. "He said he wanted the file before someone else got their hands on it. I don't know who he was referring to."

"The Arum. Hmm." Virginia gave him a big smile. "Okay, so far, so good, continue."

"I couldn't figure out how Nesbitt seemed to know all about the Solomon Group and my problems until you mentioned the church and the Solomon Group were the same. Then, I felt like a real dope. Nesbitt was getting crazier each day, and he was happy when Ann North Greenwald died. He figured things were going to be easy after that. That's when Ms. North arrived and turned everything upside down. I think Nesbitt wanted the book and file to use as leverage against someone else or because there was something else on that file about Ms. North's property. Like I said, I don't know what. He, and the Solomon Group wanted *Borealis*." Weedon looked down at the table, then back at Virginia. "You know, I actually like Ms. North, but she'll never believe that after all I've done."

"You're probably right." Virginia rested the pen on the table and stared at Weedon. "Did you kill Ann North Greenwald?" She picked up the pen and made notes.

"No. I may be a scumbag, but I'm not a murderer."

"Did Nesbitt, or whoever you talked to at the Solomon Group, mention why they wanted the computer file so fast, or specifically who wanted it?"

"No. Wait, like I said, I think Nesbitt wanted to blackmail someone or for that Arum thing. I had no idea what the Solomon Group wanted it for. I just thought of something. Maybe that the Arum thing or group, whoever they are, is a competitor. Must be important, after all, Arum means gold in Latin. It made sense once you told me Nesbitt and his church are the Solomon Group."

"Okay, now think before you answer this next questions, "Who blew up the tunnel entrance, and why were you around to see it?"

Weedon sighed. "As you know, the weather was turning, and this storm we have was closing in. I was out on Ms. North's land because I heard from... from someone in the Calvary Evangelical Chapel, that there was going to be trouble here tonight."

"Why didn't you just call Ms. North or the police?"

"And tell them what?" Weedon waved his arms. "I heard from some mysterious source at the church that there *might* be some sort of trouble here? I didn't know what kind of trouble. I didn't know who was going to cause it or how or exactly when. With my record bothering her and my antics trying to buy *Borealis*, they'd pick me up for questioning, and not investigate. I'm not sure what Ms. North would have done either."

"Good point." Virginia nodded. "Go on with the story."

"I saw all of you in that... that golf cart on steroids that Ms. North has, and followed you. I watched, and sometime after you went inside the cave entrance, another ATV arrived. Two people were in it. They had a crate on the back."

Virginia looked up from her notes. "Who were they?" She glanced at the two windows behind Weedon. Water streamed down them from the rain.

Weedon peered over his shoulder to see what she was looking at. "Not the best weather, but we do need the rain."

"Yeah, you're right. Please continue. Who tried to kill us?"

"One was that guy you decked and pretty well beat up, Blake. He's big; you can't mistake him. He had a thick cast on his right arm. He's a hired thug, and fully capable of murder. I don't think he has a lot of love for you."

Virginia grinned. "You're probably right about that. Who was the other individual?"

"The other person was short, but I couldn't make out who it was. He, or she, had on black, baggy cargo pants, a black, baggy sweatshirt, and a black loose hoodie and brown hiking boots. I never got a look at the person's face. I wasn't close enough to identify the voice either. Sorry."

"Could you tell if the person was male or female?"

"The person was short, and the outfit was really baggy. So I can't say for certain, but I'd guess it was a woman."

"Why?"

"By the short stature and the way the person moved."

"Okay." Virginia scribbled some notes. "Continue."

"They set the explosives and then left. After they were out of sight, I ran to the entrance and saw the charges. They were not just sticks of explosives like dynamite with a detonator sticking out that would be easily disarmed. They were rectangular boxes with little green lights flashing and antennae. Remotely detonated. Someone went to a lot of expense to get them. I ran, then headed for another entrance I knew about, and went looking for you all. That's when I heard the big bang. Like I said, I may be a lot of things, but letting you all die isn't in my playbook. I told you the truth about that new tunnel we came out in."

Virginia flipped through her notes then asked, "Had you seen the professors' map?"

Weedon shook his head. "No. I didn't know they had one."

"Has anyone seen your map, and where is it?"

Weedon pulled a folded sheet of paper from the right-hand, large pocket on his cargo pants and handed it to Virginia. "Here, I've noted as many specific things as I could to make it easy to follow and for reference later. It isn't to scale. I'm not a geologist or a surveyor. I noted where there were ancient wall carvings, and painting, and changes in the rocks."

Virginia took the paper and set it on the table. "Thank you. Now, did you kill Reverend Nesbitt?"

"As much as I liked his untimely passing, I did *not* hasten his trip to hell. I know; I had motive, opportunity, means, and not a good alibi. And it wasn't like I didn't think about it or wish someone would do it, but it wasn't me."

Virginia studied Weedon's demeanor. "Mr. Weedon, I believe you."

Suspicious Threads

Weedon cracked a weak smile. "Thank you, Mrs. Clark. I'm glad someone does."

"Do you have any ideas about who may have done it?"

"My money would be on someone in the hierarchy of both the Solomon Group and Calvary Evangelical Chapel, especially since they are basically the same organization. Also, the newly polished Reverend Heller had a lot to gain. He's a weasel." He sat back in his chair. "Can I go home now?"

"Not just yet. We're still talking to the other folks we found here." Virginia tilted her head. "Those sirens must be the backup deputies and the paramedics Detective Grover called."

Weedon's eyes widened. "Paramedics? Good lord, you shoot someone already?"

"No," Virginia chuckled, "I didn't shoot anyone. Detective Grover shot Heller."

"Good for the detective. Like I said, I don't like that guy, Reverend or not. Did the good detective by any chance kill him?"

"No."

"Too bad. That pompous ass even started to try and seduce Mrs. Parker, like Nesbitt did."

Virginia stared at Weedon. "Nesbitt and Jenny Parker? It's true?"

"Yeah. There was something going on between them, and it wasn't all friendly, even though they were… ahh… close."

CHAPTER 27

Virginia stood and looked down at Weedon. "Stay put. We've got a lot going on. But I'll see if I can get Natalie not to press charges against you."

He smiled. "Okay. Thank you for believing me, even after all the trouble I've caused." He sat back. "I'll be right here."

Virginia scurried to the kitchen and found Detective Grover sitting at the table with Mrs. Blair. He glanced up at Virginia. "How'd it go with Weedon?"

"Good. Got a lot of information. He identified Blake as one of the people who blew up the entrance to the caves we were in."

Grover picked his handheld radio up off the table. "I'll issue a BOLO and have him picked up. Anything else we need at the moment?"

"Yeah, hold Mrs. Blair and Reverend Heller like you said earlier. Speaking of Heller..." Virginia turned and found Heller, his arm bandaged with a bloody cloth, lying on the floor. Andy sat on a chair near him. She walked to Andy. "How's he doing?"

Andy shrugged. "He's weak. I've got it bandaged with a compress. I also tied a constricting strap... a tourniquet, above the wound. He lost a lot of blood and is still bleeding a little. Grover may have hit, or nicked, an artery."

She touched Andy's shoulder. "The paramedics and deputies should be here any minute. I heard sirens."

"Yeah, so did we. Weedon?"

"Very cooperative. He's staying in the dining room. Ask Grover if you can go watch Weedon. I'm going to see the professors."

Andy nodded. "Let me know what the professors have to say."

"Okay." Virginia walked through the kitchen toward the hallway. She noticed Blair watching her, frowning. *That self-righteous bitch is in a lot of trouble. How nice.*

Virginia walked into the living room as Natalie was letting the paramedics and sheriff's deputies inside through the front door. Virginia stepped out of the way, as the medics went by pushing a gurney carrying their red equipment boxes. Through the window, she saw a fire engine arrive. "More company."

After the firemen had come in and were in the kitchen, Virginia sat across from the two professors. Natalie sat next to Virginia. Linda stood by the front window looking out at the rain.

Virginia leaned forward. "Dr. Morrison, Dr. Shaprio, are you comfortable?"

They looked at each other, and then Morrison spoke. "If you mean being held by two menacing women with guns is comfortable, I guess so. This is an outrage. We are being held against our will. That is highly illegal."

"Well, you should be thankful one of these ladies didn't shoot you. As to being held against your will, you are right. If you remember, I arrested you."

Morrison glared. "On what charge?"

"Suspicion of attempted murder, breaking and entering, conspiracy to commit murder, conspiracy to commit fraud, aiding the manufacture of a controlled substance, and I'm sure Detective Grover and I can think of more charges. Happy?"

"You... you can't do that."

Virginia sat back and smiled. "Watch me."

Dr. Shaprio cleared his throat. "Mrs. Clark, I think what we have here is a big misunderstanding."

"Oh?" Virginia's eyebrow shot up. "Misunderstanding? Someone just tried to kill us. There are people in Ms. North's kitchen manufacturing a poison. It's the poison that killed Ann North Greenwald and Reverend Nesbitt. At the same time, I find you two here as well. Oh, I bet Ms. North revokes your permit to explore here as well."

Shaprio took a deep breath and slowly let it out. "This isn't what it seems."

"You've said that already."

Linda chuckled then turned from the window and smiled. "There is a big planter out there that's rapidly filling up with water from all this rain. We could take them outside and hold their heads under water until they either talk or... well accidents do happen."

Natalie turned toward Virginia and winked. "Yeah, as soon as the deputies leave we can dunk them like Linda said. That, or just attach a jumper cable from the tractor to their balls and—"

Morrison jumped to his feet and started to talk. When he moved, Natalie stood and aimed her .357 Magnum at him. He swallowed and sat.

Virginia shook her head. "Now, Dr. Morrison, that stupid stunt almost got you shot. If I were you, I'd sit and not do anything foolish like that again."

He flexed his fingers and nodded. "Okay. But I can't just sit and let you torture us."

"Torture? No way." Virginia feigned hurt. "They're suggesting enhanced interrogation techniques. But we won't have to do anything like that to entice you to tell us what we need to know, will we?"

Dr. Shaprio rubbed his forehead. "Our lawyer will hear about this outrage."

Linda moved next to him and said, "You have to live long enough to tell him."

Virginia waved her hand at Linda. "Linda, let's hear why the good professors think all this is a big misunderstanding, then we can decide what to do next."

Linda let out a sigh and sat in an overstuffed chair near the fireplace. "Okay, professors, I'm all ears."

Virginia flipped through pages in her notebook and then raised her pen. "Like Linda said, we're ready, professors, start talking."

Shaprio adjusted his glasses, sat back, and shook his head. "Dr. Morrison and I were approached by Calvary Evangelical Chapel a couple years ago." He frowned and looked at Morrison. "It was two years ago, wasn't it?"

Morrison nodded. "Yes, about that. Maybe two, or two and a half. I'm not exactly sure."

"At first, Nesbitt was not unlike other ministers. But he was exceptional at fund raising, and he graciously helped get us some grants for research. Two years ago, he put us in contact with the Solomon Group for grants for our academic research. They were very generous." Shaprio drummed his fingers on the armrest of the chair and continued. "Nesbitt told us he heard rumors about some caves and caverns under Ms. Ann North Greenwald's land might have some interesting features. He thought some preliminary exploration would be a good thing to do. He told us he was interested in obtaining her land for the church and figured any caverns would be a good draw and a moneymaker of the church when he got the land. He was also interested in anything unusual we might find. He never did explain what he meant by unusual. He said the development of the land would include set-asides for research and protection of important natural features. We believed him, and he actually gave us a small stipend to do the initial study and mapping until the Solomon Group funding came through."

Virginia took notes. "So, you were acting in good faith, sort-to-speak."

Shaprio nodded. "Yes. This year, Nesbitt arranged for us to be more involved with the Solomon Group, and we got a large grant to continue our studies here. Because of the grants from the Solomon Group, we got a matching grant from the federal government, the NSF, as well. That's when Ms. North gave us permission to come and continue our studies. There are some extremely interesting features in those caverns."

"You mean the ancient cave drawings, the rock formations, poisonous mushrooms, and the gold?"

Shaprio stuttered "Y... you... you know about the gold?"

"Yep."

Natalie tensed. "You mean you knew about the gold but somehow forgot to mention that little detail to me?"

"Yes," Shaprio said. "The Solomon Group was extremely interested in that and said if we wanted the money, then we couldn't tell anyone about it, including you, until it was explored further."

Natalie leaned forward. "Wait a minute, Professor. How much more involved were you with the Solomon Group?"

"About six months or so ago, we were made junior members of the board of directors. But the strange thing is, we were given reports to look at, voting forms to consider, and to provide our opinions and votes on some issues, but we never went to an actual board meeting."

"Didn't that seem weird? I'm not a big business person, just an actress, but that would have seemed real strange to me."

"Yes," Dr. Shaprio shrugged, "but we had our teaching and field work to do and didn't worry about it. It wasn't our main job, so we treated it as a way to secure research funding. As professors, we need to secure a certain amount of grants and publish every year. It was only recently that we discovered the Solomon Group has its main office and a bank account in the Caribbean. It's in the Cayman Islands. Why would they do that except to avoid taxes and some U.S. laws? Recently, we found out, quite by accident, from something Mrs. Blair said, that Calvary Evangelical Chapel's headquarters is also there, and they have the same bank and corporate officers."

Virginia looked up from her notes as she heard the kitchen door open and the sound of the paramedic's gurney being taken out. "Must be taking Heller to the hospital."

Linda stood and stepped to the side window. "Yeah, he's being loaded into the ambulance, and Mrs. Blair, in handcuffs, is being stuffed into a patrol car. I think I'll mosey to the kitchen and see what Andy and Detective Grover are doing."

Virginia looked at the hallway. "I think Andy is with Mr. Weedon. Check will you?"

"Sure." Linda moved to the hall and disappeared, her footsteps padding down the hall.

Natalie looked at Dr. Morrison. "You haven't said anything."

Morrison cleared his throat. "My colleague is covering everything quite nicely."

Shaprio rubbed his forehead. "Why don't you fill in the rest, Dr. Morrison?"

Virginia chuckled. "Being somewhat formal, are we?"

"Force of habit."

Morrison raised an eyebrow then folded his hands in his lap. "Well, once we discovered this strange confluence of organizations, we got nervous. We tried to investigate. One afternoon, at a meeting at the church, we found copies of our maps and research data. We hadn't provided the church with them. Now we knew that the church and the Solomon Group was one and the same and had stolen from us. On the maps, we had noted a special geologic feature."

Virginia raised an eyebrow. "The volcanic rock formations and the Gold?"

Morrison nodded. "We were afraid we had been... been... snookered, for lack of a better term, and may be inadvertently part of something illegal. We had heard that someone else knew of the gold before us. Nesbitt was trying to find out who some group called The Arum was. He said he heard the name was used in some document and may be on the computer file. He was afraid it was a competitor. He obviously didn't know arum is Latin for gold."

Shaprio nodded. "We tried, as board members to inquire about things. We were told to mind our own business and not say anything to anyone, or we could, and would, be implicated in something that would ruin our careers. We didn't know what to do."

Morrison interjected, "Then, Nesbitt was murdered. We panicked and went to Reverend Heller. Instead of being the little soft spoken... ahh..."

"Wimp?" Natalie said.

"Yes." Morrison nodded. "For lack of a better word. Instead of being the quiet little mouse like usual, he said we needed to accept the funding, just stick to our research, report our findings directly to him, and not interfere. He said there were a couple of people he needed to attend to and fast; then things would sort themselves out. If we stayed out of the way, we'd be okay."

"You'd be okay?" Virginia gave him a questioning look. "All of a sudden Heller is the head honcho at the church?"

"Yes."

"Who's he supposed to take care of?"

"We don't know."

Natalie tensed. "Nesbitt was after a computer file my cousin had. It had something to do with a quilt book and maybe something else. What do you know about that?"

Morrison and Shaprio exchanged confused expressions. Morrison spoke. "Nothing really. But we heard it had to do with that quilt book you mentioned, and Nesbitt wanted that file. He was blackmailing some of the church members and some outside people, and the file may have been something he needed to use against someone."

Natalie frowned. "You knew he was blackmailing people and didn't think of calling the police?"

"And tell them what? We heard rumors that there were blackmail and other scandals in the church, but we can't tell them anything specific. If they investigated, they wouldn't get very far."

Virginia rubbed her forehead, and let out a sigh. "Okay, then why are you here in Natalie's house with people cooking poison?"

Shaprio chuckled. "Misfortune really. We were getting increasingly nervous. So we went to see Mrs. Blair. She's always been nice to us. She's also big in the church and the Solomon Group, so we figured maybe she'd give us some direction or ideas as to how to extricate ourselves from the whole thing."

Virginia stopped writing. "What did she say?"

"Well, she was packing some things when we entered her office. On her desk rested an old, leather-bound notebook and a copy of our map to Ms. North's land. The book was open, and I noticed it was like a cookbook; only it was for making toxic and hallucinogenic substances. She quickly closed it and stuffed it in the box she had on her desk. I asked about it when Reverend Heller came in. He said they were investigating the use of natural substances for religious purposes."

"You believed that?"

"No." Shaprio took a breath. "I then asked about the map and the red lines that had been added. He said they were just things the church needed to know about Ms. North's land. Heller told us once they had what they needed in some computer file, and took care of a couple of loose ends; everything would be okay. He said they were going to come here and we should join them to ensure ourselves it was all above board. When he thought they were out of earshot, he said to Mrs. Blair that you and your friends were not at home and would be taken care of. We made some excuses not to come, but that's when Mrs. Blair threatened us with her small pistol."

"Pistol?" Natalie's eyes widened. "She had a gun?"

Virginia looked up from her notes. "Yes. Detective Grover relieved her of it earlier."

"Oh. Okay. So, what happened next?"

"We arrived at a gate to your land about a quarter mile down the road in one of the church vans. As we were getting out, we heard a rather loud explosion coming from the direction we were headed. We also heard a noise like an engine roaring toward us from that direction. Mrs. Blair was furious and said the people responsible for that explosion acted without her authorization, as usual, and would pay for that serious indiscretion. We quickly climbed back into the van and drove into a clump of trees further down the road. We climbed the fence. Heller led us to a rock outcropping and fiddled with something. Then a fake boulder opened, and we climbed down into a tunnel. It took us here."

Natalie tensed. "Heller knew about that tunnel, and you didn't?"

Morrison shrugged. "Yes. He knew exactly where it was. We had no idea it existed."

"Go on."

"Like I said, Heller knew you weren't home. We were told to come in here and make ourselves comfortable and not to disturb them. Oh, yeah, Heller said not to open any doors because you had them alarmed. Then, he and Mrs. Blair went into the kitchen. Every few minutes they'd stick their heads in here to see what we were doing."

Natalie tilted her head. "You didn't find this suspicious?"

Shaprio nodded. "Yes."

"Why didn't you leave, or call someone?"

"The storm had come in by then, and the phone is out. We tried that. We didn't have a car, and the lightening was furious. Walking wasn't an option. At least it wasn't a good one. And like I said, Mrs. Blair had a small, two-barreled pistol she made sure we saw. If we ran out into the rain, we'd set off the alarm and probably get shot. They said we were involved, and if we tried to tell anyone, we'd go to jail. With the storm, lightning, the threat of prison, and her gun, we figured we were better off staying here. That's when you arrived."

Virginia furrowed her brow, thinking, then looked at Natalie. "You know, they may be telling the truth."

"I agree, but who tried to kill us, and why?"

Virginia finished her notes, closed the notebook and glanced at Natalie. "Remember Mr. Blake?"

"The big nasty guy who assaulted me, you reduced to a whimpering fool, and broke his arm?"

"Yeah, that's him. He was one of the people who tried to kill us."

Natalie looked at the two nervous professors, then back at Virginia. "What do we do now? For that matter, what do we do with them?"

Virginia rubbed her chin. "I think I know the identity of the second person who tried to kill us. It's the same person Heller and Blair are blackmailing. Now to prove it."

Natalie pointed at the professors. "And what about them?"

"It is a dark and stormy night, isn't it?" Virginia watched the shocked expressions on their faces. "I'll have Detective Grover take them for further questioning and hold them until we get to the bottom of this. In the meantime, you, Linda, Andy, and I have some work to do."

CHAPTER 28

Virginia watched Detective Grover take Drs. Morrison and Shaprio, along with Weedon, without handcuffs, out to the waiting Sheriff's vehicles. She turned from the window and faced Natalie, Linda, and Andy standing in a semi-circle by the fireplace. "Well, they're on their way to the sheriff's office for debriefing."

Andy turned and looked at Virginia. "They actually going to be arrested and put in jail tonight?"

"Grover said he wanted to talk some more to Weedon, but will probably release him. As for the two professors, I think they were duped and used. They live in a whole other world. I asked Grover to do a background check for any criminal records, and if they don't have any, then to hold them for now as material witnesses. They have been cooperative. If they really were bamboozled, then they'll make great witness later, and won't have a criminal record."

"I sure hope so. I liked them." Linda moved to a chair and sat. "Looks like it was a no show for Jenny or anyone else about the computer file. Maybe it was the church folks on the whole thing."

"If anyone else came last night and saw all the lights on and the emergency vehicles around I bet they high tailed it away."

Linda shrugged. "I guess you're right. Okay, who do we go after next?"

Andy started for the hall. "While you ladies scheme, I'm going to set an alarm on that new tunnel entrance we were in, and add motion detection alarms in the basement."

Natalie touched his arm and gave him a quick kiss on the cheek. "Thank you, Andy. You've been great."

Virginia watched Andy leave, and then sat on the couch across from Linda. Natalie sat next to her. Virginia grinned. "Okay, here's what I'm thinking."

Grover slid his chair back from the metal table in the sheriff's interview room, looked at Drs. Morrison and Shaprio and crossed his arms. "Okay, gentlemen, your statements to me match what you told Special Agent Clark and with the little we got from Reverend Heller and Mrs. Blair. Your statements are being typed. We should have them for you to sign shortly."

Dr. Morrison gave a weak smile. "We're trying to be as helpful as possible. Will that help us with a judge?"

Grover started to speak when the door opened and a uniformed deputy entered with a man in a brown sport coat, and an open-necked shirt carrying a beat-up leather briefcase. The deputy spoke, "This is Mr. Jamison; he's their lawyer." He handed Jamison's card to Grover.

Grover rose and shook Jamison's hand. He glanced at his watch, 4:05. "Rather early for you, isn't it counselor?"

"Yes. Someone from the Smithsonian phoned the president of the university in the middle of the night requesting they send me. I'd like to speak with the professors. Have they been read their rights, and what are the charges?"

"Yes. The federal officer who spoke to them gave them their rights in the field, and so did I here at the station. They have given us a statement, and it is being typed now for their signatures."

"I see." Jamison set his briefcase on the table. "And the charges?"

"Originally, violation of the federal Antiquities Act, conspiracy to manufacture controlled substances, both federal felonies, burglary, another felony, and trespassing and some conspiracy charges. But they willingly cooperated, the special agent believed them, and so do I. That, and the fact they have no prior arrests, the federal charges have been put on hold, and the owner of the property declined to prosecute. Right now, they are material witnesses for a joint county and federal investigation. No formal charges are filed, yet. If they cooperate and act as witnesses for the state, my guess is none will be filed."

The lawyer stood with a shocked look on his face. "Has the U.S. Attorney been notified?"

"Yes, and he is on board with it, as is the county DA."

"You serious?" Jamison swallowed. "You actually got the U.S. Attorney and the DA out of bed in the wee hours this morning to get this done?"

"The special agent did. She doesn't want to hurt the professors' reputations or jeopardize their jobs if all this pans out. She and I think they were conned. She said since they helped us, she didn't want to hurt them."

Jamison plopped onto a chair. "This is one for the books. So, my clients are free to go?"

"As soon as they sign their statements. Oh, there are a couple of other conditions."

Jamison's eyebrow shot up. "Such as?"

Suspicious Threads

"Your clients can't leave Williamson County until further notice or without prior permission, and they are not to speak with, or associate with, anyone from Calvary Evangelical Chapel or the Solomon Group. If anyone from there does contact them, they are to notify me, or Special Agent Clark, immediately."

Jamison looked at his clients sitting across the table. They nodded. Jamison shrugged. "I guess I can't ask for more at this juncture. My clients agree to the conditions, and so do I. I would appreciate it if you'll keep me apprised of the case."

"Yes. I'll let you know of any changes, Counselor."

At eleven o'clock the following day, Linda strolled into Quilters' Corner quilt store and looked over the fabric on display. Three other women were browsing. She selected two bolts and a few yards of batting. She selected a couple of spools of high-end cotton thread and went to the cutting table.

Jenny Parker stood there finishing cutting some fabric on a blue cutting board for another customer, before turning to Linda. "Hello, Linda," Jenny said in an icy voice. "What can I do for you?"

Linda handed Jenny the bolts of fabric. "I need two yards of this one, one yard of that one, and three yards of the batting, please."

Jenny took the bolts and started to measure them. "I've been meaning to ask, how is the assessment of Ann Greenwald's quilts and her things in her studio coming along?"

"Virginia and I are almost done. Probably another few days and we'll have it all wrapped up."

"I heard Virginia found some mysterious encrypted file on Ann's computer and had managed to open it. Did it contain anything interesting that warranted being locked up so well?"

Linda set the spools of thread on the table. "Just the original manuscript of Ann's book she was writing, and something about the Arum. And another thing, Virginia and her husband found some sort of geologic formation down in a cavern on Natalie's ranch that they think may be valuable. Oh, and we caught Reverend Heller and Mrs. Blair manufacturing some sort of mushroom poison."

Jenny stopped. She placed her shaking hands on the table. "Mushroom poison?"

"Yeah. From some poison cookbook. They said it wasn't theirs. Can you believe that?"

"Where is the... the poison cookbook, now?"

"Virginia has it at her place, and later today she's planning to send it to a lab for some special tests she wants." Linda fiddled with the spools of thread. "Virginia said, if the tests are done right, they should tell her who owns the book."

"Oh. Virginia's okay?" Jenny swallowed. "Can they do that, you know, with the tests?"

"I guess so. From all the CSI type shows on TV, my guess is yes, but I'm not an expert." *She wants to know if Virginia's okay? I'll let it ride and see what happens.*

"I know what you mean. You said something about Arum. Who, or what, are they?"

Linda chuckled. "Hell if I know. It was a side note in the file. No details. Heller and the Blair woman were really concerned about it though. You have any ideas?"

"Me. No. I never heard of it before." Jenny took a breath. "Probably another developer like Mr. Weedon who wants Ms. North's land real bad." Jenny dropped the rotary cutter, and then quickly snatched it up. "You said Virginia found something that may be valuable underground, maybe that's why Mr. Weedon wanted the land so bad." Jenny resumed cutting the fabric. "I'm glad everything went so well with Ann's quilting assessment."

"Once we got everything organized, it went pretty fast."

"You said it had something Ann wrote on it?"

"Yes. Some sort of manuscript." Linda picked up the cut, folded fabric, and the sales ticket. "I guess I'll be going. Natalie and I are meeting at Virginia's for lunch just before we head to the crime lab. Have a nice day." Linda walked to the checkout counter, paid, and left the store. As she climbed into her car, she glanced over her shoulder and saw Jenny, with a phone in her hand, watching her. Linda started the car. *Couldn't be more subtle if I'd hit her with a bat.*

CHAPTER 29

After lunch, Virginia stood next to Natalie, looking out her front window, watching Linda arrive and hurry into Natalie's house.

Virginia turned as Linda flew in the door. "How'd it go?"

Linda took a second to catch her breath. "I think everything went as planned. Jenny seemed confused that you were okay. Probably because she blew up the cave entrance. The idea that the poison book was going for some scientific examination made her very nervous. She asked about the Arum, the locked files, and what was in them. When I mentioned Ann's manuscript; Jenny's hands shook. She asked if I knew what Arum was all about. She tried to pass it off as another developer like Weedon." Linda looked at Virginia and Natalie. "Okay, now that I've rattled her cage, what do we do next?"

"Where did you tell her I'd be with the poison book?"

"At your house."

"Good. Let's go to my house. I'll pick up a cookbook to use as bait and wrap it up. We'll stall until about two-thirty this afternoon, and then casually drive toward the university. Let's see who shows up."

Natalie shifted from foot to foot. "What do you want me to do?"

"Set your alarms, get your gun, and watch for anyone lurking around looking for a way to get into that tunnel we found."

Linda raised her hand. "Wait, I told Jenny we'd all be at your house for lunch."

Virginia took a breath. "Well, we can always say Natalie had something else to do. I think we may get a visitor trying to get into that cavern by way of the tunnel." She looked at Natalie. "I'd like you here to watch things and sound the alarm if my hunch is correct."

Natalie frowned. "Couldn't they get in by way of that fake rock covering the other end of it? I'd never see them there. It's too far away."

"No. Andy and Detective Grover sealed it from the inside. The way we went in was blown up, so, anyone trying to enter would have to use your basement, or find another way."

"Weedon got there using some other entrance."

"Yes. But get the tablet computer Andy gave you for the alarm system. He also set a motion alarm at the cross tunnel junction point that leads to the one we took, and the others. It's running on batteries for now but will stay live for a few months. He'll connect it to the power line later. If anyone is using the same tunnel system Weedon did, the alarm will go off. It will register on the computer, and you'll know. Call me or Detective Grover."

Natalie nodded. "Okay."

Virginia grabbed her backpack and opened the door. "Linda, shall we go? We've got some preparing to do." As Linda walked out, Virginia turned toward Natalie. "If the alarms go off, just note which ones and call us. Don't try to be a hero. These people are dangerous."

"You don't need to remind me. I'll keep an eye on the computer."

"Good."

"Oh, one more question before you go. If the alarms go off in the tunnel or in the cavern, will they just alert me, or will they sound off down there, too?"

Virginia grinned. "The noise from them will wake the dead. In the confines of the tunnels, the type of sound, and the volume Andy programmed into them, it will cause severe damage to the ears and nervous systems of the intruder, and leave them temporarily incapacitated. All you need to do is call for help."

Natalie smiled. "Good. Andy is a great guy for doing all this."

"He really likes you. He's enjoying all this, trust me." She glanced at Linda. "Shall we go to my place and get ready for a possible visit by some unscrupulous people?"

"Yes, I think so." They walked to Virginia's car and left.

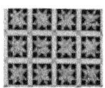

Jenny Parker hung up the telephone and dialed another number. After three rings, a male voice answered. She spoke with a nervous quiver to her voice. "Virginia has the poison book. She's having some lab tests done on it. We need to move fast. Blair and Heller are in jail being held on a million-dollar cash bond, so they are out of the picture for now." She listened, and then said, "I don't care about the damn church at this point. I'm only interested in getting that poison book and the computer file before any more problems develop. I'll take care of it. I have some motivated help. The ranch isn't something I care about and never did. If you're that concerned about it, you handle it yourself." She hung the phone up a little more abruptly than she planned.

She rose from her desk and strolled into the quilt shop. "Judy, I have to go out for a while, watch the store for me, will you?"

Judy glanced at Jenny, nodded, and then went back to checking out a customer.

Jenny went back to her office, picked up her purse, and walked out the rear door into an alley. As she went to her car, her cell phone rang. She answered it. "You know where Virginia Davies Clark lives, right? Okay, I'll meet you there. You get to the rear door and wait for my signal. I'll leave her to you; just don't get in my way." She hung up and started the car.

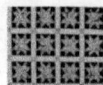

Virginia stood at the cutting table in her quilt room at home wrapping an old cookbook in brown paper. She looked at Linda. "You got that special file loaded on the red flash drive done?"

Linda looked over the monitor on the laptop. "Almost. Give me another five minutes."

"Okay. I need to get the SRH from my safe and put it on the finger of some surgical gloves for us, so it does its job, but not on us."

Linda frowned. "Huh? What is SRH?"

Virginia chuckled. "Remember last year when I went to Central America with one of the anthropologists from my museum?"

"Yeah. It was part of some investigation you were on. Something about a map being sewn in an old quilt. If I remember right, *Trail of Threads* was the code name."

"Yes." Virginia turned and leaned on the cutting table. "While we were down there, we found a certain shrub who's sap, if it came in contact with human skin, or any part of the body, caused severe gastrointestinal distress. It quickly makes your bowels unload their contents in a very violent and extremely painful manner."

"Like a laxative?"

"Yeah, but more like a shit volcano and it can... no... does hurt a lot. The victim is completely out of action for about an hour. Then, they are so weak they can't do anything for a few more hours. They should use this before a colonoscopy."

Linda smiled. "That bad? What does SRH stand for?"

"We named it that while we were down there in the jungle. It causes the proverbial shit storm. The natives had a term for it we couldn't pronounce, so we called it the Shit Releasing Hormone or SRH. The natives mix it with some liquid that makes it work faster, but we couldn't find out what it was. A chemist friend of Andy's at the university said to mix it with a chemical solvent called DMSO to get the same effect."

"Cute. How much does it take, and how long does it take, to react?"

"A drop on the skin, and about ten to twenty seconds."

Linda looked at the computer and pulled the flash drive out. "All done.

You better get your shit stuff together. It's almost show time, if we're right."

Virginia looked at the clock above her cutting table. "You're right. Turn on the CS file and shut down the computer. Put that sticker I gave you on the lid of the laptop. "I'll get the SRH and be right back. Oh, take the laptop, the flash drive, and the wrapped cookbook to the kitchen, will you?"

Linda watched Virginia hurry out of the room then looked at the sticker Virginia gave her. It had Ann's name and address on it. She shrugged and attached it to the lid. She gathered up the materials, took them to the kitchen and placed them on the table. She went to the living room and looked out the window.

Virginia proceeded to her safe and removed a small brown bottle. She carefully took it to a bathroom where she put on a rubber glove and smeared some of the SRH on the middle finger. She pulled out a small voice recorder, switched it on, and put it in her pocket. Then she picked up another glove and the bottle and headed for the kitchen to find Linda.

Linda turned from the living room window as Virginia strolled in. "Two cars just parked on opposite sides of the street on both sides of your house. One has a woman behind the wheel. The other has two men in it."

Virginia crossed the room and looked where Linda pointed. "Okay, let's gather up the stuff. We'll see what they do. But first, put this on."

Linda pulled the glove on and held her hand out. Virginia placed a few drops of the SRH on the middle finger. "Be careful and don't get any of this on you." Virginia hurried back to her safe and placed the bottle inside then returned to the living room and led Linda into the kitchen.

They placed the laptop, flash drive, and book into a cloth shopping bag and started for the back door when the doorbell rang. Virginia shook her head. "Looks like show time came a little earlier than planned." She put the bag back on the table and unlocked the rear door. Then, they walked to the front door and opened it. Jenny Parker stood in front of them holding a small, silver, semiautomatic aimed at Linda's middle. Linda stood shaking, and raised her hands in the air. Jenny looked at Virginia with a raised eyebrow. "Well, looks like I got both of you."

Virginia tilted her head. "I guess so."

Jenny shook her head, "You weren't killed in the cave after all. You lived a charmed life, until now." Virginia pointed at the gun. "Put that silly gun away, Jenny. I know why you're here."

"You do?"

"Yeah. You want Ann Greenwald's computer, the flash drive, and the poison cookbook."

"Right. How did you know?"

"Look, if you continue to stand there with a gun in your hand for much longer, a neighbor is liable to call the police. Come inside." Virginia stepped back and pulled Linda with her. "You can put your hands down Linda." They walked to the middle of the room. "Where are your two henchmen?"

"At the back of the house, in case you try to run out that way." Jenny shook her head. "I thought all of you would be killed in that cavern. I was shocked when I saw Linda at the store. How'd you get out?"

"We followed the underground river and found another maze of tunnels and caves. We managed to get out a couple of hours later."

Jenny wet her lips. "Did you find anything interesting down there?"

"Yes. A poison mushroom farm."

"Oh. You found it. Anything else?"

"Like what?"

Jenny began to breathe harder. "I don't know, unusual rock formations?"

Virginia gave her a surprised look. "Yeah, lots of funny and colorful rocks. Quartz and some other stuff. Anything in particular, you are interested in?"

"I heard there was gold down there."

Virginia started to laugh. Gold? Honey, this isn't California. It's limestone down there. That's why there are caves around here. What do they teach in Texas schools?"

Jenny tensed. "I was just curious. I had heard that… never mind. Where are Ann's computer, the flash drive, and the poison book?"

"In the kitchen."

Jenny waved the gun around. "Move it to the kitchen, ladies."

Linda, followed by Virginia walked to the kitchen with Jenny bringing up the rear with her pistol.

Virginia stopped and pointed at the table. "They are all in that bag."

Jenny slowly slinked to the table and looked in the bag. She smiled. "Nice of you to package it all up for me." She glanced back into the bag. Why is the book wrapped up?"

"Didn't want to get it contaminated before I got it to the lab."

"Oh. Now, this is what we're going to do. I'm going to open the door and let my friends in. Then, I'm leaving. They will dispose of you two. Can't have you around to tell the cops I was here."

Virginia wrinkled her nose. "Yeah, we might tell them you and Jack Blake blew up the cave entrance with the intention of killing us."

"Yes, but now they'll never know. It's too bad that didn't work."

"Depends on your point of view. If you don't mind, I have a couple of questions."

Jenny sighed. "Okay, but make it quick."

"You killed Ann Greenwald, right?"

Jenny nodded. "Yes. I used the mushroom poison to kill Ann Greenwald. She figured out I stole her manuscript and published her book under my name. That file has the manuscript and a file about Ms. North's property. It is more valuable than she thought."

Virginia nodded. "I know. I read them."

"You have? You knew?"

"Yes." Virginia rubbed her chin. "Why? Couldn't you and Ann have worked something out?"

"Not really. I stole her manuscript and published her book. She'd been talking about it for a couple of years, but never did it. But when she saw it in print she went ballistic. I should have known she'd see it. I tried to negotiate something with her, you know, split the proceeds, change it so she's a co-author, but she just wouldn't listen to reason. She was going to sue me and ruin everything. I had to do something."

"I see. How about the church and Natalie's land?"

"Reverend Nesbitt wanted it for the church, especially when a professor at the university told him he found some gold in a cave there. Personally, I don't care about that; I just wanted the computer and file so no one can trace me to Ann's murder. Nesbitt found out about my problem somehow. He was blackmailing me. I couldn't have that, especially from that pious, egotistical, jerk. At first, he was real nice, and I felt something for him. But that changed. I discovered he was a total asshole. So he had to go."

"Linda frowned. "So you killed him?"

"Yes. I couldn't go to the police."

Virginia leaned on a chair. "So, the poison book is yours?"

"Yes."

"How'd Mrs. Blair get it?"

"They stole it from me." Jenny moved to the back door and opened it. "Jack, bring your buddy and come in. I'll leave these two to you. Just remember, when you're done, I want no trace of them to be found. Got it?"

Jack Blake walked in followed by a huge man with a blond crew cut, bulging biceps, and a chest that strained his black t-shirt.

Jack's lips curled as he glared at Virginia. His voice was still raspy as he spoke. "This time there ain't any magazines around, bitch."

Jenny turned, and walked out the door, closing it behind her.

Jack pointed at Linda. "You take her and have fun, Neil. I have some unfinished business with this broad." He stepped to Virginia. "Not running or anything? Just wanting ole Jack to punish you? I'm going to make this as painful as I can."

"The last time we met, you didn't come out of it in good shape. You really want a rematch?"

"Oh, yeah." Jack's eyes narrowed. "I've been dreaming about this."

"You're going to have a nightmare." Virginia nodded. "That's right. Mad Jack Black's dick is so small that women laugh at him, so he likes beating up defenseless women to prove he's macho. I heard you were a laughing stock among the prisoners in jail. And I see you still have the cast on your arm. Nice to have a constant reminder that a woman beat you up, isn't it? Your tiny balls still hurt?"

Jack's face reddened. His jaw tightened. He grabbed Virginia's throat. He spoke through clenched teeth. "I'm going to choke the shit out of you, bitch; then I'll beat you into bloody, unrecognizable, pulp."

Virginia pulled back causing Jack to lean forward. She put her hands on his arms, and then rubbed her gloved finger across his hand.

Jack's eyes widened. His face contorted in agony. He released his grip on Virginia, doubled over in pain and grabbed his abdomen. "What the fu…?"

Virginia clenched his arm and quickly dragged him outside. His bowels cut loose. He fell to the ground as he convulsed and continued to violently fill his pants with excrement. Her nostrils contracted reflexively. The stench was overpowering. "You're outside because you aren't house trained yet."

She turned and ran back into the house. Linda was pinned to the table, bending backward, with the large man, Neil, in front of her. He had a hand on Linda's blouse and another on her throat. She clawed at his face with one hand, and grabbed his arm with her gloved hand. He turned toward the door as Virginia rushed in. His eyes were wide; his jaw hung open. "What'd you do to him?"

Virginia ran toward him.

Neil released his grip on Linda and stepped back. "Stop, or I'll…" His face contorted. "I'll kill both of you."

Virginia snarled. "That was the plan anyway, wasn't it?"

He stood staring past Virginia at Jack writhing in pain on the grass. He reached behind his back and started to pull a black semiautomatic out from under his t-shirt when Virginia slammed into him. He dropped the gun. He reached forward, tried to grab her hair, and then stiffened. His face twisted in pain. He doubled over, grabbed his stomach, and screamed.

Virginia took hold of his right arm. "Linda, grab him and let's get him outside, fast."

Linda took hold of his left arm, and with Virginia, dragged his convulsing, staggering, body into the yard. He fell onto Blake when his bowels cut loose in a violent roar. Linda looked down at the men. "Why's did that SRH stuff take so long with Neil?" She and Virginia carefully peeled off their gloves and tossed them in a garbage container on the patio.

"I don't know. Maybe some of the solvent evaporated. It finally got him though."

"What a mess. I'd love a picture of this." Linda made a distasteful face. "Good God, they really stink. Let's go back inside. Do we need to do anything with them? Tie them up or something?" She glanced back at the two men covered with feces. "I hope not."

"No." Virginia shook her head. "They aren't going anywhere or doing anything, for well over an hour or so. Even then, they'll be too weak to move or cause any trouble. Let's call Detective Grover. Maybe before the good detective gets here, we could hose them down. It'll help the smell."

As they walked back inside, Linda asked, "What about Jenny? How are you going to pin anything on her?"

Virginia pulled her small recorder out of her pocket. "Got it all on this."

"How about the computer and the flash drive?"

"The computer is an old one Andy had at the University of California at Irvine. They got new ones, and the university said he could keep the old laptop. I put some fake files on it so Jenny would think she got all of Ann's files. If she really looks at them, she'll realize she's been had. But that flash drive, if she puts it on a computer and opens it, it will load a program that will allow us to track it and the computer and also secure all the files on the computer. Then, she won't be able to use the computer or the flash drive without the password, and won't be able to turn the computer off."

"But when she finds that old cookbook of yours, she'll have a fit."

"She'll probably panic because she'll that think we're dead and the real poison book is at a crime lab."

"Good." Linda went to the phone and called Detective Grover. When she finished, she looked at Virginia. "You were pretty cool with Jenny and her gun. I was a wreck. Why didn't you get nervous?"

"I noticed the safety was on. Also, when she flashed it outside, I spotted the little window on the slide that indicates there is, or isn't, a round in the chamber. There wasn't. The gun wasn't loaded. She'd have to release the safety and rack the slide to be able to fire it, and that would give us a chance to disarm her. I don't think she knew it wasn't loaded. The way she was handling it, I figured she didn't know anything about guns, and she sure as hell couldn't fire it." Virginia looked outside at the two men writhing in their own excrement on the grass. Her cell phone rang. Virginia pulled it out of her pocket and looked at the screen. *Natalie? What happened?*

CHAPTER 30

Virginia looked at Linda. "Oh boy, just missed a call from Natalie."

"Any message?" Linda moved closer to Virginia and looked the phone's screen. "I hope she's okay."

Virginia hit redial. "Better call her, something could have happened."

She waited four rings then Natalie answered. "Virginia! Glad you called. An alarm went off. I called Detective Grover, and he's sending some deputies."

Virginia tightened her grip on the phone. "Which alarm?"

"Multiple ones. They are in the tunnels and cavern where we were. I checked the basement, and everything is secure down there."

"Okay." Virginia took a breath. "As soon a Grover and company gets here, Linda and I will hightail it out there to *Borealis*."

Natalie's voice sounded cautious. "Detective Grover's going there? Did something happen? Did Jenny show up?"

"You could say that. Jenny took the bait. She left after threatening us with a gun. We've got everything on a recording."

"Oh! That's good, right?"

"Yeah." Virginia sat on a kitchen chair. "But she brought Blake and a buddy of his to deal with Linda and me. She ordered them to kill us."

"Kill you? Are you and Linda okay?"

"Yes, but Blake and his friend aren't. I'll tell you about it when we get there."

"Okay. I'm not going anywhere."

Virginia looked up at Linda. "Natalie said the alarms went off underground. The sheriff is sending deputies. We'll go there when we wrap things up here."

"Good. How about Jenny?"

"I'll give the recorder to Grover. He can pick her up." Virginia sighed. "Now that this is over, my nerves are unraveling. Happens every time."

"Stay there; I'll get you some water." Linda hurried to the sink and returned with a glass of water. Virginia drank it and sat back. "I can't wait to see the expression on Grover's face when he sees those two in the yard."

Eight minutes later Detective Grover arrived followed by two marked sheriff's cars and the county paramedics. They all followed Virginia and Linda through the fence gate and into the yard, stopping well away from the odiferous two men groaning and writhing in excrement. Grover looked at Virginia. "What the hell happened to them?"

"They attacked us and were trying to kill us." She smiled. "But I think they had bad sushi for lunch before they got here."

Grover rubbed his forehead. "You want me to believe they came down with food poisoning at the same time, at your house, while trying to murder you two?"

Virginia stared at the men, then grinned at Grover. "Jenny Parker ordered them to kill Linda and me, but like I said, they must have had lunch before they came. You know, some of those food trucks deserve the term roach coach."

Grover, the deputies, and the paramedics looked at the two men. The senior medic laughed. "Okay, we'll let the docs at the hospital figure it out. But we need to check them first."

Linda smiled. "It'll be messy."

The lead medic glanced at his partner. "We have some jumpsuits, plastic gloves, foot covers and face masks we can use. Better get the Vaseline out, too." The men suited up, smeared Vaseline on their dust masks to diminish the odor, and examined the Blake and Neil. Finished, they stripped off their suits, stuffed them in plastic garbage bags, and nodded at Grover. "The lady is right. Looks like they've got bad stomach cramps, maybe food poisoning, and extreme dehydration. They are also very weak. We'll need to transport to the hospital."

The second paramedics asked, "How are we supposed to get them to the hospital? They aren't going in my ambulance like that. It'll take a month to clean and disinfect it."

Linda stepped close to the medic. "We'll hose them down for you."

The medic glanced at Linda with a smile. "That would probably help. What really happened to them? Poisoned?"

"Bad sushi."

Grover stepped close to the men and bent down. "You both are under arrest." He read them their rights, then looked at Virginia with apprehension. "Do you think there's any need to handcuff them?"

Virginia shook her head. "Not for about an hour, and even then, the Girl Scouts could handle them."

"Bad sushi my ass." Grover shook his head, straightened, and stared at the two men who started to moan and twitch on the filthy ground. "Whatever you did to them, you did it well."

"Thank you, Detective."

"You're not going to tell me what you did to protect yourselves, are you?"

"I already told you—"

"I know, bad sushi." Grover motioned for the paramedics to come close. "How about I get a sheriff's pickup truck, and we transport them in that? I can run it through a coin car wash afterward."

The medics looked at each other and shrugged. "Why not? It's not like they are having heart attacks, but one of us will have to suit up again."

Virginia grinned. "Better tell the hospital to have a fire hose ready to clean them up and to put newspapers down on the floor as they come in."

The lead medic laughed. "Get the truck, and let's get them out of here."

Grover keyed the mike on his radio and called for a sheriff's truck.

Twenty minutes later, after Linda hosed the men down, they left in the truck for the hospital. She and Virginia returned to the house.

Virginia grabbed her backpack from her quilt studio and met Linda by the garage door. "We'd better hot foot it to Natalie's place.

Fifteen minutes later Virginia came to a sudden stop under a sprawling old oak tree next to Natalie's garage. She noted three sheriff's vehicles parked near the house. Virginia and Linda jumped out of the car and raced toward the house.

Natalie met them at the kitchen door. "Come in. The sheriff's deputies just went into the cave tunnels through the hidden basement door we found. I haven't heard from them, yet."

Virginia nodded. "Let's wait in the cellar. I'm dying to find out who went in the caves. Maybe more of Jenny's friends."

The three women climbed down the basement stairs and stood around waiting. A while later they heard footsteps coming from the open passageway. A deputy walked through, followed by a limping Dr. Aaron Shaprio and Dr. Charles Morrison, both covered with dirt and wearing handcuffs, and two more deputies.

Virginia shook her head. "I'm very disappointed Dr. Morrison. I believed you when you said you were duped. Now it seems you were behind the growing station for the mushrooms."

Morrison frowned, raised his shackled hands, and pointed at his ear. A trickle of blood ran down his jaw.

A deputy shrugged. "We found them on the ground rolling around in pain. They were holding their ears. I think their hearing is slowly returning, but they said they have bad headaches and their ears hurt. We'll take them to the hospital before we move them to the jail."

"That was my alarms," stated Natalie. "The noise they give off can stop an elephant."

Virginia stepped closer to the two professors. "Dr. Morrison, you seem to be involved with the poison mushrooms even after what you told me."

Morrison slowly nodded, then swallowed. "I can barely hear you. I can explain about the mushrooms."

"I'm sure you can, but this time you'll need to do your explaining to a DA." She looked at Dr. Shaprio. "Looking for the gold?"

He nodded. "Yes. Can you speak up, please?"

"Sure." Virginia raised her voice. "You do realize that any minerals found here, especially gold, belong to Ms. North, don't you?"

"Yes. But I wanted to make sure this was real, and get an idea of the quality of the find."

"Is it real? There isn't any gold around here, is there?"

"Normally no. But this is kind of special. This area is mostly limestone. But there are a few ancient volcanoes in the area. For example, there's one in south Austin. There are ancient rifts or faults running through this part of Texas, as well. What we have here may be an epithermal vein."

Natalie moved closer to him. "What's that?"

Dr. Shaprio cleared his throat. "Epithermal refers to mineral deposits that form in association with hot waters. The deposits form within 1 km of the surface from minerals in very hot water. The rising hot water carries dissolved gold salts and other elements. The water boils about 300 meters below the surface and hydrogen sulfide gas escapes. This causes the gold to precipitate. The boiling zone is the target for mineral exploration. Veins commonly host the economic minerals. I spotted quartz with bits of gold, then found larger pieces."

"But it's mostly limestone down there."

"Yes. The volcano is ancient and most likely dead, now."

Natalie brightened. "So, there's a volcano on my land and possible some gold."

Shaprio nodded. "Yes, and maybe some other minerals as well."

Linda titled her head. "After the explosion down there, that spring water started to get hot."

Natalie nodded. "You're right." She looked at Shaprio. "Could that be some sort of geothermal thing you mentioned from the magma under there?"

Shaprio shrugged. "Possibly. But from what I've seen, that vein isn't very rich in minerals. You'll get some gold; how much I don't exactly know. It would need to be assayed. But it most likely won't develop into a full-scale gold mine."

One of the deputies looked at Shaprio. "If there is gold and anything else down there it belongs to this lady. What were you doing down there?"

Dr. Morrison spoke. "My colleague found the igneous rock formation and the quartz from the picture of a map when we were doing the earlier explorations with Ms. North's cousin's approval. We based our map that Ms. North has, on it. Dr. Shaprio mentioned it to Reverend Nesbitt. The

Reverend supplied some funding and helped get us grants from the Solomon Group to continue our work. He obviously knew about the gold when he pestered Ms. North, and her cousin, for the land. However, once he heard there might be gold here, he wouldn't listen to us when we said there might not be a lot of it. He became obsessed with getting the land. When he heard Mr. Weedon knew about the gold too, and wanted the land, he had a fit. Then he died. Reverend Heller wouldn't listen to us either when Dr. Shaprio said it probably wasn't a rich vein. Reverend Heller also has gold fever. He sent us back to see what the conditions were since the explosion. We came back to finish what we started."

Virginia stood, listening, and then said, "How about the mushrooms?"

"Yeah, that." Morrison shook his head. "Well, we had nothing to do with them. The times we went down there exploring before, we found wild poisonous mushrooms near the entrance in one of the caves. But they were nothing like the mushroom farm that's down there now. When we'd see Ms. Jenny Parker, she asked a lot of questions about natural poisons that may be hard to trace. She said it was for a book. During a party at the church we were invited to, I mentioned seeing a book on poisons at an antique store in south Austin and told her about the poisonous mushrooms we saw in the cave. She must have found the book and the mushrooms. After that, she didn't say, or ask anything. Later, when Ms. North's cousin died of mushroom poisoning, and then Reverend Nesbitt died of the same thing, I got nervous. When you mentioned the mushroom farm, I got even more anxious and wanted to go see if it was true. The mushroom garden I mean." He looked at the deputies. "May I ask what we're being charged with?"

The deputy answered. "Trespassing, and suspicion of murder."

Natalie rubbed her forehead. "Deputy, is it legal to have those mushrooms here?"

A sheriff's sergeant nodded. "Yes, ma'am. There is nothing illegal about them being here. It's just illegal to cultivate them to use to murder someone."

"Okay. But I think I'll destroy them as quick as I can."

The deputy held up his hand. "Ms. North, please don't touch them. We'll send some lab people to remove them. They could be evidence in two murders. I've got police tape around them."

Natalie's eyes widened. "No problem. I won't touch them. You can have them. The sooner you take them, the better I'll like it. I think Detective Grover has a sample… but you can have all the rest."

Linda stepped closer to the professors. "If Jenny wanted the mushrooms, what were Reverend Heller and Mrs. Blair doing with the cookbook and trying to extract the poison from the mushrooms?"

Morrison shook his head. "I don't know. That was strange. We asked, but they wouldn't tell us."

Virginia's cell phone rang. "Hello?"

"Agent Clark, Detective Grover here. The doc's at the hospital can't figure out what happened to the two goons who attacked you and Mrs. Chambers, except they had a violent, severe case of diarrhea. You were right, they are extremely dehydrated and exhausted, and don't have much flora, and… whatever the doc said they should have in their guts. Blake also pulled a muscle. Looks like they'll recover, but will be in the hospital for a while. There aren't enough of the proteins that caused their messy problem left in their blood. It seems they metabolized it pretty fast."

"I told you—"

"Don't say it. I mentioned it to the doc here at the hospital, and he said you were possibly right. So, if the doc is happy with that explanation, I'm good. Officially, you didn't do anything to them. They'll recover and face trial. Can you imagine what Blake's life will be like back in the county jail awaiting trial when the other inmates find out he got bested by the same woman that did him in before?"

"It won't be pretty."

"No, it won't. Oh yeah, I have deputies watching Ms. Parker's place of business and her house. She's at work right now. I just received the arrest warrant from a district judge. Want to go with me to pick her up?"

"Yes. Can I meet you there?"

"How about at that little coffee shop down the block from her store? That way we can go in together and surprise her."

"Can I bring Linda?"

"Bring the New York Philharmonic if you want. See you there in forty-five minutes."

"Okay, we'll be there." She glanced at Linda. "Want to go watch Jenny Parker get arrested?"

Linda brightened. "You bet."

Natalie watched the deputies take Morrison and Shaprio up the stairs to the police cars. She turned to Virginia. "I'm coming, too. I want to see my cousin's murderer arrested."

Virginia nodded. "Let's lock up quickly and head out. Don't forget to set the alarms."

They started for the stairs when Virginia stopped.

Linda and Natalie turned. Linda frowned. "What's wrong?"

Virginia wrinkled her brow. "I'm not sure, but something doesn't add up."

CHAPTER 31

Natalie sat on a folding chair near the stairs and said, "What doesn't add up? Jenny said she murdered my cousin and Reverend Nesbitt, and she tried to have you and Linda murdered, too."

"Right." Linda sat on the bottom step. "What's the problem?"

Virginia leaned against a support column. "You are right, but why were Heller and Blair trying to make more mushroom poison in your kitchen? What really is the professors' role in all this? Were they really duped? Nesbitt was blackmailing Jenny and Weedon, maybe others, and was pushy as hell, so we know he was a nogoodnik. That may have cost him his life." She ran her fingers through her hair. "Nesbitt had motives to get the land. One, he could use it for the church. Two, he could subdivide it and sell it for a tidy profit. Three, he thought there was gold on the land. But was he really behind all this in the first place, or was he a front for someone else? Four, there is still the Solomon Group which is really the church or the other way around. Five, Heller takes the helm of the mega-church immediately after Nesbitt's death. He had a motive. He wanted to be the big honcho but was relegated to a lower position. Is he working for someone else? Six, why did he and Blair need the poison? We really don't know exactly what Blair and Heller's involvement is except that Nesbitt and Blair are on the boards of the church and the Solomon Group, which in reality are the same thing. Seven, is Heller now the head of both organizations? Eight, who are the missing board members?" Virginia took a breath. "And most important, what, or who else are we missing?"

"I don't know." Linda stood. "Maybe when Jenny's arrested we'll get some answers."

Natalie nodded. "I agree. I'd like to see her behind bars anyway. And she hired Mr. Blake and his friend, Neil, to kill you and Linda."

"Jenny's in this really deep, and putting her away will be good, but like I said, what else are we missing?" Virginia slung her backpack up on her shoulder.

Linda turned and started up the stairs. "Let's think about it on the way to Jenny's store."

Natalie and Virginia followed her up the basement stairs.

Virginia turned the car into the parking lot of the coffee shop down the block from *Quilters' Corner* and parked. They climbed out, hurried into the coffee shop, and found Detective Grover sitting in a booth with two handheld radios in front of him. Virginia and Linda slid in across from him as Natalie sat next to him. Virginia looked at Grover. "You look tired, Detective."

"Yeah, you're right." He chuckled. "I need a vacation. This case gets crazier by the minute. We've got Reverend Heller and Mrs. Blair, both big muck mucks in a large church, in county jail. Blake and his buddy are under arrest and in the hospital. A couple of professors are being processed into the jail on lesser charges, and we have a murderer in a store down the block. Maybe this will be the end of the story."

Virginia waved the waitress over. "Three coffees, please." She waited for the waitress to leave then shook her head. "Don't count on that, Detective."

Grover looked at the donut in his hand and sighed. "Arresting Ms. Parker won't close this case?" He sagged in his seat and set the donut on the dish. "Don't tell me you've thought of something else, or someone else, to investigate."

"Arresting Jenny will solve a couple of murders, but there is more to this. Let me explain my concerns." Virginia leaned forward and told Grover her reservations, questions, and theories. She sat back. "What do you think?"

He sat staring at Virginia then looked at Linda and Natalie. "I suppose you two agree with her."

Natalie nodded and patted Grover's arm. "Yep, and don't worry, Detective, we have a plan."

Linda grinned. "Yes, we worked on it driving over here."

Grover looked at his coffee cup. "I think I need something stronger than this." He finished the donut, and then looked at Virginia. "I know I'm going to regret this, but what do you three propose?"

Virginia took a sip of coffee. "First, let's go get Jenny Parker. Then, we move to phase two."

Grover swallowed his coffee in one gulp and wiped his mouth with his paper napkin. "Okay. Phase two is what bothers me."

They paid their bill and exited the coffee shop. They walked the block to *Quilters' Corner* noticing the unmarked police cars and uniformed and plainclothes officers near the front of the shop.

Grover approached a uniformed sergeant. "What's the status?"

"Last information we received was Ms. Parker is in her office in the rear of the building. Her car is out back. There is a locked metal door on the rear of the building and this glass door here. No employees or customers inside. The front door is also locked, and the closed sign is in the window. You didn't want SWAT?"

"No." Grover looked at the building. "This will be a soft takedown. We'll wait for her to exit the building on her own. That'll be safer for our deputies and her. She has a small caliber handgun that we know of. But she's more inclined to kill using poison than firearms. According to Special Agent Clark, she likes to hire the rough stuff and is not familiar with guns, so we have that in our favor."

"The building is alarmed, and according to the security service, it's activated. So, she'll know we're coming if we try to rush her. Oh, we have another problem."

Grover rubbed his forehead. "What's that?"

"We aren't in hot pursuit," the sergeant said. "You have an arrest warrant, but no search warrant. Until we get one, we'll have to wait out here. Maybe she'll leave, and we can grab here on the street. We could also try calling her on the phone and negotiate something."

"Shit."

Virginia cleared her throat. "Gentlemen, may I suggest something?"

Grover and the sergeant turned and looked at her. The sergeant asked, "What do you have in mind?"

"I'll have Natalie call her on the phone and ask if she's seen me or Linda. Natalie can tell her Heller, or Blair, have started to talk to your people, and they now want to speak to me. And she says the cops are looking for Linda and me at places we usually go to, like her shop." Virginia looked past the men at the inside of the shop. "After telling Blake and his pal to murder us, I figure she'll try and escape."

The sergeant turned toward Grover. "I like her idea. Let's get the search warrant started and have Ms. North call Ms. Parker at the same time. Can't hurt."

Grover nodded. "I agree, and it'll help calm my ulcer. Do it."

The sergeant went to a sheriff's patrol car and radioed the information for a search warrant application. Virginia and Grover moved to his car and told Natalie and Linda what they were doing. Natalie pulled her cell phone from her purse and dialed the number for *Quilters' Corner*.

Jenny answered. "Quilter's Corner. We're presently closed."

Natalie nodded and pointed at the phone. She mouthed *it's her*. "Jenny, this is Natalie North. I'm looking for Virginia. Have you seen her?"

"No. Why would I?"

"Well, Detective Grover just called me and said Reverend Heller and

Mrs. Blair are in the county jail and are now cooperating, and they want to talk to Virginia. He said it's a break in the case, and he's got deputies going to places she frequents. I thought maybe she might have gone to your shop. Deputies will probably be there shortly looking for her."

"No, she isn't here, and I don't expect her. If I see her, I'll pass on the message."

"Okay, thanks." Natalie disconnected and looked at the others. "Okay, now what?"

Virginia leaned forward and looked out the windshield. "My guess is she'll either play it cool and not do anything, or she'll box up what she needs, like the poison book, and run. Now we wait."

After five minutes, they saw movement inside the store. Another couple minutes, and the car police radio squawked. "Unit Six to Unit Two, the suspect is exiting the building. She's carrying her purse and a box."

Grover clicked the microphone. "Any sight of a weapon?"

"Negative."

"Grab her. Be careful; she may be armed."

"Ten-four."

They waited; then Unit Six called back. "Suspect in custody. Found her pistol. She wants her lawyer."

"Of course she does. Hold her there. We're coming."

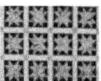

Grover pulled his vehicle into the alley and slowly drove toward the police cars behind *Quilters' Corner* and stopped. He, Virginia, Natalie, and Linda exited the vehicle and quickly stepped toward Jenny and four sheriff's deputies.

Grover walked to the deputy who held Jenny. "Has she been read her rights?"

"Yes, sir."

Virginia stopped in front of Jenny, who was now wearing handcuffs.

Jenny's face was tight and pinched. She looked shocked. Her voice broke. "You. What... how... you're here? You're supposed to be dead."

"Yes. But your plan failed. That's the second time you tried to kill me." Virginia set her backpack on the ground. "Mr. Blake, and his friend Neil, the guys you hired to kill me and Linda, are in the hospital, under guard, and will be going to jail in the next few days. I'm sure they'll talk to try and save their hides. Hiring people to commit murder is a felony. The two counts of attempted murder are felonies, too. Hiring someone to kill a federal agent is a serious federal felony. Assault with a deadly weapon and armed robbery, are both felonies. Put two actual murders on top of all those, and you've got at least seven felonies. All that because of a stolen manuscript? What got into you? Things couldn't be that bad."

"Things definitely got out of control." Jenny stiffened. "I want my lawyer."

"You'll need one. You are looking at the death penalty or life without parole at best. This is Texas, and they happily put *the* needle in people like you. I bet I can get Mr. Blake to talk and incriminate you for paying him to attack Natalie, too. He's a low life Neanderthal who would sell his grandmother out to save his skin." Virginia motioned to the deputy holding Jenny. "Take her away."

After a few steps with the deputy, Jenny stopped. "Wait. I want to talk to Virginia."

Grover motioned to the deputy to bring Jenny back.

He brought Jenny to Virginia and Grover.

Virginia took a breath. "What do you want to talk about?"

Jenny glanced down at the handcuffs, then looked at Virginia. "Can I make a deal?"

"That depends on the content of what you have to tell us, and the mood the DA and the U.S. Attorney are in. But if you give us something of value, Detective Grover and I will mention it to the court. However, right now we can't talk to you since you've asked for a lawyer."

"Okay, okay, I will temporarily waive my rights." She held up her hands. "Can you have them take these off?"

Grover shook his head. "Not out here. As the deputies have told you, you've been arrested on two counts of murder, two counts of attempted murder, and murder for hire and armed robbery. It doesn't get much worse. I'll tell you what, we'll all go to the Sheriff's office, and we can talk in a secure interview room after you've been processed. It'll be more private and comfortable for everyone, and these deputies can get back on patrol."

Jenny nodded and went with the uniformed deputies. Grover turned to Virginia, Natalie, and Linda. "I don't know what she can tell us that will be of much value, but if she's willing to talk, I think we should take her up on it. I'd like Virginia to accompany me. I'm afraid I'm going to have to ask you, Linda, and Natalie, to wait someplace else, and we can discuss what she says later."

Natalie looked at Linda. "Why don't we go shopping and maybe to dinner. Virginia and Detective Grover can find us when they're done."

Linda's face brightened. "Sounds like a plan. I'll call my husband and tell him to get himself a pizza. He thinks pizza's a food group so it won't hurt his feelings any."

Natalie looked at Virginia and smiled. "Give us a call as soon as you can. Wait. Virginia, you drove. Toss me your keys."

Virginia nodded. "Okay. Here's the keys, I'll hitch a ride with Detective Grover." She watched the two women scurry down the alley to the car.

She turned to Grover. "Shall we go to the Sheriff's office? You're driving; they have my car."

"Let's go. I wonder what Ms. Parker thinks she can tell us that will impress the DA and a judge."

"I don't know, but from her change in attitude, I expect it's important."

CHAPTER 32

Virginia paced outside the interview room waiting for Grover to bring Jenny in. Grover arrived with a uniformed deputy and a handcuffed Jenny Parker. Once they entered the room, Grover removed the restraints and had her sit at the table facing the door. He placed a recorder on the table. "Do you mind if I record this conversation?"

Jenny shook her head. "No. But turn it off when I say so."

"Okay." He switched it on. "Ms. Parker, were you read your rights and do you understand them?"

"Yes."

Grover continued, "Ms. Parker, you are waiving your rights at this time?"

"Yes, but I reserve the right to change my mind later."

"Fine."

He and Virginia sat across from her.

Virginia placed a plastic water bottle on the table and leaned back in the steel chair. "Okay, Jenny, what did you want to share with us?"

Jenny looked down at the table, then at Virginia. "Can we cut a deal?"

"Depends. What is the information about?"

Jenny fidgeted in the chair. "Okay. Reverend Nesbitt was hired as the pastor of Calvary Evangelical Chapel. He was good at raising money and had grandiose plans. But he was also a principal at the Solomon Group. They're the organization the church fronts for. There are complicated tax and some religious protections built in that I don't understand. The Solomon Group invests through the church and other shell corporations and businesses they took over. They're a rat's nest of privately held companies with stateside and offshore activities. They have criminal undertakings... like fraud, blackmail, investment and real estate scams, drugs, money laundering, and other things in multiple states. The Solomon Group, and the church have their main offices, their headquarters really, and a bank in the Cayman Islands. The board members of the Solomon Group, slash church, are: Reverend Nesbitt, Mrs. Blair, Reverend Heller, someone else who I think is the head person, another person who seemed to be a shadow, and me. I was a junior member. When I originally got involved, I wasn't aware of their criminal activities. I was flattered that the church and this big business wanted me on their boards. When I found out... well, it was too late."

Virginia gave Jenny a bewildered look. "You mentioned a shadow person. What do you mean?"

"Yeah. He always knew what was happening and would vote at meetings, but only on the phone or via a computer. I never met him in person. For that matter, I never met the chairman either."

"So, you've got someone you think is the head guy who you don't know, and this mystery person."

Jenny nodded. "Unfortunately, yes."

"Could the two people actually be one person?"

"No. I've heard them having conversations."

"How about Nesbitt?"

"Nesbitt was a born confidence man and fit the Solomon Group board and the Calvary Evangelical Chapel like a glove. He was blackmailing some parishioners, Mr. Weedon, and me. He used varying techniques, like intimidation, bullying, and strong-arm tactics to keep people in line. He'd hire thugs. That's how I learned about Blake. I don't know what rock Nesbitt was under when they found him, but it must have been a big dirty one. I think he may have been in prison. He had a few tattoos he didn't want anyone to see. But he was a great con artist. His sermons and scams could charm the socks of St. Peter. He was real smooth. When I met him for the first time, I thought he was a good man. Little did I know."

Virginia nodded. "Why did Nesbitt really want Ms. North's place?"

"For the land." Jenny shifted in her seat. "He wanted to have a church retreat, tax-free of course. And he could develop part of it, sell building lots or homes, and make a tidy profit, tax-free. The profits would be huge, especially if he got the land for nothing. That was until he found out there was a possibility of gold on the land. Then he went even crazier. He was a slimy crook and blackmailer... that nut case just had to go."

"So, killing Reverend Nesbitt was a public service?"

Jenny nodded. "Yeah, something like that."

"Okay. Now, why were Mrs. Blair and Heller trying to make your mushroom poison in Ms. North's kitchen?"

"They were making it there because I told them Blake and I blew up the entrance to the cavern you were in, and that Ms. North was with you. I figured you and Ms. North would be dead, so it was a safe place to work without being caught. I didn't know they brought the professors with them."

"I got that, but what did they intend to do with the poison?"

"Kill the professors and Mr. Weedon."

"What?" Grover almost choked. "Why?"

Jenny grinned. "They said the professors were scared and snooping around, and they had uncovered part of the operation, and therefore needed to go... permanently."

"The professors weren't part of the conspiracy?" Virginia asked.

"Not really. They were held close so Nesbitt could keep an eye on them and get their research results."

Grover frowned. "Weren't some of them on the board of the Solomon Group?"

"Yes. But they were junior members of the Solomon Group like me. We weren't privy to everything. They weren't aware of what was really going on. At least, I don't think so. I guess they got too curious and got caught."

"Why Mr. Weedon?"

"Mr. Weedon had received funding to get Ms. North's land and develop it from Solomon Group. He tried to drop out when he smelled something wrong and started to sniff around. He was also a competitor for the land. Nesbitt didn't like anyone interfering with his lavish plans. Like I said earlier, Nesbitt used intimidation, physical harm, blackmail, and murder, as his way of handling things. Weedon was as stubborn as Nesbitt, and was not just trying to get the same land as Nesbitt, but started investigating the church and the Solomon Group. Weedon had a lot of connections, and that scared Nesbitt." Jenny leaned forward. "Nesbitt's real second in command was Heller. He appeared to be the nice, mild-mannered, soft-spoken, Reverend Heller." She took a swallow of water from the bottle on the table. "He has connections with crime families in New Jersey someplace, Newark, or Elisabeth, or somewhere in that area. Oh, yeah, you'll love this; both Nesbitt and Heller's ordination credentials are from the same online church."

"Cute." Virginia took notes. "How about Mrs. Blair?"

"Oh, she's a piece of work. She's all high and mighty. She was holier than thou, uptight, Bible thumping, prude, and total bitch. Mrs. Blair is a swindler and bunko artist from way back. One of her best cons was the bump from behind routine."

Virginia and Grover exchanged glances; then she leaned on the table. "What's that?"

Jenny smirked. "You'll love this. Blair bragged about it. 'Foolproof,' she said. Here's how it works. She'd be at a stop sign, or light, or better yet, on a sloped off ramp from a freeway. Then, when someone with an expensive car was behind her, she'd back into them and scream they hit her from behind. Her car was dented in the back and the other one in front. The cops would site the poor slob she backed into. Of course, her neck hurt. Then, she and a less than honest chiropractor would show any court X-rays and examination results with the diagnosis of whiplash and neck injury. Blair and the doc would get the insurance money for the repair of the cheap car they had purchased, which they never repaired, for medical care she didn't actually get, and for hardship or punitive damages." Jenny stretched. "Sometimes the victim would want to just pay her off, so she didn't call the cops, and he wouldn't have to report it to the insurance company. When the local cops started to put the scam together, Blair and the doc would move their rip-off operation to a new city. This was a great scam in parts of California, Arizona, and Washington. She even did it in Washington, D.C. The last place she pulled this con was San Francisco. The law started to close in, so she fled to Texas and got into this church racket. I think Nesbitt recruited her."

Virginia nodded. "So, you hired Blake and his friend to kill Linda and me after you and Blake failed to kill us in the caves by blowing up the entrance."

Jenny nodded. "Afraid so."

"Who hired Blake to intimidate or hurt Natalie?"

"I think that was Weedon, but I'm not one hundred percent sure. Could have been Nesbitt. Blake's not all that bright and is just muscle for hire. He'll do anything for the right price."

Grover started to talk when the door opened, and a deputy and another man in an expensive-looking suit entered. The suit said, "I am Ms. Parker's lawyer. This conversation is terminated. My client has nothing more to say." He handed Grover his business card.

Jenny looked at the man then slumped in the chair.

Grover turned off the recorder, picked it up, and followed Virginia out.

As they walked to Grover's desk, Virginia asked, "Where'd he come from?"

"I don't know. She hasn't made any calls since we arrested her. I'll run a check on him when I get to my desk. What are you going to do now?"

"I'm calling Natalie and Linda to come and get me. Then I'm going home to see my husband and cat. Maybe Leo has some ideas."

"Leo's your cat, right?"

"Yes. He has some good ideas once in a while."

Grover shook his head. "I think I need a beer."

"Not a bad idea."

"Yeah, well now, after that little exchange with Ms. Parker, I think I'll do some more records checking on Heller, Blair, and the suit. I'll call you if I turn up anything."

As they sat in Virginia's car in the sheriff's parking lot, Virginia told Natalie and Linda what transpired with Jenny and about the lawyer showing up.

Natalie sighed. "I hoped she'd tell us everything and we'd be done with this."

Virginia, sitting in the driver's seat twisted around. "She told us enough to finish Blair and Heller for good. And with the help of social media, and the FBI and IRS, we can bring down the church. That will upset the remaining leaders of the Solomon Group, and we'll flush them out."

Natalie gave her a weary look. "How?"

"Dr. Morrison said Dr. Shaprio used a copy of a map to find that vein of rock with the traces of gold. Where did it come from? They made a crude map of your land, Natalie, to show how to get to the entrances and some of the tunnels. Obviously, they didn't have the details about the caves and tunnels on that basic map of theirs. The picture was something they got access to later. And Dr. Shaprio said Mr. Weedon knew about the gold when he was pestering you about your land."

"So?"

Linda straightened in the front passenger seat. "Where'd Dr. Shaprio get the map, and how'd Weedon know about the gold before the others, unless someone told him?"

Virginia shrugged. "Maybe he saw the actual map someplace."

"Maybe." Natalie yawned. "I could use a hot bath and some rest. Maybe we could take this up again in the morning."

"Maybe you're right." Virginia started the car. "I'll drop you guys off and head for home. I bet Andy and Leo are starving." She pulled out of the parking lot and drove toward Texas 29.

A black, dual-cab pickup pulled out of the bank parking lot across the street and fell in behind them, two cars back. It continued to follow them west on University Avenue.

As they drove west, Linda stiffened and gasped. "I know where the real map of the caves and the gold is."

Natalie leaned forward. "You do? Where?"

Linda turned around. Her eyes sparkled. "The whole map is at your house. It's on a quilt. I just remembered it. I thought it was just a very unusual pattern at the time I saw it. Colorful, too. We didn't know about the caves then. But with the earlier crude map from the professors we did see, then Weedon's taking us through the tunnels, and now remembering that special rock formation, it all fits. The actual map quilt is in Ann's quilt workroom. Matter of fact, it has a lot more of what I think are caves and tunnels and stuff on it. Maybe Ann did some exploring years ago and never told anyone. She hid the real map as a quilt. The drawing was probably an older one and not as complete. Maybe that's the real reason Jenny Parker wanted to assess the quilts."

Virginia smiled. "I knew you'd be good at cataloging Ann's quilts, and other works. But the begs another question. Why would Ann use a quilt for a map instead of just finishing the original drawing?"

"My cousin was always a security nut," Natalie said. "Double locks and such stuff. If the map indicated where the gold was, she didn't want it in any place where it could be stolen. Putting a map on a quilt that would fit in with all the others was an excellent hiding place. Maybe Nesbitt saw it and figured out what it meant, of maybe it just slipped out, and that's why his interest in them, too."

Virginia switched on the headlights. "Natalie, you still got Grover on speed dial?"

"Yeah. Why?"

"We're being followed."

CHAPTER 33

Clouds were quickly darkening the evening sky. Loud cracking of thunder made Virginia tighten her grip on the wheel. "Thunder? I don't remember anything about a thunderstorm coming. Just what we don't need right now."

"With everything that's been going on, I forgot to mention that my cell phone warned of a severe thunderstorm heading our way tonight." Linda glanced back at Natalie, who was on her phone.

Natalie muttered something into the phone then hung up. "We're on our own for a while. Grover said the storm caused some serious damage and multicar pileups north of us. Deputies and state troopers are being deployed to assist people and the authorities up there. The storm is headed our way pretty fast. He advised us to go straight home." She looked over her shoulder. "Is the car still following us?"

Virginia looked in the rearview mirror. "Yeah. And it's a big double cab, black pickup. Once we clear this traffic and get into the country, is when something may happen. That, or the driver is just trying to unnerve us."

"He's doing a good job." Natalie shoved her phone in her pocket. "What's the plan?"

Virginia cracked a smile. "The unexpected. Let's see if he continues on Texas 29 or turns at D B Woods Drive. If he follows us, we'll turn the tables on him."

Linda clenched her seatbelt. "Whatever you're planning, is it going to entail mayhem and violence?"

"Possibly."

"Good. I'm in. I'm tired of being the target all the time."

Natalie sat back. "Me too. Being the target is getting old."

Virginia held up her hand. "Easy ladies. We may have to explain things to a judge, and hunting people down usually doesn't go over well with judges, the DA, the police, or juries. We have to turn the tables on these people, but be able to say we were defending ourselves while doing it. Now, can we help it if that big truck happens to follow us down some dark place and threatens us? We'd have to defend ourselves."

Linda turned toward Virginia. "Are we going to do that?"

"No. Too dangerous. We're going to my house. As you know, it's in a gated community." Lightning flashed, followed shortly by a resounding boom. Virginia glanced out the side window. "That was close. Anyway, the only way he can get in is to tailgate us, follow someone else in, or use a code, which means he's been there before. If he follows us in, then we speed to my house. Andy's got some nifty toys to confront the person with, and we have our weapons."

Natalie leaned forward. "You said he. How do you know it's a man?"

Virginia glanced in her rearview mirror. "Just a figure of speech, but I'll bet a dinner the driver is a man."

"What if he runs us off the road before we get to your subdivision?"

"Is he prepared to confront three scared, armed women? We may have an advantage being women, and we're armed. And the cops don't like men attacking women at night or anytime. In your movies, Natalie, you fight the bad guys." She hit the Bluetooth icon on the car radio system. "I'll call Andy now." She hit the speed dial on the video screen and talked to Andy for a minute, then disconnected.

Natalie swallowed. "Yeah, but in the movies, the bad guys and I just follow the script, and we're on a movie set. I hope whoever's in that truck has read the same script we did."

Linda looked over her shoulder, took a deep breath, and then flexed her fingers. "Check your weapons, ladies. The truck is still behind us. Are we close to your place, Virginia?"

"We're almost there. Things look different at night." The barcode on the side of her car opened the gate, and she sped through. The truck raced through the gate behind them as it started to close. Virginia slowed and continued down the road. A few raindrops splattered on the windshield. "Oh boy, just like a bad movie." She turned at a stop sign and sped up. A few houses down the road, she cut into her driveway. Out of the corner of her eye, she spotted the truck run the stop sign and bear down on them. "Looks like he wants to stop us before we get inside."

Natalie clenched her revolver. "Now what?"

"Watch." Virginia slowed as she drove down her driveway, approached the garage, and stopped. The overhead door started to rise. Andy and another younger man ducked out from under the rising door pulling a cable attached to a rifle stock with a round, flat, thin box attached just below where the gun barrel would be.

The truck screeched to a stop. A figure jumped out and started running across the grass toward the house. As he got about halfway across the front yard, bright strobe lights flashed. Then the sprinklers went on. He stopped, covered his eyes, and staggered around as if confused, and the sprinklers

Suspicious Threads

stopped. Andy aimed his instrument and pulled the trigger. A loud, high-pitched sound erupted from the device. Leaves on the ground flew violently into the air. A second later, the man tumbled backward; a pistol flew from his hand; he pressed his hands to his ears and fell to the ground. The sound stopped. He lay motionless for a couple of seconds then rose on one arm. He shook his head, and then looked for his gun. He tried to move to get it when Andy stepped forward a few steps and fired another burst of focused, high-frequency sound at him. The mystery man stopped, he didn't move.

Virginia jumped out of the car, hurried to Andy, and kissed him. "Thank you, dear. That was impressive. Another toy from the university?" She glanced at the man standing near Andy. "Hi, Ed."

Ed nodded. "Hello, Virginia."

Andy grinned. "I made it for a demonstration in class next week. It worked pretty well. Hell, if you shot him, I'd have all that blood to clean up and you'd have a lot of paperwork to do. Let's go see who he is before this storm gets worse." He saw the neighbor's lights go on. "I guess our demonstration sonic gun is a little loud."

In light rain, Virginia, Linda, and Natalie, with guns drawn and aimed at the still unmoving body, advanced slowly toward him. Andy, now holding a revolver, hurried to catch up. The group stopped and stared down at the unconscious, hooded body wearing a ski mask. Natalie knelt next to the figure. "Let's see who's behind the mask." She carefully pulled back the hood and yanked off the ski mask. Rain pelted down.

CHAPTER 34

Natalie held the ski mask and stared at the unconscious man. "Mr. Weedon? What the hell was he doing? I thought he was a just a cheesy developer and another victim of Nesbitt's crazy plots."

Linda poked him with her foot. "Man, he's out cold. Can we drag him to the house?"

"I'd love to question him, but in drier conditions." Natalie ran her hand over her now wet clinging hair. "I'd like to dry off, too."

Virginia looked at Andy and Ed. "Give us a hand, please."

Andy handed Virginia his pistol. He felt Weedon's neck. "Still got a pulse. He's breathing. That's good."

He and Ed hoisted Weedon up and dragged him to the garage. Lightning flashed in the window. Andy and Ed dropped Weedon in the middle of the three-car garage as Virginia pulled her Toyota in and closed the big door.

As Andy rose, Weedon started to move. He groaned and slowly opened his eyes. He rubbed his head and rose on one arm. "What the hell? How'd I get here? What happened?"

Natalie kicked him in his leg. "You followed us. You... you came at us with a gun. Here I thought you were a good guy. You're a... a lying, two-bit, louse." She put her hands on her hips. "I thought maybe Andy had killed you with that contraption of his. No such luck. You're not very original, wearing a ski mask... that's not even done in Hollywood anymore. And you scared the hell out of us... me." She kicked his thigh again. "Bastard."

Weedon pulled back. "Stop kicking me."

Virginia leaned against her car. "Okay scumbag, you have some explaining to do."

His eyes narrowed. "You can't question me. I want a lawyer." He sat up and shook his head. "What the hell did you use on me?"

Andy smiled. "A sonic weapon."

Virginia looked around the garage, then at Weedon. "Let me explain something to you. You followed us... however the report will say stalked, judges like that, trespassed in a gated community, and you attacked us with a gun. You're lucky you're still alive."

"So, call the sheriff."

Natalie winked at Virginia, then, frowning, moved next to Weedon and bent down and cooed. "I have a better idea. We'll tie you up and take you to my barn. Then, we'll actually do what we talked about before. I'm sure you remember. Now, I'm really pissed. No one will know what happened to you. I have a few thousand acres to dispose of your body. Then again, we could just use the power tools Andy has here on you."

Weedon sat straighter, looked at the women and swallowed. "You wouldn't dare. Anyway, that would be illegal, and there are witnesses."

Ed leaned toward Andy and whispered. "What's with her barn?"

Andy chuckled. "Last time he tangled with them, they were going to take him to Natalie's barn and use the shop tools on him."

Ed's eyes widened. "Oh."

"That's what they led him to think. They weren't really going to do it."

Ed sighed. "That's good to know. Oh, you were right, Ms. North is a doll, and she's got a lot of spunk."

"She's great. She's easy to talk to and an excellent cook. I think you've noticed; she's got an outgoing personality, too. I think you and her will get along really well."

"I hope so. But she's a pretty actress. I'm sure she has a lot of men, especially with a lot of money, after her. Not sure how she'll like me."

"You'll do fine. She doesn't like the phonies and the Hollywood types. She's nice. You need to talk to her some more."

Natalie turned to Virginia. "Let's tie him up. We can use his truck to haul his sorry ass to my barn."

Virginia nodded. "Not a bad idea. Mr. Weedon, you have really pissed us off. You expect us to provide you with all your constitutional rights after what you tried to do to us?"

He tried to look smug, but failed. "Ahh... yes."

"We are wet, angry, and not in very good moods. The sheriff is busy with problems caused by the storm." She listened to water streaming from drainpipes, and then pointed at the big garage door. "From the sound of all that wind and rain out there, I think they're going to be tied up for a long time. Looks like you're stuck with us for a while."

Linda ran her hands over her wet clothes. "I think we need to secure him, and then go dry ourselves off and get comfortable. As much as I'd like to try Natalie's barn toys on him, we should wait until the storm blows over. There is no real hurry to see him bleed." She turned away and stifled a giggle.

"I like that idea," Natalie said.

Virginia shrugged. "Andy, will you and Ed help tie him up and secure him to the post over there while we ladies go dry off. I'll get my handcuffs; they'll help."

Weedon's eyes widened. "Handcuffs? That's right. You're some sort of federal cop. You can't torture me. I have rights."

"Yes, you do." Virginia sneered. "But you haven't been arrested... yet. And I don't like you. So, later, after I arrest you, tell you about your rights, and you try to escape—with a gun of course—you'll be shot. See, no torture, no fuss, just a lot of paperwork. The other ladies will be disappointed, but such is life." She headed for the house. "Keep an eye on him while I get my handcuffs."

Weedon choked. "Wh... wait. You can't do that."

Natalie kicked his leg. "Quiet." She bent down, "Any last requests?"

He swallowed. "You wouldn't really do that, would you?"

"Do what?"

"Torture or... or kill me. I saved your lives once."

"Yeah, you did that once. But normally you are lower than pond scum." Natalie straightened. "Ain't up to just me, sport. It's a group decision. So, my guess is yep." Rain pelted the roof.

Weedon gave Andy a questioning look.

Andy shrugged. "Don't ask me, pal. It's their show."

Fifteen minutes later, with Weedon handcuffed and tied to a large column in the garage, they went into the house. Natalie wrinkled her nose. "I still think I should stand guard over him."

Virginia laughed. "If you stood guard, he'd either be dead or in pieces in an hour."

"You say that like it's a bad thing," Natalie said.

Linda chuckled. "You two are quite the pair. You enjoy getting on Weedon's nerves. I should call my husband to come get me. But I'd like to know why that bastard was following us and came at us with a gun."

Natalie nodded. "Me too. Can I interrogate him?"

"No. But let's all go talk to him." Virginia picked up Leo, her cat, and proceeded to the garage. She stopped in front of Weedon with Linda and Natalie standing on either side of her.

He looked up at the women. "What now?"

Natalie bent down. "We'd like to know why you were after us and with a gun. As you pointed out, you saved our lives once. You told us the church and the Solomon Group were your nemeses."

"Before I answer that, can I ask a couple of questions?"

"What?"

"I heard Heller and Blair are in jail, and you captured Jenny Parker. Is that true?"

Natalie nodded. "Yes."

"Did any of them tell you or the sheriff anything?"

Virginia stepped closer. "Yes, but I can't tell you what they said. Oh, by the way, your friend Blake and a buddy of his are in the hospital under guard and will be going to the county jail in a few days to await trial. They'll sing like birds to save their skin."

Weedon gave her a blank look. "Blake's back in jail? Why?"

"He attacked and tried to kill Linda and me."

"Again? Blake was never the brightest bulb. I guess he didn't learn from his first encounter with you."

"I guess not." Virginia petted Leo. "It looks like you didn't either. Now, answer Natalie's question."

"Okay. Like I told you before, I needed money for my real estate development projects. Nesbitt steered me to the Solomon Group, again, like I told you before. At first, everything was great. We had quite a few successful endeavors here, and elsewhere in Texas. We were so successful they made me an officer of the Group to get me to expand their real estate holdings in Texas and Louisiana, for a fee of course. They also wanted *Borealis*. At the time, they said it was for development. But then, things went south when Ann wouldn't sell. And then, you, Ms. North, wouldn't sell either. I found out about the caves and wondered about how much of *Borealis* could safely have construction on it. Nesbitt also wanted the land for the church. I was caught between the church and the Group. That's when things got bad, at least for me. I later learned, from you, Mrs. Clark, that the church, and the Group were actually one and the same. I was unwittingly on the management board of a huge illegal racket. I tried to quit when they wanted to eliminate Ms. North, but couldn't. I got a call a short time ago. Now, with everything turning to shit, the president of the Solomon Group wants Ms. North's land, and her dead, in the next seventy-two hours, or else it's my hide. I believe him."

Virginia frowned. "Why? Why the next seventy-two hours?" She looked at her watch. "Less now."

"I don't know why. This has all spiraled out of control. It seems stupid. Maybe he didn't know about the others at the time."

"As an officer, you knew about the shady deals, right?"

"Yeah. But at first, I didn't know they were illegal. A little unorthodox at first, but not exactly illegal. The illegal ones came to my attention later. They let me in on things slowly. That way I was in over my head before I knew it."

"And as a board member, you voted on things over the phone?"

"I didn't want my involvement known, and the higher-ups agreed. I was a good front, like the church. I'd get things to review and vote on by phone, so only a select few knew who I was. But my job was real estate development like I was normally doing. The real estate stuff was legal, well, mostly legal. That's what I concentrated on."

"You knew Jenny Parker was on the board, too?"

"Yes. But she was just a junior member like me on the board. There was a difference. Some of the Group officers were also on the church board, but not all the church board members were Group officers or Group board members. Nesbitt, Blair, Heller, and someone else were involved with both boards. I was just on the Group board."

Virginia looked at Natalie and Linda. "I guess that make sense.' She looked at Weedon. "There is still one person missing. Who is the other missing church, or Solomon Group, board member?"

Weedon sat staring at the concrete, then looked up. "Now Heller is now head honcho at the church. He and Blair wanted to move up in the organization. Heller came across as the meek milquetoast, but he was a first-class bunko artist, and he's a certifiable sociopath or psychopath. I'm not sure if there's a difference."

"That we know." Virginia bent down. "You didn't answer the question."

"I don't know the answer. It's the Solomon Group president, but I don't know who he is. He ordered the hits on Ms. North."

"Okay. How'd you find us in the tunnels? You mentioned a map. Where'd you see, or get it?"

Weedon sighed. "A copy was sent to me. I was to use it to help with structuring a deal to get Ms. North's land so the church could get the gold and develop the land. Kind of a double hit. This way we could stay away from the petroglyph areas. I would get to be the developer, of course. I used it, along with my past short experience exploring the tunnels on my own, to rescue all of you."

"Who sent it to you?"

"It had to be someone Ms. North's cousin knew. I heard she knew about the caves and tunnels, had done some cave exploring over the years, and may have made a crude map. She never said anything publically about the caves. I got it with a note to use it for the deal somehow."

Linda cleared her throat. "Could the president of the Solomon Group be someone local? Someone Ann knew?"

Weedon sat staring at Linda. His face brightened. "Yes. At least I think so. I remember hearing a radio in the background during a phone conversation. He always called me, not the other way around. The number was untraceable. I tried. The voice disguised. Anyway, he called me on my cell phone when I was driving. The radio station in the background on his end was playing music, and then there was a commercial. It was the same station I had on my car radio. It was out of Austin. If I tried to call him, I got a voice mail and had to leave a message. He'd call me back."

Virginia smiled. "Thank you, Mr. Weedon, you've been extremely helpful. I'm sure the judge will take that into consideration at your trial."

She turned to Natalie. "Use your speed dial and call Detective Grover. Ask him to send deputies to pick up Mr. Weedon, and take him to jail. Hold him on a seventy-two-hour open charge for now. I'll go later and file the paperwork and charges."

Natalie put her hand over her heart and feigned shock. "Take him to jail? Seriously? My barn would be much better."

"Jail." Virginia chuckled. "Anyway, we weren't really going to hurt him, were we?"

Natalie pouted. "Well…" She looked at Weedon and grinned. "No, not really."

Weedon slumped against the column and let out a sigh. "Thank God. You ladies are both cunning and dangerous."

Virginia rubbed her cat's chin. "After Grover picks up Mr. Weedon, we have planning and work to do."

Linda leaned against Virginia's car. "We do?"

"Yeah. I know who the president of the Solomon Group is." She knelt next to Weedon. "I need you to do something for me."

CHAPTER 35

Early the next morning after the storm passed, Virginia, Linda, and Natalie stood out of sight near a university faculty office building, under an old, dripping, oak tree. The glass front doors opened, and Dr. Emerson Dunlap, the archeologist who had visited Natalie, rushed out. He carried a battered, brown leather briefcase, and with purposeful strides, pulled a wooden, wheeled, locked box. He glanced around, turned, and trudged down the wet sidewalk toward the faculty parking lot.

The three women hurried to Virginia's car parked at a nearby curb. They pulled into the street as Dr. Dunlap exited the parking lot in a faded, old blue Buick. Virginia could not guess the age of the car. They followed him at a discrete distance as he drove west on Texas 29. About ten miles west of Georgetown, he turned off onto a county road with no traffic. Virginia fell back further. "Okay, we now know for certain where he's going. He took the bait."

Natalie leaned forward from the rear seat. "Yeah, having Weedon send the message that things were heating up and that the others in custody were starting to talk to save their own skins must have panicked him."

Linda squinted ahead. "I expected him to run for the airport. He has plane reservations for a flight from Austin to Cancun, then to the Cayman Islands, and then to Argentina. You have U.S. Marshals waiting at the airport when he shows up. Why's he going to Natalie's place? Are you going to tell the marshals?"

"Yes, after we capture him. I don't want to have them stand down. If he escapes us, I want them to catch him there." Virginia increased her speed. "He's headed to Natalie's place because Weedon told him in the message that I was going to get some incriminating evidence, like the actual map he photographed, and the map quilt. He also told Dunlap I found fingerprints and something else there but didn't realize at the time the significance until now. Weedon said I'm going to get them at Natalie's house this morning and have them identified. Dr. Dunlap wants to destroy any possible evidence he may have may have left behind. We'd better speed things up; we don't know what's in that box."

"Why is he going to the trouble? He could be in Argentina by the time we connected the fingerprints to him and located whatever else it is you found. And since he'd been at Natalie's place before on university business a couple of times, they wouldn't be all that incriminating."

"You're right. But like Natalie said, he's panicking. He's not thinking straight. Dunlap's co-conspirators are in jail, and he thinks they are all talking to save their asses. He knows things are turning to shit. Even if they couldn't, he thinks one or more of them could inadvertently implicate him. I bet he'll try and leave some items linking someone else to this to throw us off even more."

As Virginia turned down Natalie's road, Natalie's cell phone sounded off like a siren. She pulled it out of her purse and looked at it. "It's my alarm system. Dunlap's trying to get into the cellar by the outside entrance."

Linda twisted around. "Can he get in?"

"I doubt it. Andy reinforced it and secured it from the inside with a special lock. Oh boy, now he's trying the back door." She pushed back in her seat as Virginia accelerated.

Virginia gripped the steering wheel. "Hang on." She whipped around a corner, and then dashed down the road through the dark tunnel formed by the shadows of massive oak and elm trees rushing by in a blur. She slowed and turned into Natalie's driveway. Virginia drove slowly up under a sprawling oak and parked. "Okay ladies, let's go, but be careful. He may be armed."

They slipped out of the car and hurried to the bushes beside the big house. They crept along the soggy ground to the back porch. Virginia, pistol in hand, carefully peered around the side of the building. She spotted Dr. Dunlap on the porch rummaging in his now open box. He stood holding a small bent bar that resembled a short crowbar. She turned to Natalie and nodded.

Natalie pressed an icon on her cell phone. The loud, shrieking alarm system sounded. Strobe lights above the door and at the top of the three-step stairs flashed. Dunlap jerked around, seemingly confused, his empty hand blocked the bright light from his eyes. He dropped the bar and yanked a pistol from inside the box. "What the... damn. Better hurry."

"Not so fast Professor." Virginia swung her gun around the side of the building aiming it at him. "Drop your weapon."

Dunlap narrowed his eyes. "Who's there?"

"Virginia Davies Clark. Drop your weapon."

"This is all a big mistake, Mrs. Clark. I can explain."

"We'll talk after you drop your weapon."

"Well, I..." He turned and sprinted down the porch away from Virginia. As he got to the stairs on the far end of the porch, he leaped off, and screamed.

Virginia heard a load thud, like a side of beef hitting the ground, and then tense cries of pain and swearing. She turned and saw only Linda behind her. "Where's Natalie?"

Linda shrugged. "I don't know. She dashed off after she pressed the alarm button."

Natalie's voice called from the far side of the porch. "I'm over here. See what I've got."

Virginia and Linda hurried around the porch and stopped in their tracks. On the ground rested a moaning Dr. Dunlap. He held his leg, which was bent in an unnatural angle. His face looked like he had run into a wall. Blood poured from a misshapen nose. Dunlap's head had a severe, bleeding cut across his forehead. His clothes were wet and splattered with blood. His gun sat in the wet grass a few yards away. Natalie stood over him holding a cracked two-by-four.

Natalie smiled at her handy work sitting on the ground in front of her. "He tried to break into my house and came at me with a gun. A girl needs to protect herself."

Virginia pointed at her ears and shouted. "Shut that noise off."

"Okay." Natalie dropped the two-by-four and pulled out her phone. She thumbed a couple of icons and the alarm silenced.

Virginia looked at Dunlap, then at Natalie. "Nice job, and you didn't even shoot him."

"It was tempting."

"How many times did you hit him?"

"I don't know. A few."

Virginia chuckled, then knelt next to Dunlap. "You blew it, Doctor. I'm a federal officer. You're under arrest."

"My leg." He grimaced and spoke like he had a stuffed-up nose. "The pain. She broke my nose. God, it hurts. My head hurts, too. I'm bleeding. Call the paramedics. That woman attacked me. I want her arrested."

"She's within her rights, so she won't be arrested. I'll call the paramedics and the sheriff. And I'm afraid you're going to miss your flight this morning."

"You don't understand."

"Let me explain some things to you, Doctor." She read him his rights. "Now that you acknowledge your rights, do you want to waive them?"

"I want the paramedics and my lawyer. God damn, my leg, nose, and my head hurt. Get me to a hospital."

"You'll live. I'll call the paramedics when I call the sheriff." Virginia stood, walked a few feet away, and made the calls. She turned and looked at Dunlap. He sat leaning his back against the bottom step of the short porch stairs looking up at Natalie. She had picked up her two-by-four. He twisted his head toward Virginia. "If she hurts me anymore I'll sue. I'm in custody."

Virginia mounted the stairs and slowly ambled toward the rear door. "I need to call the marshals at the airport and tell them we have you in custody. If you get feisty, Ms. North might be inclined to painfully augment your condition, so don't move."

Dunlap called out. "Don't leave me with this woman. She's dangerous. She'll hurt me." He eyed Linda. "She's got a gun. Don't leave me!"

Virginia eyed him contemptuously. "Ms. North's barely five feet tall, and weighs less than a hundred and twenty-five pounds, and you're what... five nine or ten and about two hundred pounds? How much of a threat can she be?"

"She broke my leg, and my nose, and hurt my head. My leg and nose are killing me."

"You trespassed, tried to break into her house, and went toward her with a gun. What did you expect? Cookies? She could have shot you. And when the inmates at the jail find out a girl her size did all that to you... well... are you familiar with the term anal retentive?" Virginia sat on the top step making Dunlap painfully twist around to see her. "Doctor, I'd like to ask some questions while we wait. As you know, you don't have to answer, but Ms. North won't like it if you don't."

He turned and glanced up at Natalie holding her board, and Linda with a pistol at her side, standing in front of him. He looked back at Virginia, grimaced, and moaned as his leg moved slightly. "What do you want to know?"

"How did the others not know you were the leader of this operation?"

"The other professors considered me just a... well... when they found the petroglyphs in the caves, they thought I'd add some more interest to the grant request. They figured I was just an old academic, but someone they could add to the grant request to make it look better. Nesbitt was helping them with grants and unwittingly brought them into the fold without their knowing it... at least at first. They got some funding and went for it. Funding for research is a big deal at universities as is publishing. Only finding the gold only made things worse. Greed set in."

"I see." Virginia motioned to Linda. "Ladies, get that box of his, and the briefcase, and let's see what he's got inside. I'm sure that will prompt even more questions."

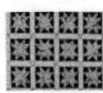

Three days later, Virginia, Natalie, Linda, and Grover sat in the parlor at Natalie's house. The ladies sipped tea.

Virginia set her cup down and looked at Natalie. "So, how are things with you and Ed?"

"He's a quantum physicist and an associate professor at the University of Texas."

"I know."

"He's smart, fun, has a nice personality, and easy to talk to, and he thinks I'm pretty and special because I'm me, and not because I'm an actress. He has treated me nicer than ninety-nine percent of the men I've known. He was nervous at first. I tried to help him get over that."

"I bet you did."

"Your husband and Ed are the one percent of terrific men. Andy is wonderful." Natalie smiled at Grover. "You too, Detective." She sat back in her chair. "Ed gave me a tour of the university, and I saw his lab. I didn't understand most of what he does in there, but he was excited to show me. He said quantum physics has to do with atomic and subatomic systems and their interaction with radiation. I'm not sure what that means, but it sounds fascinating, I think. It probably involves a lot of math. We're going to dinner tonight and to a show. I never dreamed I'd be dating a science professor. He's a lot like Andy. I can't wait to cook for him."

Virginia smiled. "Good for you. Ed is a great guy. Andy said Ed is really smitten. If you cook for him, he's finished as a bachelor."

"That's for sure." Grover finished a homemade scone, dusted off the crumbs, and took a drink of his tea. "Sounds like things are brightening up for Natalie. I'm glad. Natalie, you deserve the best." He glanced at Linda. "What about you, Mrs. Chambers?"

Linda set her teacup down. "My husband and I are taking a fifteen-day cruise out of Fort Lauderdale in two weeks. We've got a mini-suite. We're going to the western Caribbean. It should be relaxing and fun. I'll have the quilt, table runners, and wall hanging inventory finished for Natalie on Friday. And I gave Natalie the forms and pictures her agent asked for. Who knows, maybe I'll be in a movie someday."

Grover finished his scone. "Virginia, how about you?"

"I'll finish the inventory and assessment of the quilt workroom tomorrow, and I've given Natalie my pictures and forms her agent asked for, too."

Grover picked up another scone and took a drink of his tea. "So, you three managed to get Dr. Dunlap to waive his rights and talk. I would've bet he'd scream for his lawyer and refuse to say anything to anyone. I don't think I want to know how you did that. But his testimony, along with all the others, will put that gang away for years. They couldn't wait to try and make deals and basically fingered each other. The FBI and IRS are investigating them now, too. Ms. Parker's going to face multiple counts of capital murder in the first-degree, and multiple other serious felonies. If she doesn't get the death penalty, she'll be in prison until she dies." He sipped more tea. "Virginia, how'd you know Dunlap was the missing director... president, or chairman, or whatever?"

Virginia sat back. "It was something Weedon said. During our last conversation, he mentioned the leader sent him a copy of the photo of a crude map of the caverns so Weedon could subdivide and plat the property to keep development away from the petroglyph areas underground. The leader wasn't interested in the gold-bearing rocks or the other caves and tunnels, just the things of archeological interest. All the others were more interested in the gold or the real estate, not the archeological or historical stuff. The geologist was concerned about building above the caves and knew there wasn't much gold down there. The biologist was fascinated with the unique flora and fauna. The only person with knowledge, and a real interest in the petroglyphs and not the gold, was the archeologist, Dr. Dunlap. The others either didn't know or didn't care about the petroglyphs. Dunlap spotted the map at Ann's house depicting the caverns when visiting her before all this started. He knew she had explored the caves and had sketched the map. She also turned it into a quilt. He took a picture of the map. Dunlap may have seen the actual finished cave quilt, too. We figured he'd go to Natalie's house to destroy any evidence he thought he'd left behind. It was kind of stupid for him to do it, but desperate men do desperate things. He panicked."

Grover shook his head. "I still can't believe Dr. Dunlap was the organizer and leader. Why?"

Virginia took a sip of tea. "He was divorced a few years ago. That hurt him emotionally and financially. He never recovered from it and was seriously depressed. On top of that, Dr. Dunlap was an associate professor and had been for one a long time. He was getting older, and he'd been passed over three times for full professor. His academic career was not going as he planned. He knew he was on the way down and out. Dunlap's academic standing was slipping, and his research was dwindling." She set her cup down. "His teaching suffered because of his attitude. He hadn't published much of any merit in the past few years, and his grants were diminishing in number and size. Publish or perish is the term, and grant money talks at universities. Dunlap's life was basically turning to shit. So, he started padding his savings and planning his early retirement by creating this bunko outfit."

Grover nodded. "That was quite an operation for a university anthropologist to set up. How'd he do it so well?"

"Yes, it was. But he had to be a good organizer to get his Ph.D. and to do both research and teach. He was a graduate advisor and on some committees. Nesbitt was an old college friend and had the requisite personality and experience as a good conman. Nesbitt recruited the others and even got his ordination off the Internet. That way he was a valid minister. Nesbitt and Dunlap made a great pair. Nesbitt was a great swindler, and Dunlap was a good organizer. The Solomon Group real estate outfit and the church angle they set up worked here, and in other places, for some time. The church gave him some protections and great cover."

Natalie nodded. "Yeah, the church made a great front for the operation. And it's tax-free. They were quite the scammers."

"Yes. He and Nesbitt used people. But the discovery of the gold on Natalie's land sent things spiraling out of control. Greed took hold among the troops, and logical thoughts were lost to gold fever, even if there wasn't much gold down there. According to the report the Smithsonian got from the IRS, the Solomon Group and church were worth over seven hundred million dollars. Most of the money was offshore."

Linda frowned. "They had a lot of money, why continue?"

"Good question. If they had stopped the blackmail and trying to force Natalie to sell, they all could have run off to some nice, warm, quiet spot in the world, and lived like kings. Gold and greed ruined them. Heller and Blair will be the guests of the State of Texas for some time, too. I heard a few other states are interested in them as well. Guys like Jenny and Weedon were pawns in all this with their own issues and problems. They got caught up in something they didn't fully understand, and by the time they did, they were in way over their heads. Jenny panicked when she murdered Ann and tried to cover it up with other stupid activities. Jenny will be in prison for life. Weedon will also do some time, but the DA said Weedon will get some credit for helping us."

"Well, you ladies did quite well," said Grover. "We got Ann North's murderer and the whole confidence gang. I couldn't have done it without your help."

"Thank you, Detective. Another scone?" Natalie asked.

"No, thank you. I've put on some weight working this case because of you, my dear. But I have to admit, I've enjoyed working with all of you, and especially enjoyed Ms. North's cooking. But I would like to take a few scones home, if you don't mind."

"Not at all, I'll package some for you when you leave. It's a pleasure to cook and bake for someone who appreciates it."

"It sounds like you'll have someone else to cook for and be with who will appreciate you."

Natalie smiled. "I hope so."

He looked at Virginia. "What are your plans?"

"I'm thinking of going to see an old friend in California. It will be a nice rest bit from here and mysteries. What could go wrong?"

ABOUT THE AUTHOR

Dr. David Ciambrone is a retired aerospace and defense company executive, scientist, professor of engineering, and a business and environmental consultant and is now a best-selling, award-winning author living in Georgetown, Texas with his wife Kathy. He has published twenty-five (25) books: four (4) non-fiction, two (2) textbooks for a California university, and nineteen (19) mysteries and has two (2) new mysteries in work. He is the author of the Virginia Davies Quilt Mysteries.

Dave has been a speaker at writer's groups, schools, colleges, libraries, quilt guilds, writer's conferences, and business/scientific conferences internationally.

Dr. Ciambrone also wrote three newspaper columns and wrote a column for a business journal.

Dave is a member of Sisters in Crime, the San Gabriel Writer's League, the Writer's League of Texas, Mystery Writers of America, the International Thriller Writers Association, The Beacon Society, and DFW Sherlock Homes Society.

Dave was appointed a U.S. Treasury Commissioner and to the management board of the Resolution Trust Corporation (RTC) by President Clinton.

He is a Fellow of the International Oceanographic Foundation.

Visit David at

Author's Website: davidciambrone.com

Facebook: facebook.com/david.ciambrone?fref=ts

Twitter: twitter.com/mysterywriter5

LinkedIn: linkedin.com/pub/david-ciambrone-sc-d-fiof/11/ab5/bb3

Amazon: amazon.com/author/davidciambrone

Progressive Rising Phoenix Press is an independent publisher. We offer wholesale pricing and multiple binding options with no minimum purchases for schools, libraries, book clubs, and retail vendors. We offer substantial discounts on bulk orders and discounts on individual sales through our online store. Please visit our website at:
www.ProgressiveRisingPhoenix.com

*If you enjoyed reading this book, please review it on Amazon, B & N, or Goodreads.
Thank you in advance!*

www.ingramcontent.com/pod-product-compliance
Lightning Source LLC
LaVergne TN
LVHW010257260326
834688LV00044B/1326